FEARFUL SYMMETRY

A PRIDE & PREJUDICE VARIATION

GAILIE RUTH CARESS

Quills & Quartos
PUBLISHING

Edited by Debbie Styne and Serena Agusto-Cox

Cover Design by Cloudcat Design

ISBN 978-1-951033-69-9 (ebook) and 978-1-951033-70-5 (paperback)

To the memory of my father, Mark R. Fulton (1955-2009), who taught me how to live with courage. This work is a product of his many years spent praising my earliest attempts at scribbling stories.

The Tyger

Tyger! Tyger! burning bright
In the forests of the night,
What immortal hand or eye
Could frame thy fearful symmetry?

In what distant deeps or skies
Burnt the fire of thine eyes?
On what wings dare he aspire?
What the hand, dare sieze the fire?

And what shoulder, & what art,
Could twist the sinews of thy heart?
And when thy heart began to beat,
What dread hand? & what dread feet?

What the hammer? what the chain?
In what furnace was thy brain?
What the anvil? what dread grasp
Dare its deadly terrors clasp?

When the stars threw down their spears,
And water'd heaven with their tears,
Did he smile his work to see?
Did he who made the Lamb make thee?

Tyger! Tyger! burning bright
In the forests of the night,
What immortal hand or eye
Dare frame thy fearful symmetry?

-William Blake, 1794

CHAPTER ONE

Fitzwilliam Darcy had finally begun to reckon himself safe now that Miss Elizabeth Bennet had taken her recovered sister home from Netherfield Park. He began to fancy himself ready for his own leave-taking, and indeed, within hours of the departure of the Bennet sisters, he had grown restless enough to shrug off even his most congenial obligations to his host and hostess.

To his mind, it was better that he return to London before his host and friend Charles Bingley opened his manor for the ball he had promised his new neighbours in ten days' time. Unsettled as Darcy's nerves now felt, he would be glad to make his escape from the clamouring attentions of Charles's sister Caroline—the self-same woman whose imperious voice had been raised unceasingly over the servants of Netherfield as she directed the preparations for the great event with all the hauteur of an aristocrat.

This demeaning show only served to further diminish her in Darcy's eyes, and he was now ensconced firmly—and rather early—in his room where he completed his nightly ablutions in

1

silence. As he washed himself, Darcy's imagination continued to churn with possible ways of ending his sojourn at Netherfield, weighing their benefits to himself and to others. In the morning, Darcy could make his ready excuses to his friend and happily wish Bingley well in his foray into Hertfordshire society. There was surely no longer any need for his guidance, now that Bingley's family had settled so comfortably in their new neighbourhood.

Or was there still need for guidance? Darcy considered that Bingley might yet be in danger of falling victim to an unfortunate alliance in the form of the recently recovered Miss Jane Bennet, who had just left his home after a week's stay. In that time, Miss Bennet had been largely absent from their company on account of a violent cold, while her sister Miss Elizabeth had attended her needs and at times shared in the party's company —including Darcy's. Whenever he was exposed to the distracting charms of Miss Elizabeth's liveliness, Darcy soon forgot about the elder Miss Bennet lying in recovery upstairs. To Darcy's alarm, he had observed that Bingley had done the reverse. Instead, he was preoccupied with Miss Elizabeth's presence as a daily reminder of the deprivation he felt at her elder sister's absence.

Frowning, Darcy allowed his valet to help him shoulder on his robe.

Surely, Bingley's natural easiness of manner would assert itself in that boyishly capricious fashion that had so often kept him from forming serious attachments. Surely, there would be no need for—

"Will there be anything else, sir?" his valet repeated.

"I thank you, no, Roberts," Darcy managed, barely concealing his distraction.

By morning, he would have to decide either to hasten off to London or to stay on to steer Bingley clear of Miss Bennet and be entrapped into attending the ball in the process. Yet, it might not be too burdensome a prospect. Perhaps he might engage Miss Bennet's spirited sister Elizabeth for a dance, perhaps—

But, oh, that would not do!

The irony of his preoccupation with that lady did not elude him and only increased his sense of frustration. Striding to his bedside, Darcy roughly drew down the counterpane, only to reconsider dropping onto the featherbed in defeat. Instead, he paced to the window, trying to trace, through the moonlit darkness, the shape of the small estate that had served as the cradle to the woman who had come to occupy his thoughts so steadfastly. At this distance, he fancied he could just make out the outline of the roof and one of the two chimneys—only two— of which the estate could boast.

He reminded himself that any alliance with such an estate would be insupportable to the heights of society to which he had been bred. The vulgarity of her family, too, would quickly become an oppressive source of vexation and shame. To stoop so low in marriage, to make an intimate, lasting connexion with the Bennet family would surely blot the nigh-pristine Darcy family legacy, leaving a dark stain, which he fancied, even now, he could see appearing and hanging above their little manor house, thrown into the stark relief of chiaroscuro from the brightness of the round, nearly full moon.

The shadow over Longbourn was growing. Darcy blinked to clear his vision, yet it remained. Perhaps it was a cloud.

He squinted again and saw that the yonder dendrites of darkness drew upwards rapidly, not passing lazily eastward as did the paler clouds above it. With an alarm nearing shock, Darcy realised what he saw was neither vision, nor a cloud, but a growing haze of smoke—and too much of it to be accounted for by only two chimneys on a mild November evening.

It was hard to be certain, but as the seconds passed and he continued to stare, the smoke continued upwards, and he faltered. Fearing the worst, he rang the bell by his bed.

Roberts darted in from the dressing room, and Darcy immediately directed him. "Look out that window to the manor house past the edge of the Netherfield boundary. What do you see?"

Walking to the window, Roberts peered out, making full use of his neat spectacles. After a moment searching over the fields, he drew in a sudden breath and glanced anxiously back over his shoulder at his master.

"I cannot say for certain, sir, but there appears to be a great deal of smoke rising from the Longbourn estate."

Darcy had already thrown off his robe and ducked back into the dressing room, pulling on riding breeches with nary a care for Roberts's careful arrangement of them.

"Have the groom bring my horse. While you are about it, rouse Bingley's man and Hurst's too. See whether their masters have gone to bed, and if they have, beg them to awaken, at my urgent request. Make haste, man!"

Fleet-footed as Roberts was, he had never quit a room faster. Darcy, himself, had never dressed more quickly. In haste and without Roberts's skill as a valet, he jammed his nightshirt into his breeches and pulled on an overcoat.

With his boots finally on, he cast one last glance out the window towards the spread of blackness hanging above Longbourn. He turned and raced down the stairs, nearly laying Bingley flat.

His friend righted himself against the staircase and spluttered, "I say, Darcy, what the devil—"

He was relieved to see that Bingley, while somewhat brandy-addled and sleepy, was still dressed. He roused him to action at once.

"To your horse, man! Longbourn is on fire!"

CHAPTER TWO

lessedly effective in their volubility, Lydia's shouts and Mrs Bennet's shrieks managed to raise the alarm to everyone on the floors and grounds. At Elizabeth's request, the Bennets' maids had run straightaway to Lucas Lodge to secure help from Sir William and his servants. As shouts of men from Longbourn Village arose in answer to the growing clamour at the manor house, tenants came racing with their water pails, ewers, and buckets. In the midst of the chaos, Elizabeth stood on the grass, safe, shocked, and attempting to gather her wits and courage to take an accounting of the household spilling out onto the lawn.

Mary, Jane, Lydia, their mother, Mrs Hill, Mr Hill, dear old Cook, and there—yes, Papa—had all come racing out of the house in good time. With their two young maids gone off to Lucas Lodge, that left only—

"Kitty is missing!" Elizabeth cried, racing to her father, who was bent at the waist, coughing and wheezing from the smoke. As he had not been roused from above stairs with the rest of the family, Elizabeth gathered he likely had fallen asleep in his book room, perilously close to where the fire had apparently started in the sitting room.

"Kitty!" he choked in answer, wiping his eyes before another wracking cough stole his breath. "I must—"

"No, Papa," declared Elizabeth, seeing how unfit he was for such a search. "Stay with Mama. I shall go around to the back where the smoke is less. It is possible she ran that way and is looking for us even now."

Despite the bright tones in which she had expressed the possibility, she felt a sinking uncertainty within. But before her father could reply, Elizabeth was off, with her bare feet flying over the grass as she dodged many a tenant and servant who raced to douse the blaze.

"Miss Catherine is missing!" she called to them as she raced to the kitchen door. "Let me know at once if you see her!"

She yanked open the door and felt the house's heat blooming upon her face as she progressed through its aperture.

"Kitty!" she cried, peering through the haze.

The kitchen was full of smoke, and she ducked lower as she ran through it, calling out her presence to two men with buckets already farther inside. Elizabeth hurried around the corner towards the sitting room, where she stopped in shock at the edge of the door and nearly dropped the shawl she had pressed to her nose.

The sitting room was violently ablaze. There, against the farthest wall, a brightness of flame ran up like an all-consuming lattice towards the ceiling.

She stepped back from the doorway and its blistering heat in terror as one of their tenants raced into the fiery room and threw his bucket over a flaming chair by the heart of the blaze, only to dash out again.

There was no doubt in Elizabeth's mind that Kitty would have avoided this room and path if she could—and, indeed, the whole of the lower floor, which was full of creeping fire and smoke.

Elizabeth's only option was to search for her sister above stairs. Surely, she could avoid the worst of the blaze and run for the servants' stairs to the bedrooms above. She could find another way down afterwards, should the flames have spread.

She ran for the stairs, clutching her shawl securely over her mouth and nose. As she trod up the strangely warm and creaking steps, she began to call out for her sister and to listen for any answer above the crackle of the flames and the shouting of men at work to douse the fire below. Her senses seemed to fail her when she ascended onto the landing's disorienting blackness until she heard a familiar sound—Kitty's cough, muffled, as though through a door.

"Kitty! Kitty, come to me!" Elizabeth cried, unable to see her sister in the thick wafts of smoke at the top of the staircase. Her eyes watered as she staggered forward, reaching into hollow darkness towards a cry that answered her.

The floor beneath her feet turned hot, and she raced onward, heedless in haste, shouting Kitty's name. The coughing continued fainter, and Elizabeth ran towards it, arms outstretched. She felt the panels of a door in front of her face, and after a desperate few seconds' scramble, she turned a warm doorknob in her hands. As the door swept open, it made a sibilant sound that she recognised. It was the sound Mrs Bennet's chamber door made as it scraped open across the nap of a well-worn Persian rug. The realisation that she was in her mother's bedroom, which faced the rear of the house, gave Elizabeth courage to move forward in the swarming darkness.

She could not see and breathing was so difficult in the smoke that she dropped to her knees, crawling towards the coughing form on the floor near the windows. As she drew nearer, Elizabeth felt cool air hitting her face. There was a glow of faint silver light, and she guessed by the movement of the air that the windows had been thrown open, letting the smoke pour freely into the night. Her sister had certainly tried her best. Elizabeth reached for the form on the floor.

"Kitty, Kitty!" she cried, shaking her sister, who appeared to have bundled herself in sheets in an effort to protect herself from the smoke—or mayhap, had aborted an attempt to tie those sheets together as a sort of ladder for escape.

Hoarsely, Kitty's voice answered, "Lizzy?" before it was taken with another fit of wretched coughing.

Elizabeth pushed the linens away from her sister's face. "You must come with me. Come now!"

Finding Kitty weak and numb with fear, Elizabeth desperately began to unwind the sheets from Kitty's legs and arms, and grasping her sister around the ribs, tried to pull her to her feet.

Kitty swayed. Elizabeth could do naught but drag her across the floor and towards the door. The hallway without was now so full of smoke that she was forced to pull Kitty down with her to crawl across the floor towards the stairs.

Elizabeth's eyes stung and watered, her throat burned, and every muscle seemed to scream in protest as she panted, trying to fuel her way forward with every gulp of the terrible air in the hallway.

Where were the stairs? She could not see! Oh Lord, if they should be trapped here, smothering and helplessly blind in the smoking darkness!

Suddenly, she heard male voices shout below her, and she hung her will on the thought that she must keep moving towards them. Then she heard her own name, called out wildly, rising above the din from the lower floor. *"Elizabeth!"*

With all her strength, she grasped her sister to her breast and made towards the voice on her hands and knees. She pulled in a suffocating breath and cried out desperately, "Here! I am here! Please, help us!"

She shuddered as a black shape came pounding upwards towards her out of the gloom. Stupefied by terror, she froze for a moment and forced down her instinct that told her to run from it, reasoning with her last thread of logic that this dark force could only be her rescuer.

And, indeed, it was. A man dropped to his knees before her with a heavy sound in the darkness. His voice was rough when he asked, "Is this Miss Catherine with you?"

"Yes! She cannot stand!"

She felt a hand pass along her frame, blindly finding her figure and that of her sister together. With an indrawn breath as from a bellows sounding above her, the burden of Kitty's weight lifted from her side as the man rose to his feet. Their rescuer had, in one swift, shadowy gesture, taken Kitty up in his arms and put her over his shoulder. Then, she felt him reach for her again, and securing his other arm about her waist, he drew her up against his side and steered her around the bend of the landing and towards what had to be the edge of the staircase, for light suddenly arose through a rolling fog of fumes from below.

Panting hard and finding every burning breath more painful, Elizabeth reached out to steady herself against a wall and put her hand against the cast-iron handrail. She cried out in pain from the searing heat of it. Then as her naked feet hit the steps, another agony of heat assaulted her and she stumbled.

The arm about her waist tightened, pulling her closer, pulling her along. "Stay close. The heat is intense here. Do not touch the walls!"

Her rescuer's voice was hoarse, dampened by what she could now see was a white lawn kerchief tied around his face.

"We must run. Now!"

Although the soles of her feet were afire, she obeyed. Through the haze of panic, Elizabeth was steered past the flames licking at the staircase, through the servants' entrance, and back out the door into the shocking coolness and safety of the night.

In the garden, the air, so clear and fresh, burnt her lungs as she drew it in. Weakened from her efforts and starved for breath, Elizabeth fell onto the grass, gasping, tears running down her hot, sweaty, soot-stained face. She coughed uncontrollably, almost choking.

Beside her, the grass rustled as Kitty settled onto the ground, where her constant coughing became wracked, desperate, and helplessly agonised. Within that space of pity-filled moments, Elizabeth also heard the sound of her sister vomiting. She could not open her stinging eyes to look at Kitty yet, but she turned her head towards the sound with a stab of anxiety.

"Kitty! Lizzy!" cried Jane's voice, rushing nearer. "Oh, my dear sisters! How ill you must be! Father, come quickly!"

She felt Jane's gentle, cool hands on her arms for a moment before she opened her watering eyes to see Jane's face go white as she gasped and rushed to Kitty, who lay on the ground nearby.

Their rescuer knelt over her, calling hoarsely for water. Kitty, barely supporting herself on her elbows, was retching, her face a dark colour.

"Kitty took the worst of it," Elizabeth said to Jane in a rasping voice she did not recognise as her own. "She was in Mama's room and has breathed in ever so much smoke!"

Jane bent over Kitty, helping her to sit upright, wiping at her soiled face with her shawl, cooing to her and cajoling her to try and take deep breaths. Elizabeth watched, feeling half caught in a nightmare, as their shaken cook carefully carried a ladle to Jane and urged her to offer water to her sister.

Just as Jane had managed to get a few drops of water past Kitty's cracked and sputtering lips, their father appeared, looking drawn and terrified.

"Kitty, Lizzy—my girls! Are you well?" His voice was hardly above a whisper.

"I am," answered Elizabeth, her own voice weak and tight as

she struggled to a seated position, up from the coolness of the grass. "Kitty, I fear, is not."

Her father was already trying to help Jane by supporting Kitty's frame as the girl gagged and wheezed in acute misery.

"Mr Jones is on his way," her father soothed. "Please, keep trying to breathe."

"Hurts," gasped Kitty.

"I know, my child, but you must!"

"Miss Elizabeth," a voice at her side called, startling her from her worried observations. "Will you not take some water? You look truly ill."

With a start, she recognised their rescuer, who was offering her the ladle, his kerchief now drawn down around his neck and spotted with soot. It was Mr Darcy.

She stared at his face for a moment, too shocked to respond to his offer. "Sir, I thank you," Elizabeth finally managed. "Thank you for saving us at such a risk to your life."

"Pray, do not try to speak. Your throat must be enflamed," he admonished her, though his own voice sounded no less smoked or shattered. "Come now, drink. Slowly."

With shaking hands, Elizabeth cupped the proffered ladle towards her mouth and brought it to her heat-chapped lips. The crisp coolness of the well water on her tongue was a balm. She swallowed a large draught of it eagerly.

Immediately, she regretted having done so. She choked, turning her head and spitting to the side, her face growing hot from the pain in her throat and for shame at such a display in front of Mr Darcy.

"Easy, now," he said in a low voice, not unkindly. He pulled a cracked ewer to his side and refilled the ladle. "Take one sip at a time."

Gingerly, she tried again, this time with better success, although her shaking fingers made it an effort to keep the ladle steady. Awkwardly, Elizabeth wiped her mouth with the back of her hand.

Mr Darcy gasped at the sight. "Your hand!"

Elizabeth turned it over numbly, wondering at his reaction, but soon saw the evidence of his concern blazed across her palm in a raw, scarlet line.

Her mind laboured to recall the events on the staircase, as though remembering something that had happened to someone else.

"I braced myself on the railing," she said hollowly. "I must have burnt it when I did so."

He was already untying his kerchief and pouring cool water onto it. Without asking, Mr Darcy reached for her hand and began to bind it in the moist makeshift bandage. He worked surely and, to her relief, gently, wrapping the palm securely and tugging a knot carefully into place at the base of her knuckles.

"I shall have to ask the apothecary for a liniment for this when he comes. But for now—" He shook his head in needless apology for his attempts at doctoring.

"My hand and feet will be well," she reassured him. "Mr Jones needs to tend to poor Kitty." She nodded to where her father and elder sister were huddled around the coughing, whimpering second youngest daughter.

"Your feet are injured as well?" Mr Darcy asked, drawing back as though to search her for more injuries.

Her toes were modestly tucked underneath the hem of her nightgown, hidden away from sight. She had no intention of showing him. She nodded instead.

His mouth drew into a straight line, and to Elizabeth's eye, he looked almost pained. Her concern aimed towards a new object. "You also ran into the house, sir. Are you well?"

Mr Darcy might have replied, but he was prevented by the heavy clattering of a wagon cart drawing at a hasty speed up the gravel drive. Mr Bingley jumped down from the seat and unlatched the tail board, from which poured at least eight male servants, all carrying pails and rushing towards the house with purpose. Behind them on the wagon sloshed a copper tub brimming with water and two large barrels.

It was a hopeful sight, and Elizabeth was never more pleased that Mr Bingley was all that he claimed—that whatever he did, he did in a hurry.

Mr Darcy did not seem as impressed by his speed. "Bingley, it is about time you arrived!" he said sharply, standing and taking the reins of the team, which stamped nervously at the head of the cart.

"I see the blaze is already coming somewhat under control," said Mr Bingley with relief. "It took us some time to raise the alarm and fetch all the water from the pump house."

He looked a bit abashed at Mr Darcy, and then turned and made his bow to Elizabeth. "Miss Elizabeth," he said, "how do you do?"

"I am well, sir, as you see. I hope you will forgive me if I do not stand."

"Indeed, do not trouble yourself!" he replied, looking rather stricken by the evident weariness written on her face and the hoarseness of her voice. "I have my carriage coming at a pace just behind my men here. I mean to convey all your family to Netherfield until Longbourn is safely extinguished and habitable. I hope you will take some comfort there."

"Sir, you are too kind," said Elizabeth, with more composure but even greater astonishment. "You are truly the best of neighbours."

"I only wish I could have arrived sooner," Mr Bingley replied distractedly, as his eyes met Jane's over Elizabeth's shoulder.

"Miss Bennet!" he exclaimed, rushing over to Jane, where she knelt with her father over Kitty. "I see Miss Catherine is unwell."

"Most unwell, sir," said Jane anxiously. "She has taken the most smoke of all of us, I fear. One of Sir William Lucas's stable boys has already run for Mr Jones. I am afraid it will be a difficult night for her."

"It has been a difficult night for all of you," said Mr Bingley, surveying his neighbours huddling on the lawn. "Mr Bennet, if I may, I have taken the liberty of ordering my carriage for your family. I mean to invite you all to come to Netherfield at once for your comfort and care."

"I hope we are not too much of an inconvenience to you, sir, but we are grateful indeed."

CHAPTER THREE

The Bennet family quickly found themselves wrapped in quilts and lap rugs and trundling towards Netherfield to find recuperation within its walls—for some of them a second time. Along with the manor's capable housekeeper, Mrs Nicholls, Miss Bingley was there to receive them with an admirable alertness in light of the lateness of the hour, and even Elizabeth had to commend her for her presence of mind. She had prepared the basic needs within the guest rooms with astonishing speed, although some rooms would need to be shared among the sisters. When asked if she would mind being put up with Jane, Elizabeth showed all the enthusiasm her weariness would allow.

As she trod gingerly and painfully up the front steps in bare, soot-blackened feet, Elizabeth thought with a twist of dark amusement that Miss Bingley must be beyond shocked by her wild appearance. She was clad in little more than a nightgown and a borrowed counterpane with her hair in a loose braid that was presently falling apart. Positively wild, indeed! And her entire family looked much the same! Why, her father was still wearing his soot covered nightcap and dressing gown!

Behind her, Miss Bingley praised Mr Darcy's safe return, and when Elizabeth turned and beheld him for the first time in the bright light cast by the sconces and the great chandelier above, she was amazed at his appearance. The poor man must have come straight from his bed. Streaked with black across the face and hands like a chimney sweep, how little dignified he appeared!

Yet, he seemed little affected by it. He shrugged off his over-coat, fully exposing his white sleeves and his neck, naked of cravat and with several buttons undone at the collar. He then turned to Mr Bennet, enquiring as to whether a litter would be needed to bring Miss Catherine into the house, or if he would permit her to be carried in directly. Mr Bennet confessed he thought any additional fuss unnecessary, and asked if a sturdy footman could be provided to carry in the girl.

"The footmen are likely still engaged at Longbourn, but I am not yet so fatigued that I cannot manage it myself. Miss Catherine is slighter than my younger sister, Georgiana. I would be glad to be of service."

Mr Bennet's face showed some surprise, but he wearily acceded.

Elizabeth considered it quite conscientious of Mr Darcy to have mentioned his own sister at such a time. It rendered his offer innocent, which was the spirit in which she felt it ought to be taken.

She paused on the cool marble staircase in the great hall to take advantage of the relief its smooth surface provided to her burning feet and to observe the proceedings. It puzzled Elizabeth exceedingly to see a man she had deemed so haughty performing a footman's office. She was pulled from her thoughts by her youngest sister's voice.

"Shall you not come above stairs with us, Lizzy?" asked

Lydia, tarrying just long enough to take the arm of her mother, who was expressing her most rapturously grateful appreciation to Miss Bingley.

"I think I shall wait for Kitty and Jane. You and Mary and Mama should go to your rooms and try to rest."

"If you wish," said Lydia with a shrug, but before she turned away, she examined her sister with a raised brow, adding, "You look frightful, Lizzy. Pray do not stand about like that for long."

Elizabeth did not know whether to be touched or offended by Lydia's remark, so she merely smiled at her sister and promised not to stay overlong.

When she turned her attention back to the scene below, she realised Mr Darcy had gone out again. After some moments, Mrs Hurst drew back the front door to admit him and Kitty, cradled in his arms like a child, and Jane, who followed close behind them. Elizabeth turned and went ahead of him on the staircase, opening the door to the bedchamber prepared for Kitty's care. She turned down the counterpane, and with Mr Darcy's careful assistance, together with Jane, she settled Kitty onto the mattress and propped her up with pillows to ease her efforts to breathe. A new round of coughing had shaken the girl, and it was all the sisters could do to soothe her.

Jane and Elizabeth's preoccupation led them to barely hear Mr Darcy volunteer to fill the ewer in the room with water. He took it and was gone.

"Mr Darcy is very kind to do so much," said Jane, once she recalled the errand he had appointed to himself. She spoke softly as she smoothed sweat and stray hairs from Kitty's brow. It was hard to say whether Jane directed her comment to anyone in particular or merely to the room.

"Mr Bingley was also very kind to bring all his menservants and to stay on at Longbourn to supervise," Elizabeth replied.

Kitty coughed again and then she moaned. Elizabeth moved

to her side and sat on the bed, glad to be off her throbbing feet, which seemed to grow more painful by the moment.

She could not conceal her own impatient anxiety when she spoke to reassure her sister. "Mr Jones has been told to come straight here, Kitty."

"Hurts to breathe."

Jane hushed Kitty gently and took her hand. After some minutes of exhausted silence punctuated only by their little sister's coughing and wheezing and Jane's calming utterances, Mary appeared at the door.

"How does Kitty?"

"Well enough, for the moment," answered Elizabeth. "We still await Mr Jones."

"Mama sent me to ask you to beg some smelling salts of him when he does come. She swears she cannot breathe, although she certainly can talk!"

It was the most forward, true, and, yet, uncharitable thing Mary had ever said, but no one in that little room of exhausted survivors faulted her for it.

"We shall ask him. Please tell Mama to try and take some tea if Miss Bingley can spare the maid to fetch it," said Jane.

"Thank you. I shall." Mary turned and left directly.

"Should we not try to offer Kitty some water when Mr Darcy returns?" asked Elizabeth. "The heat of that upper room where she hid herself very nearly roasted her. In addition to all that smoke in her lungs, I fear her body has lost a great deal of water."

"That is certainly sensible, Miss Elizabeth," answered Mr Darcy, surprising her. He had returned with the ewer and now entered the room. From the bedside table, he took a glass and filled it.

He passed it to Elizabeth with care, instructing her pointedly. "Mind you, be sure she drinks it more slowly than you did."

Elizabeth was not of a mind to argue at his high-handed-ness, although Jane blinked with some surprise at the curious exchange. Together with Jane, Elizabeth helped raise Kitty enough to take some water. With painful effort, she was able to sip a little, though it made her ensuing coughing fit all the more wretched.

This attempt, and yet another, met with only moderate success. Rather than try Kitty's strength, Jane put a stop to the efforts for a few moments' reprieve. She passed Elizabeth the glass and told her to take a sip or two as well. Mr Darcy still hovered in the room with evident anxiety.

"Sir, have you not yet had the chance to refresh yourself somewhat?" Jane asked gently. "You, too, went into the fire. I should not like to see your injuries unmet."

Mr Darcy bowed. "You honour me with your concern, but I am well. I simply wished to be of service until Mr Jones arrives. But I see you will manage. Indeed, you must have long been wishing for my absence, and I can only justify my continued presence by real, though unavailing, concern. I shall leave you three sisters to your privacy."

"Your kindness does you credit," replied Jane with a nod.

Elizabeth, struck at that moment by a great indebtedness to him she could not express in words, extended her uninjured hand to Mr Darcy, which he took in his grasp with care, and with great solemnity, he bowed over it. Then, wishing them all good rest, he turned and quit the room.

At length, Mr Jones arrived, and following a short examina-tion, he began preparing a poultice to be applied directly to Kitty's chest. Jane did not forget the smelling salts for Mrs Bennet, and with his permission, took them from Mr Jones's bag and delivered them to the room at the end of the hall. Eliza-beth stayed as a matter of propriety while he tended to Kitty, for whom the whole ordeal seemed uncomfortable, embarrassing, and more than a little painful. The poultice he applied to her chest was an expectorant. It made her coughing worse, though the apothecary assured her it should serve, in time, to clear her lungs of ash.

While assisting Mr Jones with the application, Elizabeth's mind returned to the extraordinary succession of events she had just survived.

Of great mystery to her was the source of the fire. She could not remember if there had been a candle or any sort of flame that could have been left unextinguished in that part of the sitting room where the fire seemed to have originated just after her family had gone to bed. She also worried for her father, who was nearest to the fire at the start, and she begged Mr Jones to see to him next.

With this request and her office as assistant complete, she took her younger sister's hand and bade her rest. As Kitty's coughing became less distressing, Elizabeth allowed her mind to wander again.

The appearance of Mr Darcy in her moment of need was almost miraculous. Why had he come? How had he known to come, when the alarm had only then been raised to the Long-bourn household and grounds? What was she to make of his attention to her injuries out in the garden? And how, indeed, could a man of his pride lower himself to act as a manservant to her entire family, of whom she knew he thought so meanly?

This conundrum was not to be answered, but rather compounded, for almost an hour after Mr Jones had left Kitty and had in turn been ensconced while treating her father, Mr Darcy reappeared. This time he knocked, but he did not enter the sickroom when Elizabeth hobbled to the door on her tender feet to answer it.

"I know it grows late, Miss Elizabeth," he said with some wariness at her surprised expression, "but I could not hope to retire without delivering this to you."

He extended to her a round glass vial, containing some

unguent. "It is liniment. I took the liberty of speaking to Mr Jones regarding your burns, and he advised that this should be applied several times a day for the next week at least. I beg you will accept my best wishes for your rest and good health."

Elizabeth took it with murmured thanks, and he bowed and left her. She turned back to the sickroom, still shocked by Mr Darcy's thoughtfulness and attention. She had thought for certain he had gone to bed.

To her even greater surprise, Kitty was awake and managed to offer a thought on the exchange. "Lizzy, I think that man likes you."

CHAPTER FOUR

"*S*ir, I fear the bath I had drawn for you when you returned has gone cold," Roberts said. "Allow me to fetch some hot water."

"I have dealt with an inferno tonight. I daresay a cold bath will soothe me better." So saying, Darcy cast off his clothing, and Roberts bowed his assent and gathered the smoke-suffused articles that his master tossed aside.

"It is late indeed. If you will lay a nightshirt on the counterpane for me, I will dismiss you for the night. I shall not need you to attend me in the bath. Go to your bed, man!"

"Certainly, sir."

Darcy lowered himself into the tub with a sigh at the coolness of the water. For some time, he simply soaked, closing weary eyes against the remembrance of the heat of the flames that he had tread so close to that evening. Now removed from danger, his thoughts returned to that first fearful moment when his worst imaginings had been realised.

Upon dismounting his horse at Longbourn, Darcy had

immediately scoured his surroundings in an attempt to account for every Bennet—especially one. As he rushed towards the house, he passed by the noisy Mrs Bennet, saw the eldest Miss Bennet bending to comfort her, and Miss Lydia and her sister Mary huddled crying on the lawn a few paces away. To his concern, he saw in the grim glow from the house that a figure in a dressing gown was walking back towards the entrance to Longbourn, and he raced at once to catch up to whomever it was.

The stride told him that it was not Miss Elizabeth, and at this disappointment, his pulse began to thunder in his ears as his mind raced to other possibilities. The sight of Mr Bennet before him in a state of shocked anxiety arrested and confirmed his worst fears. He rushed to support the older gentleman, who appeared to be trying to make his way unsteadily towards the house.

"Do not detain me!" begged Mr Bennet, attempting to shake off the younger man's arm. Even as he did so, a wracking cough shook his frame. "I must go in!"

Darcy was firm with him. "Let me or a servant go inside for whatever you are seeking. You are not well. You cannot go yourself."

"I must," protested the other gentleman weakly, before his voice suddenly erupted into louder, broken tones of despair. "Lizzy has gone inside! She has gone back to find Kitty! I should not have let her get away from me!" Fighting for breath after this outburst, his knees trembled under him.

Darcy felt as though his own breath had been stolen from him. "How long has she been inside?"

"Too long!" cried Mr Bennet wretchedly, coughing once again with his face gone white as bone.

"Sir, you are unwell! Stay—no, stay here!" Darcy urged him, with more command than request. He pulled the gentleman to sit on the ground to recover his breath. He then drew himself up and pulled his handkerchief from his coat. Numb with sudden acceptance, he tied it about his nose and mouth. "I am prepared, sir, and I shall go at once!"

Thus, Mr Bennet, forced to concede, commissioned him, though in so breathless an intonation as made him almost unintelligible, to fetch his daughters to him.

Darcy was within the heat of the house in moments. The prospect of Miss Elizabeth in such peril seized him with terror unlike anything he had yet experienced in his nearly three decades of life. But as he stood on the threshold of Longbourn, the true horror that had clenched his heart had been unbearable.

It was a sheer miracle that Miss Elizabeth had heard and answered him above stairs in the blinding confusion of smoke and ash and the noise of the disjointed efforts of men fighting back the blaze below. Darcy cursed himself that he had been unable to protect her from her burns, which he knew had been the price of her courageous folly. If only she had waited for his help, if only...

But no, if she had come any later, Miss Catherine might well have perished. He could not fault Miss Elizabeth for her daring action in that regard. No, he could fault her for nothing.

His admiration for Miss Elizabeth's courage opened doors of awareness to certain other delightful attributes he had not allowed himself to dwell upon in his haste. He found renewed appreciation for the cool water of his bath as he considered them.

The shape of her figure in the thin cotton had not escaped his notice, and now he could picture it all in his vivid memory. The strong and shapely legs that propelled her into the night shown clearly through the gauzy fabric of her gown. Those dark, tumbling curls that were longer than he had imagined, escaping her braid. That taut, warm waist he had had the privilege of encircling on the stairs. The lightness of her weight, the softness of her hand, the surprising delicacy of her wrist. And there was more—more that the part of him that was essentially and primally male could appreciate.

It was better he not think of those things now, not when she was again under the same roof with him. It was unwise and a most certain path to temptation. Moreover, it was unworthy of the best parts of her nature, which he had also witnessed that night.

Miss Elizabeth had astounded him with her trust and daring by following him down into the hellish heat. He had barely regained his own breath, when she had stolen it again with her remarkable resilience, evincing such quick recovery of her clever spirits and her shining compassion. Awash in retrospective appreciation, he could now acknowledge the sheer wonder these gifts of her character had awakened in him. He had never known such a woman, one who could rush into an inferno and emerge as bold and brilliant as burnished brass, bright as any mirror.

In the borrowed light of this image, he suddenly recognised what looked back at him from the reflection he cast—a doomed man, besotted by love and admiration. He was certainly not safe from her influence now, and all the fancies he had entertained of escaping her reach now seemed absurd.

Darcy took the soap, industriously scrubbing soot from his face and hands and rinsing the smell of smoke from his hair. These activities only saved him from thinking of Miss Elizabeth for a few minutes. Cursing, he finished his ablutions rapidly and rose from the cold tub.

Drying himself, he paced to his bed and put on his night shirt, welcoming the clean linen and the absence of the acrid smell of smoke hanging about his person. Then he blew out his candle thoroughly, blinked back a sudden image of Miss Elizabeth's exhausted, tear-stained face in the blackness, and dropped to the counterpane with an agitated sigh.

As he lay in repose, Darcy wondered whether she was thinking of him now, and if she thought well of his actions tonight. He thought of her with bare feet, seeming to wait for him on the staircase at Netherfield that evening, and this hopeful image and his exhaustion carried him into dreams.

CHAPTER FIVE

*E*lizabeth awoke thirsty. After drinking a tall glass of water from the ewer Mr Darcy had brought up to the sickroom the night before, and letting Jane help her wash her hair in the bath, she felt a little better.

After towelling herself dry, she winced as she reapplied the liniment Mr Darcy had procured to her burned palm and feet. As she worked in the salve, her fingertips explored her soles carefully. Her poor feet had developed blisters and had grown more tender overnight, and she was saddened to think it might be some days yet before she could stand to walk any distance without pain. The thought encased her mind with a woeful dread, and Elizabeth strove to calm herself as her heart beat desperately inside her like a wild bird in a cage.

Yet, for still another reason, she and her sisters would soon *all* feel a little trapped. It might be some hours, they now realised, before they could divest themselves of their night-time dishabille and don their own day clothing. Their brave little chambermaid, Sarah, had promised to come with a trunk later in the day, once it was established that it was safe again to venture up the stairs of Longbourn and into the family's rooms to look for any clothing that had survived the blaze.

So it was that the Bennets prepared to break their fast above stairs together in their nightclothes in a small sitting room.

Mr Jones returned to see his patients shortly after their meal. Finding Mr Bennet much improved, and Kitty predictably, yet not intensely, feverish due to the purgative process, he then turned to Elizabeth and chided her for neglecting to inform him of her burns when they were fresh.

"The burn on your hand may blister but should mend itself well, I believe," he said after some examination, "but your soles sustained far more prolonged exposure to the heat. With the skin on your feet so damaged, I think it best I give you some cloths for dressings." He then produced a bundle of linen strips from his bag and began to show her how to wrap her feet, mindful of the shape of the arch. Elizabeth's independence could not long permit her to merely observe whilst being thus handled, and she soon insisted on performing the task.

"You see, I shall manage this new fashion quite well after all," she said pertly as she neatly tied the first bandage in a merry bow at her ankle.

"Miss Elizabeth, I know there is little you cannot manage, but take care to keep your bandages dry and clean for at least three days before attempting shoes again. You may experience some infection otherwise," Mr Jones warned her, pushing up his spectacles as he gathered his things once more into his bag. "Your feet will need to recover from the trauma of the heat, and the small blisters that have formed there will weep and drain until fresh skin is formed. I am sorry to say that scarring is likely."

"It is a good thing, then, that the scars will be in a place least likely to be seen by anyone but myself and perhaps a spider hiding in my shoe."

Mr Jones could only smile at his teasing patient, whom he had tended since her girlhood. "For a young, vain lady like yourself that is a blessing," he replied with equal impertinence.

His patient merely laughed and set herself to wrapping her next bandage.

ON THE MAIN FLOOR BELOW, MISS BINGLEY PRESIDED over subdued guests at breakfast. Darcy quietly took his coffee, bolstering his mind in preparation for the uncertainties of the new day. He had just gathered enough energy to find his appetite when Miss Bingley suddenly spoke.

"Charles, exactly how long shall we play host to the Bennets —once again?" she asked while scraping her butter knife across her toast with some aggression.

"Darcy and I shall ride out with Mr Bennet later today to survey the damage, if he is well. Should the living quarters prove safely habitable again after a few well-placed repairs as Darcy hopes, we should be at liberty to return them home within perhaps a month or two. Repairs of a more aesthetic sort can continue later."

"A month or two?" Miss Bingley repeated. "Heaven and earth! Have they no family they can go to? What about that Philips woman?"

"Should they need to stay away longer, Mr Bennet said that his brother-in-law's family in London would likely take them in."

At the mention of the Bennets' Cheapside relations, Miss Bingley offered a dramatic shudder.

"Surely this is not too terrible a task," continued Bingley. "We must all do what we can for them, and hospitality is within your gift. Even Louisa has gone to Mrs Bennet to offer her wardrobe to the ladies, which as you know is no small gesture on her part. Do they not deserve such kindness? After all, the

Bennets are our neighbours and they are our friends! If you could but think of the pleasure you might encounter in the coming weeks, I daresay you may procure delight in having opportunity again to entertain Miss Bennet here, since when last she visited, she was so ill and could not be much in company."

"If the burden should become too great," offered Darcy, "I would be glad to supplement any additional needs the family should have for the interim, Miss Bingley. I can imagine what an inconvenience it must be to suddenly be charged with the feeding of seven mouths and the entertainment of an entire household."

Miss Bingley coloured, no doubt chafing at the implication that the Bingley household's coffers were insufficient for the cost of such hospitality, or that her skills as hostess might somehow be lacking.

"That is most kind of you, but I am sure there will be no cause for that," she reassured him.

Darcy cleared his raw throat and addressed his friend. "As it is, I should be glad to bear the costs to expedite, from London, any materials needed to rebuild Longbourn. I should hate to see the Bennets put out of their home for longer than necessary after such a trial. It must make them feel acutely their lack of privacy, which they surely desire in order to recover their health and good spirits from such an event."

His example of compassion should have shamed Miss Bingley, but it seemed she was far too immersed in her annoyance with the Bennets.

"For myself, I have begun to suspect they do not mind the burden of living with their current company, as I believe it is so very much in the vein of forwarding Mrs Bennet's wishes for her daughters. In fact, I wonder at the timing of this particular accident."

Darcy's knife clattered to his plate. Too tired after a short night of sleep to check himself, he exclaimed, "You do not mean to imply the Bennets were responsible for a misfortune that nearly killed two of their daughters, do you?"

"No, indeed," replied Miss Bingley softly, "but I do mean they intend to use it to their advantage. Mark my words! Within the week, Mrs Bennet will be hinting that it is time for Charles to declare himself to Jane, and Miss Eliza will be throwing herself most shamelessly at you."

"Pardon me," said Darcy, standing abruptly, his appetite quite gone, "but I can testify that Miss Elizabeth can hardly walk, let alone throw herself about."

With that, he quit the table and left Miss Bingley at some pains to find a way to call back the words she had uttered with such ill judgment.

Later that afternoon, after a disappointingly small shipment of presentable clothing from Longbourn arrived for the Bennets to put to use, Darcy, alongside a rather worn-looking Mr Bennet and Bingley, rode sedately over the very fields he had galloped through the night before in a fever of panic.

From the exterior, Longbourn appeared to be intact, with the exception of the sitting room windows which, due to the intense heat of the fire, had cracked and burst away from their frames. Some sooty stains on the stone façade of the house were clearly visible, but it was nothing that a good scrubbing could not remedy. The team of men last night had done an admirable job of preventing a large amount of damage to the overall structure, and Darcy found himself pleasantly surprised by the evidence of their industry.

Inside, however, the sitting and dining rooms and their contents were largely destroyed and sodden with water, as were the ceilings to both rooms that had been charred right down through the horsehair plaster to the wooden beams. In places, it appeared the flooring above the rafters had been partially consumed as the fire greedily made its way to the family's apartments above. The servants' staircase Darcy had used to make his rescue also displayed enough damage to its supporting structure as to seem precarious. It was no wonder he and Elizabeth had felt the heat so acutely or that it had transferred to the railing. It appeared the fire had been smouldering right beneath their feet.

Darcy shook off the memory of it. Focusing on the destruction before him, he noted the stairs would need to have most of its blackened steps replaced, new footings fitted to the stairwell, and the wall next to it would need to be completely reframed and replastered.

After touring the tortured house for some time with its owner in compassionate silence, Darcy said, "I should be glad to draw up some figures with a builder I trust for the repairs."

Mr Bennet did not answer as they continued to pick their way through the waterlogged, littered hallway. His pondering steps led them rather absently down to his habitual haunt: his library. Darcy thought this place was the saddest of all he had yet seen in the house, for having shared a wall with the sitting room, most of the books and shelves on the eastern and southern walls had been reduced to ash by the paper-loving flames.

Mr Bennet, drawing in a heaving breath, ventured inside. Once he had progressed as far as it seemed his feet were willing to take him, he paused and picked up a heat-curled copy of Chaucer's works from his desk with an air of sadness.

"I know it must seem a daunting prospect," said Mr Bingley suddenly, "but Darcy and I had hoped you would allow us to help. I know a man who could hurry along anything you need from the timber docks."

"And as a gift to your family, I would be glad to compensate for the cost of any expedited materials," Darcy added.

"That is extremely generous of you. Your recommendation of a builder would certainly be of aid, but as to the lumber, that may be quite unnecessary," said Mr Bennet, his voice somewhat diminished and tinny from the previous evening's surfeit of smoke. "My brother Gardiner, you see, has many connexions at the docks and will certainly offer the same."

Mr Bennet rubbed at his eyes, pushing aside his spectacles. Darcy thought that the poor man appeared near tears, but Mr Bennet then blinked and seemed to set aside the strong emotion.

"I can only imagine what this house must have looked like when you and Lizzy ran into it last night to rescue Kitty."

Darcy nodded, not trusting himself to comment.

"I do not know how to thank you for my daughters' lives, sir, but I believe you may have a reward coming to you which only a higher power can bestow. I thank you for your courage."

After a moment suspended in amazement at being so honoured, Darcy took a breath. "I believe Miss Elizabeth's courage is greater than mine by half," he offered, feeling some relief in the moment when Mr Bennet smiled faintly.

"Yes, that I can certainly believe." Mr Bennet might have followed this assessment with a laugh, but as tired and worn-spirited as he was, he could only cough and lay aside his ruined book.

As the three gentlemen walked out of the house discussing how soon it might be possible for the very basics of structural reinforcements to be put in effect, they were surprised by the arrival of a hack chaise, and from it, the descending figure of a large and rotund young man clad in black.

The stranger bowed low. "I beg your pardon, gentlemen, but am I correct in calling this particular domicile Longbourn?" said he, in some evident confusion as he glanced towards the charred structure.

Mr Bennet seemed to shake himself from a stupor. "Yes,

this is Longbourn or what is left of it, and you are Reverend William Collins, I believe?"

"Indeed, I am!" said the cleric, doffing his wide-brimmed hat in an affected manner, "and I have, at the behest of my noble patroness, Lady Catherine de Bourgh, hastened to make exact the time of my promised arrival to visit upon my cousin, Mr Thomas Bennet of Longbourn. Punctuality is of utmost importance to my noble lady, and therefore, I strive to keep the clock at every turn."

Mr Bennet looked rather embarrassed. It was clear, in light of the recent destruction, that he had quite forgotten that his preening and obsequious connexion was coming to visit.

"I am Thomas Bennet, and I must apologise to you immediately for a nuisance that will affect all our plans. Longbourn has recently met with some catastrophe, sir, which a brief tour inside will show. It will be some days yet, I am afraid, before I can bring my family back into residence. I am terribly sorry to have inconvenienced you during your visit, but it happened only last night."

Mr Collins's mouth dropped open. "A catastrophe, you say?"

"Indeed, sir," answered Darcy, quickly losing patience with the man, who appeared rather simple-minded despite his elaborate capacities for speech. "A fire broke out at half past ten last night. Mr Bennet's daughters were in some danger, but have been safely removed to Netherfield Park, a neighbouring estate. I am Fitzwilliam Darcy, a guest of Mr Bingley at that estate." He nodded to indicate his friend.

"Mr Darcy? Fitzwilliam Darcy!" exclaimed Mr Collins. He bowed in an obscenely servile fashion, although his excitement did not render him silent during the gesture. He spoke, even as he rose. "Indeed, you must be he, for I now recognise in you the superior elegance, the height and bearing, the noble features, and the perfection of graciousness of your excellent and prestigious noble aunt. Such nobility in one's acquaintance is a true gift. Your aunt is a great lady, whom I serve most unreservedly in response to her generous condescension, as she has chosen to include me in her circle of acquaintance and within her beneficent influence. It is indeed a pleasure to meet the nephew of Lady Catherine de Bourgh, sir, in truth, it is!"

"Kind of you to say so, Mr Collins," responded Darcy, once Mr Collins had finished his effusions. "And how do you know my aunt?"

"By her ladyship's grace I have been given charge of the parish at Hunsford. And I am exceedingly obliged—"

"Yes, yes," interrupted Mr Bennet, "but now that you are here, we must make you comfortable. Please allow me to pay a call at the home of one of our most delightful and trusted neighbours, Sir William Lucas. I believe it would be in keeping with his good grace and warm hospitality to host you at Lucas Lodge for some days at least. I am afraid my daughters at present are recuperating from injuries from the fire and must remain in seclusion at Netherfield."

Mr Collins looked crestfallen, but to Darcy's eye, his expression was owed to a concern tainted with other considerations than the well-being of his cousins.

With some apparent thought, the parson roused himself to voice his concerns with some delicacy. "Your daughters have been injured, you say?"

"Yes, especially my second eldest, Elizabeth, and my second youngest, Catherine. They are still quite ill from the smoke and are recovering from some unfortunate burns."

"My dear sir!" cried Mr Collins, with rather more volume than pity. "I would be happy to visit when convenient and offer them my sympathies and comfort as befitting a man of the cloth. I most certainly would not shirk my duty to any cousin of mine, nor to any gently bred young woman, for that matter."

His speech was met with a nod from Mr Bennet, but Mr

Collins was not yet through. "I should ask, sir, was your eldest daughter injured at all?"

"Jane escaped perfectly unharmed."

"A blessing indeed."

The relief on Mr Collins's face could not be mistaken, and Darcy's mind worked immediately to uncover the truth of his suspicions: Mr Collins appeared to have been afraid that his pre-determined choice of wife might bear unsightly scars.

"I should be happy to call on Miss Bennet, with your blessing, of course, should she feel prepared to receive visitors," Mr Collins offered. "I assure you, I am most sensitive to the breach that has formerly caused a rift within our family, and I shall not fail to do my duty by helping to mend it through a most fortunate alliance within our family circle. Please convey to Mrs Bennet my most honourable intentions in this matter."

Bingley stifled a gasp, but he recovered himself in a moment. Darcy could only stare aghast in extreme distaste at the presumption of the parson.

"I vow I shall not hold it against any of my fair cousins that Longbourn's catastrophe has materially lessened the value of my inheritance and perhaps may yet have a detrimental effect on their own prospects."

Silence followed whilst Mr Collins clasped his hands and surveyed the property of Longbourn with a wagging head. Only one gentleman could find a measure of grace for their visitor in that moment.

"Please come with me, Mr Collins," said Bingley. "I shall instruct your driver to leave your bags here at the step. I should like to tour the house with you, as I understand it may someday fall to your keeping. You are here at a strange time, but as a neighbour to this estate who bore witness to what transpired, I shall be glad to acquaint you with all that happened last night. Mr Bennet will, I am sure, return soon from calling upon Sir William, and all will be settled."

"I would be very obliged to you, sir. I always, if I do flatter myself, endeavour to make myself content in any situation, as befits a minister of the gospel," said Mr Collins without the least uncertainty.

"Good man," replied Bingley, steering him towards the house. Mr Bennet nodded gratefully at Bingley before speaking to the driver of the hack, who agreed to take him as far as Lucas Lodge before continuing on his way.

Darcy then took leave of his friend and Mr Bennet, and he went so far as to offer to send a carriage to convey Mr Collins and his luggage to wherever he wished or needed to go. Such an offer, of course, was deemed the height of condescension—so similar to that of Lady Catherine—and was lauded fluently by Mr Collins.

Mr Bennet took his leave and made his escape. Darcy likewise took the opportunity to return to Netherfield, where he dispatched Bingley's carriage to Longbourn to assist his friend and Mr Collins with all due haste. Afterwards, Darcy sought the quietest room in the house, feeling a strong desire to withdraw and ponder all that he had learned from his tour of the destruction at the Bennet's home.

He retired to the library with a resolution to restore himself, ringing the bell for tea service in answer to his own need for some refreshment to soothe his throat. He had just settled himself on the settee and reached for the book he had abandoned two days previously—a day when he had tried his best to ignore the presence of Elizabeth Bennet in the room—when he observed he was, yet again, not alone.

From the corner of his eye, Miss Bennet appeared. "I beg your pardon, sir. I should never have intruded on your privacy had I known you intended to use the library."

"Not at all," said Darcy, recovering himself. "I have no claims on this particular room."

Miss Bennet smiled warmly at his generous pronouncement, and Darcy felt himself grow a little more at ease. He observed that she held in her arms a pair of books, and he wondered if one of them was for Miss Elizabeth. Without realising he had done it, he had asked his question aloud.

"Indeed, they both are for Elizabeth," Miss Bennet confirmed. "Poor Lizzy is feeling rather disappointed that she is unable to walk out of doors as she is wont to do. She has begged me to find her some poetry or some sort of treatise on the natural world so she can escape to nature through her meditations."

"I can well comprehend that for someone with her spirits such confinement must be very frustrating. Pray, Miss Bennet, do you think your sister would be able to take a short outing, perhaps in the garden, keeping to the path? There are benches there, and a small orchard, and she may read in the shade if she chooses. It is not far, and I believe she might manage it on foot. If not, please convey to her that I would be honoured to escort her there by any means."

Had it been any other creature to whom he had spoken so openly, Darcy would have been mortified by this desperate and obvious display of his desire to cater to Miss Elizabeth. But Jane Bennet, with her soft and pleased gaze, showed clearly in her mien that she refused to think ill of anyone for wishing to do a kindness, especially a kindness to her dearest sister. She merely smiled and, thanking him, said she felt her sister would never think to ask for such a favour, yet would likely enjoy such an adventure immensely.

"I shall suggest the outing to her, Mr Darcy. It is likely she will attempt it herself, and I do not doubt she will succeed in the journey, considering the inducement. You are very kind." With that, Miss Bennet curtseyed and left him to his book.

After half an hour's attempt to take some tea and focus on his reading, Darcy abandoned his book for the second time. Restless, he shut the volume and put it back on the shelf. With a sort of pleasant apprehension, he headed towards the back of the house to look out over the garden.

He smiled. There on the bench, looking very pleased with her success, was Miss Elizabeth, reading contentedly, her bandaged feet hidden out of his sight under her gown.

CHAPTER SIX

Despite the hodgepodge of rescued or borrowed clothing in which they were attired, and even though one of their number—young Miss Catherine—was still keeping to the sick bed, to Darcy's eye, the Bennet family's spirits appeared high as they congregated in the dining room. He mused that the call to dinner must have worked some gladdening charm to restore the party to the pleasant, everyday habits of the commonplace amidst the struggle of their unusual circumstances.

Miss Bingley had mixed as many ladies as possible in the seats between the outnumbered gentlemen. Darcy suppressed the vexation he felt at the yawning gap between himself and Miss Elizabeth that prevented conversation. In the best interests of his contentment, he resolved to enjoy his dinner.

Darcy began by patiently answering Miss Mary's questions about the state of Longbourn. In so doing, he discovered the middle Bennet daughter, while pedantic in conversation, nevertheless held a commendable concern for her home and the comfort of her family.

He also found it was pleasant to observe Miss Elizabeth at a distance. From the first moment he had reached his seat, Darcy had monitored her progress as she gingerly stepped to the table, seated herself when her father held her chair, and proceeded somewhat awkwardly to use her injured hand to eat with her utensils. With the aid of candlelight, he could see the sheen of liniment on her palm, and he was pleased to know she was using it.

He longed to ask her how she fared. More than that, he wanted to hear the sound of her voice, to hear if its pleasing tones had recovered from the effects of the searing smoke. His attention was rewarded towards the end of the meal when quiet descended momentarily upon the sated occupants of the table.

"Miss Bingley, I thank you for the delightful meal," Miss Elizabeth said, and Darcy was cheered to find her voice seemed stronger than the night before.

Miss Bingley raised an eyebrow but answered agreeably. "But of course. You are certainly welcome."

Soon after that exchange, the separation of the sexes commenced. Mr Bingley invited the men to take a nightcap in the library or to join Mr Hurst in the billiards room, and the Bennet ladies were asked to join Miss Bingley and Mrs Hurst in the music room for some practice and entertainment.

Mrs Bennet expressed a strong desire to see the room and its beautiful instrument, and she fluttered about gathering her daughters like chicks to leave their roosting perches at the table. It was nearly painful for Darcy to observe Miss Elizabeth struggling up from her chair later than the rest and, teetering in open discomfort, be forced to lean on the arm of her elder sister as they followed in Miss Bingley and Mrs Bennet's wake. As she walked out with a belaboured step, Darcy observed a glimpse of linen bandages on her feet under the hem of her dinner gown. The sensation this sight evoked was difficult to name, but he knew it was a sentiment more noble than pity.

ELIZABETH WAS FAR FROM COMFORTABLE, AND IN truth, although she strove not to show it, she felt almost unequal to the journey across the grand foyer into the smaller parlour that served as the music room. The balls of her feet had formed a series of blisters overnight that were now extremely tender under the pressure of walking, and Elizabeth worried at any moment that she would need to stop and adjust her bandages. Yet, in this company, she knew there was no privacy to do so. She wished in vain that she had not been so stubborn and had remained above stairs.

Although Elizabeth believed she had adequately concealed her discomfort, Jane perceptively slowed her steps beside her and wordlessly passed an arm around her waist, supporting more of Elizabeth's weight as they made their way.

For an hour, they sat and listened to Miss Bingley exhibit on the pianoforte—very correctly and energetically done, with good fingering and execution—and to Mary, who did her best in turn. Mrs Bennet spent this time attempting to glean Mrs Hurst's knowledge of the latest fashions in town that she had observed in her recent visit, which Mrs Hurst proved happy to supply. All seemed genial enough, but Elizabeth could not observe such pleasantry without sinking self-consciously into mortifying reflection as she surveyed the scene. Once again, her family's misfortunes had cast an imposition upon the Bingley sisters, and her own growing discomfort only compounded her sense of helpless dependency.

It seemed more discomfiture was to come, for Miss Bingley had begun to talk very pointedly to Jane about the great enjoyment her brother had in attending fashionable balls and gatherings in some of the higher circles of London, fairly intimidating her listener through her descriptions of their superiority and grandeur. Vainly did Elizabeth strive to assert a measure of her native wit in order to help her sister deflect some of Miss Bingley's comments, but she found her painful feet to be a source of constant interruption to her concentration. Perhaps, she considered, it would not be inappropriate to help Jane to withdraw from the uncomfortable tête-à-tête—and at the same time, to secure an escape from her own suffering.

"Miss Bingley, I am sorry to interrupt," said Elizabeth when there was a moment's pause, "but I require Jane's assistance. My burns have given me some pain just now that I know I can only attend to in my chamber. I beg your pardon for taking Jane from you, yet I am afraid I simply must retire."

"Oh, poor Miss Eliza! I had quite forgotten how very injured you were," Miss Bingley replied. "Of course you must be excused, and you must do as you will to meet your needs. Shall I summon a footman to assist you?"

"I do not think it will be necessary. I have managed the stairs before. I thank you, Miss Bingley."

"Not at all," replied her hostess, who rose when Jane did, as both made a curtsey. Jane went to Elizabeth and helped her to her feet, which now seemed rather more swollen than she had last perceived them to be.

Their progress to the stairs was slow, as Elizabeth strove to set her weight to each foot carefully with each step through the hall. Jane became noticeably concerned at the sight of her sister's pain, made more obvious by Elizabeth's increasing reliance on her arm.

"Lizzy, perhaps we ought to send for a footman or for our father."

Elizabeth gritted her teeth. "If I can but reach the stairs, I shall do well on my own. I shall hold onto the rail, as I did last night. Surely, there can be no new difficulty."

Jane conceded, and after some effort, they made their way to the staircase, where Elizabeth reached for the handrail and pulled herself up to the first step.

Elizabeth gasped, alarmed as a peculiar sensation of pain and hot moisture suddenly pulsed from the ball of her right foot. At once, Jane took the next stair to help hold her sister upright from above.

"I think I have ruptured a blister, Jane. Hold on to me a moment more, please."

Slowly bringing her left foot up to the step to join her right, she carefully shifted her weight again, and holding the rail, raised her right foot behind her for inspection. A spot of rust coloured blood now stained the linen, threatening to soil the polished staircase. She groaned in mortified frustration.

"Here now, Lizzy, what is the matter?" said a voice, surprising both women from their private conference. It was their father, who had just emerged from the library with Mr Darcy.

Elizabeth hurried to lower her foot so that neither her father nor his companion could view the damage she had done to herself. She was grateful for the long hem on her uncomfortable gown borrowed from Mrs Hurst.

"It is nothing," she prevaricated. "It is only more difficult to run about as I should wish. I shall be well, merely a little slow."

Mr Bennet may have accepted this fib with naught but a wry expression, but it seemed that Jane would not allow it to pass. She left Elizabeth holding onto the bannister and hastened to her father's side in supplication.

"I fear Lizzy has done herself more injury. I beg you would help me assist her, Papa. She needs to retire."

"I see," replied Mr Bennet gravely.

Mr Darcy raised his eyebrows in surprised concern, and Mr Bennet turned to him. "My daughter, despite her notable injuries, suffers most greatly from her own stubbornness." He approached and took Elizabeth's arm, giving it a comforting pat. "Now, now, my girl, do not protest. Will you not allow your old papa to help you up the stairs?"

Elizabeth looked into his concerned face and wilted in defeat. "I fear I have no choice."

Mr Bennet smiled at her, gave a small cough that sounded almost apologetic, and then encircled her with his arm. "Put your arm around me, dear girl. Up we go."

Leaning on her father, Elizabeth took the next four steps with rather the same difficulty she had experienced with Jane. Mr Bennet grew immediately more concerned, and pausing on the last step they had surmounted, said to her, "Has it truly grown so much more painful since last evening?"

"I do not know why, but it has," Elizabeth whispered, her eyes glistening with tears of frustration and pain. "It feels intolerable at the moment. I must have aggravated the wound somehow."

"Then let us take a moment to rest, my dear. Come, sit next to me, and when this new pain passes, we shall try to climb the last few steps quickly."

Elizabeth nodded, and with his help, she carefully eased herself down to sit on the step. In doing so, however, she had unwittingly allowed her feet to slide from under her hem, exposing her bandaged soles to those below her for but a moment.

Jane gasped aloud at the sight. "Lizzy, your feet are bleeding!"

If the preceding display of pain and discomfort had not already arrested Mr Darcy's attention, then this pronouncement proved to have captured it completely. He moved quickly from the edge of the foyer to approach the staircase.

"Given that further attempts to ascend could produce more damage to these injuries, would it not be much safer for Miss Elizabeth to be taken off her feet?"

"Mr Darcy, I am afraid I may be past such an age where I could safely carry the girl pig-a-back up the stairs, such as I used to do," said Mr Bennet.

"You are perfectly right, Papa," Elizabeth agreed, before lifting her eyes to Mr Darcy. "I thank you for your concern, but

I believe I shall manage very well in a moment. I simply need to rest."

"Forgive me, Miss Elizabeth, but I disagree," said Mr Darcy, placing his foot on the bottom step of the stair in an attitude of implacability. "You risk rending flesh that has only just begun to heal."

"I think Mr Darcy is right. It is best we fetch a footman to bring you above stairs," said Jane, gently but firmly.

Elizabeth felt rather betrayed that Jane should oppose her. "I have no wish to be fetched up to my room like a pail of water by one of Mr Bingley's men! I can—"

"Come now, we must insist," interrupted Mr Darcy in a tone rather darker than Jane's. "You could be up the stairs and comfortable in an instant, if you would but allow those who care for you to render assistance."

Elizabeth drew in a sharp breath of ready retort, but her father held up his hand, forestalling further argument.

"I have heard enough. My child, you must be sensible, and I rather think your champion has the right of it here. You must be carried. I am sorry that you must suffer the indignity, for I know you will not take it lightly."

Seeing no friendly assistance to secure her side of the argument among the little band gathered around her on the steps, Elizabeth sighed. "Very well, Papa. Call a footman, if that is your wish."

"If you would permit me, Mr Bennet, I rather think Miss Elizabeth is no greater a burden than was Miss Catherine," said Mr Darcy, indicating his purpose and utterly surprising Elizabeth.

"We must not depend upon you to carry every Bennet lady in the house up these stairs, however inclined you may feel to the exercise," Mr Bennet replied.

Darcy did not shrink. "It is no burden."

"Then, Lizzy, let us waste no more of Mr Darcy's evening. I

am afraid he has taken orders upon himself for your service. Jane and I shall go up with you."

"Papa—"

But Mr Darcy was already at her side. Having secured her father's consent, he now appeared determined to fulfil his purpose. "Miss Elizabeth, with your permission?" he requested, bowing and indicating his intention by the open sweep of his hands.

Numb with mortified irritation, Elizabeth could do no more than nod. In moments, she felt herself being gathered to his chest, and then she was elevated some feet above the staircase, which under Darcy's steady tread, receded rapidly from beneath her.

Elizabeth found the confines of her new situation both distressing and fascinating. Aside from her father or her uncle, she had never been held in the embrace of any man. At this proximity, her senses felt overwhelmed by the invasive assault of unfamiliar stimuli such forced intimacy invited.

Although her embarrassment kept her from meeting his gaze, she could take in the fine stubble of his beard that followed the line of his jaw, the bright linen of his cravat near her nose, and the fine texture of his coat at her ear. Elizabeth noted, too, the firmness of his arms, the nimbleness of his grasp, and the rhythm of his walk that rocked her slightly as they progressed, punctuated by the contraction and expansion of his breathing at a pace slightly more accelerated than her own. And lastly, she became aware of his scent, which carried with it such depth of information—the cedar clinging to his clothing, and some exotic, spiced fragrance that must have come from the oils in his soap—and layered beneath all of this, wafting from his skin, the unnameable scent of something decidedly male that was strange to her, given her cloistered world of close female society.

With a start, she felt vibration in her ribcage as Mr Darcy

spoke, his deep voice rumbling from his chest and through her own.

"When we came upon you, I was just speaking to your father of Longbourn, Miss Elizabeth," he said once they had reached the landing. "I received this afternoon a response to my express to a builder I trust, who provided within his reply some figures for your father, and Mr Bennet has chosen to engage his services. I have sent for him to come, and he expects to arrive in Meryton within the week. Then repairs within your home can begin."

Elizabeth thought Mr Darcy very clever to distract them both from the unexpected intimacy of their short journey by speaking to her of home.

"That is wonderful news. Pray, did the builder also tell how long he thought such repairs might take?"

She watched in some fascination as his lips shaped his reply to her question, hardly aware of her own wayward observation that there was something rather pleasing about his mouth when he spoke.

"He could not, in good conscience, offer any specifics until he had seen the damage with his own eyes, of course, but from my notes, he did not think it overlong before you could find yourselves in an agreeable state to return home, at which point less essential renovations could be enacted. If supplies and men arrive soon, I daresay it will be only six or eight weeks hence when you will be unpacking your trunks in your own rooms."

The idea delighted her greatly, and as they passed as one through her chamber door, Elizabeth could see that Jane, who entered before them with Mr Bennet, had heard all and was pleased as well.

"That is excellent news indeed, Mr Darcy," said her sister, who motioned for him to place Elizabeth onto a sewing chair.

Elizabeth's body had gone rigid at the prospect of being

deposited, like some awkward package, onto a chair. Mercifully, her release was quick and surprisingly graceful.

Mr Darcy then bowed and moved to make his exit. "I wish you both good evening," he said to the women. Then to Mr Bennet, he added, "We can complete arrangements regarding Mr Higgins back in the library, if you wish."

"Certainly, sir. I believe we have given the ladies plenty to discuss," said Mr Bennet lightly, and he followed as Mr Darcy retreated from the room.

CHAPTER SEVEN

The next morning Darcy finished a pile of business correspondence with little pleasure. Yet, he picked up the last letter—the one he knew would take him the longest to answer—with delight. It had come from his sister, Georgiana, full of her satisfaction to hear his account of his visit, which had included a report of Miss Elizabeth Bennet's stay at Netherfield during Miss Bennet's illness.

As he read her response, he sighed, wondering how best to share his latest—and no doubt alarming—news of the great personal risk he had taken just two evenings prior to secure the lives of Miss Elizabeth and her younger sister.

The sound of the pianoforte from the music room downstairs drew his attention from the desk. Looking about the sitting room to ensure he was alone, he stood and stretched his shoulders. He briefly listened to the soft resonance of the music, conjecturing which lady might be at the instrument before he again regarded his sister's letter.

After a moment of consideration as to how to proceed, he

decided that it was best to write of a subject while in its presence.

Tucking his pen into the inkwell and carefully rolling up some paper, he took both with him as he walked across the hall and down the stairs to the music room door, drawn almost closed as Miss Mary and Miss Elizabeth practised. After listening a moment, Darcy cleared his throat.

"Pardon my interruption, ladies, but I was having trouble finding enough light to write this letter to my sister on this cloudy morning. Would you mind if I shared the music room with you? I shall keep only to the window, there." He felt foolish even offering such a poor excuse.

Miss Elizabeth nodded. "We are happy to share the room, but I fear for your powers of concentration. We are not the quietest of students."

"Nor should you be," he replied. "As music students, you must experiment with sound as a necessity. I do not mind it. My sister practises constantly when I am at home writing my correspondence, and it is no strain for me to forge onward."

He took his seat as the ladies resumed. Miss Elizabeth asked her sister to repeat the last section of the aria again.

"Take Mr Darcy's advice, Mary. Experiment with the sound of the accented separation, and see where it leads you."

Miss Mary returned to the instrument, and Darcy took up his pen.

He wrote with steady concentration for several minutes, hoping to convey his assurances, even as he related the dreadful events of scarcely two days prior. It was the sort of news he would have preferred to have told his sister to her face so that he could comfort her. He could readily imagine her shock and anxiety once she realised the very real danger in which he had placed himself. Darcy also anticipated how her tender, compassionate heart would be touched with worry for the ongoing welfare of the Bennets, and most especially those who had been injured. Without wishing to draw too much of her alarm towards Miss Catherine's condition, he requested Georgiana's prayers for a complete recovery.

He stopped his pen and listened to Miss Elizabeth singing softly and expressively as she and Miss Mary returned to the first lines of Pergolesi's aria. As Darcy examined Elizabeth's now-familiar features, he was pleased to see that her expressions revealed an easiness of spirit, but her awkward seating on the bench betrayed her acute discomfort.

He took up his letter again.

Pray also, I beg you, for Miss Elizabeth, for I have learnt she sustained some burns to her hand and feet in the incident from which she now suffers pain. Perhaps even more troublesome is that such injuries have infringed upon her much-cherished liberty to venture wherever she chooses.

Cautious not to centre his concern upon Miss Elizabeth overmuch, yet no longer wishing to conceal his admiration, Darcy decided to merely close his letter and let Georgiana make of it what she would.

I took note from your last missive that you have received glowing reports on your progress on the pianoforte from your new master. I am delighted you have taken so much care to learn an instrument that often brought such pleasure to our mother. I know she would be proud of your efforts! Pray continue in your endeavours, for I selfishly wish to have the delight of listening to you.

You are always in my prayers, my dearest girl, and never far from my thoughts. I look forward to seeing you soon for Christmas.

Your loving brother,
Fitzwilliam

Sighing, Darcy sat back, listening to the song as the duet recommenced. When the page before him was dry, he folded his letter, and perceiving an echoing rustle of paper, looked up to find Miss Mary industriously reshuffling the pages of the aria to return them in proper order to Miss Bingley's collection. Miss Elizabeth was preoccupied with cautiously rising from the bench with one hand on the pianoforte's edge.

"May I assist you, Miss Elizabeth?" he offered.

She froze, then offered him a small smile. "Do not trouble yourself, sir. My feet are much improved."

"I am glad to hear it," he answered, heartened by the news, but also disappointed that he could not be of some use to her in a way that might afford some contact. Turning aside his wayward thoughts, Darcy glanced at Miss Mary and said, "I believe I would be remiss not to thank you both for an hour's entertainment."

Miss Mary adjusted her spectacles and looked at him in some surprise before addressing his compliment. "Sir, you are welcome, but I believe music should be a gift bestowed freely on any listener."

Having already shared some conversation at the previous evening's dinner with the girl, Darcy was not surprised to be addressed in such a didactic fashion. "Indeed, but I thank you for the privilege, just the same."

She curtseyed and turned away to offer her sister some assistance in leaving the room. Elizabeth declined and said she would be along to attend to Miss Kitty in a moment.

Inwardly, Darcy exulted, although he was privately concerned that standing as she was so unsteadily by the piano, her pain might force her from the room at any time. As he crisped the folds of his finished letter, he began to wonder if he had the power to detain his delightful companion many moments more.

He quickly searched his mind for a topic. "Miss Elizabeth, I hope you do not mind that I have taken the liberty of disclosing the events of the past two days to my sister. I believe Georgiana would wish to know of my involvement and to learn of your family's safety and current comfort."

He inwardly rejoiced when Elizabeth turned towards him and replied, "Of course, although I wonder that she would, beyond her obvious care for your welfare, wonder overmuch about the fate of my family, seeing as we are so wholly unconnected."

"The circumstances of your previous visit to Netherfield were enough to excite her curiosity about you and your family, particularly after I related to her your devoted relationship to your elder sister, and how you had travelled hither."

Elizabeth blushed. "Surely, she must think me a curiosity—that I should shock Miss Bingley with my sudden and soiled appearance after traipsing across such muddy farmland!"

"Not at all. Rather, she thinks it displayed a noteworthy affection for your sister. That is nothing for which you should blush."

His praise made Elizabeth fall silent. Darcy forged onward, determined to restore their conversation. "I fear, however, that the tale of the extraordinary events of two evenings past will stretch my sister's fervent belief in my truthfulness to its limits. She might find it believable, based on her knowledge of your strong sisterly affection, that you would race back into Longbourn to rescue a sister, but Georgiana might be hard-pressed to envision her ordinarily cautious brother daring the blaze without a more careful plan of action!"

"I saw no true fear in you. Would you, in a moment of such 'cautious' thinking, have rather remained outdoors than have entered the house?"

"Had I been rational, I might have at least brought a pail of water to clear a partial path," he admitted. "As it was, I made do with only a handkerchief."

"Indeed, you looked a veritable burglar as you came up those stairs out of the darkness and smoke!" She laughed. "I was afraid when I first saw you, so much so that I had to force myself not to run, as my instincts instructed me to do."

"Did I truly frighten you?" Darcy said in amazement and with some regret.

"Yes, although part of my terror may have been a result of being already frightened half out of my wits!"

"As could naturally be expected! Still, I ought to have given some thought to that."

"Far be it from me to reproach any action of yours that night, Mr Darcy. You have no need for regret," she said with great sincerity.

"You are very kind, but no mortal action is perfect."

"True, but some mortal actions are praiseworthy none-theless," Elizabeth said, sounding like her gentle elder sister as her voice grew in warmth. "If you believe Miss Darcy may have trouble taking your likeness in the role of hero for such an adventure, ought I to enclose a statement of support to verify your account, should it ever be brought to trial?"

She stepped on careful cat-feet to the table before him and drew up his abandoned pen. With an arch smile that made him laugh outright, Elizabeth took up the only remaining blank page before him and pressed her purloined pen to paper.

"You need not do that," he said with a smile. "Truly, my word is good enough for my sister. I only wish to spare Georgiana the shock of such a singular night's events that she will uncover on reading this missive."

"Ah, so you require no corroboration?"

"Not as evidence, no."

"Pity! I should have written her a lovely little note, which would have amused and shocked her still more."

"Then I should not postpone such an experience for her, nor any pleasure of yours, if it be your wish to shock and amuse, which I fancy is a turn of your mind that cannot fail to please you."

Miss Elizabeth seemed emboldened by his challenge, and giving him a teasing glance, she bent over the desk and wrote.

> *I, Elizabeth Bennet, enclose this statement in support of the veracity of the contents of this letter and of the claims herein. Mr Darcy is all he declares to be, and has done all he claims to have effected on the night of the 17th—unless, of course, he should have claimed to have rescued four damsels instead of two, or to have summoned rain clouds to douse flames, which he has no art to enchant!*
>
>   *Signed to witness, this 19th November,*
>   *EB*

With a flourish, she trimmed the note and handed it to him. "There, enclose it if you will, but entreat your sister not to judge the quality of my hand too harshly, for it was lately burnt."

"You have my word," he answered, taking the letter from her. Smothering a new wave of chuckles, Darcy added a hasty postscript to his own letter to note the enclosure.

Her modesty reasserted itself as she flushed anew in some embarrassment at her own actions, and he imagined, at some surprise at his sudden whimsy. However, Darcy was unperturbed as he sealed her note within his own. Then, he bowed to her.

For all his seeming aplomb, Darcy felt rather dazed and elated as he posted his letter for London. To have effectually endorsed a correspondence between Georgiana and Elizabeth, to have her volunteer a message—however as a turn of humour —was a wonder! That she would tease him in order to delight him and his sister! It was all almost too fantastical to believe.

Their flirtation had been more overt than any Darcy had dared before with her or with any lady, and despite its clear danger to both her raised expectations and his, he could not reprimand himself. He was far too well pleased.

CHAPTER EIGHT

Resting above stairs at Kitty's bedside, Elizabeth could scarcely believe her own audacity—but neither could she account for Mr Darcy's, except as an extraordinary measure done to indulge her own vain concept of cleverness and to amuse his sister. Such a measure gave evidence not only of an unlooked-for piece of playfulness within Mr Darcy but also a willingness to open a friendship between Miss Darcy and herself. Such a connexion, Elizabeth thought, must be insupportable to such a prideful man!

Yet, since the fire, had she seen any evidence of Mr Darcy's fearsome pride? The very pride she had pressed him to defend only a few days ago? She paused to consider.

Since Sunday night, Elizabeth had seen nothing but gentleness, anxious concern, and willingness to share his company and confidences as she had never seen him venture before. Could it all be done out of pity for her family and her injuries? Could it be a result of the forced moments of trust forged between them in the crucible of his rescue?

Neither cause seemed fully sufficient to create openness and humility in a man so given to reticence and superiority. What could account for it? She could rest her mind only on her supposition that the man could not be so completely ill-tempered as he had first appeared at the Meryton assembly.

Elizabeth's mind was little settled by dinner that evening, when all the families again convened around Miss Bingley's splendid table. She scarcely managed to lift her eyes to him when Mr Darcy offered to escort her and Mary in to dinner, though she did not hesitate to rely a little on his arm to spare her still tender feet more abuse.

Elizabeth was gratified to see Jane and Mr Bingley defy the previous evening's seating arrangements by sitting together. That happy observation gave her the courage she needed to face another meal in such mixed company.

She slid down into her chair with a sigh that was covered by the effusions of her mother, who had opened dinner conversation with the announcement that the whole company had been invited to one of her sister's card and dinner parties at the Philipses' home the following evening.

"For, although her apartment has not enough bedrooms to take us all in," explained Mrs Bennet, "my sister has a delightful sitting room, and she makes such clever arrangements in her dining room so as to ensure everyone is seated at table."

"That is very kind of Mrs Philips," answered Mr Bingley at once. "I should be glad to come." He smiled brilliantly at Jane.

"Indeed, it will be jolly good fun after being cooped up here like hens all day," said Lydia. Before Elizabeth had time to fully drown in the mortification of Lydia's display of ingratitude, her sister continued. "I so long to see the officers, who I am sure my aunt will invite. I daresay they miss me too! Oh Mama, may I walk into town tomorrow morning to call on my friends?"

"That would be just the thing! But I fear that for Kitty, such an adventure would be too much. It is regrettable that she must remain at home until her fever is fully gone," said Mrs Bennet, "and, of course, Lizzy must stay home as well, at least until we are conveyed to the Philipses' by carriage. Her burns are dreadful."

"La, who cares about that!" Lydia sniffed. "I had much rather go alone, and then all the officers will speak only to me."

"But you must be accompanied," said Mrs Bennet artfully. "Jane may go, too, and Mary, if she wishes, and I would be vastly contented if a gentleman would escort you. Mr Bingley would certainly do, if he is not occupied."

Jane blushed furiously at her mother's presumption, but her doting lover saved her.

"I would be happy to, Mrs Bennet!" cried Mr Bingley. "I rather think it would do me good to walk about town and see what has come lately from London."

"I have no need of such trifles," said Mary. "I would much rather stay in and read. It might do Kitty some good if she were to listen to me read aloud, for she hardly reads enough."

Mr Bennet chose that moment to attempt to close the subject. "It all sounds settled. Jane, Lydia, you will go tomorrow with Mr Bingley, as he is so good to offer his escort. I daresay there will be enough entertainments in Meryton for you, and it will be good to show the neighbours that we have not all of us gone up in smoke."

"Oh, Mr Bennet!" cried his wife, "you are so good to our girls! But it brings to mind another person who ought to see us now. Poor Mr Collins has come with the express purpose of meeting us all and calling on our daughters, and he has not had a proper chance since he arrived."

To Elizabeth's horror, her mother then turned to Miss Bingley. "If you would be so good, we should love to have Mr Collins at Netherfield to dine some evening."

The indelicacy of asking their hostess such a thing while

they were all at table—and where she could not with seeming grace refuse—stole all colour and breath from Elizabeth. She looked anxiously at her father, hoping in vain he would correct her mother, and saw, not far from her father, Mr Darcy glowering with his eyes downcast.

Miss Bingley took a moment to collect herself. "I daresay it can hardly be a difficult task to host one man," said she at length and very coldly. "Invite him to dine here on Thursday, if he is not otherwise engaged."

Mrs Bennet at least had the grace to thank her hostess warmly before turning and crowing, "There, Lizzy! Will that not be a fine thing? Mr Collins will have occasion to meet you, and now that you are back in looks, he will no doubt fall in love with you."

Elizabeth wished she could sink straight through her chair and disappear into the floor. "Mama, please—"

Mr Darcy's voice, pitched to carry farther, interrupted her. "Mr Bennet, if you recall, I sent an express yesterday to Mr Higgins asking him to come with his team as soon as may be to assess and begin work on Longbourn. I received word this evening that Mr Higgins will arrive tomorrow in Meryton. Would you be so kind as to reserve your next two afternoons in anticipation of meeting with him during his assessments?"

Mr Bennet blinked, turning from his mirth over his family's antics to give Mr Darcy his full attention. "I would be happy to. Heaven knows I am at my leisure and at your disposal. I received a note this morning, and I think it likely that my brother-in-law, Mr Edward Gardiner, will also come from London soon and stay with the Philipses, likely two or three days hence, to see what assistance he can lend at Longbourn as we order supplies. The timing will serve us well."

"Papa, I should like to accompany you to see Longbourn when next you go," Elizabeth began in an eager tone. "I must learn what I can do to salvage the furniture, the household items, and books. I may be of use in ordering fabric or thread, or rebinding pages—" Elizabeth fell silent, anxious now at perceiving Mr Darcy's eyes on her as well as her own father's, both alight with concern.

"You ought to be mindful of your feet," her father chided her gently. "Longbourn is not yet safe for you to go running about in bandages. You must be well enough to wear your boots, or you may not come at all."

"In two more days, I shall manage perfectly well."

Mr Bennet chuckled. "I see you are determined. I shall not reject your request outright, Lizzy, but I advise you to wait until Thursday to ask me again. Your proof must be offered on the day of your proposed adventure."

Elizabeth nodded, seeing his good sense, and she was surprised to note that Mr Darcy nodded as well, approving her father's answer in accord with what, she assumed, were his own feelings of caution.

Once more, Elizabeth examined her feelings on Mr Darcy's unsolicited opinion. Whereas once she might have considered such participation from him an impertinence, she now saw his expression as evidence that he retained some concern for her well-being. She felt no irritation towards him, only a sensation of unexpected tenderness, which both soothed and surprised her.

Buoyed by the unexpected sensation, Elizabeth gave both men a teasing look. "I suppose this *evidence* I am to offer must be something substantial to satisfy such stringency. What must I do to assure you that my feet are sound? Shall I dance a reel? Shall I perform a leg race against one of the dogs?"

"I think a jig would serve perfectly. I should hate to see you being chased by a bird dog. It is most unladylike, my dear," her father said with a chuckle.

"Caesar would best you regardless," said Mr Darcy dryly. "My dog is a rather competitive lout."

For the first time that evening, Elizabeth felt at liberty to laugh aloud. Her merriment only multiplied when she saw Miss Bingley turn with an aghast expression, and she recalled that lady had once declared that to laugh at Mr Darcy would be impossible.

For the first time that evening, Elizabeth felt at liberty to laugh aloud. Her merriment only redoubled when she saw Mary hurrying away with an abstracted look, and she recalled that they had once declared that to laugh at Mr. Darcy would be impossible.

CHAPTER NINE

O n Wednesday morning, Kitty, whose fever had broken and who had awoken hoarse but exultant, was seated with the entire Bennet family for breakfast when the post arrived. To Elizabeth's surprise, the footman delivered to her two letters. The first was a short note written in the familiar hand of Charlotte Lucas, declaring her intense desire to call upon Elizabeth as soon as she felt well. The second was a letter of some greater substance, judging by its thickness, written in a dainty hand unknown to her, directed to Netherfield from Darcy House in London. She read its first lines with astonishment.

Miss Elizabeth Bennet,

   Be not alarmed, madam, at my haste and presumption in writing you after having read your extraordinary statement enclosed within my brother's express this evening. There is so much I wish to know about you—an entreaty with which I hesitate to burden you, since we have not yet been introduced. Be assured that this letter, despite its untoward delivery, is born of

*an eager and sincere wish to further our acquaintance, limited as
I am by our awkward correspondence!*

That Miss Darcy should write to her was entirely unexpected. Such a thing was hardly ever done between two women
who had never met, but upon examining her feelings, Elizabeth
decided at once that she felt none of the insult usually associ-
ated with such a breach of etiquette. After all, it was she who
had written first by enclosing her joke of a letter within Mr
Darcy's. She eagerly read on, curious to know better this daring
yet hesitant stranger.

*My brother has hardly ever written of any other lady of his
acquaintance, but since meeting you and your family, his past
two letters have been full of stories of your adventures in Hertfordshire that have done nothing but delight me and make me
impatient for the liberty to travel north myself and make your
acquaintance.*

Elizabeth was forced to stop reading and put the letter in
her lap, for Mr Darcy himself had entered the room. He made
his way to a seat near Mr Bennet and began to take his coffee.
Elizabeth at once sensed his eyes on her and with a twinge of
anxiety, she wondered whether she should reveal to him that
Miss Darcy had written to her.

In only a moment, however, the footman approached Mr
Darcy and handed him a letter with directions scripted in the
same dainty hand. A happy expression shone in his countenance as he tucked the letter into his waistcoat.

Seeing him at his ease, Elizabeth began to contrive some
way to responsibly alert him to her own piece of correspondence in a manner that would not betray his sister's actions to
those seated around the table. An opportunity presented itself

when Elizabeth asked her father to pass the scones and her voice seemed to stir Mr Darcy's notice, and he addressed her.

"I see Miss Catherine is feeling better this morning." Mr Darcy nodded to the end of the table where Kitty was wrapped in a cluster of shawls and delighted sisters.

"Indeed, sir. She has declared her wish to be free of the sickbed and has been granted the opportunity to come down for breakfast, if she vows to rest again until the afternoon."

"My own sister has just written, no doubt seeking information as to Miss Catherine's condition. I shall be glad to convey such satisfactory news to her."

"That is good of you—and of Miss Darcy too. Please do so until I have your leave to convey my own assurances and my warm regards to your sister."

Elizabeth had cautiously veiled her request for permission to write to Miss Darcy, and so she was pleased when Mr Darcy responded with a raised brow and eager nod that indicated his understanding.

Mr Bingley then directed a question to him from across the table, and Mr Darcy was prevented from saying anything further.

When the plates from breakfast were taken up, Elizabeth struggled a moment to rise with one hand stuffed with new letters, using her other to brace herself against the table as she forced her complaining feet to bear her up again. Her chair suddenly slid back, and she glanced around to find that Mr Darcy had come to assist her. He wordlessly offered her his arm, which she took without hesitation.

"Thank you," she murmured.

"My pleasure, Miss Elizabeth."

His kindness helped her recover from her embarrassment, and when her courage returned, Elizabeth decided to risk further disclosure.

"I hope you were not surprised by my request for permission to write to Miss Darcy myself in response to her concerns. It may have been too forward."

"Indeed, it was not," he assured her, and in a quick movement, he removed his sister's letter from his waistcoat. "I daresay half of this will be devoted to her requests to hear news of how you and your family fare. Georgiana has a tender heart and no doubt feels great concern for you all. I imagine she may also feel some sense of association with you since receiving the note that was enclosed with mine."

Elizabeth paused to look up at him. "Yes, I was very bold," she admitted. "I daresay I have set a bad example as the elder lady of this correspondence. For I, too, received a letter from Miss Darcy this morning, which I have just opened out of curiosity."

"My sister—my shy little Georgiana—has written to you?"

"With great self-mortification and genuine feeling, she has," Elizabeth said. "Miss Darcy is very kind." She offered the letter in question for his examination, but he did not take it.

"I certainly take no exception to you two writing to each other. I believe Georgiana would relish the connexion and would benefit greatly from your confidence. Pray, do not hesitate to return the gesture. She no doubt waits anxiously in hopes of hearing from you."

Elizabeth was pleased at the compliment such assurances presented. She thanked him and promised to reply faithfully, before turning to help Jane escort Kitty back to the sick room. Distracted still by thoughts of Mr Darcy, her cheeks burned all the way up the stairs.

"Lizzy, are you quite well?" Jane asked, pressing on Kitty's arm to stall their progress on the stairs.

Kitty turned to Elizabeth with some alarm. "Oh, I forgot what Lydia told me about your injured feet! I am sorry. You do not need to help me go up if it pains you, Lizzy," Kitty protested before bending at the waist under the force of a sudden, hacking cough.

Elizabeth rubbed her back and helped her right herself. "It is nothing, I assure you. Come, Kitty, let us get you to bed."

The ladies reached the summit of their climb, and once they gained the sickroom, Elizabeth was able to let her mind wander as she and Jane removed Kitty's shoes and took out her hair pins so she could rest comfortably.

Elizabeth wondered anew about the young girl, so close to Kitty in age, who had written to her. Mr Darcy's comment had described Miss Darcy's enthusiasm for her friendship and had likewise told Elizabeth much about Mr Darcy's approbation of her. That he should feel his sister would 'benefit greatly' from confiding in her, that he should so unreservedly give consent to their correspondence, testified to an esteem Elizabeth would never have expected from a man who at first had found her merely 'tolerable' and who had seemed only last week determined to show disapprobation for her every action and argument.

Elizabeth examined her own perception. Had she been wrong in her earliest assumptions regarding his behaviour, or had Mr Darcy changed so materially? She decided it might be best to discover her answers by reading the rest of Miss Darcy's letter when she had the opportunity. For the present, she soothed Kitty's latest episode of coughing with a draught to help her rest. The exertion from her excursion downstairs had clearly exhausted Kitty, for she was asleep in barely a trice. Soon, Elizabeth and Jane began to whisper confidences, as was their wont.

Once Elizabeth had sufficiently teased her sister about Mr Bingley's ongoing interest in Jane's quality of sleep at every breakfast since the fire, Jane turned the conversation by sharing the news that she had received some post of her own that morning in the form of a letter from their aunt in London.

"Aunt Gardiner seemed so anxious, Lizzy. I think I should reply to her letter immediately to allay her fears. Her mind must be wild imagining our suffering, and I would not have her think the worst."

"My own note from Charlotte was much the same. Ought we not find some pens and paper, then?"

United in their tasks, the two sisters made their way to the little sitting room on the other end of the wing the Bingley sisters often favoured. There they found Miss Bingley's fine escritoire abounding with the tools they required to attend to their correspondence.

Once Jane was engaged in writing her response to Mrs Gardiner at the coffee table nearby, Elizabeth removed Miss Darcy's letter. She perused it closely, finding the lines that had shocked her upon her first reading them at the breakfast table and then venturing onward.

Rest assured I have not your courage and would never, beyond this letter, tax you with such an infringement on your kindness as to call! I do realise I am full young to be anything nearer a friend to you than a slight acquaintance made through your connexion to my brother. But I do own that another motive, nearer to this mark of friendship, has made me write my brother today in addition to writing you. To wit, I wish dearly to be of use to you and your sisters in this time of distress.

I can only imagine how it must be to have such a calamity enter your home and force you out of it. Then in addition to all these trials, have to suffer injury, and after your return home, to be burdened by yet many weeks or months in which your home is in a state of continual disruption to effect a restoration. We have seen our own fires in the tenants' homes and outbuildings at Pemberley, and I have learnt to do what I can to give assistance.

If you find you would rather have some time away from home whilst repairs are wrought, I would gladly entertain you and your family in town. It has been some time since Fitzwilliam and I had a house party, and I believe that the devastation of a friend's home would make such an invitation imperative.

But I fear I am overreaching and making myself quite ridiculous and impertinent. I would not for anything in the world offend or embarrass you. Rather, I think I embarrass myself.

Please receive my offer as I have intended it—a wish to be a comfort and a helper in a difficult time. I may not have my brother's heroism, but I have learnt at his knee and by his loving example to be of assistance whenever I can. I cannot praise him overmuch, for he has instilled in me the virtues our parents cherished and has taught me to treasure them as well. Fitzwilliam is truly the best of brothers and the best of men!

I hope I do not do injustice to Fitzwilliam's attempts to raise me well by so flagrantly trespassing too long on your patience and kindness. But by all his reports of your compassion, wit, and playful sweetness, I confess I feel myself somewhat safe in writing to you. For if I do not succeed in gaining your regard and receptivity to this correspondence, then at least I know that your kind heart is too warm for me to risk your cold censure for my overstep!

I can only hope you will be moved enough by my boldness to return it in kind. I shall wait to hear news of you, either through my brother or by your own hand.

Your unacquainted friend with sincerest regards,
Georgiana Darcy

By the time she had finished reading this epistle, Elizabeth's emotions had moved beyond astonished curiosity, into perplexed pleasure, and then to eagerness. Yet, she was uncertain as to how to answer the girl who thought so well of her and yet was a stranger.

While she could with all good grace and gratefulness receive Miss Darcy's kind wishes and return her desire to meet, Eliza-

beth felt she could not respond to the young woman's astonishing offer of hospitality and assistance without first
discovering the wishes of the lady's brother and of her own
parents.

What was clear was that Miss Darcy was a sweet girl and was
just as her brother described her—tender-hearted and shy. Yet,
how bold was she when she felt herself able to be of assistance!

The thought struck Elizabeth then—how remarkably like
her brother was Miss Darcy!

But could Mr Darcy, in being similar to his sister in some
ways, be described in other ways as bold, yet tender-hearted,
and even shy? Was the influence of one sibling's letter so
vibrantly colouring her perspective on the other's behaviour?

Her first impression of Mr Darcy certainly seemed to
require a fair reassessment. Had she misjudged him for what
was only a moment of pique, an utterance borne of a natural
reticence, goaded by Mr Bingley's insistence into a breed of irritation before he had even come to know her? Certainly, her
former belief that he had formed a disapproving attitude
towards her, had judged her for her appearance and behaviour
during her first stay at Netherfield, now revealed itself as
unfounded. By Miss Darcy's account, her brother's opinion of
Elizabeth was one wholly of approbation. He had not written
to express disapproval of her. By Miss Darcy's own words, he
had expressed quite the opposite.

Elizabeth did not know what to think, and she strove and
struggled in her confusion to know herself as well as to
know him.

She stood and awkwardly paced the room, but finding
Jane's concerned eye on her, she sat again, and availed herself of
a distraction by answering the letter from Charlotte.

As she filled her pen, she wondered whether or not to share
her confidence regarding her deeper acquaintance with the
Darcys. Uncertainty forced her to write first of the most

pressing matters—answering Charlotte's concerns with reassurances and thanking her for her family's kindness in hosting Mr
Collins. Her page filled surprisingly quickly, and Elizabeth
decided that any conversation about the Darcys ought best to
be done face-to-face than by letter, where opinions might be
shaped by the limitations of her pen. She seized on her best
chance to arrange a visit with Charlotte as she wrote her last few
lines.

If I should gain my father's permission to accompany him
tomorrow morning to view Longbourn, I shall be glad to come
and call at Lucas Lodge before dinner preparations. I hope to see
you very soon, and until then, I remain,
Yours &c,
Elizabeth

She had begun to fold her note when Jane looked up from
her own correspondence. "I have just finished this letter, Lizzy,
but would you like to add a postscript? Aunt Gardiner asked
particularly about you, but she was afraid to write directly,
should your burned hand make it difficult for you to answer. I
told her you are much recovered, but a few words from you
would ease her mind greatly."

"I should be glad to!" Elizabeth replied, and bending over
her sister's letter, she wrote a note of reassurance to her beloved
aunt.

As she blew on the ink to set it, she could not help but read
a few lines of Jane's response in the body of the letter itself.

"*. . . we owe Mr Darcy a debt of gratitude for the lives of Lizzy*
and Kitty. I confess, Aunt, that his care of Lizzy yet continues . .
."

Elizabeth raised her eyes to her sister. "I noticed that you mentioned Mr Darcy in your letter. I must own that I did something rather shocking the other day that I ought to share with you, as it now has come to bear repercussions."

"Oh no, I hope you and Mr Darcy have not had another misunderstanding!"

"No, something rather more shocking. I have committed a faux pas of a wholly other sort by collaborating with Mr Darcy in his writing of a letter to his sister not two days ago."

At Jane's look of astonishment, Elizabeth continued. "Mr Darcy had been writing his letter above stairs in the music room while Mary and I were practising and mentioned that he feared his report to his sister of the events of the fire would cause her some anxiety. I offered to write a note to her, not only commenting on the claims of his account from my own view, but also to introduce some levity into the letter. In a moment of impertinence, I wrote a trifling little slip that I hoped would cheer her, and he willingly enclosed it within his missive. He even laughed!"

Jane hesitated a moment before replying. "I am sure that because you received Mr Darcy's tacit permission with his sponsorship of your enclosure you did nothing strictly untoward."

"Perhaps, but alas, I have set Miss Darcy a bad example, for this very morning I received a long letter from her. I have already told Mr Darcy of it, and he again affirmed that he had no reservations if we should wish to correspond. But what Miss Darcy has written is truly astounding. Indeed, I believe she is as soft-hearted as you, but perhaps you should read it for yourself." Elizabeth handed Jane the letter, and Jane read it complete.

"This is indeed a great gesture of civility! Miss Darcy writes with the most charming mix of restrained eagerness and overwhelming sweetness of address that I have scarcely ever read. And with what an accounting of goodness does she credit to her brother—and to you! I believe now that Mr Darcy must have written a great deal about you in order for her to form such a pleasing sketch of your character and temper. I daresay it is an accurate sketch too."

"Certainly it is a far kinder portrait than my initial rendering of her brother's character," Elizabeth confessed. "But Jane, what should I answer regarding Miss Darcy's offer of assistance? She is truly too good and I fear somewhat misguided. She allows for too much liberality on the part of her brother, who must naturally approve of any such scheme before they are carried forward. What she offers—it is too much—and I can only think that it reflects her lack of information regarding the degree of acquaintance that exists between Mr Darcy and myself."

Her sister frowned thoughtfully. "I think I understand you. You believe she presumes, simply because Mr Darcy has written of you so often, that he has formed some attachment, or even an understanding with you, that would render her offer more appropriate, considering the future degree of intimacy Miss Darcy believes you might someday enjoy with her family."

Elizabeth had not considered such a perspective. She bit her lip. "If she believes so, then it is too embarrassing even to contemplate how I could go about correcting her assumptions."

"Perhaps she does not assume that much, Lizzy," Jane said slyly, "at least, not on her brother's part. I have noticed that Mr Darcy certainly pays you a great deal of attention."

Elizabeth looked away and carefully refolded her letter. "Since the fire, I own he has offered his assistance at every occasion, but I believe he does it out of some sense of obligation or gallantry pertaining to his role as a rescuer."

"I disagree. Otherwise he would pay the same amount of attention to Kitty, but he has hardly said a word to her."

"I do not know what to think. He is not an easy man to read. His reportedly glowing accounts of my character in his letters to Miss Darcy show that while I may not be an object of his affection, I may hold his respect. His approval of our corre-spondence also demonstrates some level of esteem for me."

"In any case, proof of esteem is an excellent way to begin a friendship, do you not think? It is prudent to claim no closer connexion at this time than either of you may feel."

Elizabeth nodded. "I agree that is certainly the most sensible way to proceed. I suppose I ought to go to Mr Darcy—however indelicate it may be—and have a conversation with him regarding his sister's desires to be of use to us. But, oh Jane, I think I must be very careful not to give offence, for I certainly take none from her kind offer!"

"I know you will do just as you ought. You need only approach him with the same kindness Miss Darcy has shown you, and all will be well."

"I hope you are right," said Elizabeth. "I should not like to lose their good opinion."

Thus resolved, the sisters returned to their room to help Jane prepare for her outing to Meryton. Before taking her leave, Jane took Elizabeth's note for Charlotte Lucas, intending to deliver it on the way. She then asked Elizabeth if there was anything she might desire from town.

Elizabeth shook her head sadly. "I daresay now is not the time for buying trifles. I dread to think what it will cost our father to restore our home."

"You are right. I shall endeavour to curb Lydia from any wasteful spending!"

After embracing her sister, Elizabeth followed Jane to the landing where she watched her gracefully descend the stairs and meet Mr Bingley and Lydia in the vestibule below. With high hopes of an outing in little more than a day, Elizabeth was able to wave her more sure-footed sisters off on their trip to town with Mr Bingley without resentment.

CHAPTER TEN

The walking party from Netherfield stopped to pay a call to Mrs Philips and thank her for her invitation to dinner and cards. Mr Bingley stepped forward and communicated his happy acceptance and the regrets of his sisters and Mr Darcy. The former had claimed other obligations, but the latter had genuinely pressing matters regarding his own estate that he had put aside these many days while he offered his services to the Bennets.

Mrs Philips showed all her joy and pleasure in anticipating Mr Bingley's presence, and she hastened to make known to Lydia, particularly, that she had also invited several officers, including a new one, whom she had seen with Mr Denny only yesterday as the two had walked up and down the street together.

"Oh Aunt, if you noticed him, he must have been handsome!" Lydia exclaimed. "You must tell me, for Kitty will certainly want to know, and she quite depends upon my news."

"Oh yes, he is very handsome! He looked to me like a gentleman of quality. And he was not a youth, but a man with a fine, tall figure," Mrs Philips said with an encouraging wink.

Lydia tittered with delight. "Excellent news! And what is his name? Where did he come from? Do you know anything else about him?"

Mrs Philips had a ready supply of information. It was Mr Denny who had brought his friend, called Wickham, from London, and that Mr Wickham had taken his commission in the regiment only days before.

Jane turned the conversation. "And did you include all the officers of the regiment in your invitation for tonight?"

"Of course. I made specific mention that Mr Wickham should be included when I spoke with Mrs Forster. She is such a lively, pretty young thing. If you have not yet met her, Jane, I can make an introduction. And Lizzy, too, if she is able to attend. Oh my, I had not even thought to ask. How are Lizzy's feet faring? Can she walk?"

"Her feet sometimes do cause her pain, but she has made good progress and has taken short walks around the house at Netherfield."

"I am glad to hear it," Mrs Philips declared. Then she turned again to Mr Bingley. "You, sir, are kindness itself for taking in all my dear Bennet relations. Would that I had more bedrooms here, I should take them all! But you may have heard our brother is to come from London. I daresay he will take them all home with him, once his wife has made the arrangements."

"I should be disappointed if they take their leave of Netherfield too soon," Mr Bingley said with a slight bow to Mrs Philips and a grin at Jane. "I could not countenance sending them on when the ladies are only just recovered, and when their company has been so pleasing. We have become quite a merry party, have we not, ladies?"

Lydia exclaimed, "Oh yes! And we shall be merrier still

when we return to Netherfield, for I shall tell Mama and Kitty the news from the regiment. But oh, Kitty will be disappointed. Think of all the fun she will be missing!"

Mr Bingley could only smile at such enthusiasm, and taking the opportunity to make their farewells until the evening, offered each Bennet sister an arm.

As they took to the street, Lydia made to dart away towards the milliner's shop, but Jane arrested her retreat. "Lydia! The time! We must go home to change if we are to return soon to our aunt and uncle's for dinner!"

Lydia became subdued at this reminder, but she came along with them willingly enough. Her spirits recovered once they passed the pales of Netherfield's orchard, and she recalled all the news she had to tell.

AT THE PARTY, MRS PHILIPS FUSSED OVER ELIZABETH upon her arrival, loudly enumerating her worries for her niece's injuries. Although Elizabeth staunchly proclaimed the soundness of her feet, tucked inside a pair of Lydia's slightly larger shoes, she was nonetheless bidden to sit and remain seated as soon as she disembarked the carriage. This order perturbed her to no small degree, as she felt herself greatly in a mood to mix with the diverse company crammed into the little drawing room of the Philipses' apartment.

After a few bids at cards, Elizabeth and her family supped well with the sociable company, which included Colonel Forster and his new bride, whom Elizabeth thought a bit too young and feather-headed to be married. Mrs Forster's friendship with Lydia appeared already solid, and the two of them sniggered away and flirted with the officers across their plates in such a fashion as Elizabeth could hardly countenance.

She soon sought relief from their antics, which she found in the glowing visage of her elder sister. Jane was happily ensconced with Mr Bingley at the corner of the supper table, where he spoke to her almost exclusively. Such behaviour caused quite a stir, for it had not gone unnoticed that Mr Bingley had remained by Jane's side since he had handed her down from the carriage that evening. During the separation of the sexes that followed dinner, it was with great embarrassment that Elizabeth overheard her mother and her aunt speculating in a most animated fashion as to when that young man would propose to their lovely Jane.

When the gentlemen returned to the room, Elizabeth felt a great relief. The officers gathered there were in general a very creditable, gentlemanlike set, but the new one called Mr Wickham was far beyond them all in person, countenance, air, and walk. Indeed, it was Mr Wickham, with his handsome face and gentlemanly comportment, who instantly claimed the attention of almost every young woman in the room the moment he entered it.

Elizabeth followed him with her eyes out of innate feminine curiosity, but she was impeded by Mr Denny, who at her aunt's insistence, escorted her to the settee in the middle of the room and bade her rest her feet, despite her protests. From that vantage point, she watched as several pleasant tables of cards were again made up.

"You must pardon me," Mr Denny began, "for my officiousness in seating you here. I have never been asked by a hostess before to ensure a lady's comfort at a party, and I find myself uncertain if I have made your experience this evening better or worse."

Elizabeth answered charitably. "You meant well, I am sure. I suppose my status as an invalid comes with one benefit—I have not yet been called upon to exert my meagre talents at the pianoforte. We shall see how long I may escape such an obligation!"

Mr Denny chuckled. "As you are not able to play or mix

easily in company, I suppose I shall have to bring some company to you."

Having taken such orders upon himself, Mr Denny did his duty well and introduced her to his new, fine-looking friend, Mr Wickham.

CHAPTER ELEVEN

"*M*iss Bennet, how do you do?" said Mr Wickham, bowing to her with a charming flourish. Immediately, Elizabeth sensed in him a liveliness of manner that she must appreciate for its similarity to her own.

"I am well, sir, although my dear aunt has sequestered me to this couch due to some unfounded anxieties about my feet. I am sure Mr Denny or Mrs Forster has told you of the fire at our home," she replied in a light tone, hoping she would not have to burden her new acquaintance with the tale.

"Indeed, and I was delighted to hear that your family all came out of it well. I do not wish to burden you if you do not wish to speak of it, but I have just heard tonight from Mrs Philips that your injuries were tendered as the price of a very noble victory—the rescue of your sister. Is she well? Is she here tonight?"

"Kitty is improving but is not yet well enough to join us tonight. She is still recovering at Netherfield Park. Mr Bingley has been our host there these past few days."

"How kind of him to show such hospitality to his neighbours," observed Mr Wickham, nodding in Mr Bingley's direction in an attitude of respect.

Elizabeth's agreement was as warm as her growing approbation for her companion. "He is very kind to do so, especially when he is only just settled in the neighbourhood."

"That is generosity indeed! And what of his other guests?" said Mr Wickham lightly. "I hope they do not think so poorly of the company of militiamen as to avoid joining us?"

"Oh no, sir, certainly not," exclaimed Elizabeth at once, not wishing him to think for a moment that anyone in Hertfordshire would be in the least bit unwelcoming to him. But then she realised that she was being teased, for Mr Wickham smiled at her in such a way that proclaimed some triumph at seeing her rush so passionately to soothe his concern.

Elizabeth could do naught but act in accordance with her own teasing nature. "Mr Bingley's sisters are ladies of most determined fashion. When they sent their regrets, I confess I did rather wonder at their refusal. I attributed it at first to their distaste for our *local* wardrobe, rather than the colour of our new *redcoats*. But if you think they are avoiding our men-at-arms, then it is certainly their loss!"

Elizabeth grew more serious. "But Mr Bingley's friend, who is staying with him, must truly be excused. Mr Darcy spent a good deal of time assisting my father with the arrangements for making repairs to our home, and I daresay he would have come with his friend tonight had it not been for the more pressing concerns of his own estate that he has been forced to neglect out of kindness."

"Ah, Mr Darcy is staying with Mr Bingley, then?" Mr Wickham enquired, his face gone suddenly pale.

"I understand he came up from London with Mr Bingley to see the fields and the manor house of the estate his friend has let."

"How long has Mr Darcy been staying there?"

"About a month."

"And are you well acquainted with him?"

Elizabeth was undecided how to answer. She paused just long enough to reassure herself that she had not misread his initial reaction. She was certain he had looked shocked but a moment ago and then became hesitant afterwards. She wished to put him at ease, but she was also wild with curiosity to understand why Mr Wickham should appear so unsettled at the mention of Mr Darcy's name.

"I am acquainted with him, but ours is an unusual association. I owe him my life, for it was Mr Darcy who reached Longbourn first upon noticing the fire from a window at Netherfield. Once he had heard I had gone back into the house to look for my sister, he went inside to retrieve us safely. I suppose that while I do not know Mr Darcy well, I know enough to think well of him."

As she spoke, Mr Wickham watched her very closely, as though to look for any signs of interest or attachment in her response. He then favoured her with a wry smile. "As well you might, Miss Elizabeth. I do recall that when we played as boys, Darcy always did like to act the hero."

It was now Elizabeth's turn to show her astonishment. "You were childhood playmates?"

"I was raised at his father's estate in Derbyshire. My father was old Mr Darcy's steward. The late Mr Darcy was one of the best men that ever breathed and the truest friend I ever had." Here, he frowned and clasped his hands in his lap, looking at his interlaced fingers with an air of such sadness as could only move Elizabeth to concern.

"I can never be in company with Fitzwilliam Darcy without being grieved to the soul by a thousand tender recollections," continued Mr Wickham. He looked up steadily at her as he confided, "I am afraid to say that his behaviour to myself has been scandalous, but I believe I could forgive him anything and everything, except for what he has done in disappointing the hopes and disgracing the memory of his father."

Elizabeth forced her dropped jaw to close. "I am all astonishment."

"The world is blinded to Mr Darcy's true nature by his fortune and consequence or frightened by what some have called his high and imposing manners—too frightened to come to know him. And so it is that the world often sees him only as he chooses to be seen."

Elizabeth could only feel distressed by this assessment. Perhaps it was because Mr Wickham's description of Mr Darcy's manners reminded her so exactly of her own initial dislike of him as well as her own poor first rendering of his character. She found strangely little pleasure in the intimation that her original impressions regarding Mr Darcy may have been correct.

Seeking revelations that would cause her less discomfiture, Elizabeth turned her questions to the subject of the man before her instead. "May I ask, sir, if you were raised in Derbyshire, how you came now to be in Meryton in the regiment?"

Wickham smiled and explained. "The prospect of employment in a respectable regiment and the promise of good, constant society certainly gave strong inducement to my choice. But I was not intended for a military life. I was brought up for the church, and I should at this time have been in possession of a most valuable living, had it pleased the gentleman we were speaking of just now."

Elizabeth could scarcely breathe upon hearing of all unchristian acts that Mr Darcy should have denied this man something as revered as a church living.

Mr Wickham bowed his head stiffly, as though the action pained him. "The late Mr Darcy bequeathed me the next presentation of the best living in his will. He was my godfather and excessively attached to me. He meant to provide for me amply and thought he had done it, but when the living fell, it was given elsewhere by his son."

"Good heavens," murmured Elizabeth, for a level of doubt began to rise within her. Why on earth would Mr Darcy disregard his father's wishes? She probed further. "How could the elder Mr Darcy's will be disregarded? Why did you not seek legal redress?"

"There was an informality in the terms of the bequest that gave me no hope from the law. A man of honour could not have doubted the intention, but Mr Darcy chose to treat it as merely a conditional recommendation and to assert that I had forfeited all claim to it by extravagance and imprudence. That living became vacant two years ago, exactly as I was of an age to hold it, and it was given to another. I cannot accuse myself of having done anything to deserve to lose it, but I have an unguarded temper, and I may have spoken my opinion of him, and to him, too freely. I can recall nothing worse. But the fact remains that we are very different sorts of men, and Darcy hates me."

"Hates you? I cannot imagine that." Elizabeth's attention had been caught not only by the spark of rancour in Mr Wickham's declaration but also his account that Mr Darcy had denied him the living because of Mr Wickham's extravagance and imprudence.

She knew enough of Mr Darcy's character to believe that if he had indeed done Mr Wickham such an injury, he would have ample reason to act in such a fashion. It was true that Mr Darcy had once boasted of his implacable resentment, but he was also a rational man, and therefore his contempt must have developed from some logical cause.

But what might that cause be? Were the failings that Wickham had listed sufficient to justify the denial of such a living? Were these *all* the failings of character that Mr Wickham might have?

"Perhaps it is not hatred he feels," amended Wickham, who

continued with some eagerness, "but a thorough, determined dislike of me—a dislike I cannot but attribute in some measure to jealousy. Had the late Mr Darcy liked me less, his son might have borne me better, but his father's uncommon attachment to me irritated him. Darcy had not a temper to bear that sort of competition—the sort of preference which was often given me."

Elizabeth considered her previous line of thought for a moment. "I do remember Mr Darcy boasting at Netherfield of having an unforgiving temper."

"I shall not trust myself to remark on the subject," replied Mr Wickham. "I can hardly be just to him."

His statement, Elizabeth thought, certainly had merit, but she was convinced of only two things. First, that Mr Wickham clearly seemed to feel as though Mr Darcy had wronged him unjustly, and second, that the motives Mr Wickham offered for such ill-treatment seemed far too slight an irritation to compel a man like Mr Darcy to take such cruel measures against anyone.

What could it benefit a man in Mr Darcy's position to do such a thing against a man so below his consequence in the world? Mr Darcy stood to inherit Pemberley and held all the privileges given to an only son and heir—great gifts indeed, which far surpassed any jealousy he might feel of the friendship between Mr Wickham and his father.

The motives of such an action were not the only features of Mr Wickham's argument that appeared suspect. Elizabeth considered such cruelty beneath what she knew of Mr Darcy's character and habits. She could not envision him carrying out such a scheme with active malice. Indeed, it went sharply against the established pattern she had witnessed of his propensity to give assistance—even to such undeserving people as her family, so wholly unconnected to him—rather than to take away any aid that was in his power to grant. She could not imagine it of him.

"To treat in such a manner the godson, the friend, the favourite of his father!" she half whispered, adding louder, "And one who had been a companion from childhood, connected and raised together in the closest manner!"

Mr Wickham, apparently believing he had her sympathies, unwittingly gave voice to words that corroborated Elizabeth's thoughts. "We were born in the same parish, within the same park. The greatest part of our youth was passed together in the same house, sharing the same amusements, objects of the same parental care.

"My father began life in the same profession as your uncle Mr Philips, but he gave up everything to be of use to the late Mr Darcy. My father esteemed that man, and he devoted all his time to the care of the Pemberley property. Mr Darcy often acknowledged himself under the greatest obligation for my father's active management, and when, immediately before my father's death, Mr Darcy gave him a voluntary promise of providing for me, I am convinced he felt it to be as much a debt of gratitude to my father as a display of his affection for me."

Learning of the depth of their familial connexion and affections, Elizabeth felt herself now at war with all she had observed and heard of the current Mr Darcy while at Netherfield.

Specifically, she was caught by how principled he seemed, how selfless he could be, and how much good his sister had reported of him. Her mind reviewed some words she had read and re-read just that morning in Miss Darcy's letter.

I cannot praise him overmuch, for he has instilled in me the virtues our parents cherished and has taught me to treasure them as well. Fitzwilliam is truly the best of brothers and the best of men!

Elizabeth realised she had lapsed into silence as she strove to find any common ground with Mr Wickham on the subject of

Mr Darcy's character. She hit upon the one flaw in Mr Darcy she had observed—and she hoped it would be enough to encourage Mr Wickham to continue his flow of information.

"I have encountered a fearsome pride in Mr Darcy, and I admit he once wielded it to wound my vanity. In his dealings with you, I wonder that Mr Darcy would so neglect his pride, for he should have been too proud to stoop to such dishonesty."

Mr Wickham chuckled. "Ah yes, that Darcy pride! It is plain to any who know him, for it guides almost everything he does."

Elizabeth wanted to know what good he could say of Mr Darcy. "Can such abominable pride as you have witnessed ever have done him good?"

"It has often led him to be liberal and generous, to give his money freely, to display hospitality, to assist his tenants, and relieve the poor. Family pride, and filial pride—for he is very proud of what his father was—have done this. Not to appear to disgrace his family or lose the honour and influence of the Pemberley estate is a powerful motive. He has also brotherly pride, which united with his natural affection for his sister, makes him a very kind and careful guardian to her."

Now, Mr Wickham had touched upon a person of great interest, whose kindness and goodness had shown itself, and whose youthful innocence and lack of exposure to society could surely give rise to no defamation, and of whom Elizabeth felt certain that her companion could have no cause, if he were truthful at all, to say any wrong.

"What sort of girl is Miss Darcy?" she asked plainly, then waited eagerly to weigh his next words against the balance of her feelings.

He shook his head. "I wish I could call her amiable, but she is too much like her brother—very, very proud. As a child, she was affectionate and pleasing—and extremely fond of me. I devoted hours and hours to her amusement. But Miss Darcy is nothing to me now. She is a handsome girl of about fifteen or sixteen, and I understand, highly accomplished. Since her father's death, her home has been in London, where she lives with a companion who supervises her education."

At these remarks, Elizabeth's doubt and suspicion returned at once, leaping to a level of vexation. Miss Darcy very, very proud? Now this was too much to believe, though she had but one letter from the girl as substantiating proof against this unfair charge.

As her hackles rose in defence of her newest friend, Elizabeth felt herself in danger of causing offence to Mr Wickham and by doing so, chasing him away along with any answers he could provide. Because she knew she was incapable of denying herself an outlet for her rising agitation, she set out to continue her interrogation of him in a fashion most likely to catch him unprepared. Elizabeth teased him in such a charming manner that her piercing sarcasm passed by his notice utterly undetected.

"I am astonished at what such a gentle spirit as yourself has endured," she said in a tone of sweet commiseration. "I only hope Mr Darcy will never meet another man like you—so affable, so apt to speak well of others, and so far in his power as you have been. Mr Darcy must be a villain to conceal his misdeeds to those who know him well, and you must surely be an angel for uncovering them so openly before me, who is almost a stranger to you. I thank you for the warning!

"But I am troubled, quite troubled, by what you have said, for now there is another who may be his next victim." Here, Elizabeth glanced meaningfully across the room at her sister's doting companion before continuing. "I can only hope Mr Bingley, who bears your likeness in temperament, is never ill-used by his friend, whom he relies on for his counsel and in whose goodness he so firmly believes. Mr Bingley cannot know

—not even after all their years of acquaintance—what kind of man Mr Darcy truly is."

"Most likely not," said Mr Wickham, without hesitation and seemingly without reading into the double meanings and subtle barbs couched within her words. "But Mr Darcy can please where he chooses. He does not want abilities. He can be an agreeable companion if he thinks it worth his while. Among those who are at all his equals in consequence, he is a very different man than he is to the less prosperous. His pride never deserts him, but with the rich, he is liberal-minded, just, sincere, rational, honourable, and, perhaps, even agreeable."

"Yet, even with the less wealthy, he has shown some of these virtues," said Elizabeth before she could stop herself. Seeing his frown, she softened her mistake with a smile. "You have far more charity in you than I would have in your situation were I not myself so indebted to the man. The injustice is quite shocking, considering the disparity between his treatment of you and me! For, in one moment, Mr Darcy rescued two girls of no connexion to him from a fire at nearly the cost of his life, when not long before, he had thrown a man, practically a brother, out into the night over a slight to his pride. Shocking! Mr Darcy deserves to be publicly disgraced, if not to be straightaway sent to Bedlam for what appears to be madness of the most perverse and unstable sort."

Drawing breath after this pronouncement, Elizabeth put her hand to her mouth to conceal her laugh at the absurd picture she had presented.

Mr Wickham chuckled lightly. "Some time or other he will be shown for what he is—but it shall not be by me," he promised. "Until I can forget his father, I can never defy or expose him."

Elizabeth was strangely pleased to hear this man contradict himself so openly by vowing never to expose Mr Darcy—which his own complaints to Elizabeth seemed exactly calculated to accomplish. Her sly amusement at his ironic admission gave Elizabeth the serenity to smile at Mr Wickham and turn the conversation to less unnerving topics.

Nevertheless, when the room's occupants shifted and drifted apart, and the night's entertainments drew to a close, Elizabeth was glad to be on her way to Netherfield. Her relief surprised her, and she strove to find the answer for it. After all, Mr Wickham had shown her every attention and charm that evening, and had she met him under any other circumstances, she might have gone off with her head full of him. Now, however, the opposite was true. She wished to rid her head of Mr Wickham, and instead think only of Mr Darcy.

Elizabeth knew she would not rest well until she had searched all her resources for evidence to refute the charges that had been laid at Mr Darcy's door. While Jane sighed in her sleep beneath the counterpane, Elizabeth's sense of justice burned bright within her as she turned Miss Darcy's letter over and bent to read its lines once again in the flickering glow of the fireplace. She reread Miss Darcy's words regarding her brother's goodness and his love for the things his parents treasured. She thought again of those moments when Mr Darcy's pride had done far more good than harm, at least in relation to her family. She also meditated at length on Mr Wickham's tale, and inspected those instances where his account was marred by incongruity with what she knew of Mr Darcy's character, and where Mr Wickham revealed less desirable facets of his own character in the telling.

Fairness demanded no less than this valiant attempt to uncover the truth of these matters. For it seemed abhorrently wrong for Elizabeth to begin the week giving thanks to Mr Darcy for preserving her from certain death in smoke and ash— and then, a mere four days later, to stand breathing in clean air, safe again in the cradle of the world, and thinking ill of him.

CHAPTER TWELVE

Thursday morning dawned too early for one occupant of Netherfield. Elizabeth arose late from her bed, washed her tired face, and with a yawn, unwound her dressings to examine her injuries. This was done with some anxious anticipation, for she was hopeful to find her feet recovered enough to bear the pressure of walking in boots during a visit to Longbourn later in the day.

Exploring her soles, she found a series of red calluses on the balls of her feet that did not bother her, but on her heels, a few raw patches still proved tender where the blisters had ruptured.

Nevertheless, she was determined. Seeing her sister already awake and arranging her hair before the mirror, Elizabeth asked, "Do you still have those scissors Miss Bingley loaned to you?"

Jane gave Elizabeth a look of curiosity, but she fetched the borrowed sewing scissors, nonetheless.

Elizabeth took a few lengths of the bandage and crouched with it on the floor. Using her discarded slippers as a guide, she cut out a double-backed pattern of her own shoe prints from the linen. Then, going to her hatbox, she retrieved some cotton and stuffed each linen pattern. She was just threading her needle to sew the makeshift boot liners closed when Jane's interest transformed into concern.

"I know what you are about! Your feet are not healed enough for this adventure, are they? Pray think of what further injury you might do to yourself! I beg you to leave inspecting our home for another day."

"No, Jane," said Elizabeth, already running thread and needle into the fabric. "I cannot put off my duty. I must go and help our father today."

"If you cannot wear your boots in comfort, you should not go. Papa said so. It is wrong of you to conceal the fact that you are too injured for this outing!"

"I shall feel perfectly at ease in my boots. Do you not see I mean to take precautions?" She held up one of her creations. "I shall walk on these, light as air, and no harm will come to me."

Jane looked doubtful. "Are you certain that a bit of padding will prove sufficient?"

"Let me finish them, and we shall see. May I borrow your woollen stockings? I mean to secure the padding inside each one. I should hate for these cushions to shift about in my boots."

In a little over half an hour, after some rapid sewing and Jane's help to finish dressing, Elizabeth's plan was tested. Lacing on her boots and finding the fit snug, yet tolerable, Elizabeth stood and executed a twirl before her sister, arms outstretched in elated satisfaction at her own artfulness.

"There, you see!"

"Very well. You have persuaded me. But I am not the only one you must convince."

Elizabeth picked up her reticule and bonnet, beckoning Jane to come with her into the hallway. "Papa will not be the wiser," she declared, as she set out. "He will have no cause for concern."

They walked for a moment in silence until Jane paused at the top of the staircase. "I was not only speaking of Papa. Mr Darcy ordered the carriage for your outing at breakfast today, and I daresay he means to go with you and our father to meet the builder."

Elizabeth's colour rose, but so did her courage. "I am not afraid of Mr Darcy, Jane."

"Nor should you be, but you might excite his suspicions. He is every bit as clever as you are, and you can be certain he will observe you carefully."

"That is just as well," Elizabeth said, adding quietly, "for I mean to observe *him*."

She left Jane in Mr Bingley's company, for he and his sisters were already awaiting her in the parlour, where they were to receive some neighbourhood callers.

Elizabeth continued onward to the abandoned breakfast table and sideboard, where she paused to avail herself of a pastry before setting off in search of her father. She did not need to venture far. He was in the library, examining some figures set before him with a frown deeply etched in his brow.

"Good morning, Papa," Elizabeth said brightly, taking in his troubled expression and trying to cheer him.

Mr Bennet sat back in the chair, crossing his arms over his chest. "Ah, Lizzy. I see you intend to prove your point to me first thing this morning. You have managed to get into your boots."

Elizabeth held up her bonnet. "I am prepared to leave whenever you are ready."

"You ought to fetch a kerchief, for the air there is not of the best quality. And to protect your gown, you will certainly wish to bring an apron."

"I am not concerned about a little soot, but I shall fetch my kerchief and beg a maid for an apron, if it will satisfy you. When shall we depart?"

"Mr Darcy has already gone to get his notebook and confirm the readiness of the carriage. We had hoped to be on our way in twenty minutes or so."

"I daresay bringing a notebook of my own is not a bad idea. I shall need to make lists. I am not sure where I could borrow one, though."

"You might find one at home—that is, if every bit of paper there was not rendered into charcoal," said her father in a weary tone.

Elizabeth placed a hand on his shoulder. Perceiving the deeper worry in his words, she strove to reassure him. "We shall manage, Papa. We truly shall."

Her father took her hand and gave it a gentle squeeze. "You are a good girl, my Lizzy." He offered her a weak smile and then released her. "Now, be off with you, so we can be on our way."

Her eagerness made quick work of her errands, and once sufficiently attired, Elizabeth, her father, and Mr Darcy were in a carriage rolling towards Longbourn. As they approached the familiar bend in the lane, she felt a rising sense of trepidation. When she finally looked upon her home, Elizabeth was glad to see that its creamy stone facade appeared intact, although she immediately noted the scorch marks on it and the shattered window. As they came to a stop before the house, she could readily perceive movement within.

Her father took her hand as she disembarked from the carriage, and Mr Darcy followed behind as they approached Longbourn's stoop.

It was odd to be greeted at their own home by a man she had never met, but upon opening the door, that gentleman immediately tugged off his gloves and pulled his forelock.

"Mr Bennet, Mr Darcy, ma'am," he said, meeting her eye with a quick, bright glance that showed good humour. There was a stripe of soot on his brow, and he wore a smudged and heavy work shirt, rather than a coat. It was apparent he had been hard at work throughout the morning.

Mr Darcy stepped forward and took the man's large, calloused hand. "Mr Higgins, it is good to see you and your team already at work. Mr Bennet is come with his daughter to take inventory within the damaged rooms of the house." Here, he paused and indicated Elizabeth. She reflexively curtseyed, and the man bowed to her in a rustic expression of good manners.

When Mr Higgins straightened, Mr Darcy continued. "We do not mean to get in the way of your crew with our visit today, Higgins. Is there a room where Mr Bennet and Miss Elizabeth could begin their inventory without interrupting your repairs?"

Elizabeth watched this exchange with some fascination, for instead of greeting his foreman with distant superiority, she had witnessed Mr Darcy approach him with more warmth, courtesy, and assurance than she had ever seen him meet others nearer his station in society. Here, where there was much of substance to be accomplished and where interactions fostered honourable transaction, his expressions were as open and earnest as his conversation was plentiful and direct.

Elizabeth realised she now beheld Mr Darcy in his element —thinking and acting like a good master by directing his energies towards the needs of an estate—and he did himself credit. She found further corroboration of this impression when she perceived that Mr Higgins did not react with any surprise to Mr Darcy's manner.

"Well, sir, we've set ourselves up in the parlour here," he nodded to the right, indicating the sitting room, "and I expect we'll move into the library towards the afternoon to see where that wall was burnt through, take its measure, put in some supports, and tear the rest of it down. I expect you could start in the library first, then trade places with us once we finish removin' these rafters in the parlour and settin' in the temporary supports for the ceilin' and that wall between it and the dinin' room. It's near gone, as well."

"Thank you, Higgins," Mr Darcy said, before stepping aside and nodding to Elizabeth and her father to precede him down the hallway.

Elizabeth risked a glance into the sitting room as she passed its door. Once her eyes moved past the men at work, she could not fail to notice the blackened walls, charred furniture, and the curled and crumpled ashes sprawled on the floor where there once had lain her grandmother's rug. She stiffened at the sight, understanding for the first time the loss of her family history among the everyday trappings in her home. Indeed, even as she breathed in to steady her emotions, she could taste the cloying, smoky remains of her family's past.

She stared around the room before her until she was roused by her father's hand on her arm, and then she spoke. "I think I had best find some paper or a notebook. I fear I shall be making a rather long list."

With that, Elizabeth disappeared into the old music room, finding there only more destruction. The wall it shared with the sitting room had been eaten almost cleanly away by the flames, and the pianoforte pressed against it gaped open to reveal a maw full of ashes and blackened ivory teeth. She reached out with a shaking hand and touched a key, only to be met with silence.

"Poor Mary. This was more than an instrument to her. This was a friend."

Unsure how she would find the strength to grieve her younger sister with such news of her beloved pianoforte's demise, she moved away to the far shelves. There, barely within reach on the highest tier, Elizabeth found some surviving sheaves of music. She pulled them down, along with a tumble of ash, which surprised her blinking eyes and choked her breath. She sputtered and coughed as she rifled through the pile to find some useful pages.

She met her father in his library and revealed her bounty—a handful of blank staff-paper in lieu of a notebook—but his attention was directed elsewhere. The state of her father's old sanctuary stole her breath away again.

The ruined wall was the first to meet her eye, shot through with blackened ribs of shelving. Upon each shelf were row upon row of the charred grey spines of books that had been reached by flames and consumed in place. Her father's beloved desk was warped from heat under its lacquering and burnt badly on one side where its footings had been eaten away to the point it looked in danger of collapsing. His battered old armchair near the fireplace, too, had been rendered into an upright lump of blistered leather, little resembling its former self.

The loss that moved Elizabeth to greatest distress—even above all the beloved books—was the devastation of the little table and the ivory chess set that she and her father had played upon for so many years. Tearfully, she approached it and fingered the white queen that once had been pristine, now scorched brown from the heat. Many of the corresponding black teak pieces had been further darkened by the flames, and the board itself was in cinders upon the ruined table.

Hands shaking, Elizabeth set down the chess piece, tied a kerchief over her mouth and nose, and went to work. She listed what titles of the books she could still read, guessed at the rest by their position, and then went on to note the damaged furniture, ruined drapes, picture frames filled with curling watercolours, and fire-bitten embroidery samplers. So much was completely beyond repair. As Elizabeth glanced back to her father's chess set, she considered with a small hope that it could possibly be made useful again with a new board and a heavy application of paint to the chess pieces, but it would never be as beautiful as before. Nothing in her home ever would be.

Mr Bennet laboured at her side, pulling down books that

sometimes dissolved into ashes in his hands. Elizabeth set aside the tomes that had nestled on shelves at the edges of the fire and might someday be rebound. It was dirty work, and soon Elizabeth's hands were covered with soot. She had to take pains to keep the dark spots already on her hem from spreading elsewhere. She was glad of her borrowed apron.

"Mr and Mrs Hill have been stripping the rooms upstairs to clean each item, article by article," said her father, as he picked up a magnifying glass and tried to polish off the soot upon it with his handkerchief. "Mrs Hill assures me that in the rooms where the floors are sound, much is as it was, albeit in need of laundering, dusting, or scouring."

"That, at least, is good news," said Elizabeth, forcing a smile. Mr Bennet nodded and turned back to jiggle open his desk's warped drawers. Once successful, he began sorting through the mass of his disorganised papers. Elizabeth offered to assist him, but he declined, so after taking a moment to stretch her spine, she turned again to her own employment.

Mr Darcy had given them some privacy during their time in the library by returning to the workmen and seeking information about what materials would need to be ordered for them by Mr Gardiner when he arrived from London. After two hours of occupation, taking measurements and hearing advice regarding needed equipment from Mr Higgins, Mr Darcy returned to the library with his own notebook, with the top page covered over in notes and measures, orders for different cuts of lumber and hardwood, as well as the odd joints, bolts, nails, plaster, and daub.

Elizabeth peered over his shoulder when her father did, silently reading all that was written in his bold, neat hand and wondering how on earth they would afford it all, even with her uncle's sources and possible assistance with funds.

"I see you have used this past hour well," said Mr Darcy as he surveyed the little piles Elizabeth had formed and sorted.

"I am almost afraid to look into the dining room," she sighed, straightening her notes and smearing them with soot in the process. She shook her head. "There will be a great deal to do there as well."

"I hope you would not attempt it all today. This sort of work is often very taxing because of the strain of the environment."

Mr Bennet clapped ashes off his hands and seconded Mr Darcy's advice. "Indeed, Lizzy. And did you not say that you still wished to call on Charlotte Lucas?"

Elizabeth pulled the kerchief down from about her nose and laughed. "I confess when I thought of making my visit, I did not realise I would hardly be fit to be seen by the time I had fixed on calling this afternoon. Do you think there might be some water in the kitchen so I may wash?"

"One of your stable lads may still be hereabouts. He has been taking care of the animals in the pens and outbuildings," said Mr Darcy. "I could ask him to draw you some, since he has set himself to that task once today already."

Elizabeth realised she had completely forgotten about the other poor living creatures on their estate. She was very glad Mr Darcy had spared a thought for them.

"Yes, please tell Seth that I would be grateful. Thank you, sir."

Darcy bowed, and again left her to her work and thoughts. Her meditations were interrupted, however, when the Bennets' own dear cook entered the library, wiping her hands on her apron and looking uncomfortable at being so far from her usual territory.

"Beggin' your pardon, Mr Bennet, Miss Elizabeth," said old Mrs Linville, "but I've been in the kitchen sortin' the larder. Some cheeses and things got a bit warm in the pantry, and they've set to spoilin' something awful. I've started to throw out some that couldn't be fed to the hogs, but there's other things

—vegetables and 'taters and such—that are still all right, but I think could turn before the family can come back here to eat 'em. What would you like me to do with 'em?"

Elizabeth turned to Mrs Linville. "I shall be glad to make up some baskets with anything fit to be taken to the tenants. It is the least we can do to thank them for the assistance they gave us on that terrible night!"

Elizabeth smiled encouragingly at her father and excused herself, glad to have a task that would remove her from the soot and sadness of the library for a time.

As she passed through the hall in the wake of her family's conscientious cook, she peered into the sitting room and noted that the workmen had paused for a repast. She was glad they had managed to take a little ease, as it was well past noon. Elizabeth might have taken some refreshments herself had she not been assailed by the rancid smell of rotten cheese from the moment she entered the kitchen. One glance at Mrs Linville, who held her apron to her nose with a slightly green complexion, showed that her nausea was shared.

"I cleaned up the cheese as best I could," explained that good lady, "but the spoilt smell won't air out. I reckon it's melted right onto the shelves in the larder."

Elizabeth nodded. In her acute discomfiture, she was forced to breathe through her mouth until she could adjust to the odour as they set to their task.

Later, while she was helping sort through the vegetables in the foul-smelling larder and the dry goods in the pantry, their tow-headed stable lad returned with a bucket of water. It would be nearly an hour before Elizabeth and the cook finished their task and made baskets ready for the tenants on the land. When all was finally prepared and they showed the baskets to the boy, Elizabeth observed Seth's smile and was glad some good had come of the waste and spoil of the day.

As Elizabeth scrubbed her hands and face at the work

counter and attempted to make herself presentable to visit Charlotte, Mr Darcy stepped through the doorway.

"Oh, I see young Seth found you," he said by way of both explanation and apology, and he turned aside to give Elizabeth some privacy as she dabbed her face dry with a rag.

Elizabeth hastily finished and pushed her damp curls back from her face. "Indeed, and I am most grateful to him. He just left to take some baskets of food from our larder to his sister to be distributed to the rest of our tenants."

"That was thoughtful of you. I confess in such events as these, my mind considers first the most immediate losses of capital in property, rather than the household tasks and human comforts which would be, in most cases, handled by an effective mistress of an estate. I am not surprised that you responded with such thoughtfulness, Miss Elizabeth."

She blushed, feeling unable to accept his praise. "I must confess I was reminded of my duties by our cook. I was pleased to see her here—so devoted and reliably kind. Although I was raised to run a household, I find I was not prepared for such an event as this one."

He nodded his understanding. "Nor could you be. Still, the work is to your credit."

"Thank you," she said, not knowing how else to respond.

"Do you still intend to call on your friend at Lucas Lodge?"

"I do, if I do not look too frightful. I wrote to Miss Lucas yesterday promising to come for a bit of refreshment in the mid-afternoon. If I walk down the lane now, I may still make good on my promise."

She wrung out the rag she had used on her face and offered it to him, indicating with a silent gesture that his cheek needed attention.

With a frown, Mr Darcy took it and obediently dabbed at the spot on his face, his expression thoughtful. "I should drive you in the carriage. You ought not walk too far after all your

work this morning, for your feet have only lately been restored."
As he said this, he did not look at her, but instead focused his
attention on the dirty marks on his hands, and he began to
attack them briskly with the cloth.

"Sir, it is barely a mile—"

"—and you are already tired." He spared her a dark look,
which softened at her chagrin. He shook his head and returned
to scrubbing at his hands.

Elizabeth expelled a breath, fighting the temptation to
argue further. "I am quite well, although I confess to feeling
rather peckish, but my dear friend has promised to remedy that
at the Lodge."

He paused, stilling his hands. "Did you eat anything at all?
You were not at the table this morning."

"I awoke late. It was my own fault. I did manage a few bites
of pastry before we left."

"Could I get you something from the basket we brought in?
Your father has already availed himself of some cold ham and
cheese."

"Cheese! Oh heavens!" She wrinkled her nose in immediate
reaction. "Forgive me, but I think I have had all I can bear for
now of that. Can you not smell it?"

"Is *that* what I smell?" he asked, glancing around with no
small degree of disgust.

Elizabeth could not help but laugh at his expression. Once
her helpless chuckles subsided, she responded to his query.

"I fear I shall be unable to so much as look at a wedge of
cheese without being henceforth reminded of my experience
today. Hungry as I am, I shall forgo such a repast at present.
Truly, sir, I shall be well until I reach Lucas Lodge."

Mr Darcy tossed the rag back into the bucket with surprisingly good aim, startling her with the action and with his rather
scolding tone as he said, "Such obstinance, Miss Bennet! Whatever shall I do with you?"

"Do with me?" she exclaimed with a laugh of surprise. "Why, nothing! I am my own mistress, and must compensate for my own whims and follies."

Mr Darcy glanced meaningfully over her shoulder towards the passage where the servants' stairs stood charred, a stark reminder of just where her courage-born folly had led her before.

"Perhaps in most cases," he acceded, bowing before he continued, somewhat awkwardly, "but allow me, where I can offer it, to render assistance to ensure that your follies do you no real harm. Shall we not take the carriage so that you may arrive at Lucas Lodge before your friend is called to dress for dinner?"

There was little chance, she knew, of her dissuading him from the course he presented. She had seen already that his mind was set when he was certain he was right, and Elizabeth had little time to waste in arguing the point.

In a few industrious minutes, she had taken off her filthy apron, put on her clean gloves, secured her warm spencer and wrap, fruitlessly shaken her hem—that was sooty but would have to do—and met Mr Darcy outside, where he was speaking to the stable boy while they examined the team and traces together.

Seth had apparently returned and, seeing Mr Darcy occupied with the horses, had taken it upon himself to act as their tiger and had ensured that the team was once again hitched to the carriage. After a satisfactory examination of the lad's work, Mr Darcy clapped him on the back, making the boy grin before he tugged his forelock and scuttled around to the rear of the carriage, where he climbed onto the platform above the dumb irons, taking hold of the strap.

As Mr Darcy approached Elizabeth to hand her in, she glanced around for their driver and belatedly recalled that Mr Darcy had dismissed him that morning, asking the man to return at three o'clock to convey them back to Netherfield for dinner. With Seth on the tail of the conveyance, she was to be the only passenger in the carriage.

Just as Mr Darcy extended his hand to assist her up the carriage steps, she hesitated.

"Are you driving the team, Mr Darcy?" she asked, clasping her hands in front of herself and looking up at him with a far deeper sort of enquiry on her face.

"I am," he replied with an expression of wariness that showed his uncertainty as to the motivation behind her question.

"There is something particular I wished to discuss with you. Would you mind terribly if I rode with you upon the coachman's seat?"

His face showed all his surprise, but he wordlessly led her towards the carriage and, making a sling of his hands, boosted her up to the coachman's step. As she gained her footing, she reached for the seat irons and pulled herself onto the unfamiliar perch.

With greater agility gained through experience and longer legs, Darcy alighted beside her on the narrow seat and took up the reins. He paused only to adjust his beaver to shade his eyes and glance at her to ensure that she was securely settled. Then he started the team forward with a signal from the reins and a clipped, "Step up."

As the horses moved forward with eagerness, Elizabeth saw him adjust his hold to hamper the team's pace. She knew he was waiting for her to speak.

CHAPTER THIRTEEN

Elizabeth stared straight ahead, gathering her courage. "I must thank you, sir, for two things I now enjoy. The first, being my life and that of my sister. I realise I have not yet properly thanked you for it."

Silent until now, Darcy did not abide her gratitude without objection. "But you have, and you need not—"

"The second," she persisted, "is the thanks I owe you for the new friend I have gained through correspondence. Your sister is delightful, sir. But I wanted to apprise you of some of the very great extensions of her kindness in her letter to me. Were you aware that Miss Darcy has offered to host my family in London?"

Elizabeth laughed at his astonished expression. "I had thought not! But you may rest easy, for I have not replied to her scheme with any agreement. I am attempting to find the words to politely decline without causing her to feel embarrassment, for Miss Darcy was only doing what she thought best, in these circumstances, to be kind and helpful."

"You are very understanding, Miss Elizabeth," said Mr

Darcy gravely. "I am glad you took the offer in the spirit it was given. Georgiana certainly meant no offence—no offence at all."

"And none was taken, sir. She is right in thinking that my family and I might wish for some temporary lodgings, but I believe my aunt and uncle Gardiner will wish to host us in London. We cannot trespass much longer on poor Mr Bingley's generosity."

"Bingley takes great pleasure in being of help to his friends and neighbours. You cannot trespass where you are welcome."

"Mr Bingley is everything kind and neighbourly, but it is best if we stay with family. I am sure he will understand, as will your sister, when we remove ourselves to reside with our relations once they are prepared to receive us."

Mr Darcy nodded, looking ahead of them down the lane, which was rapidly drawing up to the lawn before Lucas Lodge. "If you express your wishes to Georgiana in that way, she will certainly find no fault in your reasoning. Do not worry about injuring her feelings, however. She knows whatever you write in response to her will be kindly meant."

Elizabeth smiled at that. "I can well believe it! You gave your sister a far more flattering impression of my nature than I feel I rightfully deserve."

"I believe a week ago I observed that you have a propensity for wilful misunderstanding—a propensity that extends, I suppose, even to yourself," he said in a voice so droll that she looked at him askance. In response, Darcy tipped his hat at her with a small smile.

He is teasing me with this dark attempt at humour, Elizabeth thought. His manner had reached her in so disjointed a mix of archness and dryness that Elizabeth could not help but chuckle.

Mr Darcy gave her a rueful glance. "Forgive me. You would have phrased that far better than I."

"Indeed not. I am afraid my teasing is never quite so effective. I have no talent for gravity and so would have failed to carry my point."

"I never thought seriousness of manner could be considered a talent."

"Of course it is. Did not the Romans laud it as a virtue? *Pietas, dignitas, virtus, et—*"

"*Gravitas,*" he finished.

"Exactly. I am sure we have both done our Latin tutors proud."

As the carriage approached the drive to the front of Lucas Lodge, it was their easy smiles, even more than their unconventional arrangement on the coachman's seat that must have surprised Charlotte Lucas as she caught sight of them from the doorway where she awaited her friend.

"Elizabeth!" she exclaimed. "And Mr Darcy!"

Mr Darcy descended from the seat and once before her on the ground, he bowed. "Miss Lucas."

"How good of you to deliver my dear friend to me, sir," said she, curtseying to him. Charlotte then addressed his companion. "Eliza, it is such a blessing to see you out and about."

"And it is so good to see you, my dear Charlotte!" Elizabeth replied as she stood and gave her hand to Mr Darcy. She clambered down to the coachman's step, where she paused and contemplated her most graceful form of descent to the ground a few feet below.

Mr Darcy shook his head and released her fingers. He brought his hands instead to her waist. "With your permission?"

She nodded, and for the second time that week, allowed him to lift her. This time, it was merely a brief exchange while he swung her down to the ground.

"I am delighted you have come," Charlotte said, kissing Elizabeth's cheek and offering her arm. She looked up at her friend's tall companion and offered, "Mr Darcy, you are more than welcome to join us. There is nothing formal in the gathering, you understand, but we can offer some refreshments."

"I thank you, but forgive me," he replied, bowing to her. "I should return to Longbourn and assist Mr Bennet. Would it be convenient if we both returned to collect Miss Elizabeth in an hour?"

Charlotte's crooked grin nearly made her friend blush. "Oh, an hour will do, I suppose," she acceded.

When Mr Darcy resumed his place in the driver's seat and signalled the team to turn about, Charlotte fixed her eyes meaningfully on Elizabeth and began to lead her towards the house.

"There is much I wish to know, if you would indulge me," she prompted.

As they passed together into the vestibule of Lucas Lodge, Elizabeth lifted an eyebrow at Charlotte's unrestrained curiosity. "You will not be disappointed, for I confess that was a part of my design in coming today. Ask me anything, for I shall tell you all."

Charlotte motioned for her to turn around as she helped Elizabeth to remove her wrap and spencer. "It may be difficult for us to share confidences until after I have helped Mother serve the tea," Charlotte advised her in a whisper, "for as you know, Mr Collins is—"

"Ah, there you are, Miss Lucas!" exclaimed the very object of their discussion, meeting them in the foyer and bowing with effusion. "And dare I presume that your companion is my fair cousin who you have been awaiting?"

"It is, sir," said Charlotte, recovering herself with good grace. "Mr Collins, allow me to introduce my dear friend, Miss Elizabeth Bennet, the second eldest of the daughters of Longbourn."

As Elizabeth curtseyed, she observed Mr Collins as he swept his wide frame into a bow. In looks, he was exactly what she had expected: plain and broad-faced, larger than her father, and much younger, but without the benefit of physical grace that the vigour and athleticism of youth might have gifted him. As Mr Collins righted his rather portly frame, Elizabeth had to hide a smile, for she saw at once that he was taking her measure as well and was eminently more pleased with what he saw.

"Miss Lucas has done me the honour of describing you and your sisters, Miss Elizabeth," said he, nodding in a magnanimous fashion to Charlotte. "Although I certainly never doubted her—all honesty and goodness that she is—I am nevertheless delighted to find her rendering of you remarkably accurate. You are uniformly charming!"

Charlotte stepped forward. "She certainly is, sir. Now that you have made each other's acquaintance, may I have the pleasure of inviting you into the drawing room for some refreshments—perhaps some tea? We may converse more comfortably there."

With great alacrity and a plenitude of affable words, Mr Collins accepted her invitation, and they all sat down together as the tea things were set out. Lady Lucas and Mr Collins declared themselves vastly happy to see Elizabeth looking so well, and before Elizabeth had touched her plate, the conversation launched forward as questions about the fire, both delicate and indelicate, were laid before her by Mr Collins and, from the corner, an anxious and surprisingly talkative Maria Lucas.

Elizabeth did her best to answer them all with tolerable equanimity, but Mr Collins's frequent interjections chafed at her nerves. Her father's summation of the man had been entirely correct, for she detected such a lack of sense, marked with puffed-up self-importance, as to render him a comical and even pitiable character were he not so tedious in company.

"Such a frightful thing to happen!" he declared, once she had finished telling them all of how Kitty had struggled to breathe and given them many sleepless hours during that first night of their refuge at Netherfield. "But you must have both felt such gratitude to Mr Darcy, who in his generous condescension, risked his life to bring you from the house, and to Mr Bingley, who threw open his doors to bring you into his home. Not that such behaviour by gentlemen is unexpected, and especially, of a nephew of Lady Catherine de Bourgh, who is in all circumstances the most amiable, helpful, and obliging."

Elizabeth replied, "Yes, we are greatly indebted to both gentlemen."

"I am glad that they both have garnered your esteem, Eliza," said Charlotte slyly. She smiled as she sipped the last of her tea, and set it aside with an impatience Elizabeth had never seen in her friend before. "Now, all this talk of the fire must have you anxious for fresh air, I think. Would you take a turn in the garden with me?"

Elizabeth knew at once what Charlotte had planned. "Nothing would satisfy me better," she said, rising immediately and making a curtsey to Lady Lucas and her company.

"Mr Collins, while the ladies are out for a few moments, could you tell me what a clergyman would be expected to do, should such a fire ever happen within his parish?" said Lady Lucas.

Elizabeth and her friend had already made their happy escape and were out laughing breathlessly in the garden.

"What pure genius, Charlotte!"

"I fancy myself clever on occasion, though not as often as you," her friend quipped, beaming in equal delight at her scheme's success. "Now, Eliza, you must reward me for my efforts. Do be serious, and tell me more. What has happened at Netherfield since you came there? What of Mr Bingley and Jane? And what of you and your solicitous Mr Darcy?"

"Such an inquisition! May I beg your leave to answer one question at a time?"

"Only if you agree to answer them all."

Elizabeth gave her aching feet some rest by settling herself on the bench near the rose bushes. "Prepare yourself for some shocking revelations, then, if I am to answer each one in full."

Charlotte sat next to her and took her hand. "I should not demand it all of you, if any of it is painful in the telling."

"None of it is taxing now. The worst of it, at any rate, I have already told you. When we arrived at Netherfield, it was quite late, and I daresay Miss Bingley was quite put out to have all of us invading her household—with Jane and I returning a second time. She had only just gotten rid of us! But Mr Bingley—oh, Jane is so smitten, and for good reason. He stayed on for hours that night to oversee those putting out the fire at the house while Jane and I stayed up with Kitty after Mr Darcy had helped us get her to bed."

Charlotte gasped. "Mr Darcy was in her bedroom?"

"All of Mr Bingley's servants were at Longbourn helping with the fire, with the exception of the maids. And my poor father could hardly have carried Kitty all the way up the stairs at his age and with such horrible coughing as he suffered that night. As Mr Hurst was nowhere to be seen, it all fell to poor Mr Darcy," Elizabeth explained. "He had to bring her up the stairs to the sickroom himself. Once Jane and I had tucked her into bed, he then fetched water for us. Truly, he was very kind to act in the role of manservant."

"Perhaps the necessity forced Mr Darcy to bend some of his scruples of rank. I am grateful for that! But you, my poor Eliza! How wretched and miserable you must have felt that night with your injuries so fresh. I had forgotten to ask about your feet and your hands. Are you truly better now?"

"I am, as you see. And it was only this hand that was burnt," she said, holding it up. "My feet were in bandages until yesterday evening. The first night, they were hot to the touch and not painful. I suppose I was still in a state of shock, now that I revisit it. The pain came later, and might have been far worse, but Mr Darcy brought liniment for me directly from Mr

Jones, who was much needed by Kitty and by my father too. Mr Jones was only free to examine me the next morning."

"How very kind of Mr Darcy to think of your discomfort at such a time. How did he learn of your burns?"

"He was with me when I burned my hand, and I was barefoot the whole night. I now look back on it with more mortification for my modesty than I felt at the time, I confess."

"There were too many other, more pressing causes for worry on that evening, I am sure," Charlotte said, reaching to give Elizabeth's uninjured hand a commiserating squeeze. "I can only imagine what you must have done, and thought, and suffered. And yet, how striking it is to me that amidst all the chaos, Mr Darcy should take it upon himself to procure you some remedy for your comfort. Has he asked you about your burns every night and every day since then?" Charlotte smiled in such a conspiratorial fashion that Elizabeth could not help but roll her eyes.

"A pair of burned feet and the resultant hobbling about do not make a woman most attractive, dear Charlotte. I declare you are getting carried away with such notions! Mr Darcy has indeed been very kind and on that evening, quite gallant, but I expect nothing more from him than his civility and charity."

"Then you are a simpleton indeed, for what man can resist a pretty damsel in distress?"

Elizabeth shook her head in wry disbelief.

Charlotte sighed. "Very well. I suppose he did not have much opportunity to see you at your disadvantage. Were you long in bed with your feet bound in bandages?"

"Oh no, for you know me well. I cannot keep to a sickbed, so I did my best to hobble to dinner the very next night, whether it proved wise of me or not."

"That must have been quite painful."

Elizabeth bit her lip at the memory. "I was very foolish to try to do so much that night. After dinner, I begged Jane to help me escape to our room, but I began bleeding through my bandages as I attempted to climb the stairs! Jane and my father had to assist me, and even then, it was such a painful process, that Mr Darcy...intervened."

Charlotte shifted forward in her seat in anticipation. "In what manner?"

"You will be quite shocked by it," Elizabeth warned.

"I think I have already deduced it. You certainly did not flinch when he helped you down from the driver's platform today. Was this the first time he has assisted you?"

Elizabeth flushed. "It was not. My father decided Mr Darcy was very sensible to offer to carry me up the staircase."

"Oh Eliza! This is above everything!" exclaimed Charlotte. "You have transported me to romantic thinking, which is not often done. So, on this rare and momentous occasion, you must and will tell me all!"

"There is not much to tell, Charlotte. I was irritated at Mr Darcy's officiousness at first, but as I realised how very easy such a chore was for him, and since he would keep me distracted by talking to me of Longbourn while I was aloft, it was not so trying as it might have been."

"No, I daresay being carried up a marble staircase by a handsome, young gentleman who was too enamoured to let a footman touch you—for I am certain there were plenty of Mr Bingley's men to be found on that occasion—was not so very *trying* at all."

Elizabeth's mind was overpowered again with the memory of his close, warm scent. She could do naught but shake her head to clear it. Once recovered, she demurred quietly, "He is not enamoured, Charlotte."

"Yet, you made a very pretty picture sitting on that coachman's seat together as you came up the front drive. And now he is back at Longbourn, helping your father manage the estate. I would not be surprised if Mr Darcy's next strategy was to find a way to introduce you to his relations, and before you know it, I shall be very satisfied indeed to learn that his courtship of you has neatly ended, and you have accepted him."

"Charlotte!" gasped Elizabeth, thinking of Miss Darcy's letter with some new wonder, and then censuring herself. "That sort of speculation is not amusing! I hope you will be satisfied to learn that I do not dislike him nearly as much as I have done these past weeks and that he seems to have forgiven me my deficiencies as well. You and I both know that Mr Darcy cannot intend to pursue me."

"Have it as you will. I suppose I must content myself for the present to learn merely that your opinions of each other have bettered themselves."

"Thank you. Now that you have finished your examination of the matter, do you think we ought to go back inside?"

Elizabeth had been tempted to talk to her friend of Mr Wickham, but seeing now that Charlotte would take such a conversation as further proof that her interest in Mr Darcy was developing, Elizabeth thought it best to abandon such a topic.

"I hardly think it necessary, unless you wish to take proper leave of Mr Collins. Here, we can stand watch for your Mr Darcy to return to carry you off again."

Elizabeth suddenly felt quite hot. "He is not *my* Mr Darcy! For heaven's sake!"

"Do lower your voice. I was only teasing you! But I see I have hit upon something and will therefore be silent—for now. Come, let us go inside, and you may take a proper leave if you wish. If I am not mistaken, I hear a carriage coming down the lane, and we shall soon have the gentlemen upon us."

In spite of her alacrity to have the niceties completed, Mr Collins detained Elizabeth in the sitting room during her leave-taking to express how much his anticipation of their coming dinner at Netherfield had increased since the happenstance of their meeting. As he said this, he gave her such a fawning smile and determined glance that Elizabeth felt a little ill as she responded with her own far less effusive regards and made her curtsey.

Her father stood by the carriage door to hand her in while Mr Darcy tipped his hat to her from his position on horseback as postilion. It seemed the carriage would contain only father and daughter on their return to Netherfield, which suited Elizabeth's frayed nerves rather well.

CHAPTER FOURTEEN

$\mathscr{N}$etherfield was quiet when they returned, for the Bennet ladies had retired to dress carefully for dinner after having spent part of their day being entertained by Mr Bingley and his sisters. Elizabeth, tired and sooty, likewise made her way above stairs to her chamber to take off her boots, apply more liniment to her feet, wash, and change.

Upon entering the room, she found their maid, Sarah, faced with the daunting task of readying, with such a scarcity of proper clothing and adornments, so many ladies for dinner in time for the event an hour hence.

Elizabeth divested herself of her boots with only a little discomfort and availed herself of the ewer and stand in the corner of the room, using Miss Bingley's expensive rose-oil soap to wash as thoroughly as she could in the cold water. A bath would have to wait, much as she desired one.

Smoothing down her hair, she donned some old satin slippers and worked the buttons on a fresh dinner gown. Elizabeth then slipped from the room so their maid could continue to attend to Jane's hair while Mrs Bennet hovered anxiously, directing the harried abigail on how best to arrange her eldest daughter's coiffure to please Mr Bingley.

Seeking solace and a chance to rest until she could claim Sarah to help with her own hair, Elizabeth sought sanctuary in the library. Finding it empty, she shut the door behind her, sighed deeply, and picked restlessly through the books until she came across a recent copy of *The Examiner* tucked between two rough old volumes. Amused at the radical publication's presence in an otherwise unremarkable collection of literature, she took it to the settee facing the window on the far wall. As she relaxed in the late afternoon sunlight, she gave in to the temptation to pull her feet up onto the seat and recline as she read, secure that the high back of the settee would guard her from the view of others who might enter through the door behind her.

While Elizabeth idly flipped through the publication, her mind focused on a blot of darkness on the edge of one page, which looked to her like soot. Nervously, she checked her fingers but remembered she had scrubbed them since returning from Longbourn.

Longbourn. She could no longer focus on her reading but began to worry anxiously over the coming months of hard work and expense needed to set their home to rights. She dwelled on these unsettling meditations for longer than she thought, closing her eyes at last in exhaustion as the sunlight slanting through the panes began to fade away.

Voices in the hallway approached and receded, some raised in frustration as Elizabeth failed to answer their entreaties to show herself and come prepare for dinner. Jane ducked briefly into the doorway to peer about, but in the gathering darkness, she could have perceived nothing.

Minutes later, another click signalled the doorknob had turned, and the firm tread of a gentleman's steps followed, but trapped in a dream, Elizabeth did not hear them.

DARCY SUSPECTED THAT MISS ELIZABETH, MISSING for nearly an hour, had likely turned to the library in search of quiet. He frowned as he glanced around the room, initially unable to see her until the glow from the hallway sconces caught upon a lock of brunette hair curled against the arm of the settee.

Not wishing to startle her, Darcy came softly around the side of her couch, all the while smiling with the realisation that Elizabeth's seemingly boundless energy indeed had its limits. It was good that she was resting after their outing. It had been an eventful one for the both of them.

His smile only grew when she was finally within his sight. Reclining in a most unladylike yet wholly feminine way, Elizabeth lounged deep in slumber upon the cushions with her feet drawn up against the opposing arm of the settee. The softly suffused shadows and her position gave him an excellent view of many of her finest features—the dusky eyelashes he had so long admired, her lovely décolletage, the delicate dip of her waist, and her shapely hip and thigh.

Tearing his eyes away from her pleasing figure, he noted the publication still clutched in her hand, and his curiosity ignited. He held his breath as he bent nearer to discover its title. He was instantly diverted by her choice in reading material, a publication crammed full of controversial and witty essays that he had brought to Netherfield himself. He deduced that Elizabeth had likely stolen away from the chaotic preparations for dinner for just a moment's thoughtful repose, only to fall asleep in the middle of her reading.

Darcy regretfully recalled his duty. He ought not to linger when her family was looking for her. He ought not to be the one who awakened her, for it would only cause her embarrassment. It would be best to find one of her sisters directly.

He turned carefully on his heel, ready to retreat in silence, when Elizabeth exhaled sharply. Darcy froze on the spot and returned his eyes to her, warily searching for signs of awareness.

Her eyes remained closed, and her body, once her sigh subsided, remained still. But her face, at first so peaceful, had transformed into an expression of pain and anxiety. As he watched, her brow contracted, her lower lip quivered, and from the corners of her eyes, tears began to gather and shimmer on her closed lashes.

It was clear her dreams had now taken a decidedly unpleasant turn. As he watched her breath catch and release in a silent sob, his posture turned steely under the shock of her obvious distress. He ought to immediately fulfil his quest to find her sister—preferably Miss Bennet—and bring her quickly to awaken and attend Elizabeth.

But he felt unable to leave her now. Not when tears began to slide down her alabaster cheeks. And certainly not when she began to tremble from an onslaught of invisible terrors.

The darkness made him bold. Hesitantly, Darcy moved within arm's reach of her, drawing in a breath. Extending his hand, he drew the backs of his fingers gingerly down her forearm before withdrawing instantly. Her response to his touch was immediate—the muscles of her frame locked, then released, as her eyes, dewy and dark, flew open.

He met her bewildered gaze uncertainly and bowed, not able to think of any posture less intimidating. In soft tones, he pronounced her name and his guilt. "Miss Elizabeth, pray forgive me." She sat up hastily. "I should have brought your sister to awaken you. You were in the clutches of some terrifying dream, and you seemed most distressed, so I took it upon myself to release you from it."

As though conjured back by his explanation, an echo of Elizabeth's dream caused pain to flicker across her face. Closing her eyes against it, she drew in a deep breath. When she opened her eyes again, they grew wide with alarm as she noted the fading sunlight.

"It appears I have slept the last of the daylight away! It must be time to dine."

"It is," confirmed Darcy, producing a handkerchief and handing it to her.

She took the bit of silk he offered. Darcy noted that, although she was fighting for composure, she seemed still somewhat enthralled by the dark dream she had just escaped.

As he watched her touch his handkerchief to her face with a shaking hand, he continued. "May I bring something for you? Perhaps a glass of wine? Shall I get you one?"

"No, no," she protested, continuing to dab her damp face with the cloth. "I assure you I am well."

"Shall I call for your maid?"

Elizabeth shook her head. "No—that is not—unless—" Here, she paused and patted her hair. With a mortified expression, she looked up at him as he shifted from foot to foot in the pale light. "Do I look dreadful?"

Such bluntness forced him to check an unexpected laugh. Composing himself, he shook his head. "You never look dreadful, Miss Elizabeth."

She sat upright on the settee and raised a brow at him. "Tolerable, then, I suppose? But not handsome enough to be tempting?"

She allowed his handkerchief to fall to her lap as she nonchalantly removed some loose hair pins from her nape.

Caught by her unmistakable recitation as much as by her mystifying transformation from grief into such playful ease, Darcy grasped for some form of response. After a beat of heavy silence, he offered gravely, "I hardly looked at you at the assembly, if that is the conversation to which you refer. I ought never to have uttered such an ill-considered remark, not even to keep Bingley's attempts—"

She waved his white handkerchief dismissively like a surrendering flag before she handed it back to him.

"I was teasing you, sir, but I think I can tell well enough that my appearance needs some attention before I present myself to those in the dining room. Since I find I have no time to return to my room to properly have it addressed by a maid, could I trouble you to locate Jane for me?"

Eager for both an occupation and a graceful exit, Darcy bowed and immediately went to perform his task. He found Miss Bennet pacing the hall, calling softly for her missing sister. With a nod and tilt of his head as a signal, he drew her worried eye.

"You will find your sister in the library, Miss Bennet," he informed her, once she had drawn near.

Her round, china-blue eyes lit with puzzlement and surprise. "Why, I looked there for her only ten minutes ago. Are you certain, sir?"

"Completely. I unwittingly discovered her on the settee. She," he paused, wondering how much to reveal, "seemed distressed. I offered to find you."

"I am glad you did." Jane curtseyed to him and at once turned to hurry down towards the library.

Mr Darcy, already dressed for dinner, turned into the foyer, where many of their party had already gathered. He greeted his hosts and the Bennets with the happy news that Miss Elizabeth had been found.

Miss Bingley addressed him directly. "Well, I am glad she has been located at last!" cried that lady as she claimed his arm. In a more confederate tone, she added, "It is abominably rude for a guest to make the food go cold. Mr Collins has arrived, you see, and so, we are all assembled. We may now go into dinner."

Mr Darcy felt all the rudeness of the circumstance but on the hostess's side. "Should the Miss Bennets not be escorted to the table? Miss Bennet has gone to attend her sister, who seems unwell."

Miss Bingley tutted. "They may escort each other, if they so choose."

Darcy had no recourse but to acquiesce to the mistress of the house and so went into the dining room with Miss Bingley's firm grasp keeping him captive. His mind, however, was free to think on the exchange of only some moments before in the dimness of the library.

The sight of Elizabeth's tears had unnerved him, and although she had recovered her playful manner soon enough, he found anxiety still sat stiffly on his shoulders as he took his seat at the table and awaited some sign of her.

Elizabeth and her sister did indeed walk in together some minutes later, and with surprising timeliness, for the soup had not yet been brought out.

It eased his mind to find Elizabeth looking so well. Darcy could see that Miss Bennet had done a marvellous piece of work in restoring order to her sister's hair. He might have been content to admire her for a moment longer, but the matron of Longbourn turned on her daughter.

"Lizzy, must you run wild so near to dinner?" said Mrs Bennet loud enough to arrest Elizabeth's attention, and indeed, half the room's. "Gracious heavens, girl! Where have you been?"

"I was quite fatigued after my visit to Longbourn today, Mama," whispered Elizabeth. "I did not mean to fall asleep in the library, and I am sorry for it, but I am well now."

Mrs Bennet huffed in displeasure. "Well, you had best use the restorative to advantage. Be charming to Mr Collins."

CHAPTER FIFTEEN

"Cousin Elizabeth, how well you look this evening," said Mr Collins at her side. "I do hope you have recovered sufficiently from your outing today." His words themselves were gracious, but his manner was ingratiating as he leaned towards her.

Elizabeth took a breath before responding. "I am much recovered now, sir. I apologise for being late, but it seems the exertion took more of my strength than I anticipated."

The footmen came to the table bearing the soup course, and Elizabeth hoped Mr Collins would eat, rather than talk. But it was not to be. The man was determined to do both and all at once.

"Marvellous soup!" exclaimed he to Miss Bingley, with the spoon just barely out of his mouth. "I daresay your cook is nearly so fine as the one employed at my patroness's estate at Rosings."

Miss Bingley merely inclined her head at the poor compliment, for she, too, was occupied with eating and was determined to show her superior breeding through ladylike silence.

Mr Collins needed no encouragement to continue. "It is a grand house indeed, and since coming to take up my appointment at the parsonage this spring, I have had occasion to dine with the ladies of the house on no less than two occasions. Lady Catherine even condescended to send a note to me last Saturday to help her make up a quadrille. Such affability as I have enjoyed is beyond expression!"

As he said this, he favoured Elizabeth with a smile, which she, with some anxiety, returned with a nod.

At Elizabeth's uncharacteristic silence, Mrs Bennet put in encouragingly, "That is all very proper and civil I am sure, and I daresay her ladyship is a very agreeable woman. It is a pity that great ladies in general are not more like her. Does she live near you, sir?"

Mr Collins's smile was wreathed with more pleasure than borrowed grandness should grant. "The garden in which stands my humble abode is separated only by a lane from Rosings Park."

Mrs Bennet looked to Elizabeth to further the conversation. Her daughter merely shifted in her seat as she nervously stirred her soup without glancing up, so Mrs Bennet sallied forth again. "I think you said she was a widow, sir? Has she any family living with her?"

"Lady Catherine has a daughter. She is the heiress of Rosings Park, a very extensive property."

"Ah!" cried Mrs Bennet, shaking her head, "then she is better off than many girls. And what sort of young lady is she? Is she handsome?"

Elizabeth set down her soup spoon and stared at her mother, as though seeing her for the first time. Her lack of tact, in such mixed company, truly knew no bounds.

Yet Mr Collins seemed pleased to be applied to for this information, which he provided after sending a meaningful glance at Mr Darcy that made that gentleman clench his jaw.

"She is most charming indeed. Lady Catherine, herself, says that in point of true beauty, Miss de Bourgh is far superior to the handsomest of her sex because there is that in her features which marks the young woman of distinguished birth. She is unfortunately of a sickly constitution, which has prevented her from making progress in many accomplishments, as I am informed by the lady who superintended her education and who still resides with them. But she is perfectly amiable and often condescends to drive by my humble abode in her little phaeton."

"Has Miss de Bourgh been presented?" Miss Bingley asked. "I do not remember her name among the ladies at court."

"Her indifferent state of health unhappily prevents her being in town, and by that means, as I told Lady Catherine myself one day, she has deprived the British court of its brightest ornament. Her ladyship seemed pleased with the idea, and you may imagine that I am happy on every occasion to offer those little delicate compliments that are always acceptable to ladies. I have more than once observed to Lady Catherine that her charming daughter seemed born to be a duchess, and that the most elevated rank, instead of giving her consequence, would be adorned by her."

Elizabeth blushed at the sycophantic idiocy so near to her and nearly recoiled when Mr Collins shifted his chair closer to hers and gave her another smile—this one still slightly moist with soup.

Elizabeth directed a desperate glance to her father that she hoped he would interpret correctly. He met her eye with a twinkling glint of mirth in his own.

"I am sure you judge very properly," observed Mr Bennet, "and it is happy for you that you possess the talent of flattering with delicacy. May I ask whether these pleasing attentions proceed from the impulse of the moment or are the result of previous study?"

"They arise chiefly from what is passing at the time, and though I sometimes amuse myself with arranging such little elegant compliments as may be adapted to ordinary occasions, I always wish to give them as unstudied an air as possible."

As Mr Collins answered, he stole another bold glance at Elizabeth, which made her pause over her soup and replace her yet again uneaten spoonful in the bowl. Hungry as she had been upon awakening in the library, she had been unable to find any source of appetite at this most discomfiting of dinner parties. Her embarrassment at Mr Collins's every word, compounded by his eyes constantly on her as he spoke, had quite put her off her food.

Her untouched bowl of soup was taken back up as the next course came out, and during this exchange of dishes, Elizabeth sought a new partner in her attempts to turn the conversation away from Mr Collins's mortifying monologue.

She feared her father would only encourage the man to continue on in the same ridiculous fashion, so she looked to Jane for some assistance. Finding her pleasantly engaged with Mr Bingley, Elizabeth looked farther down the table to where Kitty was coughing quietly while Lydia regaled her about some young officer's foolish behaviour from the evening at the Philipses'. The Hursts merely seemed content in the prospect of the coming food. Miss Bingley looked upon all these proceedings with evident distaste, while Mary, seated at her other side, was patiently listening as Mr Collins wore on, and Elizabeth knew she was not likely to contribute in any meaningful way except to observe on some moral point of order.

And so, she looked across the table to her only other possible champion: Mr Darcy. That gentleman's visage bore an expression of disdainful hauteur, which signified, Elizabeth presumed, he had absolutely no wish to further conversation with the parson and would persist in abstinence from the exchange. Much as this frustrated her, she found she could hardly blame him for his cold silence.

With a sigh, Elizabeth took a sip of wine and tried to remove her thoughts from those before her. Such an action was doomed to fail, however, now that she found herself the object of Mr Collins's intense fascination.

"Have you much travelled beyond Hertfordshire, Miss Elizabeth?" he asked, with such eagerness she could see no sense in forestalling him.

"I have not ventured far. I have been to London to visit my aunt and uncle Gardiner once during a recent Season, and many times throughout my girlhood. Beyond that, I confess I have not had much occasion to stir from our little county."

"Ah, so you have never seen the beauties of Kent! Perhaps you will be extended the privilege someday, and you might then experience the beneficence of Lady Catherine de Bourgh for yourself. There are many beauties to be seen around the park, and Rosings is simply exquisite. You would no doubt greatly enjoy the hospitality of its mistress at her table."

Elizabeth's face went white at his insinuation. "I am sure that her ladyship is very gracious, but I would have no occasion to visit Kent."

Mrs Bennet cleared her throat and glared at Elizabeth upon hearing this discouraging denial, but Elizabeth refused to shrink.

"You are very young, if you will pardon my saying so, Cousin—if I may call you such," replied Mr Collins, with an air of commiserating condescension. "There is much that life could bring to you yet, which the present would seem to offer up as fantastical. You may someday enjoy many advantages that you, in your modesty and simple upbringing, have not yet imagined or dreamt. Why, just four years ago when I entered seminary, I could never have conceived that I would someday be in the service of a lady of such eminence and nobility, or that I would have such a comfortable parsonage and garden to call home, or so many other Providential blessings as I now enjoy."

He smiled at her and in tones of sympathy, added, "Indeed, I imagine you must feel a great deal of uncertainty in your present situation. Perhaps in your current deprivation, you cannot fathom such security or bounty ever being offered to you."

Elizabeth envisioned the dark remnants of her dream—Longbourn a bitter, ashen shell, her father dying from the toil and grief of trying to restore it, her family, harrowed, hungry, and spent, unable to survive the loss of home, protector, and provisions.

Sweat broke out upon her brow. Elizabeth clutched the table edge, taking a breath, striving for some semblance of equanimity, but it was too late. The embers of fear from her bleak dream had been kindled to bright anger by Mr Collins's implications. As she seethed, she reasoned that Mr Collins had only foolishly awakened the monster of her greatest anxieties in an attempt to court her interest with his position as a potential provider. It only stung her now with her emotions so aggrieved, so tender in these short hours after her intimate work in the disastrous ruins that had been Longbourn's most lively rooms. He surely did not mean to do her injury with his thoughtless talk.

Reminding herself of his ignorance, Elizabeth retreated from the fray by sinking back into her chair. As she released her breath, her vision unaccountably swam.

Mr Collins dropped his fork and wrung his hands, obviously realising his misstep. "My poor cousin! You do look unwell."

Elizabeth pressed a hand to her face and replied tightly, "I—I *am* unwell. Forgive me, Mr Collins. I must excuse myself."

With that, she abruptly stood, curtseyed, and without

meeting anyone's eye, Elizabeth turned from the table and went out into the hall.

She had gained the staircase before she felt the need to sit down again. When Jane found her there moments later, Elizabeth was too tired and troubled to do more than raise her head from her hands to meet her sister's concerned gaze.

Jane sat down next to her and gently took Elizabeth's hand in a gesture of reassurance. Her sister regarded her in quiet compassion while Elizabeth continued her struggle for composure.

After some moments of silence, Elizabeth whispered, "Jane, what am I to do? If we are unable to restore Longbourn—if Papa loses a great deal of money in the attempt, and we fall into debt..."

Jane brushed the curls and even a few tears back from Elizabeth's cheek.

"It is possible—in fact, it is probable that we shall have some substantial debts to repay." Elizabeth stared down at her empty hands helplessly. When she spoke again, her tone was dark and bitter. "Perhaps I ought to do this. Perhaps I ought to allow that odious man to court me—to marry me. But dear lord, how I loathe the thought! Better that I had been turned to cinders in the fire." She was openly crying now.

"Lizzy, no! You must not say such things!" Jane shushed and soothed her sister, pulling her into her arms. Resting her cheek upon Elizabeth's crown, she reassured her. "And as to a marriage that would make you unhappy—my dear, it will not come to that. Father will never allow it."

Elizabeth continued to weep into her hands, leaving Jane to find ways beyond words to offer comfort. She stroked Elizabeth's hair and pressed her tightly, striving to calm her in the old ways she had done when they were children.

After a few minutes, Elizabeth quieted, then spoke. "I ought to go to bed. I should not let anyone see me like this."

"You are frightfully pale. I think I shall go up with you."

"No, I am well," Elizabeth said, but when she struggled to her feet, she found herself mistaken. Black motes swam in her vision, and she hurried to grasp the stair rail at the same moment Jane's hand caught her arm to steady her.

"You are chilled through!"

"I am faint, if I am honest," said Elizabeth. "I cannot account for it, except that I have not eaten more than a pastry at breakfast and a few swallows of tea with Charlotte. Just let me sit a moment, Jane," she said at length.

Jane helped her sister to sit upon the step again. Then she straightened and placed her hand on Elizabeth's shoulder in a manner that brooked no argument. "I told you this morning that it was too soon for such an outing, did I not? You are over-wrought, Lizzy. I must leave you now to call for a footman. Stay where you are."

"No! Jane, please! I can manage on my own. Just let me stay here a moment longer."

"Persist in this foolishness, and I shall fetch Mr Darcy to carry you again."

"I shall be mortified if you trouble him again on my account. Please do not!"

"Then stay where you are!"

In a few minutes, Jane returned with a cordial young footman, and Elizabeth was obliged to take his arm as she progressed up the stairs. Jane followed for propriety, and once she had sat Elizabeth down and dismissed the footman, she shut the door and helped her sister undress.

"Do not worry for me," Elizabeth pleaded while Jane worked her buttons. "Return to dinner. I am well now, truly, I am."

"You must rest, that much is certain. But you should take a little sustenance before you sleep. I shall request for a maid to bring up a tray directly. Pray promise me you will eat something."

After Jane laid aside Elizabeth's gown, she turned back to her and lifted her chin, compelling her to meet her eyes. "Truly, Lizzy, I have never seen you thus. You worry me so."

Seeing the concern in Jane's normally serene countenance, Elizabeth had little recourse but to give her promise.

Ten minutes saw the errand done, and Sarah tapped upon the door. Feeling exhausted, Elizabeth bade her enter, rather than rising to answer it.

Sarah bustled in with a tray. "Miss Elizabeth, I hear you are unwell."

"No, only foolish. I have not eaten a proper meal today to equal my exertions."

Sarah nodded and uncovered the tray. "I heard you went back up to Longbourn. It cannot have been easy for you. I have brought some soup and some warm bread and butter, if that will satisfy."

Elizabeth nodded at such thoughtfulness and admitted that any repast would be a fair deal better than an empty stomach. She ate the simple fare willingly, finding herself much hungrier once away from the cloying attentions of Mr Collins. Afterwards, she quickly fell into the untroubled sleep of the truly weary.

CHAPTER SIXTEEN

*T*hose who remained at the table were more subdued after Elizabeth left it. Miss Bennet returned and assured those gathered that her sister was well but simply overwhelmed by the events of the day. By way of soliloquy, Mr Collins steered the conversation to the Lucases and their hospitality, of Meryton and its surrounds, and regrettably, back to Rosings again. Mercifully, the final course was soon served and eaten, and the ladies withdrew while the gentlemen took themselves off to the library.

After finding himself the object of Mr Collins's many obsequious compliments and fawning effusions, Darcy was relieved to escape to the sitting room and to rejoin the ladies. He and Mr Bingley went immediately to Miss Bennet to seek details of her sister's condition.

"I have just been to our room to observe her for myself," said Miss Bennet. "She has eaten and fallen asleep. I own I am relieved—much relieved."

"Did she have nothing served to her at Lucas Lodge? I am

very surprised that Miss Lucas did not see to her friend's needs," Darcy observed with some concern.

"With all the attention Mr Collins gave her, she likely found herself too distracted to eat."

Darcy's consternation was evident. "I see."

"But a night of sleep shall put all to rights, surely," Mr Bingley said hopefully.

"That is certain," replied Miss Bennet, favouring him with a smile. "Elizabeth has proven time and again that she is not formed for illness or ill-spirits. She has always been the strongest of us all." To Mr Darcy, she said, "I am sure she will be quite well by the time she awakens tomorrow."

Darcy could have no doubt that Miss Bennet had some suspicion of his harbouring a tendre for her sister. While he could readily accept the fact of it himself, he was not yet willing to acknowledge it to others, and he allowed Bingley to express his pleasure for him.

Both men, however, were struck with surprise when Miss Bennet's characteristically composed spirits suddenly seemed to falter.

"I—I must confess that I have lately placed too much faith in Elizabeth's strength. She may be our bravest sister, but I am the eldest, and the household burdens of Longbourn should naturally fall to me."

Mr Bingley began to protest, but Darcy broke in. "It was Miss Elizabeth's particular wish to go and be of use to your father, and you could hardly have swayed her from that desire."

Miss Bennet was firm in her contrition. "Perhaps not, but I could have easily accompanied her."

"She had others with her today. In addition to myself, Mr Bennet and Miss Lucas attended her. We each trusted that Miss Elizabeth would apply her good sense and that the hospitality at Lucas Lodge would give her sustenance and enliven her spirits.

Whether you had attended her or not, the outcome may have been the same."

Miss Bennet took up her teacup and regarded Darcy over its rim. "I see what you are about, sir."

"You do?"

"Yes. You wish to lay the blame upon the circumstances alone. But Elizabeth has been my charge almost since her birth. As an elder brother, I am sure you understand the responsibility that I feel acutely for Elizabeth's welfare, one which I shall continue to feel by instinct, regardless of any eloquent argument to the contrary."

Darcy's mind darkened at the memory of a young girl shattered at Ramsgate. After a breath to recover himself, he bowed. "I understand you perfectly."

ELIZABETH AWOKE HUNGRY AND WAS CONFOUNDED to discover, judging by the darkness outside her window, it was too early for breakfast. She took advantage of the quiet, however, by catching their maid as she refreshed the fire in the dark, and whispering for bath water to be sent up. Quietly, so as not to awaken Jane, she pulled on yesterday's day dress and a borrowed wrap. She descended the stairs in the dark and removed to the gardens to await the sunrise.

She walked outside and entered what sailors call the nautical dawn—that time of day when the earth is dark, and only the sky and the water display the coming light. Elizabeth stepped into the garden and stood watching the clouds take colour as the amorphous flowerbeds and hedges around her remained a silvered black. She did not wander far, not trusting her feet to know the way without tripping. Instead, she breathed in the clean air, enjoying the sensation of her own warm breath kindling against the chill of the morning air upon her face.

A thrush awakened somewhere in the brush, and she heard

it call softly. As she waited for another bird to answer, the sun continued its ascent, bringing with it a palette of golds and reds that lent more brightness to her surroundings. Shapes near her feet became distinguishable, then rendered with clarity and colour.

Elizabeth walked a little farther, trailing her hands along the hedges and feeling the tenacious last vestiges of blooms and leaves with her fingertips. Soon, all but the strongest evergreens would be drab and colourless.

When she felt the first warm rays of true sunlight upon her face, a recollection of the routines of those within Netherfield returned to her. Rather than risk being discovered in yesterday's dress with her hair in disarray, Elizabeth knew she ought to find her room again. Her heart gave an aubade to the fragile beauty around her as she slowly returned to the sleepy house and to her long-awaited bath.

She found Jane awake and sitting up in bed, staring at the tub as the maid filled it. She turned in surprise as Elizabeth entered.

"I hope Sarah did not wake you, Jane."

"She did not, but I was worried to find you gone. Are you feeling well this morning?"

Elizabeth toed off her shoes. "With a little breakfast after my warm bath, I believe I shall be as refreshed as I could ever hope to be."

"I am relieved. But—oh! Do not tell me you wore that dress to walk out this morning. It is filthy!"

With Jane's assistance, Elizabeth found herself soaking in the bath in mere moments. Soon, the last of the previous day's tensions began to leave her body as she aimlessly chased the slippery soap at the bottom of the basin with her foot.

She roused herself at the sound of the maid's voice. "Shall I wash your hair, Miss Elizabeth?"

Elizabeth could not resist the offer. And so it was that while

Jane brushed her hair before the mirror across the room, Elizabeth reclined in the tub, tipping her head back as the gentle maid worked soap through her hair and rinsed it with a mixture of rose hip oil and diluted wine vinegar, banishing the lingering odour of smoke from her work at Longbourn. After one more rinse of water, Jane came to the tub and helped her sister wrap her wet hair.

Shivering in the open air, Elizabeth donned a clean chemise and joined her sister before the fireplace. Then she stood still while Jane gently pressed the dampness from her dark curls, an act the sisters had performed for each other since they were girls.

Elizabeth's voice was muffled from beneath the towel. "I am sorry to have caused you such worry last night."

Jane's hands stilled for a moment. "I worry only for your happiness. I have never seen you cry so, not even when you were very small."

Elizabeth straightened and let the towel fall to her shoulders. Brushing her damp hair from her eyes, she confessed, "I worry for my happiness, too, Jane. But now that I have reflected on it, I have decided that I shall not be trapped into thinking the very worst until it comes. After all, even if I do marry Mr Collins, I shall still have the grand expanse of Rosings Park to ramble in—where I may become hopelessly lost. I shall be sure to do so frequently!"

Jane laughed, relieved to have her spirited sister restored to her.

Both ladies came down to breakfast an hour later. Elizabeth was happy to find it a far more cordial meal than the past evening's dinner had been—due, no doubt, to the absence of Mr Collins. Her father was at table, as were Mr Bingley and Mr Darcy, who rose and bowed as she and Jane entered the room.

As Elizabeth poured herself some tea, she met Mr Darcy's dark gaze and knew he was examining her for signs of lingering illness in his own quiet way. She had just favoured him with a small smile and a raised brow to evince her good spirits when her father's voice captured her attention.

"I hope you have recovered from last night's attack of missish nerves."

Elizabeth sighed. In some ways, her father would never change. "I am well, Papa. Nearly ten hours of rest and quiet have put me to rights."

"I hope today's company will suit you better. Did you know that we expect your uncle Gardiner to arrive at the Philipses' this afternoon?"

"I had heard a hopeful rumour that he was to arrive today." She stirred her tea. "Might I call upon our relations in Meryton this afternoon directly when he comes? I so long to see my uncle."

"I shall send a note to Mr Philips and ask him to convey that we should both like to visit," her father offered. "But you understand that your uncle would have only just arrived. You ought not besiege him at once with too many enquiries. I am sure his good counsel will touch upon every needful issue once he has had sufficient time to recover from the road."

Although eager to see her uncle, Elizabeth had no intention of smothering him as her father supposed. "Do you know how long Uncle Gardiner intends to stay on with the Philipses?"

"At least until Tuesday, at which time, he hopes to receive word from your aunt Gardiner that their home will be ready to receive all of us in town. Then we will go to London with him."

Across the table, Mr Bingley's teacup clattered abruptly. "Will you leave Netherfield so soon?" he asked with some anxiety, glancing from Jane to her father and back again.

"My good sir, you know we cannot trespass longer on your kindness," said Mr Bennet. "Our family wishes to give us their hospitality as an expression of their affection and care for us, which will make our stay with them as pleasant as our quarters shall be snug."

"Indeed, we shall make quite a merry party at Gracechurch Street," agreed Jane, "although we certainly have experienced every source of happiness and comfort at Netherfield with you as our host." She smiled at Mr Bingley.

"Then I shall only express my wish that we shall meet again soon in town, nearer the Christmas season." Jane raised her eyes to Mr Bingley's expectant face but remained silent.

Elizabeth, sparing her sister, said, "We shall meet again gladly."

Shortly after she ate, Elizabeth excused herself and went to find some quiet employment. As she wandered into a vacant sitting room, she espied the escritoire and, remembering she was still a letter in Miss Darcy's debt, gathered some sheets of paper. The grandeur of the locale to which her letter was destined did not escape her, but before any feeling of intimidation could forestall her, the memory of her new correspondent's kind words spurred her onward with warmth and assurance.

Dear Miss Darcy,

I am a shameful correspondent to neglect my response to your sweet letter for so many days. Your words have won my gratitude and my frankness, so I shall confide to you all my thoughts upon receiving your note, and by these reflections, attempt to procure your pardon for my delay in replying to you.

When I first opened your letter, my surprise was quickly succeeded by my admiration for the warmth and kindness of your address as well as your eagerness to help a stranger so far removed from your acquaintance and sphere. The goodness of your brother's example has indeed been well represented by your charity and courage, and I find I am glad to know you, if only but a little, through our correspondence.

In order to avoid giving any offence to your brother by

accepting such a missive in secret, I looked for an opportunity to alert Mr Darcy to the arrival of your letter and to ask for his permission to respond. Being unable to deny you any pleasure, he acceded at once to my request and gave his support to our correspondence.

For some days I kept and reread your letter while I recovered from my injuries. My spirits were sorely tested shortly after, during a visit to examine the damage that had been done to our home. I spent most of a day at Longbourn, taking note of what had been lost and realising that nothing will ever be as it was before. Much of our family's history, along with many articles of dear memory, have been lost in the disaster, and I felt these components of my life to have vanished into ashes as well.

Despite my susceptibility at such a time to crestfallen spirits, when I consider your words and my own heartfelt response to them, I must tell you what comfort I found in your letter. For, although I am tempted to feel quite small and diminished by this loss, I recall that I have been distinguished in a remarkable manner by the epistle of a lady quite unknown to me, and I cannot but be flattered into thinking myself not quite so insignificant in the world. Although I am not so perfect a creature as you seem to imagine, I thank you for the reminder, the attention, and the kindness you have given me.

In regard to your extraordinary offer of hospitality, I am exceedingly grateful, and I am happy to perceive in it the implication that you might wish to meet face-to-face. However, regarding my family's future lodgings, I must inform you that my uncle and aunt in London are anxious to open their home to my family and will do so very soon—next week, in fact. At such a time as this, I am sure you understand that the consolation of family is the spirit's greatest balm. I would, however, delight to presume upon your friendship by seeking a chance to call upon you while I am in town. I shall apply to your brother for permission to visit you whenever you deem convenient. I am all antici-

pation to meet you in London, where I hope to take your hand in true friendship, and afterwards, tax you with my healthy appetite for conversation and laughter.

Your friend in Hertfordshire,
  Elizabeth Bennet

Happily occupied by her writing, Elizabeth failed to notice the invasion of the parlour by a creature altogether unexpected. Before she had even breathed upon her pages to dry the ink, a dapple-eared dog had padded quietly into the room and come to sit at her feet. When Elizabeth began to fold her letter, the thump of a tail on the floor alerted her to his presence.

"Why, good day," greeted Elizabeth, smiling and reaching down to pat the friendly animal. Recognising her companion as the one with whom she had passed a playful morning near Mr Bingley's orchards a week ago, she scratched along the furry pathway down the line of his spine and asked, "How did you come here—Caesar, is it?"

Mr Darcy's hound rose to his feet in order to better express his delight at her attention with such wagging and frisking as betrayed his pleasure. Elizabeth laughed at his antics but feared for the fine furniture of the parlour as he pranced about, heedless of Miss Bingley's expensive delicate displays.

"Shall we go outside, sir? If you will wait for me but one moment, I shall gather my boots and spencer and give this letter to a footman to post. Then we may romp in the fields. Will you stay until I fetch you?"

Caesar, hearing in the tone of her voice some offer of exciting merit, barked his immediate assent.

Elizabeth sealed her letter, rose, and turned from the room with Caesar pattering behind her. As she reached the stairs, she hesitated, debating as to whether or not the animal might be permitted so near the families' sleeping quarters.

"Caesar, you must stay here. Stay!" she urged him, putting out her hand. Caesar licked it.

"No, boy. Here—sit. Sit!"

When he complied, Elizabeth nodded. "Good boy. Stay!"

Examining the hound and finding Caesar was somewhat calmer, Elizabeth began to climb the steps to gather her things. As she progressed, her suspicions were stirred when she heard movement behind her echoing on the marble landing below.

"No, boy! Stay!" she commanded, whirling around on the step.

"If you insist, Miss Elizabeth," said a surprised Mr Darcy, putting up his hands in surrender and arresting his progress below her.

"Oh! Forgive me, sir," Elizabeth apologised, her colour rising at once. "I was speaking to Caesar."

"I believe you will find him obeying my orders and lying down, as I have found he has never shown the will to master the command to 'stay'."

"Ah," said Elizabeth, peering beyond and below Mr Darcy to where the dog was lying belly-down upon the cool marble of the foyer and peering up at both of them curiously. She bit back a smile. "I cannot much blame him. I have never mastered that particular command myself. I was going for a walk, and I hoped to take Caesar with me."

Darcy nodded and ascended to the step below Elizabeth's, bringing his gaze nearly level to her own. His eyes searched her face. "If you are well enough for such an excursion, I am certain Caesar would welcome the exercise." He looked back at the hound that returned his master's regard with raised ears and a thump of the tail. "As would I. May I accompany you and perhaps keep your companion from running off into the next county?"

Elizabeth hid her astonishment. "You may, but only if you

will indulge me and explain why you think poor Caesar would ever feel the need to run away from me."

"Quite simply, madam, it is because you are not as challenging to catch as a rabbit, which has always proven a temptation to Caesar above all other things."

"You have never seen me run in open country, sir," she challenged. "I may be every bit as swift as a hare."

Mr Darcy smiled. "I shall expect you to be quick, then, as you gather your things."

"I shall bound away soon enough, but I shall be detained by one more errand." Elizabeth brought her letter between them. She fluttered her missive teasingly in the air before her as though fanning her cheeks. "I must first post my letter to your sister if she is to receive it before Sunday."

The intensity of Mr Darcy's gaze increased. Before she had time to react, he had caught her hand by the wrist with a gentle but firm grasp. While Elizabeth was shocked into stillness, he neatly plucked the note from her fingers.

Darcy grinned in triumph as he released her. "I shall post it now," he said lightly, saluting her with his prize. "Bingley's man is presently in the foyer."

She gave him her curtsey. "You had best be about it, then, before I return," she said pertly, as she turned and sprinted up the stairs.

CHAPTER SEVENTEEN

Elizabeth returned downstairs in her boots and spencer. When she reached the bottom step, she found Mr Darcy in the foyer in his field boots, dropped on bended knee and vigorously scratching Caesar behind both flopping ears. The dog's expression was one of ecstasy as his tongue lolled past his teeth, and his tail churned enthusiastically upon the floor. Hearing her footsteps, Mr Darcy drew to his feet, and Caesar looked up in abrupt confusion, only to have his pleasure return in full tail-wagging measure at the sight of Elizabeth in outdoor clothing.

Mr Darcy opened the front door, and his faithful hound, requiring no further invitation, ran out immediately. Elizabeth smiled and hurried out after him, leaving Mr Darcy to follow.

Caesar ventured to the nearest tree to sniff out a suitable toy, and pawing at a loose stick on the ground, he put it in his mouth and bounded to Elizabeth, whining in anticipation.

Elizabeth bent to snatch the stick, throwing it some distance ahead. Before she and Mr Darcy had progressed many more steps, however, Caesar had already retrieved it and came prancing back to them.

Mr Darcy grinned. "You want a challenge, boy?"

Caesar barked again, circling his master's legs. Elizabeth stifled a smile and matched their pace, absorbed in the spectacle of their playful camaraderie.

Mr Darcy hurled the stick nearly twice the distance Elizabeth had, and they both looked on in amusement as Caesar tore up the ground running after it.

Mr Darcy turned to her. "Should we take to the path? Caesar will follow us."

"I should be glad to. With my family leaving soon for London, I fear this may be my last opportunity to tour this park in mild weather for quite some time. I was able to venture out only briefly at sunrise to enjoy the peace and quiet. It was quite an effective restorative."

Mr Darcy touched the brim of his hat in acknowledgement and lowered it slightly against the pale light. "Will you miss such morning outings when winter comes?"

"I always do. I am not suited to indoor confinement, stale fires, draughts by windows, and cold feet. I have thought sometimes that I should seek a warmer clime—in India perhaps—where I might give some emigrated British girls an unconventional version of an English education."

"Do you imagine you might serve them as a governess or open your own school?"

"Oh, I should start simply, I expect, and work as a governess. One cannot establish a school without gaining a reputation of some kind first."

"You sound as though you have given this some thought," he said in surprise, just as Caesar caught up to them.

Elizabeth reached down and, grabbing hold of one end of Caesar's stick, gave it a tug, which the pup resisted. "I have thought of it more often in recent days especially, I confess. It has not escaped me that I do my family very little good going on as I have been." She paused for breath as she fought against the dog's brute strength. "I promised myself long ago that I shall not marry except for affection. But what good shall I serve as a spinster and an additional mouth to feed, especially in such times as my family will face, when funds shall soon be needed to restore our home?"

She surprised herself by confiding this. Yet she found, on this remarkable morning, that Mr Darcy's laconic nature and unusually relaxed manner invited her speech, almost too unguardedly.

Frustrated and embarrassed by her own candour, she wrenched the stick free and threw it forcefully into the hedge. Caesar barked sharply and dove in after it.

She felt Mr Darcy's eyes upon her as she continued walking, and he fell quietly into step beside her again.

"I feel I should apologise," she said, after they had gone some way in silence. "I have spoken out of turn. I have often envied men their ability to make their own way in the world, and I sometimes find fault with both the world and myself for having not been born to different circumstances."

"None of us can control the first assets granted us by Fate," observed Mr Darcy, "but you have acted as well as you can and have already been of great assistance to your father. There are many young ladies who would not have taken upon themselves as much as you have done."

"I could take on more. I simply lack the courage to do it. Sensibly, I should either face the lot that has been cast for me or sacrifice myself in another manner that might better benefit my family."

Without speaking more plainly, Elizabeth imagined Mr Darcy comprehended her well enough, for had they not dined only last evening with Longbourn's heir presumptive?

Elizabeth bent down and patted the felt-like fur on Caesar's knobby head. "Why cannot mankind be like the creatures of the earth and merely do as Nature would intend for us every day? Do you think Caesar ever wonders about his future, Mr Darcy?"

He shook his head. "Not for a moment."

"I am frightfully jealous of you, Caesar," Elizabeth said softly to the dog, laughing ruefully at herself. Caesar did not take much notice of her words, lost as he was to everything but his pleasure while Elizabeth rubbed his ears vigorously as she had seen his master do.

Mr Darcy stood aside, smiling at their exchange, until Elizabeth again began to walk, and Caesar came to him for more attention. He took control of the stick this time, and after weighing it in his hand, let it sail into the air far ahead of them.

Elizabeth did not watch where it landed. She retreated into her thoughts once more as both dog and projectile flew past her.

"India is not so hospitable as you seem to imagine," said Mr Darcy suddenly. "It is often miserably hot. There is typhus and a plenitude of other strange diseases you will not find on English soil. Moreover, the snakes, tigers, and elephants are a constant hazard. If you are not born to such environs, making oneself habituated to life there can be difficult."

"Have you been to India?"

"My cousin has. He is a colonel in His Majesty's army. I am sure he could speak to you on the subject far more fluently than I and with greater objectivity."

"I am sure he could. But if he is off fighting against Napoleon in some campaign, I doubt I shall meet your cousin very soon."

"He will be on leave once December begins. I am sure he will come to visit Georgiana in town. If you still remain there at that time of year, my sister and I shall be pleased to introduce you."

"I would be glad to make his acquaintance," replied Elizabeth before adding with some wonder, "and I think it very kind of him to visit his young cousin so directly upon his return."

"Colonel Fitzwilliam and I share guardianship of my sister and have done so since my father's death some five years ago. His affection for Georgiana has always been genuine, and at times, his protective feelings towards her have been even more fervent than my own."

"That inclination must come as part of one's duty as a soldier," mused Elizabeth, trying to envision what threats might justify such careful protection of Miss Darcy. "A good colonel will always imagine and prepare for the worst in any situation."

"Would that his fears were only imagined," muttered Mr Darcy.

Elizabeth stopped suddenly, her curiosity ignited by his wayward comment. "Was she ever in danger?"

Mr Darcy stalked past her, shaking his head. "I ought not have said anything at all. It is not my tale to tell," he said in some regret, and to Elizabeth's ear, some distress. "Georgiana may confide in you, if she so chooses, but I cannot decide for her."

She hastened to catch up to him. "I hope she is no longer in jeopardy. Can you not at least tell me that?"

"Yes, Georgiana is quite safe now. I could hardly stray so far from her if that were not the case. But she is not herself. She has been quite dispirited since—since it happened."

Elizabeth observed his stricken expression in mute compassion for a moment. "I see. I am sorry to hear it."

He turned to her, the distressed lines of his face softening in appeal. "I know your society will be of great benefit to Georgiana, Miss Elizabeth. I hope you will still consider calling on her once you are in London."

"Of course! I told her in my letter that I would be glad to do so."

"That is kind of you."

They walked again for some time in near silence, broken only by the imploring whines and triumphant barks of their canine companion.

Sensing that Mr Darcy had returned somewhat to his ease due to her promise and realising that he had shown a generous measure of trust in her by giving her what information he could regarding his sister, Elizabeth gathered her courage to ask for his assistance in solving the disconcerting mystery that only days ago had been thrust upon her.

As she shaded her eyes to watch another one of Mr Darcy's long volleys fly into the distance, she said suddenly, "I wish to seek your advice regarding an acquaintance I made recently among the militia quartered in Meryton."

"Is this acquaintance someone I might know?"

"He did claim to know you. He claimed to know many things about you, in fact, although I doubted much of it was true," Elizabeth said haltingly. "He said that you and he had grown up together in Derbyshire."

Darcy's colour rose, and he turned at once to face her. "George Wickham is here? In Hertfordshire?"

"Then you do know him?"

"Yes, as much as the admission pains me, I do." Mr Darcy glowered at the ground. "And I am sorry if Wickham importuned you in any way, Miss Elizabeth. He is, as you appear to have guessed, not a man to be trusted."

Elizabeth measured his obvious displeasure. "I thought as much. When he spoke to me and gave me to know of his history, I thought his story too glib, too practised by half. He has easy, unguarded manners that would have given me every impression of good breeding, except that I could not escape the impropriety of his sharing so much of his life's struggles with me, a veritable stranger."

Mr Darcy sighed with relief. "Wickham does indeed have the happy manners that enable him to make friends easily.

Whether he is capable of keeping them is less certain." His expression clouded, and he drew his hand across his mouth in troubled thought. But at last, he gazed at her in pained sincerity. "The offences he has committed against my family, and indeed against the world, have been the source of great misery to many."

Such an indictment! "Should the populace of Meryton be concerned?" she asked anxiously.

Caesar returned again at that moment with his stick. Mr Darcy duly captured it, but rather than throwing it, he used it to swipe at the hedge as he passed. "The tradesmen of the town should certainly be warned not to extend Wickham any credit. I have claimed enough of his debts myself to know his habits. And I feel as though I should also warn Colonel Forster to be sure to observe him carefully in society."

"And why is that?" said Elizabeth, catching her breath as she strove to keep up with him, for he had lengthened his stride.

Mr Darcy's eyes drew once more to the ground, and his steps, which had begun to outpace hers, slowed until he came to a full stop on the path. He looked at her earnestly, opened his mouth as though to speak, and then paced away from her again with Caesar in tow. Elizabeth watched him in silent apprehension, growing more and more uneasy about what he might relate, before she hurried after him.

She recognised, amidst the unravelling of Mr Wickham's tale, that she now beheld the evidence of the greatest weight against him. In Mr Darcy's discomposure, she found the mark of a man with a true and awful burden to relate, which contrasted sharply with the buoyant, almost cheerful countenance of one who had voiced so many lies.

After going ahead a short distance on the pathway, Mr Darcy collected himself and turned about. In a more measured pace, he came to stand before her, addressing her with some composure at last.

"I would not speak too completely of Mr Wickham's nature to any woman, being that it is indelicate," he began, seeking her gaze, "but I rely upon your superior understanding to infer my meaning when I ask you to ensure that your sisters are never alone with him—or yourself, for that matter."

Elizabeth blanched. "Sir, what I must deduce from this warning is indeed a damaging accusation."

"I can provide the names of victims and witnesses for you to interview if you so require. Further, I can affirm I observed him myself when we were at Cambridge together, where Wickham's vicious habits and licentious propensities proved themselves as dissolute as any I have ever witnessed."

"Is that why you denied him the living at the rectory?"

Mr Darcy blinked in surprise. "Wickham spoke to you of that?"

"He did indeed. He spun quite a long, sad tale."

"I should not be surprised," said Mr Darcy, shaking his head. "Did he also tell you that he refused the living and asked instead to be compensated for it? That he claimed an intention to study the law? I confess I rather wished than believed him to be sincere—so relieved was I that Wickham was not to join the church. And although I greatly doubted he would apply the funds to his proposed purpose, I acceded to his request to remunerate him accordingly. It was only a little over two years ago that this arrangement was transacted, and I can show you in my steward's books his signature verifying acceptance of this substitution in place of my father's preferment."

Elizabeth tried to reassure him with her earnest expression that she needed no such evidence. His word, weighted as it was already by the recommendation of his character, was enough for her.

Mr Darcy paused, for he was being baited by Caesar's whines to cast the poor dog's prize once more. Caesar raced off again in pursuit of it.

"And so now Wickham is in the militia," Mr Darcy said almost absently as he stared after his reckless hound. "I wish I could say I was astounded to be led by this intelligence to believe that he has now certainly also dispensed with the three thousand pounds that I granted him directly in lieu of the living. I know full well of his penchant for idleness. He would only enlist and face the rigours of military life out of most dire necessity. I fear, given his habits, he must have played his funds away through poor hands in some gaming hell, and perhaps he even now feels the weight of debts stacked against him."

Elizabeth was dumbstruck as she calculated the living expenses she knew her family incurred in one year. "Why, Mr Wickham could have lived contentedly, with some small comforts, had he invested those funds with any care."

"In addition to his love of gaming tables, Wickham has ever been a spendthrift and eager to live lavishly. I am afraid my father indulged him as a boy, unwittingly feeding that appetite in the child to the degree that the man now considers such extravagance his due."

"And that is why he hates you? Because it is *your* due?" she asked unthinkingly.

Abruptly, Mr Darcy's open countenance transformed into a more guarded expression. "My estate and fortune are hardly mine alone. All of it was entrusted to me by those who gained their fortunes long before my birth, who intended for me to leave it as an inheritance for generations still to come. It would be the height of selfishness to fritter it away in my few decades of life for mere pleasure's sake."

Elizabeth reddened. "I did not mean to imply—"

"I know you did not," Mr Darcy interrupted her. He pulled off his hat, and in some agitation, ran his fingers through his dark hair. "This is a subject I have considered a great deal. The aristocracy is active in its own destruction, living with little consideration for the sacrifices of its predecessors or the hardships that future generations may face. I shall not allow such wastefulness. No, not at Pemberley—not while my children, or my sister's children, and their children after, all depend upon my diligence, not to mention those hundreds of people who daily tend and rely upon the land and properties I hold for their survival."

Elizabeth felt ashamed of herself for her previous bias against Mr Darcy, even as she was overtaken by wonder at her companion and the burdens of his fate. True, she had known he had a great house, fortune, and properties—all this she had heard said and had repeated herself, and at times she had even mocked them as sources of his pride.

Hearing of his holdings and fortune from his own lips, she felt the weight of it all profoundly. Elizabeth could almost see the burden of it upon his countenance as she stared at his face in the dappled sunlight, where the shadows had marked the lines of his furrowed brow. As a brother, a landlord, a master, how many peoples' happiness were in his guardianship? How much of pleasure or pain it was in his power to bestow? How much good or evil must be done by him? How deeply he seemed to feel it—and how favourably this sensibility vouched for his character!

"I never understood you properly before," Elizabeth admitted aloud, causing his eyes to meet hers. "I never understood you properly when you said, 'Pride, where there is a true superiority of mind, will always be under good regulation.' There is much, I think, that you could be proud of, Mr Darcy —in the things you own, and in what you accomplish. But how tenuous that balance would prove, should you ever become too assured of the permanence of either!"

"Yes, exactly. Those were my thoughts precisely when I uttered those words to you."

"Then I am glad I have taken the opportunity to re-examine them," she answered quietly.

They resumed their walk in a silence that edged beyond the merely companionable. As they ambled, their path turned its pleasant course back towards the great house. Soon they broke again beyond the wilder trees and into the orchard lining the drive, and Caesar began barking in a tone that signalled some discovery.

"There must be a carriage coming," Elizabeth said, perceiving it at a distance that hindered the sound of its rumbling progression, "although I have no inkling as to who might come to call so early. Do you?"

Mr Darcy surveyed the carriage as it grew closer. "No, and neither do I recognise the conveyance."

Elizabeth shaded her eyes against the sunlight that defied her bonnet's brim, observing the carriage until she could distinguish the trunk and bandboxes secured to its roof.

"I do know it!" she exclaimed.

Without a thought, Elizabeth gathered up her skirts and hastened towards the conveyance in a most indecorous fashion. When her feet met the even ground upon the lawn, she ran.

CHAPTER EIGHTEEN

The carriage drew to a halt, at which time Elizabeth, now out of breath, came to a full stop before it. Two familiar, fashionably dressed persons emerged, and Elizabeth at once fell into the embrace of the lady. Tears welled in the woman's eyes as she released Elizabeth in order to study her better.

"Oh Lizzy! I am so relieved to see you!" Mrs Gardiner exclaimed, and without pause, again enfolded Elizabeth into her arms with little notice or care for the stranger bearing witness.

"My dear girl, I am so glad to see you well," seconded Mr Gardiner, handing a handkerchief to his wife.

Elizabeth came forward to press a kiss to her uncle's cheek. "I am surprised you came so soon. And Aunt, how unexpected, yet delightful, that you should accompany him!"

"Neither of us could rest easy at home, but now that I have seen you, I am satisfied that my prayers have been answered. You look truly well, my dear, and seem in good spirits."

Mrs Gardiner paused, and the couple glanced beyond Elizabeth to her tall companion as he approached their reunion.

"Pray, forgive us, sir," said Mr Gardiner, bowing to the newcomer and addressing him. "We have come unannounced, with no excuse for our call but our concern. I find I must apologise for our intrusion with the same fervour with which I must thank you for your hospitality to our relations."

Elizabeth stepped forward between the men. "I am remiss as well, Uncle," she declared, "for not properly introducing you to this gentleman. He is not, as you have supposed, Mr Bingley." She turned to the younger gentleman. "Mr Darcy, may I introduce to you my aunt and uncle, Mr and Mrs Edward Gardiner?"

Elizabeth's relations demonstrated their good breeding, making their proper respects despite their obvious discomfiture.

"Mr and Mrs Gardiner," Mr Darcy responded, smiling slightly as he bowed in answer.

"I also must apologise to you for not preventing my husband from mistaking you just now, Mr Darcy," said Mrs Gardiner. "Hailing from Lambton, I bore the advantage of recognising the likeness of your late father in your appearance. He was regarded as a very good man and, as events have lately shown, you are in many ways like him. It is indeed a pleasure to make your acquaintance."

"You honour me, Mrs Gardiner. Such confusion as your husband suffered is easily understood. Were I your host, my approach just now would have been to properly welcome you to Netherfield. But I have no excuse but my own curiosity to justify following Miss Elizabeth to meet you here."

Mr Gardiner chuckled. "Let us not weary ourselves by debating who is the intruder. For here we are, unannounced and unexpected in Mr Bingley's park—having arrived too early for calls!"

"I shall be glad to remedy your predicament by making your visit known to my friend," Mr Darcy volunteered. "And I may safely guarantee, sir, that Mr Bingley's amiable disposition will allow him to feel nothing but delight at the news of your arrival." His assurances earned him smiles from Elizabeth and both of her relatives. "I shall be gone but a moment to fetch him, with your leave."

"We are much obliged to you, sir," replied Mr Gardiner.

Elizabeth turned to watch Mr Darcy make short work of the front steps of the great house with his long stride. As she observed his graceful and efficient passage, her heart felt unaccountably soft and full, and she smiled in unconscious amusement when she spotted Caesar dutifully rushing along to join his master as he entered the house.

"Elizabeth, is this the 'proud, disagreeable' Mr Darcy of whom you wrote to me a month ago?" said her aunt, recalling her attention. "Why, he is all ease and friendliness. He has no false dignity at all!"

"I would not have expected such attention from so great a man," agreed her uncle. "Upon my word, he seems remarkably good-humoured and kind."

"I gave myself the disadvantage of judging Mr Darcy from an unfair first impression that prolonged company with that gentleman has since forced me to discredit," said Elizabeth, shaking her head. "And what is more, I owe him due consideration out of gratitude, for I can hardly continue to dislike the man who saved my life! For that alone, I could sing his praises all day long if you wish."

"I think you could," said her aunt, peering closely at her niece. "You did not tell me that Mr Darcy is uncommonly handsome," she continued in a tone of playful chiding. "As to his having some appearance of pride, I cannot find that it damages his aspect in the slightest."

"Now *you* are singing his praises, my dear," Mr Gardiner teased his wife.

Mrs Gardiner feigned innocence. "I am merely noting what

I find. And I am not wrong, am I, Lizzy? You cannot tell me you do not think him handsome."

"Aunt, I—"

At that moment, Netherfield's great doors flew open, and Mr Bingley's eager step was heard upon the portico, followed only by the pattering of footfalls from the larger party of Mr and Mrs Bennet, Mr Darcy, Jane, and Mary.

"Mr Bingley!" called Elizabeth, relieved by the distraction, "may I introduce my aunt and uncle?"

The acquaintance was made with pleasure, and once all this was expressed, Mr Bingley invited the Gardiners to come directly into the house. Tea and coffee were brought to the parlour for refreshment, and as the rest of the Bennets converged, conversation with their relatives flowed easily under Mr Bingley's affable hospitality.

The men all took up a post near the mantlepiece, acquainting Mr Gardiner with the latest news regarding the condition of Longbourn, while the ladies embraced, exclaimed, and poured cups of tea.

"It does my heart good to see you all so well," Mrs Gardiner said, "but where are my youngest nieces?"

As though she had summoned them, Lydia fluttered into the room and announced, "Kitty is coming down, but she will need a seat, for she will be out of breath! Make room, would you, Lizzy?"

"Oh Kitty, come, let me look at you!" Mrs Gardiner demanded the moment Kitty emerged from the hall, still wrapped up in shawls. Her aunt cupped her face and studied her closely, tutting aloud. "Oh, you poor child! You still look pale."

"She certainly does!" concurred Mrs Bennet. "I cannot countenance Kitty mixing much in company just now. Why, if she were to catch a cold, who knows what might happen? Her poor chest cannot handle so much as another rattle. I know not what to do but to keep her close to me. Had I a set of leading strings, I would tie her up again."

"Aunt Gardiner, you must talk some sense to my mother," Kitty complained. "She will not even allow me to receive callers when they come to Netherfield!"

"Now, now, Kitty, you have had a terrible week of it and are only just recovered," her uncle observed kindly.

The next moment, everyone glanced up when Miss Bingley and the Hursts finally appeared in the parlour. All discussion paused for the requisite performance of more introductions.

"Charmed," said Miss Bingley with the barest civility, bobbing to the Gardiners, once Mr Bennet had performed his office.

"My sister informs me that her family has received every comfort and kindness from you as their hostess here, ma'am," said Mr Gardiner as he rose up from his bow. "We are so grateful for your hospitality until we could open our home to them. You are very kind."

"It was no trouble, I assure you. We have very capable servants here at Netherfield, which, I am pleased to say, allows us to keep many guests in comfort," Miss Bingley replied stiffly.

"Indeed, you seem very well-settled here already, although I heard you have only been here but a month," complimented Mrs Gardiner.

There was an unexpected lull after that statement. "Yes, that is true," tittered Mrs Hurst into the silence, peering nervously at her sister, who seemed to have suddenly found her bracelets more interesting than her guests. "We came up from our home in London near Michaelmas."

"The neighbourhood has certainly been blessed by your arrival," Mrs Gardiner responded warmly.

It was then Miss Bingley's desire to ask the Gardiners of their home, and she exerted herself to enquire with a look that anticipated her satisfaction in forcing them to confess to its want of size and good neighbourhood.

"Our house is certainly not so large as Netherfield or even as Longbourn," replied Mrs Gardiner evenly. "But it is on a very pleasant street and close to Mr Gardiner's place of business, so we are content. We have four children—two girls and two boys—and I have sent them to stay with my sister for a week until the Bennets are all settled with us. We hope to remove the Bennets to London on Tuesday if that is convenient, Miss Bingley."

"Oh yes, that is hardly a trouble to me. I hope you will all be content to take refuge together in your little house in *Cheapside*," said Miss Bingley. The coldness of Miss Bingley's response was not lost on her brother, who let his spoon fall to his saucer with a clatter before he sallied into the conversation with a quick change of topic.

"Miss Bennet was just telling me this morning how much she looks forward to spending time with you, and what a merry party you always make at Gracechurch Street. Do you not sometimes host the Bennets at Christmas, and they you, at Longbourn?"

"While our tradition has been to stay for Christmas at Longbourn, we have at other times hosted the ladies for visits in the spring and fall. That is why we were able to prepare for their coming with such relative ease, for it has all been arranged in years before," replied Mrs Gardiner with some relief at his good grace.

Her husband nodded, adding, "I daresay we shall have a very joyful time. Our children will be delighted to have their cousins already there to play with them, especially Jane and Lizzy, who quite dote upon them." Here, Mr Gardiner gave his favourites a smile and added with praise, "Such good girls they are, very loving and obliging."

"We shall be happy to see them again as well," declared Elizabeth. "Little Thomas loves to go down to the Thames to see the trade ships and ferries. I daresay Samuel is almost big enough to come with us if I carry him part of the way. I shall show the boys how to make and race their own paper boats if the weather is mild."

Jane nodded, adding, "And I look forward to instructing the girls. Amanda is learning to read, and Rebecca, the elder sister, is learning to draw and sew. I think we shall enjoy many pleasant hours practising it all, in addition to the dancing and frivolity certain to be found during the holidays."

Although such cheerful prospects made Elizabeth and Jane smile, their younger sister Mary approached their aunt with a look of such distress that Mrs Gardiner frowned in concern.

"Oh, Mary dear, whatever is the matter?"

"I—I am so sorry to tell you this, but the songbook I had bought to practise with Rebecca burnt in the fire and so did our pianoforte. In my last letter, I promised her that we could work on a duet from it, and now I must disappoint her and break my word."

"I am sure you will both be disappointed, but Rebecca is old enough to understand. But what a shame about your instrument! You will have as much access to ours as you wish when you come."

"Thank you, Aunt," Mary replied, embracing her.

"Of course!" replied Mrs Gardiner just before the clock chimed.

"The time!" said Mr Gardiner. "I am afraid my sister will be distressed if she does not receive us soon in Meryton. I had not told her we would call on you this morning. In any event, we hope to see you again later today. I cannot be trusted to convey any details, but you may expect a note from Mr and Mrs Philips."

Mrs Gardiner then turned to their hosts and expressed

again all their pleasure and gratitude, curtseying most deeply to Mr Bingley.

They made their farewells at the door, with Mr Darcy and Mr Bingley bowing their good-byes and the Bennets more warmly embracing their relations as they took their leave.

When the door was shut, those who remained within returned to their employments. Mr Bennet disappeared into the study. Mary and Kitty removed above stairs to read. Lydia went to her mother's room to remake a singed bonnet, while Jane and Elizabeth took out their workbaskets to repair the remains of some outer clothing recovered from Longbourn.

As Elizabeth rifled through the collection of thread, she allowed her mind to wander away from the unpleasant prospect of sewing towards some very pleasant reflections on her morning's ramble.

DARCY AND BINGLEY REPAIRED TO THE LIBRARY TO discuss business, but even as they entered that room, Miss Bingley invaded their territory in a flurry of lace and bright cloth to solicit Mr Darcy for his assistance.

"I cannot find anything of worth to read, sir," she complained, "and my mind is laden with more nonsense than I can stand after spending my morning with such tedious company!"

Darcy rose silently, went to the shelf and, plucking up a collection of Samuel Johnson's essays, pressed the volume into Miss Bingley's hand. He then sat down and turned back to Bingley, not trusting himself to speak to her.

"Why, Mr Darcy, is there any reason why you would wish for me to read from Dr Johnson in particular?" Miss Bingley entreated.

"I would direct you, madam, to his work, 'Conversation'. It seemed as though you were rather out of practice this morning when the Gardiners visited," replied Darcy artlessly. "Indeed, some may feel that much of what you said was badly done."

"Badly done!" cried she in perplexed astonishment.

Bingley turned to address his sister. "Darcy is perfectly right, Caroline. I do not know what possessed you to show such ill-grace to the Gardiners, but I would not have it so again."

"Oh Charles, do you really care what that tradesman and his wife may think of you? I certainly do not!"

Bingley's cheeks reddened. "I would. I do!" he declared. "They are Miss Bennet's favourite relations, and I saw for myself that they are kind and sensible people. I would not for the world make them uncomfortable in my home, and I was quite ashamed of you today for making them feel so unwelcome. Indeed, they are doing you a kindness in removing the Bennets from this house, since their presence here gives you so little pleasure. For that, at least, I had hoped you might spare them your incivility."

"I was as civil to them as the slight acquaintance required, for I am not in a rage to connect myself with that family, and it alarms me that it appears you are! Jane Bennet can bring nothing to you in marriage—nothing at all—except her pretty face and the misery of her relations. The Bennets will hang upon you for every penny of their existence once they realise that their little estate will no longer be of any good to them."

"That is patently unkind and untrue!" declared Bingley hotly before in some real anxiety, he turned to his friend and enquired, "Darcy, you would not say the house is beyond repair, would you?"

"No, the Bennets will merely have to economise in order to afford the necessary repairs, and so they shall."

"You see, Caroline?" exclaimed her brother triumphantly.

"I speak the truth. Mark my words. Even if they are not now, the Bennets will soon become the worst of fortune hunters. I feel very little sympathy towards them, except for dear

Jane, of course, who is faultless in this matter. Nevertheless, I pray you will not let misguided compassion turn into misguided passion. Jane is not for you. The Bennets are not for you. You would do well to learn to see their kind for what they are!"

Bingley leapt to his feet, and Darcy, who had withstood quite enough, decided to intervene at once before the siblings' squabble deteriorated further.

Turning to Miss Bingley, Darcy spoke with cold solemnity. "Were there not a gulf between your situation and theirs and your comfort and their homelessness at present, I would not have quarrelled with you about any liberties of manner you may have taken today, but as it stands, your incivility has revealed an irrational and uncharitable contempt. Have you no proper feeling?"

Miss Bingley, stunned into silence by his rebuke, dropped her book to the floor with a thump and quit the room.

Mr Darcy, seeing her truly affected for once, turned in surprised contrition to his friend. "I ought not have spoken to your sister so, Bingley. My temper bested my judgment, and I overstepped by correcting her. I apologise."

His friend shook his head. "You were not the least in the wrong to advise her. I only wish that Caroline would listen to me as she does to you."

"My words today have proved that she has absolutely nothing in her power to attract my admiration after such an ill-judged display. As a brother, your words could not have wounded her hopes so much as mine have done just now. Would that my admonishment gave her some impetus to examine herself and see her prejudice in a proper light!"

"I thank you for speaking as you did. An argument with Caroline always gets my blood up, and anything I would wish to say is lost with my composure." Bingley went to the side-board and poured them both a measure of brandy. Bringing a glass to his friend, he raised his own. "To the betterment of all our characters—and the calming of our nerves," he declared.

Darcy raised his glass. "Hear, hear."

AFTER SUCH AN EVENTFUL MORNING, ELIZABETH AND Jane repaired to a sunny spot in the parlour to chat about the arrival of the Gardiners and to anticipate their own efforts in restoring Longbourn to its former comforts over the coming weeks.

"Do you think you can reupholster the entire chair yourself, Lizzy?" Jane asked, pulling the book on pattern making into her lap and studying the page her sister had opened.

Elizabeth shrugged. "With some careful measuring for the pattern pieces, how can it be different than tailoring a well-fitted jacket? I know Papa's old chair was covered in leather, but I have neither the skill nor the tools to recover it with the same. I should ask our aunt about where to find a suitable sort of brocade or some other sturdy material that will bear needlework. I would hate to make a jumble of it by choosing the wrong fabric."

There was a gentle rap on the door frame, and the sisters looked up in surprise. "Mr Bingley," they said together, in a chorus that made the gentleman chuckle, even as he returned the greeting.

"I am sorry to interrupt you, ladies," he began uneasily, "but I could not face the rest of the day without coming to offer my apologies to both of you for my sister's behaviour this morning. I have spoken with Caroline, and I truly believe she feels regret for her discourtesy to your aunt and uncle. As your host, I feel responsible for their treatment in my home. It should never have happened."

"You are kindness itself, Mr Bingley," said Jane. "My aunt

and uncle know your character well, sir, and do not reproach you."

Her sweetness seemed to leave him breathless for a moment, but then he asked, "And do they think so charitably of me because they have received some good report, Miss Bennet?"

"Well, I certainly have said very little to them about you, Mr Bingley—so you may surmise rightly regarding their source of information," said Elizabeth cheerfully. Deciding she would soon be in the way, she collected her book and a few loose patterns as she prepared to remove to the other end of the room. "But perhaps you may ask my sister for yourself."

As Elizabeth settled by the tea table on the edge of the room, she made a great show of spreading her book and papers before her in a studious attitude.

"Miss Bennet, I meant what I said," Mr Bingley began. "I fervently hope my sister's behaviour has not damaged your congenial feelings towards me."

"Oh no, sir! Absolutely not!" Jane said with feeling. "You need never feel any concern about that."

Bingley shifted from foot to foot before moving to approach closer. "That is a comfort to me," he confided in such a low tone that Elizabeth struggled to hear. "And if your feelings for me have not suffered any injury today, I am grateful, for I am relying upon them to support my cause just now. For there is—there is something very particular I wish to ask you."

Elizabeth heard Jane draw in a quavering breath, and she decided to risk a glance at the couple. When she looked up, Jane had turned towards her admirer, her eyes full of disbelieving hope. Whatever Jane could see in Mr Bingley's gaze must have helped her gather her courage.

"You may ask me anything, sir. I feel compelled to assure you that my feelings and my thoughts do favour you and any cause you might wish to further, for I think you the best of men, Mr Bingley—the very best of men."

Elizabeth did not dare even to breathe, frozen in astonishment by the knowledge of what such a confession from her reticent sister must have cost her. When Mr Bingley spoke again, his voice was steeped in hushed reverence.

"I am flattered you hold me in such regard, in spite of my failings, and my feelings towards you are very similar. I think you an angel among women, the best and fairest and kindest of your sex. You must know how much I admire you, how much I adore you, Miss Bennet!"

Elizabeth covered her mouth to smother her delight. Such a declaration must only be honoured by privacy, she thought, and so she rose swiftly and crept past the couple towards the door.

As Elizabeth quietly pulled the door nearly closed, she glimpsed through the gap to see her sister's suitor dropping down to one knee. She left them in the knowledge that their interview could only conclude in happiness.

CHAPTER NINETEEN

*A*fter Mr Bingley presented himself to Mr Bennet in the study, the afternoon that followed was full of celebratory cheer. If Miss Bingley's absence was noted, it was not mentioned, for there was nothing that seemed worthy to dampen the happiness within the house. Mrs Bennet was elated, and she praised her soon-to-be son-in-law to the skies before engaging her mind to the task of finding Jane's wedding clothes in London.

"I declare it will be a pleasure to dress Jane so beautifully, for she will be the loveliest bride ever to be seen!"

"I shall not disagree with you on that point, madam," said Mr Bingley.

"Will she be able to marry from Longbourn, do you think, Papa?" Elizabeth asked.

"It will be difficult," he said, considering it. "The house itself may not be ready to be occupied until just after the New Year, and even then, it may not be wise to have us all there at once whilst repairs are still taking place. It might be best done with some assistance from Mrs Philips, if she is willing."

"Why yes!" Mrs Bennet cried. "My sister would be delighted to host the wedding breakfast, since the dining room at Longbourn may not be fit to bear company. Oh, that it could be at Longbourn, though! But at least Jane shall have the comfort of all her family there."

"I shall be perfectly content with any arrangements," Jane declared, taking Mr Bingley's hand under the table in response to his infectious smile. "But I do not wish to inconvenience anyone in our family on a day that should be so full of pleasure."

"It will be no inconvenience at all, I am sure," Mrs Bennet continued. "My sister will leap at the opportunity to be of assistance on such a happy occasion. After all, she has a real affection for all my dear girls and for you, sweet Jane, especially."

Mrs Bennet's reassurances were as good as gospel, for when the Bennets and Mr Bingley arrived that afternoon, Mrs Philips received them and their news with great surprise, but as Mrs Bennet had portended, her pleasure instantly equalled that of her sister's upon hearing her good information. She rang for tea immediately and pressed the maid to bring it out on their finest china.

"Such a fine match, my dear niece! I am positively brimming with delight!"

Jane blushed when her mother stepped forward. "And so am I, dear sister! But you must know, it is not certain that Longbourn will be ready for any such event this winter. I thought of your lovely apartments here, and—"

"Say no more," her sister interrupted. "Leave the wedding breakfast to me, Fanny! I shall see it done right!"

As Mrs Philips launched into the wedding day plans with her sister and the younger Bennet girls actively interjecting their own opinions, the Gardiners quietly came to Jane and Mr

Bingley to express their delight. Elizabeth approached the group.

"I hope you will come along when we shop for Jane's trousseau in London, Lizzy. We shall need your voice in support of Jane's choices, for I fear your mother is already making plans about what Jane will need, and it entails a great deal of lace!"

"I shall be delighted to be of any assistance," she replied with a laugh.

"Wonderful! And Jane," Mrs Gardiner added, attracting her eldest niece's attention again. "I have already told your mother that I shall brook no argument regarding who will pay for the wedding clothes. You are our first niece to marry, and it is our delight to indulge you. After all, your aunt Philips insists upon giving your wedding breakfast, so it is the least we can do."

"Oh, Aunt, you are truly kind!" exclaimed Jane. "I do not know what to do, except to thank you, which seems hardly adequate."

"Your joy is sufficient for us," Mr Gardiner replied merrily before Jane rose on tiptoe to kiss his cheek and her aunt's as well.

With so much to discuss, their party was invited to stay on to dine. Mrs Philips, knowing Mr Bingley had other guests who would miss him that evening, declared her intention to immediately pen a note to Netherfield inviting Miss Bingley and the Hursts to join them for an impromptu dinner party.

"Kindly remember Mr Darcy as well," Elizabeth advised her aunt, after Mr Bingley responded to the plan with distracted affability. "He is Mr Bingley's dearest friend."

With a nod, Mrs Philips dutifully included him in her note and immediately commissioned a boy to take it to Netherfield and await a reply.

Mrs Gardiner observed this succession of proceedings with a raised brow. She approached Elizabeth with curiosity. "With so much news to account for, we have not had much opportunity to confide in each other. I wonder if you would indulge me by walking out with me when the tea things are cleared. It will be good for me to take some air after having spent so much of the early morning hours in a carriage."

Elizabeth agreed and the two ladies made their way outside and onto the street in Meryton some minutes later. At first, their conversation settled upon all that had happened on the evening of the fire, lingering on those points that Elizabeth had already shared with Charlotte, and acknowledging the ways Mr Darcy had aided her father and herself on the day they visited Longbourn. Much like Elizabeth's friend, Mrs Gardiner expressed some pointed opinions on the gallant behaviour of Mr Darcy.

"He has taken on a great deal for your sake," observed Mrs Gardiner.

"For all our sakes," Elizabeth corrected.

"As I see it, Mr Darcy's attentiveness on the night of the fire and on the evenings following show a marked interest. And a man with so large an estate of his own to manage need not trouble himself to assist your father with Longbourn—not unless he has reasons to desire to expedite relief for your family. His condescension seems to show an invested concern for your future."

"Could it not be possible that his sensibilities of kindness and charity on my family's behalf have been touched acutely by the destruction he witnessed first-hand at our home?"

"Perhaps," said Mrs Gardiner with a smile. "And you have already shown that you are willing to place a great deal of faith in his capacity for such benevolence. I wonder why you do so now, when you once described him as a cold, proud creature? What new proof have you of his good character beyond his bravery on the night of the fire and his apparent interest in restoring Longbourn?"

"I know he has been more than generous and fair to a man who did not deserve it. A man who, when I first met him, tried to discredit Mr Darcy with many lies, even though Mr Darcy had shown him nothing but kindness—and certainly more kindness than that man deserved."

Elizabeth then began to tell her aunt in detail what Mr Darcy had disclosed to her of Mr Wickham only that morning and what Mr Wickham had so wickedly tried to lead Elizabeth to believe not long before.

Mrs Gardiner had but a moment to marvel at these revelations before her niece continued. "And although we have never met face-to-face, I know also that Mr Darcy's sister, though very young, has quite an expansive sense of charity as well, for she unexpectedly wrote to me after the fire and offered not only her sympathies but her hospitality to my family as well. So you see, Aunt, the Darcys are people of splendid kindness—that is all. Mr Darcy is not expressly devoted to me."

"Let me understand you, Lizzy," said her aunt carefully. "Mr Darcy goes into a fire and rescues you—"

"—and my sister."

"Assists you with your injuries—"

"—after he had already carried Kitty up the stairs."

"And then carries you up the stairs some nights later," continued Mrs Gardiner. "He allows his younger sister to correspond with you. Then, he spends a morning with you—"

"—and my father!"

"—at Longbourn, before driving you quite unchaperoned to Lucas Lodge. And this morning, before your uncle and I arrived, he had joined you on your morning walk, again unchaperoned, with an evident desire for your company. And he had shared much of his past history with you on that walk, evidently taking so much delight in your company that he followed you right into our party without a thought. Does not this behaviour seem singularly attentive to you?"

Elizabeth was silent, wishing and fearing to believe it. A remembrance of doubt roused her, and she offered it slowly.

"I know Mr Darcy feels no particular attraction to me. Do you not remember what I told you he said at the assembly?"

"Yes, I do remember what you wrote in your letter," her aunt conceded. "And did you ever challenge him about that remark?"

"You know my impertinent nature would not allow for it to remain long unanswered."

"And?"

"Mr Darcy apologised. He said he could not justify saying it, aside from his desire to rebuff Mr Bingley's requests that he dance with women beyond his acquaintance."

Mrs Gardiner's look was thoughtful. They walked on for a few moments before she spoke again.

"I must be satisfied, then, on only one point: that you are thinking more carefully on this matter. But let us not debate Mr Darcy's feelings further, especially since he has not declared himself. Nothing of his affections can be certain or may ever be, so it is useless now to speculate."

Elizabeth was forced to own that this was true. She nodded and her aunt continued in a manner softened by concern.

"What I dearly wish to learn will prove far more reliable, since I may apply to you directly for an answer. What are your feelings towards Mr Darcy, Lizzy?"

"I—I confess I hardly know," she answered. "I judged him so unfairly at first, but now I own that I admire and esteem him as a man of great character and intelligence. I should like, at least, to call him a friend."

Her aunt drew Elizabeth's arm within her own, giving it a pat. "You are too sensible a girl to fall in love merely because you are warned against it, so I am not afraid to speak openly. Lizzy, I would have you be on your guard. Do not give yourself over too quickly to an affection that has as yet no foundation. Mr Darcy has made no declaration. I have nothing to say against him. He seems a most honourable young man, and if he can love you without a significant dowry—or even a respectable standing, should the worst happen with Longbourn—I should think you could not do better, and he could find no better angel.

"But as it is, you must not let your fancy take hold of you. You have sense, and we all expect you to use it so that you do not find yourself the victim of disappointed hopes, given unintentionally, by so great a man. Mr Darcy's position carries with it the shared burdens of heavy responsibility and the undeniably influential force of his peers' high expectations. My dear niece, I urge you to be careful and to prepare yourself that he may yet bow to these pressures."

Elizabeth responded with a breathless laugh, and her words came out a bit sharply. "You are being serious indeed!"

Mrs Gardiner drew them a little aside and gave her niece a look that conveyed her understanding of Elizabeth's agitation. She gently squeezed her hands. "Yes, and I hope to engage you to be serious likewise, for your sake. I would not see you wounded by your own strong-willed affections, Lizzy, for you are dear to me."

Elizabeth's hands trembled slightly as she returned her aunt's gesture. Then, gathering her resolve, she lifted her chin, took her aunt's arm again, and guided her back onto their route.

"You need not be alarmed. I shall take care of myself and of my friend Mr Darcy too. I shall not use the allurements in my power to pursue his affections or even to hope for them, if he does not first give me a determined reason to do so. And I shall endeavour not to weep the loss if he does not attempt to woo me.

"At present, I am not in love with Mr Darcy—no, I certainly am not. But he is, beyond all comparison, the most honourable, clever, and handsome man I have ever met. And should he wish to court me, I know I must prepare for disapproval in equal measure to my pleasure. For did I not today witness a small portion of the sort of coldness I might expect from the *ton* upon our union, if indeed we should ever wed?" Here, Elizabeth shook her head and smiled bitterly at the all-too-recent memory of Miss Bingley's twisted expression of disdain directed at her relations.

"I should not like to bring misery upon myself by falling hopelessly in love with such a man, only to suffer disappointment should his courage fail him or should duty weaken his devotion. I have settled sensibly on caution, and at present, Mr Darcy and I are only friends. All that I can promise you, therefore, is not to be in a hurry to believe myself his first object. When I am in company with him, I shall not be wishing for signs of his affection."

"Perhaps it would be best if you do not seek for him to come more often than is needed or than he himself would attempt, should he truly wish to pursue you," her aunt suggested.

Elizabeth lowered her gaze with a conscious smile. "I see the good sense in all you say, but I fear it shall be on Mr Bingley's account that Mr Darcy will so frequently be thrown into our company, regardless of whether he harbours any tender feelings for me. But despite this, I shall try to do what I think wisest. I can promise you that I shall be careful with my own heart."

Her aunt expressed her satisfaction on hearing such an oath, and Elizabeth, a little discomposed by her frankness, nevertheless thanked Mrs Gardiner for her kindness and advice. The object of their walk thus completed, they turned back to the house.

ELIZABETH'S PROMISE WAS TO BE TESTED BARELY TWO hours later, after she had done her best to tidy her appearance for dinner and had descended from her aunt Philips's guest room to await the arrival of the rest of Mr Bingley's party. When the clatter of carriage wheels could be heard in the street outside, Elizabeth made herself remain with the rest of her party while her aunt and uncle Philips left to go and greet the newcomers at the door.

It was in this moment, as her fingers clenched the armrests of her chair, that Elizabeth saw most clearly what she had sought to deny to her aunt—that she did indeed possess all the dangerous signs of tender feelings for Mr Darcy. She was now exquisitely sensitive to every sound in the entryway that could be attributed to his progress. She eagerly awaited his appearance in the parlour and anticipated his words of greeting. She expected pleasure in beholding his handsome face, whose expressions were every day growing more comprehensible and dear to her.

His firm, familiar tread upon the hardwoods recalled her from her thoughts, and Elizabeth rose to greet him with a smile bedimmed by caution as she bobbed a hasty curtsey.

Once Mr Darcy had given her an answering bow, he addressed her directly. "I hope you are well," he said in a voice so gentled it did not carry much farther beyond her. "The day has been exciting for you and your family. I hope it has not been too taxing so soon after your recovery."

"I am well, I assure you. I was merely distracted by my aunt's advice, which I am trying to embrace," she confessed mysteriously, casting her aunt a sly glance. "I shall be racing Caesar over the grounds again tomorrow. You may depend upon it."

"Was that what you were up to this morning, Lizzy?" asked Mrs Gardiner. "When you came running up to the carriage, I could scarcely believe my eyes. Were you racing Mr Darcy's dog?"

"Oh no, not precisely," her niece answered with a guilty

expression. "Caesar has been taught to heel, and Mr Darcy had ordered him to remain, but I am not so biddable. I ran because I wished to and I could."

"It would hardly be a fair race, Miss Elizabeth," observed Mr Darcy. "Poor Caesar would be devastated to know that you could best him due to a lack of proper discipline, a virtue I impress upon him at every turn."

All promises to her aunt forgotten at his teasing sally, Elizabeth answered playfully, "'A lack of proper discipline,' you say! Dear me! Do you mean to impugn my parents with such an indictment, or do you mean to impugn yourself for failing to detain me?"

"Neither," said he, with equal quickness. "I would instead marvel at how rapidly you move to assert blame upon others when it is your own particular wilfulness at fault."

Elizabeth clapped her hands. "Well said, Mr Darcy! I own it to be so. You might add to my list of faults, then, a certain high-spirited self-indulgence, to which I often fall victim."

"That is a failing indeed, but you will be forgiven for it."

"That is charitable of you, sir. Yet, with such a failing to stain my character, may I ask why I should be absolved of it?"

Mr Darcy's answer and his smile came without hesitation. "I can supply two reasons. First, because it does no particular injury to anyone except perhaps to yourself, and second, because I can laugh at it, whereas you have owned you cannot laugh at any of *my* faults. I feel there must be some measure of justice applied to the balance between us, and therefore I am obliged to offer you pardon."

Mrs Gardiner interrupted. "Our dear Elizabeth is indeed high-spirited, and we have often lamented it for her sake at the same time as we have enjoyed observing its amusing fruits. It has been a mark of her character since childhood, beyond even the customary energy and enthusiasm of youth. I believe Elizabeth has mentioned to me that you have a younger sister, Mr Darcy.

Are such high spirits familiar to you as an aspect of your sister's nature?"

"Georgiana has always had her playful moments. She is twelve years my junior, so I have had many years to enjoy her childhood diversions when I was not away at school. But she is now a young lady nearly grown. Georgiana will be sixteen this spring and has much settled in her spirits."

"I am sure she has grown very elegant," Elizabeth commented, turning the conversation to a less lively topic, which would have the added benefit of learning more about Miss Darcy. "I hope that I might come to emulate your sister. She has such a gentle spirit, which I hope will temper my wildness, rather than working the reverse. You may wish for a better correspondent and friend for your sister, sir, but time and any future meetings in London will tell."

"On the contrary," said he with a wry smile, "my sister has a singularly dour, elder brother and needs an example of good humour. I would not have her adopt such unrelenting solemnity as you have marked in me."

Elizabeth allowed herself to feel flattered by his candour. Beside her, her aunt's creased brow betrayed her concern, even as she smiled at Mr Darcy.

They were then called in to dine, and Elizabeth, touched by the incandescent joy of the newly engaged couple at the centre of their attention, prepared her heart to contentedly reflect its glow, rather than to wish for a bright affection of her own.

CHAPTER TWENTY

On Saturday, the entire party at Netherfield gathered in the front sitting room to enjoy its large fireplace during a day that had turned cold, dreary, and wet—the first sign of winter's anticipated arrival. The occupants had all found suitable occupations for a morning indoors.

Mr Darcy was hard at work at the escritoire in the far corner, largely ignoring the faint bits of conversation buzzing around him. His back was to the fire, giving better light to his ledger books as he worked his calculations. In one of the chairs farther removed from the blaze, Elizabeth tried to keep her stitching even as she alternately squinted down at her work in the poor light from the window and studied Mr Darcy with occasional stolen glances.

Such furtive attention had become a habitual activity. In the past week, Elizabeth's ears had learnt to favour the sound of his voice, her eyes sought delight in his countenance, and her mind and her heart had been so stirred by the many tokens of his intelligence and kindness as to arouse both to keen interest and affectionate regard. Study of him had become her most joyful diversion. She could not be in the same room with him without becoming absorbed in his expressions and his doings.

Catching herself again watching him, Elizabeth resolutely bent to resume her mending. She attempted to regain her concentration to no avail, for her mind was more agreeably entertained by the diverting discovery that Mr Darcy seemed rather too large for the escritoire he occupied. His shoulders were nearly wider than the writing surface, and the length of his legs and large feet quite extended beyond the supports of the desk. But his own proportions, though grander than those of most men and certainly grander than the rather feminine design of the desk, were so balanced as to lend his figure grace. It was far too easy for Elizabeth to become lost in her admiration, and she sought to check herself.

She had just finished a row of stitching when a rustle from Mr Darcy's corner caused her attempts at self-control to fail. Elizabeth glanced up to watch his hands alternately spread and move over the pages, and she was lost again to diverting inspection. His hands were far too large to be considered elegant. Yet, they were cleverly formed, with a firm grip that Elizabeth felt suited his decisive nature far better.

She could not look away when Mr Darcy rolled the stiffness out of his shoulders. He had been working long in that attitude, she surmised, since he had been there before Miss Bingley had directed her guests into the room following breakfast. Now that so many were gathered in his working place—which perhaps might have been Miss Bingley's design—Mr Darcy had drawn his brows together in concentration. He seemed determined to finish his task.

His strained expression stirred her, and Elizabeth measured the emotions that roused within her and sought to understand them. Now that she had spoken to her aunt and had become better acquainted with her growing attraction to Mr Darcy, Elizabeth was prepared to own that her tender feelings towards him were stronger than they ought to be. Her first desire was to ease his discomfort, to lighten his burden, to give him aid in any way she could—even to ease the tension in his shoulders with her own hands. Were Jane suffering so, she would have done it. But the notion that she might attend him presented itself as something so wholly improper that Elizabeth nearly dropped her sewing.

As she fumbled with her threads in a flustered manner, Mr Darcy glanced at her and seemed amused. He raised a speculative brow, but Elizabeth immediately turned away towards the window to rethread her needle.

The sound of the wind and rain suddenly increased, and those conversing in the room were forced to talk louder. Mrs Bennet had already complained that the rain had prevented a visit between the Gardiners and Bennets during morning calls, and finding the sound of the water slapping against the house disturbing to her nerves, she complained of it again.

The rain did not, however, prevent the arrival of one unexpected visitor whose determination and lack of sense rendered him quite impervious to the discomforts of such a journey.

"Mr Collins! We are very glad you have come to visit and on such a day, too," cried Mrs Bennet, smothering her alarm at his somewhat sodden appearance with effusions of welcome.

"Madam," replied he, bowing and dripping a little upon Miss Bingley's fine carpet as he swept off his wide-brimmed hat and handed it to the footman who had anxiously trailed after him from the vestibule. "I am come today to enquire after Miss Elizabeth's health, for she took such a sudden illness when last I visited as to impress upon me the necessity of calling again to confirm her recovery."

"That is very kind of you, sir," said Miss Bingley with fawning warmth. "Pray, do stay and take some tea, and make yourself quite at home. As you see, there is a seat just there—near Miss Elizabeth's chair."

Mr Collins met this invitation with deep bows. But Elizabeth, who had risen from her sewing to curtsey with the other ladies upon his entry, immediately sank back into her seat, glancing alternately at Miss Bingley and her mother with no small expression of alarm. Too late, she found herself once again in Mr Collins's close company as he approached her with a plodding step.

"Cousin Elizabeth, I am delighted to find you well, and I wished to express to you my humblest apologies if aught I said or did on Thursday contributed to your illness," he said without further greeting. "And I wish to offer you some comfort by informing you that in addition to becoming the focus of many meditations as to how best to seek your forgiveness, you have also been the subject of my particular prayers for God's healing and grace. As one who wishes for you only blessings and the happiest of lives, I would greatly desire during the course of this morning to request a private audience with you in the hopes of securing at least one of these objects." With a smile at Mrs Bennet, he added, "I shall, of course, request such permission from your honoured parents as required for an audience of this intimate kind."

Elizabeth, aghast, could not immediately respond, so her mother leapt into the silence.

"But of course! Lizzy, go into the music room at once and await Mr Collins."

"Mama, there is nothing Mr Collins can say to me that others may not hear," Elizabeth pleaded, too much now in dread of her suitor to feel concerned by exposing their conversation in front of their party.

Her mother's response was sharp and biting. "I insist that you go now and hear Mr Collins—and that you answer him as you should!"

In terror at this prospect, Elizabeth sought Jane's gaze across the room, silently begging her sister to accompany her.

When she stood up trembling, Jane stood, too, but Mrs Bennet put out a hand to detain her.

"What are you about, Jane? Stay where you are and keep Mr Bingley company. I insist upon it," hissed Mrs Bennet.

Elizabeth's gaze offered her sister all clemency as Jane settled obediently back into her seat. Elizabeth then took a tremulous breath, gave her mother a level stare, and resolutely turned from the room.

Behind her, Miss Bingley smiled meanly.

DARCY, AT FIRST SUSPENDED IN DREAD AT THE realisation that his aunt's parson likely meant to propose to Elizabeth, now set aside his ledger book and bent his mind towards calculations of an entirely different sort.

As Mr Collins bowed to the company and opened his mouth to make his excuses to follow his cousin, Darcy spoke, causing him to freeze in his tracks.

"Before you are gone from us, I would speak to you of a matter pressing to her ladyship's concerns." It was not a request, for as he spoke it, Darcy stood and gave the parson the fullness of his dark and flinty gaze. "It should take only a few moments of your time."

"Of course, Mr Darcy!" sputtered Collins, bowing twice in confused submission.

Darcy gestured for Mr Collins to follow him from the room, and the rector at once complied, following doggishly on his heels to the study. From her chair, Mrs Bennet huffed at both men in consternation at the timing of such a request as they went out.

When they arrived in the study, Darcy took a seat behind the desk and beckoned Mr Collins to take the facing chair. Mr Collins's nervousness bubbled over into unprompted speech.

"Sir, if I may say—"

"I would rather you did not. I would come to my point first. It is my understanding that you came into Hertfordshire under direction from my aunt to seek out a proper wife to join you in your work in her parish. Is that not so?"

"You deduce splendidly, sir," replied Mr Collins, who would have gone on, except that Darcy's expression now bound him to silence.

"I would imagine that my aunt has impressed upon you the importance of finding a woman of excellent character, of good family, and whose comportment would befit the humility and unimpeachable respectability befitting the wife of a clergyman. Is that correct?"

Mr Collins nodded mutely.

Darcy's eyes narrowed as he leaned forward over his steepled fingers. "You choose exceedingly ill, Mr Collins, if Miss Elizabeth Bennet is now your object. My aunt would find much to despise in Miss Elizabeth's impertinence and wilful independence were she to hold such a station as parson's wife at the Hunsford parish. Have you never noticed these defects in Miss Elizabeth?"

"I confess I have not had much occasion to observe them, sir," replied Mr Collins with growing alarm. "But while these faults may present themselves in Miss Elizabeth in such a setting as Hertfordshire, would not her behaviour in Kent be rightly tempered by the sense of natural awe excited in every person by her ladyship's authority and standing? Indeed, I would think Miss Elizabeth's other, better virtues would teach her to mend such defects as an act of respect, especially once she came to understand how much was provided for her by the beneficent generosity of Lady Catherine de Bourgh."

"Upon my word, sir," replied Mr Darcy with exasperation, holding up his hand to forestall further foolishness, "your hope is indeed extraordinary in view of what I must now relate. I am obliged to inform you that my own standing in society has certainly proven insufficient inducement to curb Miss Elizabeth's sharp tongue. On more than one occasion, she has gone so far as to discredit my opinions in public, challenge my character, and enter into open debate against me as though she were my equal."

"Has she indeed?" Mr Collins gasped, his mouth gaping wide in horrified shock. "I do see now how very mistaken I was in her character. Very mistaken! I thank you, sir, for the kindness of your forethought in sharing this information with me before I made a most grievous error, which would have proven in time to be of great and lasting annoyance to my noble patroness. I would not see her ladyship offended for the world, I assure you, and certainly not by any wife of mine! I shall go at once to inform my cousin that my intentions must, by necessity, shift away from her in consideration of such vanity and pride as this behaviour demonstrates."

"Very reasonable, Mr Collins," said Darcy, forcing back the small smirk tugging at his lips.

Darcy was thanked again and again for his candour and thoughtfulness in giving such advice, and Mr Collins, having been granted his advisor's leave repeatedly, turned and quit the room after several bows.

In the music room, Elizabeth's nerves were in an awful state. She dreaded the coming interview, and her vexation had grown as the clock behind her continued to tick away without the appearance of her would-be suitor. She had just risen from her chair to run from the room when Mr Collins at last appeared in the doorway and blocked her only means of escape.

He gestured for her to be seated with a sweep of his hand. "My dear cousin," he began solemnly, "my attentions to you of late have been too marked to be mistaken, but I have just learned that there has been some mistake! Let me begin by recounting to you my reasons for coming into Hertfordshire with the design of selecting a wife, as I certainly did. It may be advisable for me to begin with my reasons for seeking marriage."

"Mr Collins, there is no—"

His face clouded at this interruption, and Elizabeth at once went silent at his unexpectedly forbidding expression.

He continued with grave dignity. "Though my reasons for wishing to marry are several, one most pertinent today is that it is the particular advice and recommendation of the very noble lady whom I have the honour of calling patroness. Twice she has condescended to give me her opinion on this subject, and it was the very Saturday night before I left Hunsford when she said, 'Mr Collins, you must marry. A clergyman like you must marry. Choose properly, choose a gentlewoman for my sake and for your own. Let her be an active, useful sort of person, not brought up too high, but able to make a small income go a good way. This is my advice. Find such a woman as soon as you can, bring her to Hunsford, and I shall visit her.'

"So, desirous of meeting her requirements and also of healing the breach created by the entail of Longbourn, I left Kent to seek a wife among the daughters of your household. Blinded by your charms almost at our earliest introduction, I singled you out as the companion of my future life. Although I had little occasion to observe the workings of your mind and character, I began to fancy that your vivacity would be acceptable to my patroness, especially when tempered with the silence and respect that her ladyship's rank would inevitably excite."

Mr Collins's face took on a look of pained thoughtfulness. "I now unhappily discover myself to be mistaken, for only just now, I was given advice from the highest authority at hand regarding this matter—the advice of a gentleman who has, in sharing a house and neighbourhood with you, been of your acquaintance above several weeks and whose powers of observation must indeed be considerable, given the greatness of mind, which his lineage has bestowed upon him."

Elizabeth wondered, supposed, and was silent.

"Mr Darcy, who is Lady Catherine de Bourgh's most valued nephew, spoke to me himself just moments before I entered this room, and he acquainted me with such failings of your character as I deemed weighty enough to justify my throwing off any notions to form an alliance with you. Indeed, I now deem it my duty as your cousin and most notably as a clergyman to alert you to these faults in your sinful nature that will inevitably expose you to censure by those in a position of rank and may affect your own future prospects if they are observed by other gentlemen of any standing."

Elizabeth suddenly burned with curiosity. "Your words affect me deeply, and my interest and concern are all aflame. Pray, Mr Collins, I beg of you to be frank with me, and I shall thank you in advance for any insight you may relay to me from the mouth of Mr Darcy."

"It is a privilege indeed to have such notice given to my concerns by such a man, but in this he greatly resembles his aunt. Given the quality of his discernment, I must not fail in my duty to you, madam, and therefore shall give you all the benefits to be found in his most attentive correction.

"Mr Darcy has informed me that you have a certain 'wilful independence' in your character which refuses to bend before the dignities of rank and superior breeding. It was with great astonishment on my part that he gave me to know that on more than one occasion, you have willingly and most impertinently challenged Mr Darcy's opinions. And more damaging still, that you have exposed yourself to ridicule by so attempting—before others—to compare the workings of your mind to that of such an educated gentleman. Beyond this, he tells me you have also called into question the merits of his character within your discourse in a manner most unbecoming in a lady. Such misbehaviour on your part reveals too much pride in your own vain ignorance."

As Mr Collins paused to recover his breath—a need becoming more and more urgent as his haranguing increased in volume—Elizabeth tried to paint upon her face an expression of contrition, but she was helpless to do more than cover her mouth to hide her rising mirth.

"All of these failings have caused me to reconsider most carefully those offers I had hoped to make to you today. But of greatest weight in my consideration was Mr Darcy's opinion that such behaviour as you exhibit would be most repulsive to his noble aunt, and indeed, in her eyes, would render you most unfit for assuming the role of parson's wife. Miss Elizabeth, I am afraid that hardly any man would deem such qualities fitting in a wife, and I urge you now to examine your behaviour and your conscience before you are wholly beyond the reach of amendment!"

As unexpected as this reproof was to Elizabeth, relief nevertheless mounted within her breast, and she had to force down her own laughter, even as he rebuked her. Her eyes began to sting and water with the effort.

Seeing some evidence of what he perceived to be distress, Mr Collins softened his tone but did not relent in his correction. "Cousin Elizabeth, you have missed a great opportunity due to your poor judgment. My situation in life, my connexion to the family of de Bourgh, and my relationship to your own, are circumstances highly in my favour as a suitor, and these offerings have all bypassed you, due to your own neglect of character. Further, you should take into consideration that despite your manifold attractions, it is by no means certain that another offer of marriage may ever be made to you if you do not reform. I must conclude, Cousin, by repeating my hope that you will attend to your improvement and by expressing my desire that you will forgive me for failing to offer you that which my behaviour might have led you to anticipate and that might have benefitted your situation greatly, had your own behaviour been better."

At this last declaration, he appeared to have finished. Mr Collins bowed solemnly and turned to go but not before pausing to add, "And pray, allow me to observe that the notice of Mr Darcy in most helpfully pointing out your faults holds further merit for your consideration. It would befit you to offer him your apologies for your past misdeeds and to tender him gratitude for his correction, even as I myself saw fit to thank him for his information."

Elizabeth's eyes danced as she struggled to hold back yet another laugh. "Mr Darcy is goodness itself, and I find that today's events have even more fully impressed upon me the true superiority of his mind above my own. I shall not neglect any duty to him, I assure you."

Mr Collins bowed again in satisfied approval, and Elizabeth dropped a curtsey. He went out at last, and as the door swung closed behind him, Elizabeth helplessly clutched her sides as laughter overwhelmed her. After some minutes of unrestrained mirth, Elizabeth dabbed at her eyes and cleared her throat. Heady feelings of relief and happiness would not abate, and she could not contain her wild delight at her sudden freedom.

As carefree as a child, she came into the study, beaming to discover Mr Darcy there alone and in an attitude of concentration, since he had retrieved his ledger books.

Elizabeth bit her lip, hiding her smile as he looked up and drew to his feet. With an expression of perfect ease, Mr Darcy crossed his arms over his chest and regarded her with one dark eyebrow raised, much in the manner of a war general awaiting with confident anticipation the news of his assured victory.

"I have come to tell you that I must honour my promise to Mr Collins."

In an instant, his face transfigured to horrified astonishment, his arms came uncrossed, and he seemed to fall a little forward as he braced his palms upon the desk. "What? What did you say?"

"I promised him I would apologise to you for ever having questioned the opinions and workings of your mind," Elizabeth explained. "Indeed, I find it is just that I do so. I own freely that your mind holds no equal for me—for that was the prettiest piece of cleverness I have ever witnessed!"

At her pronouncement, Elizabeth surrendered once more to helpless laughter that only increased as she watched the astonishment melt from Mr Darcy's face into understanding and finally, amusement.

As his restraint dissolved into hearty chuckles that matched her own, Elizabeth eventually caught her breath.

"I also promised him that I would thank you for pointing out my faults in such a fashion. It was most well done, sir. Your reproofs could not have been better timed."

"I assure you, it was my pleasure to discredit you so soundly," Mr Darcy said with a slightly wicked grin.

Elizabeth laughed again in delight and came around the table to stand before him. Mr Darcy straightened in surprise and looked rather perplexed as she proffered her hand. When he dutifully took it up without hesitation, she tightened her grasp and shook hands with him warmly.

"I find myself marvelling that I owe you once again for snatching me from a fate no less perilous to my life and happiness than that which we faced at Longbourn."

As she spoke, she smiled, but seeing him somewhat discomfited by her proximity and praise, Elizabeth was forced to recall with anxiety what her aunt had told her—that there was no firm reason to suppose that Mr Darcy held any real affection for her. She, therefore, restrained herself from showing him what was in her heart.

"You could not have acted better today in defence of my sanity were you my own brother. I am fully convinced I can find in no other man a truer friend. I thank you most sincerely, Mr Darcy."

Then, before her courage could abandon her, she did as her heart directed and gave him some token of her affection in the only fashion she could. Elizabeth rose upon her toes and brushed a brief and grateful kiss upon his cheek, much as she might have given to her uncle or her father—or a brother.

Mr Darcy stepped back from her, and said quietly and with a fullness of feeling, "I am ever at your service, Miss Elizabeth."

"And I, yours," said she, curtseying to him with her own colour high at her act of boldness. She then turned and hurried from the room.

CHAPTER TWENTY-ONE

Following his interview with Elizabeth, the rector returned to his hosts and expressed his satisfaction in meeting with his cousin—and then, with surprising quickness, gave his civil farewells to the Bennets and made his exit. Mr Collins did not seem a disappointed man, but he had tendered no hint to either of Elizabeth's parents whether his proposal had been accepted.

"Whatever could he be about, Mr Bennet?" his wife exclaimed. "Not a word to you, or to me, or to anybody, about what was said! Am I to have another daughter married this winter or not?"

Mr Bennet returned to his paper and merely shrugged. "How fortunate that the daughter in question is still within the house. I imagine she may hold the information you seek."

In indignation at her husband's apparent indifference and overburdened with unanswered hopes, Mrs Bennet sought out Elizabeth. She gained good information from her younger daughters that they had seen her taking the stairs, so Mrs Bennet soon found her. Elizabeth sat on a sofa in the little parlour on the landing favoured by the women of the house. She had taken advantage of the limited light of the window and was humming to herself, absorbed in whittling at a pencil above a spread of old newspapers ripe for pattern making. Mrs Bennet greeted her daughter and sat down beside her.

"So, now, Lizzy, have you accepted Mr Collins, and are you not now relieved to have done so?" Mrs Bennet asked.

Elizabeth drew in a breath, perceiving how this news might pain her mother. "Mr Collins did not offer for me. There was nothing to accept."

"He—what? And why should he not? What did you say, what did you do, to make him lose his nerve? Lizzy, speak! Do not shake your head so. Oh, you did not encourage him in the slightest, did you? Must you frighten away so eligible a man and the heir to our own estate? And now what are we to do? Your alliance was the best hope we had of keeping and restoring Longbourn for the future. Did you not think of that?"

Before her mother could scold her further, Elizabeth stood. "There was nothing I could do to encourage Mr Collins! His mind was settled against me before he even reached the room."

With great agitation, Mrs Bennet rose, wringing her hands. To Elizabeth's surprise, she saw her mother had begun to cry.

With a compassion beyond any she had felt before for the woman who had borne her, Elizabeth gently took her mother's arm and led her to the sofa again. Once she had settled, Mrs Bennet peered up at her second daughter's concerned face.

"The man must be a fool. That is all there can be of it," her mother muttered softly. "Did he not gain any notion of your abilities when he saw you at the Lucases'? Does he not, in his predicament of a damaged inheritance, value the industry of a wife unafraid of work? Does he not know that you keep so much knowledge of the estate he would inherit and that you have been a help to your father? Does that mean nothing to him, as the next master? More fool he! And how dare he come here to raise our hopes, only to dismiss you!"

Having never known her mother to value these unfeminine qualities in her before, Elizabeth pressed her mother's hand in gratitude for this rare concession. The fire had changed even her mother's perspective it seemed, and Elizabeth felt strangely glad.

Seeing her mother still in tears, she sought to soothe her. "Mama, he did me no injury."

Mrs Bennet snorted, even as she dabbed at her eyes most daintily. "No, I suppose you had no wish to marry him, and it is just as well for him that you did not. No doubt he will seek a bride with a bit more dowry. It may be in his plans to benefit the recovery of his future estate in that way."

"Regardless of his plans, Mr Collins deemed me unworthy to be his wife, and I have no cause to repine."

"Well, at least I shall have Jane well settled. But Lizzy, what am I to do for you and your sisters? Mr Bingley is as kind as he may be, but having four—nay, *five*—unmarried sisters will be a trial! And your father can give me no answer, will spare not a bit of guidance, as to what I am to do, should any more tragedy befall us."

At another time in her life, Elizabeth might have defended her father, but now she felt his failures keenly. When had he ever made plans to add to any of their dowries, to lay aside funds for emergencies, or for expansion or repairs of Longbourn? He had never innovated, invested, or done anything beyond following long tradition to benefit and grow his estate. Now was not a time to persevere in honouring his indolence, when the effects of his neglect now weighed so heavily upon them all.

Elizabeth shook her head, not knowing what to say, so instead of offering words of encouragement, she embraced the woman beside her with compassion that was both sincere and sweet.

Sometime later, when Elizabeth was alone again and tracing out patterns for the reupholstering of her father's chair, her mind caught on the strange sense of gratitude she felt for the providential actions of Mr Collins. The man had somehow managed to fulfil his wish of healing a breach in her family, for he had unwittingly brought reconciliation between mother and child.

Satisfied with the work accomplished, Elizabeth set aside her finished patterns, dusted off her hands, and washed and dressed for dinner. By the time she returned downstairs, the rain had stopped, and Mr Bingley announced that Mr Darcy had gone off to Meryton to dine with Colonel Forster.

"After we had dined with the colonel, I had not thought Darcy had made a great friendship or had any further sort of business connected with the man," Mr Bingley reflected. "But when I asked Darcy about his plan to dine with the colonel again tonight, he became almost mulishly mysterious. I take it that whatever he means to discuss with the colonel must have some weight, but it is not a burden he is willing to share."

When Elizabeth recalled Mr Darcy's professed intention to discuss Mr Wickham's history with Colonel Forster, she could only smile at Mr Bingley's bemusement and say, "I have come to think that your friend's reticence pairs most inconveniently with his vast sense of responsibility. He would rather see a thing done than speak to others of how he might go about it. But I suppose that is part of his charm."

"His charm!" Bingley laughed, his face alight with amused affection. "I had not thought on it, but having seen many men of his circle speak and not act, I suppose it is a boon to be able to rely upon Darcy to do the opposite."

The party was soon called into dinner, and Miss Bingley took the opportunity to speak to Elizabeth about the events of the morning.

"Miss Eliza, I found Mr Collins a most determined suitor to

call on you on such a rainy day. How gallant of him! Am I mistaken, or am I soon to wish you joy?"

"Alas, no, Miss Bingley," said Elizabeth, smiling to herself. "It seems another lady might suit him better, but I wish him well."

"Indeed? Well, that is a disappointment."

"It is just as well that the news of Jane's engagement is not overshadowed. We have all enjoyed sharing their happiness, have we not?"

Miss Bingley, who had greeted the news of her brother's engagement with displeasure to his face in private, was now forced to fawn over it before her guests. Elizabeth spared a glance at Mr Bingley as he listened to his sister play the toad-eater with amusement, and hid her own smile behind her napkin.

CHAPTER TWENTY-TWO

*A*fter spending much of the prior evening's dinner missing his steady presence, Elizabeth was amply rewarded by seeing Mr Darcy at breakfast. His restrained civility towards the crowded table was by now such a habit that Elizabeth merely smiled at it. Lacking privacy, she decided to seek an occasion later to learn of his reception at the Forsters', and to gauge his assurances that Mr Wickham's worst vices might not be repeated in Meryton.

Such an opportunity eluded her all morning, for the entire company at Netherfield soon shuffled into carriages to attend Sunday service. Their neighbours, who had quickly learnt from Mrs Philips of Jane's engagement, could not talk enough of such news with the Bennet ladies, and Elizabeth spent all of her time in the churchyard expressing her joy for Jane and Mr Bingley to each of them. When she was finally settled in the chapel, Elizabeth sat quietly in her pew and stole glances at Mr Darcy in his elegant grey coat and listened to his warm baritone lifted up in a hymn.

When their party returned to Netherfield, Miss Bingley's offering of refreshments created clusters of chatter in the salon. Elizabeth hoped she might have her chance to speak to Mr Darcy at last, for she had spotted him in a comfortable chair, contentedly situated with his tea and a plate of biscuits. At her approach, he made to rise.

"Oh no, sir! We had better not risk an accident over a mere formality," Elizabeth forestalled him graciously, nodding towards his carefully balanced plate and then to her own teacup in her palm.

"I should not wish to leave a lady unacknowledged," Mr Darcy declared, "but I suppose some informality may be excused, given our prolonged shared occupation of Netherfield."

Elizabeth indulged his droll observation with a laugh. As she settled herself into the chair matching his, she observed, "It is above half a month now, as of today, since I have invaded Netherfield. You are very good to countenance so much unplanned company during your visit with your friend."

"I had not expected my time in such a quiet county to be so eventful, I admit. But I cannot regret coming, for I have been honoured to find myself being of use to Bingley, to your family, and to more besides," Mr Darcy reflected, catching her eye before leaning forward and lowering his voice. "Regarding our mutual acquaintance, it seems some mischief was already afoot, as I learnt from my discussion with Colonel Forster and his wife. Wickham has styled himself as the younger son of a gentleman, and he has already had some credit extended to him by the local shopkeepers who believed his shallow pockets were tied to a deeper purse. Colonel Forster was surprised to learn that Wickham was only the son of my father's steward and is now suspicious of the scoundrel."

"I am glad your mission was successful. My little village will be spared a great disservice by your diligence, Mr Darcy, though they are ignorant of it."

"It is no more than I ought to have done."

At his protest, Elizabeth could not keep from revealing some of her admiration, if only to assuage her feelings for the man before her. "Only the best sort of man would take on such an errand when it could easily have been ignored. I thank you, sir, on behalf of my friends in Meryton. There is much I owe you for the wonders you have worked."

Mr Darcy looked more troubled than pleased. Elizabeth wanted to tease him into levity to ease away the severity from his expression, but her chance was spoilt by her youngest sister.

Lydia nearly bounced with impatience as she approached. "I must have you speak to Mama, Lizzy! I want to go into the village to call on my friends tomorrow, for we shall be leaving soon and for heaven knows how long! But she says I must stay here to pack for our trip to town!"

"Lydia, a moment, please," said Elizabeth in exasperation, before turning to Mr Darcy and bobbing a curtsey. "Pray excuse me. It seems I am needed."

Her conference with Lydia soon gathered more participants as Kitty drew alongside them, and then Mary, seeing a chance to offer advice, drew nigh. Elizabeth listened but a moment to their prattling before she cleared her throat.

"It is the honour due foremost to Mama and to Jane as a newly engaged woman to take their leave of the neighbourhood," Elizabeth said. "However, I believe that Mary and I shall have sufficient help from the maids to ensure all is tidied up. I can offer Mama our assurances that you and Kitty might be spared from packing, but it is she who must grant permission."

The girls agreed to this scheme, and they applied to Mrs Bennet for approval. Mr Bingley gallantly offered his carriage, and so the arrangements for Monday's farewell tour were completed in time for the ladies to go up to rest and dress for dinner.

AFTER THEIR MEAL, DARCY FACED THE AWFUL prospect of the loss of Elizabeth Bennet's company, for it was a Sunday evening, and he had few other distractions.

The books he rifled through could not hold his attention, and conversation, though it was attempted by various persons and on diverse subjects, had proven impossible. He stalked about the room in a fashion rather reminiscent of his early days in Hertfordshire when he had been cautious to distance himself from Elizabeth and her charms. Now, he stood aloof, not to guard against his growing feelings, but to suppress an ardour already grown and to think most carefully of the conundrum in which he found himself.

Far from wishing to distance himself from Elizabeth, Darcy desired to progress ever dearer in her affection, for he could not long abide being her heart's *brother*. How such an appellation haunted him! How he sought to defy it!

With mortification, he realised that his reluctance in declaring himself had somehow spoilt his chance to win her. For in the wake of his silence, his gallant actions towards her had spoken not of courtship, but courtesy. It now seemed Elizabeth regarded him with more friendly gratitude than affection, and, therefore, had not prepared her heart for the expectation of his love. Could her heart yet open and yield to him? Darcy's uncertainty was agony, and the only remedy to his condition—the securing of Elizabeth's passionate regard—seemed soon to pass beyond his reach.

In less than thirty hours, Elizabeth would be gone to London, and he might only have occasion to call upon her with his sister in crowded company. He might perhaps share some more direct conversation with her when she came to call upon

Georgiana, but in such a setting it would be highly improper of him to flirt or woo her. It was unlikely they would meet socially otherwise, since Elizabeth's position would be far beneath his circle.

Certainly, he and Elizabeth would never find themselves alone together in a dark library again! Darcy cursed himself a fool.

AS THE EVENING WORE ON AND MR DARCY'S SILENCE stretched out ominously despite the lively conversation Elizabeth attempted to instigate within their company, she began to realise her love for him must be in vain. As she reflected upon it, he had hardly spoken a word to her all day. Her own folly in looking before their parting for some sign of tenderness sat heavy on Elizabeth's heart until the weight of it became instructive. As she went to bed that night, she endeavoured to school herself not to hope for some evidence of his affection.

When Monday dawned, Elizabeth's subdued spirits fell further with the onerous tasks the day presented. While her mother, Jane, Kitty, and Lydia went to take their leave of their friends in Meryton, Elizabeth was to go again to Longbourn. She would be accompanied this time by her aunt and uncle, her father, and Mary. There they would reunite with Mr and Mrs Hill and their housemaids to gather what clothes and articles they could for the family's indefinite sojourn in London.

Upon their arrival home, Elizabeth and her relations were pleasantly surprised by the efficiencies already performed. Mr and Mrs Hill had seen to what preparations they could manage just as soon as Mr Higgins had declared the above-stairs floor joists sufficiently reinforced and safe to bear the strain of some activity. The dear Hills had worked directly with the scullery maid and had scoured, scrubbed, laundered, ironed, aired, and placed what was serviceable into trunks.

The women gathered and began organising what was needed for their winter away, while the men went to confirm the details of an order containing the most needed materials for the next stage of repairs with Mr Higgins.

With far more ease and less soot than Elizabeth had imagined, the Bennet party completed their tasks. As they boarded the carriage to return to Netherfield that afternoon, Mr Bingley's footmen met them with a wagon on Longbourn's drive, and Elizabeth watched as they went into the house to retrieve the heaviest trunks. She did not envy them tomorrow's task of strapping them to the roofs of their carriages for the journey to London.

When Elizabeth returned to the drawing room at Netherfield, she was surprised not only to find some refreshments thoughtfully set out but also to discern among the greetings offered to her the earnest tones of Mr Darcy.

"I trust your morning's business was concluded successfully?" he asked as he straightened from his bow.

"Yes, sir," Elizabeth replied, reaching towards the table and taking a teacup in hand. She smiled as she reported, "Mr Higgins's forethought in reinforcing the upper floor allowed us access to most of our rooms to find what was needed. You did well to recommend his services."

"I am glad though not surprised to hear it. Higgins has a reputation for careful plans carried out with expediency. He has proven as much with his work on my aunt's property. It yet may be that we see your sister holding court at her own table for her wedding breakfast."

Elizabeth smiled at him over her cup and rebalanced it on the saucer, her mind following his neat turn of conversation towards the topic of her sister's nuptials.

"I am sure that would please Jane immensely and my mother no less so," Elizabeth replied. She glanced meaningfully across the room at Mr Bingley, who was laughing with Jane, the perfect picture of felicity and thriving affection. "Although I know the location of such arrangements will not ultimately matter, especially not to your friend."

"No, indeed. I think him extremely fortunate in his choice of wife," said Mr Darcy, following her eyes to observe the beaming couple. "His happiness could not be more complete or certain."

He gestured towards the mate to his own chair. Once she had taken that seat with an eagerness she thought she hid rather well, she said, "In that respect, they are well-matched."

She looked askance at Miss Bingley, who watched her closely from her position near the teapot. "Although some might say that your friend chose badly in terms of fortune."

Mr Darcy lowered his voice. "Fortune, while not immaterial to the *nouveau riche*, is not the only consideration. Your sister is gently born, an attribute my friend cannot claim."

"That might be true," replied Elizabeth, "but what benefit would there be to wed a gentlewoman who lacks fortune and whose family boasts no real connexions of value?" She shook her head. "I fail to see how their union could assist him—or his sister—in any plans to achieve high standing in society."

Mr Darcy frowned. "Connexions can be built upon, just as homes can be rebuilt," he said evenly.

Elizabeth bit her lip. "If by 'connexions' you mean to say that Jane and Mr Bingley may make many advantageous friendships, then you would be right. They are each so obliging and good-natured that they will always keep within a generous circle of acquaintance. Yet friendship only carries so far. Those connexions by blood and marriage are of greatest significance to those in your sphere. You cannot deny it."

"I cannot. Friendship between families, while important in one generation, often does not stand in the next, as blood does. Bloodlines and marital alliances are indeed deemed essential—

and I fear only in this one resolution does our wastrel peerage seek to provide for its own future."

"Perhaps Miss Bingley will marry a lord," Elizabeth quipped, taking another sip of her tea.

Mr Darcy shook his head and chuckled before taking up his own cup, allowing Elizabeth a reprieve from his conversation so that she could enjoy her refreshments and try again to content herself with only his friendship.

CHAPTER TWENTY-THREE

𝒜s the tea things were cleared away, the arrival of a footman immediately drew attention. The liveried young man sought Miss Bingley's permission to present the latest post, as many letters had not arrived in time for dispersal at breakfast. Permission was granted, and he returned with many missives from a vast circle of their acquaintance bidding the Bennets a fond journey, offered in response to the notes Jane and Mrs Bennet had sent on Friday to those they knew they could not visit directly prior to their leaving the neighbourhood.

Mrs Bennet claimed the pile of correspondence with all the esurience of a cat offered the top layer of cream. To Elizabeth's dismay, her mother began opening some of them and exclaiming to the room over the neighbourly felicitations offered to Jane and Mr Bingley.

"They are so frightfully jealous of you, Jane—they must be —but they do say such kind things. You ought to read it for yourself," she went on, handing Jane one of many notes. "Such kind attention from all our neighbours is so unexpected, yet so welcome. Look how many letters there are! Here is one from Hetty Marshall! And look, Mrs Lathrop sends a kind word as well. And here, this one comes almost from the next county—and here—"

Mrs Bennet paused, puzzling over the directions written on one missive, and then taking up another. "Why, Elizabeth, here are two letters addressed to you. I wonder who should have occasion to write to you? Oh, but this one is only from Charlotte Lucas—that hand I know. But now, this one is written in a very dainty, elegant hand. Who might have sent this, Lizzy?"

Her daughter blushed to have the details of her correspondence bandied about. "Mama, pray give the letters to me, and I shall look into the matter directly," said Elizabeth evenly, attempting composure.

Mrs Bennet tutted her disappointment but reached over to hand Elizabeth the letters. As she did, Miss Bingley stepped forward to prevent Elizabeth from relying on Mr Darcy, whose seat was nearer, to close the gap between mother and daughter.

As soon as Miss Bingley's fingers closed on the letters, her eyes sought out the penmanship on the note in question. Astonishment creased her brow. She then turned to Elizabeth with a sour expression.

"Why, Miss Elizabeth, I had no idea you were on such intimate terms with a certain young lady in London," Miss Bingley sneered as she reluctantly did her office.

As Elizabeth silently received the letters, she marvelled at the speed of the reply from Miss Darcy.

Mr Darcy peered unobtrusively over her shoulder from where he sat. "I had forgotten you had replied to Georgiana," he said in evident cheer at this sign of his sister's eagerness.

The effect of Mr Darcy's obvious pleasure and his intelligence that it was his sister who had written *first* turned Miss Bingley's colour.

"Dear Georgiana is very kind to condescend to continue the

correspondence," Miss Bingley said. "Such charity of spirit is to be commended."

"I daresay," said Elizabeth absently, not even looking up as she turned the letter over in her hands. When Miss Bingley alighted too closely nearby, Elizabeth stood. "Pray, excuse me," she said to her interloper. Then to Mr Darcy, she explained, "I feel I should attend to this correspondence before further travel preparations prevent me."

Having made her way to the settee removed from the rest of the company, Elizabeth opened her letter from Miss Darcy.

Dear Miss Elizabeth,

When I read from my brother's letter that Tuesday was to mark the day of your departure, I could not resist the opportunity to write once more to wish you and your family well on your journey and to extend to you the welcome of Darcy House at any time during your stay in London. I have thought many times about what entertainments we might enjoy whilst you are in town, and I find your admission that you have an 'appetite for conversation and laughter' most promising, for I confess it is rare that I have the opportunity to visit with ladies who speak of subjects other than the weather or the latest fashion. Not that these topics are without interest but merely that they are so often visited and worn out! Be assured that I would never neglect to discuss these things with you, if you should wish it, for I am sure your original mind would find ways to embroider the most thread-bare of topics.

Am I correct in my assumptions? My brother never exaggerates, and he has written on the originality of your mind to such an extent that I consider you as much a curiosity as a worthy friend. In naming you such, I know that I show my impertinence, but somehow I feel assured that you are rather more amused than wounded by my frankness. I hope I shall always honour your feelings.

I am not a fine writer, but I attempted to arrange my feelings as best I could when I penned my first missive to you. I, therefore, rejoiced to read that the warmth of my concern touched you in your distress. I am also delighted to have learnt from my brother's last letter that you seem much recovered, as well as your father and your sister. It is of great relief to know that your family has not suffered worse through this unhappy accident than the initial incident wrought!

I beg you would send a note as soon as you have settled in town, for even as I look forward to my brother's return, such a wish is paired with the certainty that he will make good on our introduction at the first opportunity.

Pray stay well until we meet. I wish you safe travels and a warm reception in Gracechurch Street, where I hope you may find ample rest and many joys to treasure from the season.

To this rather extended farewell, I can only add my sincere friendship.

Georgiana Darcy

Elizabeth sat back with a smile and refolded the letter. Her correspondent was certainly kind, and Elizabeth was pleased to find she was clearly as capable of wit as her brother. There was much in the anticipation of their future meetings to bring Elizabeth prospects of delight, not just the hope of finding a new friend, but also the chance to be drawn into the circle of Mr Darcy again while in London.

That thought, and the unfairness of it towards Miss Darcy, made Elizabeth sit up guiltily. In this attitude, she turned with some chagrin to Charlotte's letter, feeling yet more disappointment in herself for placing the correspondence of her new friend in precedence above her dearest and oldest one. She opened it at once and read.

My dear Eliza,

I know it is unlikely that you will be able to take your leave of us yourself, so I wanted to write and wish you well and to urge our continued correspondence. Much has happened to upset your mind that I think can only find proper relief through shared confidences.

I have some unfortunate news myself to share. Mr Collins, as you know, had gone to visit your family on a day most unfit for such a venture. As a consequence, he returned to us somewhat altered on Saturday night. I knew at once that he would take ill, and so he did, shortly after dinner that evening.

Sunday morning he spent confined to his room for so long that he was missed at breakfast. We began to worry he would miss church, and so when the chambermaid who refreshed his fire told us he appeared to her most unwell, my father sent for Mr Jones.

Elizabeth frowned. How could she have been ignorant of the fact that none of the Lucases had been at church yesterday —nor Mr Collins? Her distraction, in the form of Mr Darcy sitting in the pew in front of her, must have been extreme. She bent again to the letter.

As I write this, he has not greatly improved, although Mr Jones is convinced that his violent cold has not reached his lungs and will easily be taken in hand. Our servants have been attending his needs, but I have looked in on him myself to observe his progress. His fever has taken a distressing hold. He is restless and speaks to his patroness as though she were present. I confess my compassion has been stirred, for he seems so friendless in his illness. I intend to read to him and see if he will rest more quietly if his mind perceives some company in the room. I shall keep you abreast of his condition, as I know it will be of some concern for your family.

Elizabeth shook her head, little surprised by her sensible

friend's charitable yet practical approach to Mr Collins's care. But the poor Lucases! What kindness they had shown to host Mr Collins in the first place, and now they must nurse him! Would that Mr Collins had simply returned to Kent upon seeing Longbourn in disrepair, rather than remaining in the neighbourhood! Charlotte and her kin were truly goodness itself.

> *Once you are in London, I pray you will write to give me word of your safe arrival and all of your news. Until then, I remain—*

> *Yours &c.*
> CL

Elizabeth read this last request and felt resolved to do just as Charlotte asked. To be better able to reply to both her friends as soon as may be, Elizabeth put away her letters with care in the very top compartment of her trunk.

And it was well that she did so. Tuesday morning came altogether too soon and too chaotically.

Lydia and Kitty began the day by arguing over whose wraps were whose, and whether or not the other would ride to London in the Bennets' worn carriage or the Gardiners' newer, better-sprung borrowed carriage. Mary, disgusted by their quarrelling, insisted upon rescuing a few books from the younger girls' tightly packed trunk to read during the journey, thereby upsetting the articles within and earning the consternation of both her sisters.

"Girls! Girls!" chastised Mrs Bennet. "Help Mary put those things away again, and do not fight! Not today! My poor nerves cannot abide it! Now, where on earth has Sarah gone? I need our maid in my room now for I must know if she has packed my dinner gloves away with my striped bonnet and my good shawl!"

Jane, seeing how her mother's pending apoplexy might inconvenience many, at once set out to calm her mother's anxiety.

"I am sure Sarah did as you instructed, but she is assisting Lizzy now in retrieving our workbaskets that I left downstairs. Come, I shall go with you to your room to ensure your band box contains everything. My own trunk is packed, so I have a moment to spare."

Jane then redirected her mother's attention, thus mitigating one small part of the pandemonium caused by so many ladies preparing for a journey.

In the vestibule, Miss Bingley stood in the midst of the storm, coolly directing her servants and lending speed to the carriage loading process in such a fashion as to be admired for its efficiency.

To better avoid so much unhappy clamour, Elizabeth went in search of any belongings to be found among their rooms above stairs and in the lower drawing room of the house. Having secured the Bennet ladies' workbaskets, a missing hat, a wayward glove, and her own pelisse, she went to the library in search of her father.

"Ah Lizzy," he said by way of greeting as he set down a glass of Mr Bingley's fine port despite the indecency of the early hour. "I am bidding farewell to the last bit of peace I may find for a long time. I hope you do not disapprove."

Elizabeth replied in some confusion, "But, Papa, I thought you might come back to Longbourn by yourself after a few weeks to see to the reconstruction and to enjoy some quiet."

"I still plan to do so, but you make it sound as though I would find it a pleasurable journey. Not so! Neither does the prospect of it erase those many weeks unbroken in which I must anticipate close quarters with not only the full multitude of my own children but also my brother-in-law's, and all within the crucible of compressed time for my wife's ostentatious wedding plans."

A sharp and sudden pang of annoyance warred with Elizabeth's sympathy. The patience of each of her family members would be sorely tested in the coming weeks of confinement, but at least her father had the power as a man to travel back to Longbourn, to remove himself if he so chose. He also had more right to be of use in restoring their home than could she, his child. The thought of these ample sources of consolation within his reach, the very sources he seemed reluctant to take upon himself, increased the bitter tension in her breast.

Rather than answer her father, Elizabeth turned towards the window and looked out upon the front sweep where the carriages were waiting. The tops and rear racks of both conveyances were filled to overflowing as servants scurried about. Mr Bingley and Mr Darcy were also occupied by giving direction to the footmen as to the placement of the last few of the Bennets' scanty yet seemingly endless belongings. Then, to Elizabeth's surprise, the gentlemen began testing and resecuring the luggage strapped to the tops of the carriages.

Elizabeth watched in transfixed fascination for several moments. Mr Darcy's height certainly gave him the advantage in this particular task. Next to the more compact Mr Bingley, who went to the rear of the nearest carriage to stand up on the dumb irons to gain the requisite height to examine the roof, Mr Darcy's figure effortlessly gifted him a long and careful reach. He managed most of his inspections whilst standing on the ground, only needing occasionally to rise on point of toe to readjust a strap around a trunk or bundle. Although his service in such a low office as carriage groom should have diminished him, Elizabeth thought she had seldom seen him looking so grand.

She turned back to the room with a sigh. "It is nearly time

to go. I think everything is packed tightly. We need only assemble now."

Her father picked up a newspaper from the side table. "Be off with you, then, my dear," he replied as he rustled the leaves open. The rest of his dismissal came from behind the pages. "I shall follow once I have my overcoat and finish my farewells here."

Elizabeth turned slowly from the room feeling chilled.

AFTER ENSURING THAT ALL THE LADIES IN THE hallway had their wraps and spencers for their journey through the brisk November morning, Elizabeth and Jane led their sisters and mother outside to bid their farewells on the portico. She was mollified to see that her mother and most of her sisters made an effort to speak their proper thanks to Miss Bingley, who received such gratitude with stiffness. But Miss Bingley's manner did soften when Jane spoke to her, enough that she clasped hands with her future sister in a moment of charity and even wished her a fair journey. To Elizabeth, she gave a curtsey as both acknowledgement and dismissal.

The Hursts also bowed and curtseyed somewhat formally, although Mrs Hurst made so free as to take Elizabeth, Jane, and Mrs Bennet's hands and wished them well with some warmth.

Mr Bingley, however, pumped each hand vigorously, expressed a jovial wish to see them soon, and seemed almost distressed by their expressions of gratitude.

He was very bold when Jane came to him, and took both of her hands in his and kissed them on their dainty gloves. Before he released his betrothed, Mr Bingley gave Jane a sort of sad smile of longing. He begged her patience while he closed his house at Netherfield and declared he would follow her to town in the coming week.

More was said as the road and some plans for the winter

were discussed, but Elizabeth was insensible to it as she strained her worried eyes towards the house for some sign of her father. Finally, the door opened, and Mr Bennet emerged at last, still pulling on his gloves.

Elizabeth gave herself leave then to look for her opportunity and was surprised when Kitty approached to offer it.

"Lizzy, would you come with me to say farewell to Mr Darcy? I never know how to speak to him, but I am certain I might not have come out so well the night of the fire without his help."

A wish so near to Elizabeth's heart could not have been more easily granted, and so she took her sister's arm gratefully and approached Mr Darcy where he stood by the carriages, saying farewell to the Gardiners. She waited to gain his attention.

"Mr Darcy," Elizabeth said softly, sinking into a curtsey which her sister repeated beside her, "Kitty and I could not think of going without expressing our special gratitude to you."

"It is not necessary," said he. "I was glad to be of service."

"Service?" echoed Kitty, "I could not call it that. I—we— are alive, because of what you did, sir." She looked up at him and curtseyed again, with a reverence that Elizabeth had never seen before. Kitty could not bring herself to speak after that, but her silence was nevertheless full of meaning.

"We thank you from our hearts, Mr Darcy," said Elizabeth for both of them. Kitty nodded to second the offering.

"You are most welcome, Miss Elizabeth, Miss Catherine."

Kitty, pink in both cheeks, nodded and turned back to join her sisters, who were still sorting out their placement in the carriages. But Elizabeth, unsure of how soon she might meet Mr Darcy again, remained a moment, mute before him.

"I was disconcerted to have a letter from my sister delivered only this morning, Miss Elizabeth," he said suddenly. "I had rather thought that yesterday, when you received yours, she would have thought to send one directly for me as well. But it seems her enthusiasm for her new friendship has nearly made her forget her poor brother. My little note it seems was an afterthought, which bespoke more of her eagerness to see you than me."

"I confess I have looked forward to meeting Miss Darcy as well. I understand she will have to await your return to London for that introduction to take place, however."

Something in her tone of voice must have directed him to answer the query he found within it. "I intend to return to town just ahead of Bingley, in about four or five days. I shall be sure to bring Georgiana to the Gardiners' home, perhaps as early as next week."

Elizabeth nodded and fiddled with her gloves, feeling shy at the pleasure she felt when he spoke of his plans. As she looked upon Mr Darcy's slight smile, she felt herself being jostled by her family as they began to file past her into the carriages.

With intention, she spoke her last words to Mr Darcy before they would meet again in London. "I am all anticipation."

As Elizabeth moved to pass him, he started up beside her and came to stand next to the carriage. From his expression, his purpose and expectation could not be doubted. In answer, she gave Mr Darcy her hand as she mounted the steps. As his fingers left hers, she fought silently for composure as she nestled in among her sisters.

She turned one last time to look at him as he stepped back. He and Mr Bingley stood just outside the doors, each intent on taking their last vision of the ladies within. Jane was pink with the attention, and Elizabeth scarcely less so.

What is he about? Teasing, teasing man!

Their conveyance started forward with a lurch, and they were off to London.

CHAPTER TWENTY-FOUR

It took several more days to feel settled in the house at Gracechurch Street. Elizabeth managed to see to her unpacking efficiently and to write notes to Charlotte and Miss Darcy in notice of her family's safe arrival. In these brief letters, Elizabeth remarked on amusing misadventures of their journey that she saw fit to share in addition to the pleasantries such friendly notes must always carry. She endeavoured valiantly to keep the anxiety that had begun to oppress her away from such communications.

To be away from Longbourn during its repairs and to remember it either in terror or in disarray, weighed on her heart heavily. There was much Elizabeth felt she might be able to accomplish in the restoration of her home, and her energies chafed at her removal from the site. And while Elizabeth might have expected her sisters, mother, and father, to be relieved to be away from such burdensome duties, their dullness and irascibility assured her that they felt a bereavement akin to her own.

"I do so wish we could have had our Christmas celebrations at Longbourn as always," her mother opined to Mr Bennet.

"Do you think it may be possible next year? We always hosted my brother's family, and it is strange to see the tradition reversed."

"I am no soothsayer, my dear, else I might have better read any omens that foretold of the fire," he replied ruefully. "The coming year may bring an entirely new position for us. Much as I cannot abide such change, it now seems our lot."

Such low spirits were only natural, and their kind hosts, perceiving them, made every attempt to revive the spirits of their guests. Since their house had far fewer bedrooms available than Netherfield, there were many thoughtful ways the Gardiners sought to ensure the comfort of their visitors while closely quartered. Elizabeth was relieved to be sharing a bed only with Jane, although the little bedroom was forced to admit Mary as well, who slept on a comfortable chaise in the corner. Kitty and Lydia were to share a bedroom with the Gardiners' eldest daughter, Rebecca, which their little cousin, fascinated by the doings of older girls, was sure to view as a treat.

For perhaps the first time in Elizabeth's memory, her parents were to share a single bedroom. It was with little wonder, thought Elizabeth wryly upon reflection, that her father had taken to Mr Bingley's port to fortify himself before their removal from Netherfield.

Aside from the vexations of such close company that would only feel closer after the children returned from Mrs Gardiner's sister's care, there was one additional bit of news that made Elizabeth's first week in London less than pleasant. It was to be found in Charlotte's letter, which arrived on Friday, too soon to have been sent in answer to Elizabeth's notice of safe arrival in London.

Elizabeth had opened it out of curiosity at breakfast, only to wish she had not. She read it at the table.

Dear Eliza,

I find I write with haste to acquaint you with news which may leave you surprised. First, I must report that Mr Collins reached a point of certain recovery on Tuesday afternoon, which Mr Jones indicated and Mr Collins himself confirmed by the return of his energies and appetite. We had him downstairs to dine that very evening, although he was urged to bed soon after.

Then, this morning at breakfast as we were all gathered, Mr Collins approached my mother with the particular wish of having a private audience with me. You may imagine my surprise! But the request was granted, and so I met him in the drawing room to hear what he might say.

Mr Collins began very solemnly by thanking me for my kindness to him during his illness and immediately followed this acknowledgement by expressing his belief that my gentleness in taking to nurse-care and my attentiveness to the comforts of a relative stranger could only endear me to his parishioners and to his patroness. He then concluded by offering me his proposal of marriage.

What could I do, after seven and twenty years without offer and without hope of useful employment, but tender my acceptance? And so it was done, and at half past ten this morning, I became an engaged woman.

I can well imagine what you are thinking now, Eliza, but when you have had time to consider it, I hope you will be satisfied with what I have done. I am not romantic, you know. I never was. I ask only for a comfortable home, and considering Mr Collins's character, connexions, and situation in life, I am convinced that my chance of happiness with him is as fair as most anyone can boast upon entering the married state.

Elizabeth's astonishment was so profound that she could not help but press a hand to her mouth and let the letter fall to her plate.

"Lizzy, what is this?" demanded her mother. "What news? I

see by the hand it is from Miss Lucas, is it not? What news does she have?"

"Charlotte is engaged."

"Engaged to whom? I can think of no man who has paid her particular attention. Indeed, the only gentleman the Lucases have entertained beyond the usual neighbourhood has been—" She hit upon it. "Why, is it Mr Collins?"

"Yes, it is most unexpected," said Elizabeth hollowly. Elizabeth immediately understood that her friend had lowered herself to agree to marry a man so humiliatingly ridiculous as to never merit any consideration. Such a man! So little sense! Such misery she foresaw for Charlotte! It was too much.

It was also too much for Mrs Bennet. "Engaged to Mr Collins! What! And it was just this past week that he declined to offer for you! Oh that artful girl! She has managed to turn his eye, and she will someday be mistress of Longbourn!"

A look of despondency overtook Mrs Bennet's countenance as the last of her hopes was extinguished. "I had always cherished the thought that a daughter of mine might one day inherit my place." After this admission, she became nearly pensive, and the quiet was unlike her.

"We may at least be happy that he has chosen a woman who has the willingness and aptitude to help in both the house and estate," Elizabeth offered. "Charlotte does not want for abilities, and she is sensible almost to a fault. Mr Collins could do far worse."

"That Lucas girl is clever, I grant you. But he could have done better, had he not been a fool," Mrs Bennet replied sourly. "Oh, but I still cannot be pleased that there are to be no more Bennets at Longbourn! It feels a twice failure on my part."

Perceiving some reawakened grief in her mother, Elizabeth could only pat her hand before that unhappy matron rose and left the table.

THE SUBSEQUENT TWO DAYS PROCEEDED IN A subdued way, but on Monday morning, brighter prospects for enjoyment arrived in two forms: the return of the Gardiners' children and a note from Miss Darcy, brought to their door by a smartly liveried footman.

The first effect was immediate and widely pronounced, for the playful distraction the children provided at their home-coming rendered even Mrs Bennet more cheerful. The second impacted Elizabeth's feelings and the preparations of Mrs Gardiner as hostess once Elizabeth shared with her the most salient part of the message in Miss Darcy's missive.

"'My brother is to arrive in London within a day. I hope I do not impose, for I had hoped to prevail upon him to attend me so that I may call upon you in Gracechurch Street. He has promised to do his duty and perform an introduction to you at last,'" read Mrs Gardiner aloud, her eyes wide.

"To have such people as the Darcys calling upon us! I should never have imagined it, but we shall make them very welcome, Elizabeth, I assure you. Mr Darcy and his sister shall be given every honour."

"Thank you, Aunt. I shall be as helpful to you today as I can, for there has been such a change in the house."

"I imagine Mr and Miss Darcy may forgive us for a little disorder," said Mrs Gardiner. "They are aware of our circum-stances, and we need not feel ashamed of them."

Elizabeth glanced around the little parlour, watching the children chattering away in excited tones with Jane, while the littlest one clambered about on her lap. The picture their little company presented was very dear.

"No, indeed, we need not," she agreed softly.

THE HOUR FOR CALLERS ARRIVED THE NEXT DAY, AND Elizabeth listened with anticipation for the sounds of visitors in the front hall. In these moments of quiet, she thanked her good fortune that only an hour earlier, her mother had seen fit to take Jane shopping with her two youngest sisters in tow. Because she and Mary had been in the midst of directing Rebecca's piano lesson, they had been allowed to remain in the house.

It was only after Elizabeth had put the music sheets away that she heard her guests announced. She was glad to find her aunt readying herself where she stood across the room, tucking away a work basket and smoothing her gown.

Footsteps and voices approached, and at last she saw Miss Darcy. It was an odd thing after their brief correspondence to behold her much-imagined friend standing within the aperture of her aunt's parlour door. Miss Darcy was, and was not, as Elizabeth had pictured her. Elizabeth had conjectured she would be somewhat tall and that her eyes would likely be dark, but the golden tones of her light brown hair, the straight, yet unremarkable line of her nose, and the round, doe-like eyes of the girl were unexpected, for they were fashioned so unlike Mr Darcy's.

As the young lady held her brother's arm, Elizabeth saw in her posture an endearingly familiar stiffness—an aloofness softened by the near inscrutable expression of anxious shyness about the girl's eyes. She was indeed Mr Darcy's sister. Elizabeth could be nothing but welcoming to her.

"Miss Darcy, what a true pleasure!" she declared, coming forward as Mr Darcy offered the introduction. She gave her newest friend her hand, which was accepted and squeezed with evident delight. The two ladies curtseyed as one to each other while thus connected.

"Miss Elizabeth, I am so pleased, so delighted to meet you at last," she managed to say with a slight blush at her own eagerness. Her entire being seemed to beam and tremble as her stiffness flowed away from her in a rush of relief and happiness.

"It seems as though I have known you a long time," Elizabeth observed, "but yet, how good it is to see your face at last!"

"I feel the same," said Miss Darcy.

"Am I, then, as you imagined me?" asked Elizabeth playfully. "Your brother, I am sure, did his best to warn you that I am nothing remarkable to look at, but I should hope, at least, that he has prepared you for my tendency towards impertinence. It is my most distinguishing feature."

Silent and smiling in his observance until now, Mr Darcy chuckled and shook his head, while Miss Darcy looked up at him in alarmed confusion.

"Oh no! My brother certainly never said—and he would never say anything of the sort—and it is not so! I declare, you are very pretty!"

Elizabeth squeezed Miss Darcy's hand again in comfort and apology before she released it. She fought to stifle an urge to laugh. "I was only teasing you. But I shall not do so again until you have gotten used to my ways if it makes you uneasy. I am sure your brother would never say anything ungentlemanly of me to you."

"Indeed not," seconded Mr Darcy.

Elizabeth let further opportunity to vex him pass. Her heart was too much in bloom to offer thorns, so glad was she to see him. Taking a breath, she turned back to her new friend.

"Well, now I shall endeavour to prove that I can be perfectly well-bred, since I have already shown myself at my most incorrigible. Allow me to introduce you to my aunt."

In a few moments it was done, and Mrs Gardiner invited Miss Darcy to sit between herself and Elizabeth on the sofa, while Mr Darcy settled into Mr Gardiner's reading chair.

Miss Darcy, being in possession of a share of knowledge of the family through Elizabeth and her brother's letters, entered into conversation readily. Within a quarter of an hour, she seemed quite at home, and when Rebecca and Mary joined them, she regaled her new friends with a few recollections of her earliest lessons at the piano.

"I began my first pieces very simply, mostly with traditional carols and such as you might do, Miss Rebecca. I then moved on to the fashionable pieces you hear at most gatherings, where ladies exhibit what they have learned at home. It has only been lately that I have begun to experiment with the modern German composers."

"And do you much prefer those pieces?" asked Mary, with sudden interest.

Mary was not to be answered, for Mrs Bennet then returned with Jane, Kitty, and Lydia in a flurry of bright muslin and woollen wraps.

"Oh my dear sister, I do not know how you manage these London streets! The bustle is frightful!" Mrs Bennet exclaimed, before coming to a halt in the middle of the room at the sight of Mr Darcy in the chair and a young lady on the sofa. "Why, forgive me, I did not know you had company."

"You find us with a delightful pair of callers," said Mrs Gardiner smoothly. "May I introduce Miss Darcy to you? Mr Darcy, I believe you know."

Upon completing the requisite introductions, the Bennet ladies sought places to better admire the expensive cut and fabric of Miss Darcy's gown.

"I adore the trimming on your sleeves," declared Lydia, studying her new acquaintance with an unmistakable mixture of envy and awe.

"We have just come from the modiste, Miss Darcy," explained Jane. "We were looking at trimming for some items in my trousseau. With my sister and Mr Darcy as your informants, I am sure you must have heard that I am to marry your brother's good friend Mr Bingley."

"Yes, he did tell me of your happy news. I heartily wish you joy. I am sure you will be very happy. Mr Bingley is a fine man."

Jane replied in pleasant agreement, and Mrs Bennet, too

excited by the subject of the wedding, decided she must add to the conversation.

"He is so amiable and so good to my dear Jane! So patient, too, with all the arrangements we must make, for it is hard to plan a wedding, being so far from home."

"I imagine so," replied Miss Darcy. After a moment, she added, "I was very sorry to hear of the fire at your home. Are you all in good health now?"

"You are the sweetest child!" exclaimed Mrs Bennet brightly. "We are all well, although there have been discomforts and shifting about here and there as a consequence of being taken in by friends and family. I find it all so unsettling, but then Mr Bingley and my dear brother Gardiner and his wife have been so good to us."

"It has been a joy having the house so full of company," answered Mrs Gardiner, reaching for the pot to refresh Miss Darcy's tea and to serve the new arrivals. "There is no shortage of companionship to be found, and it is so agreeable to have family with us at Christmas."

Turning to Miss Darcy, she poured a little more and asked, "Do you and your brother often entertain family and friends during the Christmas season?"

Miss Darcy blushed. "I am not an accomplished hostess, but I have an aunt who is very much inclined to host parties with family and friends to which we are often invited. My brother sees many friends as well. I am not yet out, and so I am not much in wider company."

"Not yet out!" exclaimed Lydia. "The injustice! Why, you must be at least a year older than I am. I cannot imagine the fun you are missing, and what fine beaux you could have."

"That may be," acceded Miss Darcy, "but I confess the prospect terrifies me a little—being out for one's first Season in London, I mean. You must tell me what it is like to come out in Hertfordshire, Miss Lydia."

Such an entreaty could not but charm Lydia back into good spirits. "La, one only has to dress for and attend a local assembly and prepare a dance card. The ladies who are out will introduce you to those around the hall, and if you greet the men you meet with a smile, you need only wait for your card to fill!"

"Lydia," whispered Elizabeth in a cautioning tone.

Miss Darcy blinked in surprise at such candour. "I thank you, Miss Lydia."

Mr Darcy cleared his throat. "Ladies, I am glad we could visit you today, but I am sure your family will desire to rest after their outing this morning," he said evenly. "It might be best if we were to take our leave of you until a more convenient time."

Miss Darcy rose at once. "It was a pleasure meeting all of you," she said. She turned to smile at Elizabeth as she dropped a curtsey, which was returned by each of the ladies in the room. Her brother bowed in his turn.

Catching her brother's eye, Miss Darcy turned one last time to Elizabeth and Mrs Gardiner and offered, "We would be glad to receive you at any time. You are very welcome."

"We would be glad to call on you, Miss Darcy," replied Elizabeth with warmth. She and her aunt curtseyed again in acknowledgement of the honour.

Miss Darcy gave her farewells and took her brother's arm.

When they had gone, Lydia hurried across the room to the window facing the street.

"I did not see their carriage when we came in, but look—it is drawing up now! How fine it is!"

Elizabeth would not be reduced to gawking out of windows, but she did glance. It was a very fine conveyance, but the gleaming paint was spotted with more dirt than one might suppose three or four miles across the city might merit. Had Mr Darcy come straight from his journey from Netherfield to bring his sister to meet her?

The supposition teased at her hopes and her vanity, but at her aunt's approach, Elizabeth hastily put aside her speculation.

"That went rather well, do you not think?" said Mrs Gardiner, sounding pleased. "I should never have imagined growing up in Lambton and glimpsing Pemberley from afar that I would one day host the Darcys in my own sitting room."

"And Miss Darcy was a sweet sort of girl," opined Kitty. "Not at all what I thought. She was not haughty in the least, though she likely has a larger dowry than Miss Bingley! I should like to see more of her."

"Oh yes!" agreed Lydia. "The next time we go shopping, we should invite her. Did you not see the lace on her sleeves? I have never seen the like. What fine taste she must have!"

"She must visit a most exclusive modiste," added Mrs Bennet.

Mary sounded wistful when she declared, "Oh, but if only I could hear her exhibit on the pianoforte! I heard Miss Bingley speak of her talent. I have not had the chance to hear something by the modern German composers, but I understand so much of it is astoundingly complex. It would take someone of great skill to master one of their pieces, I should think."

Elizabeth could only smile. "Perhaps you may have such opportunities, for our winter here may be long. Miss Darcy is indeed a very kind young lady, so she may indulge you. But do have a care, and pray do not overwhelm her! We have only just had a call from her today."

CHAPTER TWENTY-FIVE

*N*o less eager herself to return the call, Elizabeth was happy for the privilege to attend Miss Darcy on Thursday at the Darcys' elegant home on Grosvenor Street. When she was ushered inside with Mrs Gardiner, she beheld a foyer with richly framed landscapes on the walls. The long, clerestory windows with their billowy curtains pulled in the light and made the marble tile gleam as it spread out beneath a graceful spiralling staircase. As Mrs Gardiner helped to divest Elizabeth of her wraps and pass them to a waiting servant, Elizabeth took a moment to glance upward and admire the painted ceiling that swept into the leaded glass skylight above the curving stairs. Every view she had of the house spoke of serenity as much as style, and it pleased her.

When they were brought to Miss Darcy's charming sitting room, Elizabeth found both siblings waiting to receive them by a glowing fireplace. She was also delighted to find that Mr Darcy seemed once again eager to further the budding friendship between his sister and herself. Once they had opportunity to be introduced to the very genteel Mrs Annesley, Miss Darcy's companion, Mr Darcy himself led the conversation. He introduced the topic of theatre, which could only lead to the comparisons such a subject invites—plays seen and read, comedies versus tragedies, actors of differing merits and acclaim, and the plots that appealed to each of the room's occupants.

"I confess myself surprised to hear you are a lover of some of the tragedies, Miss Elizabeth," said Miss Darcy after Elizabeth had named a few of her favourites. "You seem someone who would enjoy comedies instead, as you have said you 'dearly love to laugh'."

Elizabeth was thoughtful for a moment. "There is something rather more substantial in tragedies, I think. Although I do own that comedies often make me laugh, I find the lovers' quarrels and the absurd plots in so many of them to be jarringly contrived in comparison to real life."

"How so?" challenged Mr Darcy.

"Need I mention an example like *A Midsummer Night's Dream*?" Elizabeth answered wryly, as she turned her face towards his. "The constant interference of fairies renders the story completely ridiculous—including that memorable moment when one character grows a pair of donkey ears —all of which seems a contrivance to court laughter rather than portray an accurate tale of courtship and its follies."

Mr Darcy sat back a little in his wingback chair and folded his arms. "Is not revelry in the ridiculous the essential point of comedy?"

Elizabeth lifted her chin but smiled at his casual confidence. "*Commedia,* as I understand it, was first presented in poetic form and was meant to depict the authentic foibles of humanity. Farce twists it to the point of absurd spectacle, and that is what I see in many plays, especially the newer ones I have read."

"*Commedia* was much bandied about as a word by Dante in his time, yet it has an older definition. *Komoidia*, from the ancient Greeks, refers to an 'amusing spectacle'. And so from its inception farce, as you call it, and comedy are one and the same. I cannot see the discrepancy."

Miss Darcy gave a timid sigh of relief as her brother settled back in his seat in satisfaction. She looked to Mrs Annesley with uncertainty, perhaps for help in changing the topic of discussion, but Elizabeth, not yet willing to concede, exerted herself for one last sally.

"I may not be able to call upon ancient Greek etymology in my defence," Elizabeth rebutted with a tart look, "but I believe Aristotle could. I have read my father's translations of his work. He gives evidence that comedy as an art ran parallel to tragedy, and likewise had its purpose in purifying us of certain faults in our nature through ridicule, rather than the pity and terror utilised in tragedy. Would it not then follow that those faults that are ridiculed should at least bear some semblance to our everyday life?"

The dimple in his cheek twitched a moment before Mr Darcy responded. "You have made a rather apt argument. If tragedy must be realistic to be truly heart-breaking, so comedy must also have realistic portrayals of folly to achieve true humour. At times, I too have struggled to find amusement in the farcical elements of comedy that tend to be ridiculous. It is far more humorous to see portrayed some shocking and true portraits of the realities of our experience."

Elizabeth sat a little taller on the plush sofa as she sensed her success. "And so you find truth in the adage, *Castigat ridendo mores*. For how can we correct our customs or our characters, unless we point out their absurdity and laugh at them? But I forget to whom I speak, for you are not an object to be laughed at!"

Mr Darcy seized the harmless barb and sent it back. "Are you not laughing at me now, Miss Elizabeth? Am I mistaken?"

"If I am laughing, it is only because I have learnt the nature of comedy. *Sic probo*, Mr Darcy," replied Elizabeth with a mischievous grin.

Mr Darcy gave her a look of eloquent exasperation.

This exchange had made Miss Darcy turn a little pale, and even Mrs Gardiner was on the verge of saying something to smooth any unsettled spirits when Mr Darcy quite suddenly began to laugh.

"And so you use more Latin to crow your victory!" he objected in the midst of his mirth. "If my Greek must be banned, that cannot be permitted. Fairness demands it, especially since you have bested me again."

Elizabeth, having now seen the alarmed looks from her female companions, at once retired with a soft protest. "I did not think we were in any contest, sir."

"Well, Miss Darcy," said Mrs Gardiner in a decided change of topic, "you mentioned yesterday that you have a beautiful pianoforte that you practise upon here at Darcy House. Might we importune you to see it?"

"What a lovely idea," said Miss Darcy with relief. "Let us go there now. Brother, I hope you will excuse us. We ladies may tarry there some time, as there is music I would like to show to Miss Elizabeth. I know you are very busy today."

Mr Darcy opened his mouth to object, but he realised he could not gracefully protest his sister's surprising dismissal. Masking his disappointment, he rose with the ladies, bowed to them, and wished them good day. But as he turned from the room, he determined he would enquire later as to why Georgiana had sought to separate him from their company.

IN THE COMING DAYS, DARCY'S CONCERNS OF ESTATE often detained him due in large measure to his long autumn sojourn in Hertfordshire. He was therefore bound to bear the burden of frustration when he could not take Georgiana to Gracechurch Street for another call, as his appointments of business crowded his calendar at every acceptable hour.

But his sister gave him to know that while she felt perfectly comfortable calling with Mrs Annesley, Miss Elizabeth had also offered to call again at Darcy House early the following week. This intelligence yielded a prospect which Darcy looked forward to as much as his sister.

Having Elizabeth in his home—perching on his sofa, sipping her tea from his mother's favourite china—had given Darcy a strange satisfaction. By contrast, her departure from his house after that first visit had unsettled him more than he should like. Her continued absence created a discomfiting sensation of hollowness that permeated his being, a loss alarmingly impossible to ignore.

He recognised within these pangs the symptoms of a growing appetite for contact with her. When they had been at Netherfield after the disaster, Darcy had a daily opportunity not only to speak to Elizabeth exclusively and to linger closely in her company, but also to find ready excuses to make a physical connexion—to offer her his arm as they walked, to brush his shoulder against hers when they sat at table, and twice, to take her in his arms to assist her—and on that one, unforgettable occasion when he had been able to caress her bare arm to rouse her from her dreams in the library. From these interactions, his senses had gained pleasing knowledge of the softness of Elizabeth's skin, the intoxicating scent of her hair, the arresting suppleness of her figure, and the delicate, fine-boned lattice of her frame coupled with her surprising strength.

Darcy now grieved the loss of such chances to touch her again—and not only for reasons of selfish gratification. He also repined the loss because those moments had manifested a real tenderness between them—a tenderness that he hoped might, in time, cause Elizabeth to open her heart to him. Now he had only one mode of persuasion to transform her admiration for him into real affection, and that was through her favoured mode of discourse: contentious flirtation. Given his habits of guarded reticence as well as the continual presence of others in their meetings, he knew this sort of wooing might prove the most difficult of all.

When Darcy arrived home the following Monday from his solicitor's office to discover that Elizabeth had visited that very morning while he was out, he could not conceal his disappointment. He had missed a chance meeting.

"Fitzwilliam, you are not unhappy that I spent the morning with Miss Elizabeth, are you?" asked Georgiana.

"No, no, dearest. Not at all," he assured her. "I am glad you are friends. I only wish I could have seen the two of you together. I am sure you had an enjoyable time."

"We certainly did! Mrs Annesley and I were delighted to find that Miss Elizabeth has a beautiful singing voice, and so we made up some rather clever arrangements for duets for her to practise with me. She insisted I do most of the playing, for she swears her skill at the pianoforte is not equal to mine, although I see nothing to the assertion. Our styles differ, that is all. But I was pleased not to have to sing in company, for her voice is by far superior to mine in sweetness and expression. There was some beautiful music when we rehearsed, which pleased us both."

Darcy could well imagine such scenes, for they beckoned feelings of longing within him. "You will have to contrive a way to perform together for me, Georgiana, for I am so sorry to have missed it," he said with regret.

"Of course! I am sure Miss Elizabeth will not mind indulging you. She did ask after your health and was so kind as to wish you a good day, if I would convey it," his sister babbled happily.

"That was thoughtful of her," said he, swallowing and casting about for a subject that caused him less distress.

His sister's questing gaze seemed to speak sympathy. "I thought such attention to you very kind indeed, since I know she seemed upset during your last conversation with her."

Darcy felt an immediate stab of alarm. "Upset?"

"Yes! Why, she even went so far as to argue with you when you spoke against her. I could see she was upset. That is why I took her to the music room with Mrs Gardiner. Did you not think she seemed perturbed?"

Darcy had to restrain himself from laughing, for he could easily recall Elizabeth's sly smiles and her cheerful victory. "Dearest, I think you mistake her nature. Elizabeth loves a good debate as much as I do."

His casual use of her name, which he unthinkingly overlooked, gave Georgiana pause. "She does?" she asked.

"Hers is a very lively nature, and such debates please her spirits and exercise her mind, which as you have seen, is oftentimes more nimble than mine."

"So, you were not—you were not arguing?"

"No, we were merely taking up a debate with an understanding that we both have an affinity for the amusement. She has sometimes endeavoured to strike up such arguments with me before, merely for our mutual entertainment."

"So, Miss Elizabeth was never angry with you? And you were never angry with her?"

"Not at all! I confess to you, Georgiana, that all I ever felt towards her was admiration, even as she all but threw Aristotle and Santeuil in my face."

His sister's thoughtful gaze returned, and with it came a slow smile of understanding. "You do admire her, do you not?"

Darcy could feel himself colouring. To discuss such a thing with his little sister! Yet, as he looked at her, he realised that he could do far worse than to take on Georgiana as an ally.

"Yes. Well—no, that is not the word," he replied, rising from his chair and pacing to the window. For a moment, he was silent. When he turned back to his sister, he saw her brow crinkle in confusion. She looked up at him in silent appeal.

He could not hold back his answer. "I do not admire Elizabeth. I utterly adore her."

CHAPTER TWENTY-SIX

The Bennet family had more opportunities to meet the Gardiners' acquaintance than they had perhaps presumed. Among these callers, of course, came Mr Bingley, who could now hardly bear any separation from his beloved. His visits became so constant and so welcome that Mrs Gardiner got in the habit of preparing his coffee before he even raised the knocker on their door.

On one such morning, Mr Bingley arrived only moments before the Darcys' carriage pulled up on the street. Mrs Gardiner directed her maid to bring out more cups and saucers, and she hurriedly tasked her children with removing their toys from the parlour rug to the nursery.

The Darcys paid no mind to the disorderliness of the children. Indeed, Miss Darcy seemed to enjoy their curiosity and even welcomed the overtures of young Rebecca, who asked her for advice on what to attempt next on the pianoforte. Mr Darcy smiled indulgently as the youngest Master Gardiner rolled a toy wagon full of soldiers right under his chair.

Elizabeth was smothering a chuckle at the scene when Miss

Darcy turned to her, fidgeting nervously. "I hesitated at first to ask this, but then I reminded myself of your ease in company, Miss Elizabeth. And my brother, of course, has approved."

Elizabeth raised her gaze to Miss Darcy expectantly as the girl pulled at her gloves. It was clear Miss Darcy was quite apprehensive, so she gave the girl her most encouraging smile.

"On Thursday, Fitzwilliam will be out to the opera and a dinner party. Mrs Annesley has planned to spend the evening dining with her sister. I should love to have a companion for the evening at Darcy House, at least through supper, since Mrs Annesley will return late. Would you mind spending the evening with me, Miss Elizabeth? We shall be quite left to ourselves, but I am sure we shall find some means of entertainment and dinner besides."

"I shall be delighted to join you! I am certain that my kind aunt can spare me for one evening."

Miss Darcy beamed as Mr Darcy expressed his pleasure that all was settled, and he offered to send a carriage for Elizabeth.

"There will be no need," Mrs Gardiner said once she had heard the plan. "On Thursday, Mr Gardiner and I shall be dining with his business associate Mr Burns and his family. It will be no trouble for us to take you to dine with Miss Darcy and then to collect you afterwards. Would that be agreeable, sir?"

"Most agreeable," answered Mr Darcy, looking quite satisfied. "And on behalf of my sister and myself, I thank you."

ON THE EVENING OF THE YOUNG LADIES' DINNER, Elizabeth shivered as she stepped down from the Gardiners' hired conveyance and made her way up the fine stone steps to the door of Darcy House where her young hostess and a fire welcomed her warmly.

"We shall keep a wary eye out for the weather," Mr

Gardiner declared. "There looks to be a promise of rain or perhaps snow, cold as it now grows. I should like to return to collect Elizabeth before ten, in any event."

Miss Darcy expressed her agreement, and upon bidding farewell to the Gardiners, took Elizabeth by the hand and fairly raced with her to the pianoforte to engage in her favourite duet before dinner.

Elizabeth not only had the delight of playing her part in the score far better than before, but she also had the privilege of hearing more details of Pemberley as they sat down to dinner.

"Although I have been to some grand houses, I maintain that Pemberley is the most beautifully situated home in all of England! Whenever I am in town, I find myself missing my quiet summers there—the streams and the lake, the hills and the woods, our lovely conservatory, and all my favourite servants. Mrs Reynolds is our housekeeper there, and after my mother died, she had far more of a hand in raising me than any governess I ever had and with more real affection. Pemberley has always been my happiest home. I do hope you will come to visit me there sometime!"

"With such a commendation, I can hardly refuse!" Elizabeth laughed. "You have described my chief enjoyment at any estate—a beautiful park—with such brilliance that I can scarcely wait. A happy home is a beautiful home, in my opinion, but I am sure that Pemberley has its beauties of architecture besides."

"Oh yes, and my brother has given me so much liberty in setting up and decorating my own apartments. I quite adore my rooms. And while the house's scale may be grand, it looks far more harmonious in its surrounds than some of the imposing manors I have seen. They seem to be made enormous on purpose, so as to dwarf their surrounds and any visitors besides."

Elizabeth continued to quiz Miss Darcy on the house's

history and the delights of the Peaks surrounding it, only to declare, "You will quite make me fall in love with all that Derbyshire has to offer!"

Their pleasant evening of food and sweets and music continued until the clock tolled the hour that should have brought the Gardiners to the house to reclaim their niece. When another half an hour advanced, Elizabeth expressed her concern.

"I do believe that we may have had some rain," said Miss Darcy. "I thought I heard a tapping on the roof when we went up to the gallery to see the sketches I made of Pemberley."

"They might have been delayed, then," said Elizabeth. "I hope I do not inconvenience you."

"Never, never!" she declared stoutly. "You are welcome to stay however long you wish. I have no pressing engagements beyond my own bed."

At this, Elizabeth suggested they attempt another piece she spotted as a duet. It was one she had once practised, so she felt readily prepared to attempt either the top or bottom line. Another three-quarters of an hour's amusement commenced, until at a pause to reshuffle the music to start again, they heard some clamouring from the great doors in the hall.

"Ah, that must be my aunt and uncle," Elizabeth surmised. "I imagine they must be fatigued. I should hurry home, but do not mistake my eagerness to depart for anything but compassion for my tired relations. I have enjoyed myself immensely this evening."

"A moment if you will," said Miss Darcy, who had gone a few steps into the hall to listen. "I hear my brother! I had thought he would be much later. Whatever can be the matter?"

Driven by curiosity, the ladies put away their music sheaves and toed lightly into the hall towards the edge of the winding staircase. On the lower landing was Mr Darcy, emerging from a swirling dark opera cloak spotted with white.

"Is it snowing?" enquired Miss Darcy.

"It is more than snow—it is ice, and it is encasing the streets as we speak. Our poor driver was beside himself keeping the horses apace and upright," said Mr Darcy, shaking out his hat from which snowflakes as well as some heavier crystals fell onto the marble floor. "Miss Elizabeth, I fear now is not the time for you to return to Gracechurch Street. I barely got home myself, and I can readily believe that many others are sheltering where they are, for the streets are shockingly empty."

Miss Darcy turned to her friend. "I share my brother's concern. I fear that even if your aunt and uncle come for you, you would all be in danger on the road. A lame horse on such a freezing night would be a disaster. I must ask you to stay on as our guest."

The offer was not unwelcome, although Elizabeth was mindful that she, with no proper chaperone beyond the houseful of servants, would stay in the home of an unmarried man—and the object of her own tender regard, no less. As *Miss Darcy's* guest, it would not be decidedly improper, but her sense of modesty made her blush as she agreed to the night's arrangements.

In short order, the Darcys' new guest had a room quite properly located next to the absent Mrs Annesley's at the far end of the family wing. As the hour grew later and Elizabeth despaired of her aunt and uncle appearing, her kind hosts urged her to retire, and she accepted the night rail Miss Darcy's abigail soon brought to her.

Elizabeth felt grateful, but for an hour she lay unsettled, and she thought she might never be able to sleep. Her commodious environs soon soothed her, for with a warm brick wrapped at her feet, and fine linens all around her, even her own fluttering heart had no recourse but to quiet into a deeper rhythm. As she exhaled a deep breath, Elizabeth shut her eyes and began to distract herself by imagining what it might be like to be one of the Darcy family, someone used to this house and its ways. She could hear maids stoking the last fires for the night, the feet of a footman bringing more wood down the hall, doors shutting softly, and the susurration of voices. She even thought she could distinguish the distant murmur of Mr Darcy's voice, which only added to her sense of comfort as she drifted deeper into her bed's downy warmth.

THERE WAS A WEAK SUN ON THE OVERCAST MORNING that followed, and Elizabeth, judging the time to be early, contemplated going back to sleep until a light knock on her door roused her to fuller awareness. A chambermaid had come to freshen the coals in the brazier and to bring a note for her. Elizabeth could only pity the poor post-boy who had been sent slipping about into the streets to bring it thither as she opened the tightly folded letter.

> *Dear Elizabeth,*
>
> *We find ourselves unwitting overnight guests at the Burnses' home. While they are as delightful hosts as yours may be, we are aware that your situation is regrettably discomfiting and will seek to remedy it as quickly as we are able and the weather allows. Please express our gratitude to Miss Darcy for your safety and comfort.*
>
> *With greatest apologies,*
> *Your loving aunt and uncle*

Elizabeth had not expected any other news, so she could feel no disappointment—not here, where she was able to dress and breakfast in delightful comfort, and where her morning of snow-bound detention found ample sources of cheer in the company of Miss Darcy, who assumed the unusual role of her guest's teacher.

It had intimidated Elizabeth at first when a beautiful set of watercolours was shown to her, but once she understood that Miss Darcy's only expectation was that she merely experiment with the art, Elizabeth relaxed into the activity. The young ladies found much amusement at Elizabeth's disordered attempts to capture a bowl of winter apples and oranges.

Their giggling had apparently drawn the curiosity of the master of the house. Mr Darcy had endeavoured to find some morning occupation by seeing to his business correspondence in his library, but upon hearing the warm and lively company down the hall, his feet soon took him to the door of his sister's sitting room.

When Mr Darcy arrived, Elizabeth's back was to him. From there, he was able to view her work and the utter bungle she had made of the image on the cold press paper. He knocked on the doorframe and was invited in by his sister.

"I promise I shall not interrupt," he vowed solemnly. "I shall keep to the chair by the fire with my book, so I do not disturb your artistry."

Elizabeth suppressed a smile as Mr Darcy dropped into the armchair directly in her line of vision and stretched his long legs out comfortably towards the blaze in a manner so unguarded as to seem nearly boyish. Indeed, his easy, idling manner gave Elizabeth an unsettling sensation of warmth despite her own distance from the hearth.

Flustered by her response to the man, Elizabeth decided to vex him a little. "If in promising to keep still and quiet, you hope you might render yourself so easy a subject as to inspire me to attempt your portrait, I must issue you fair warning that any impressions of your visage shall be forever disfigured." She teasingly saluted him with her brush.

"Doubtless," he agreed, turning an eye towards her dripping still life.

Elizabeth permitted herself to laugh, proving herself unscathed by his critical assessment. She bent again to her work in hopes of salvaging the image. After several fruitless attempts with both a blotter and brush, she turned to her young teacher in appeal.

"I cannot seem to control my brush well enough for the precision required. I think my fingers are simply fatigued!"

"Likely it is merely that your wrist is unused to this occupation. If it troubles you, you might take a few moments' change of activity," Miss Darcy suggested, before adding thoughtfully, "and use less water next time."

"Perhaps I should take a turn about the room," Elizabeth allowed, setting aside her tools. With a smile she added, "An acquaintance we share once told me that such an occupation was most refreshing after one has long been in one attitude."

"And who might that have been?" her hostess asked.

Mr Darcy answered her without so much as glancing up from his reading. "Miss Bingley."

"It is the only advice of hers I have ever taken to heart, I am afraid to say," replied Elizabeth with arch sweetness.

She took one last look at her sorry workmanship, then rose and meandered across the room to the window, drawn by the bright glow of whiteness without. Her breath fogged the lace of frost on the pane as she approached and stared out. It took her eyes a moment to detect the faint delineation between the pale white-grey sky from the snow on the ground, and from those planes of snow to the outlines of ice-encased trees and drift-bound outbuildings. Some of these drifts shifted minutely in swirls of windy motion, but beyond that, nothing moved without.

"It has stopped snowing," Elizabeth observed.

"Has it at last?" replied Mr Darcy.

She did not need to turn away from the window to know that he had set aside his book. She could hear the pages close and the quick rustle of his clothing as Mr Darcy rose fluidly from his chair. In moments, he was standing by her side, peering out.

"I believe I would like to go out and explore," Elizabeth announced without turning from the window.

"Out of doors?" Miss Darcy exclaimed behind her. "But it is freezing, Elizabeth! Why on earth should you wish to go?"

"*Elizabeth*, is it now?" remarked her brother slyly.

Elizabeth grinned and replied, "We must allow some informality in such circumstances. And in any case, *Georgiana*, there is much to be desired in such an outing! Have you never wished to amble into heavy snow and feel its resistance like deep water? To see trees encased in ice as thick and clear as glass? To explore a drift like the snowy summit of a mountain? To slide your feet on ice like a swan landing on a pond?"

"Only if I could be guaranteed that I could stay warm! I hate to be cold!"

"Oh, but it is worth the endeavour," declared Elizabeth passionately, "if only to be in fresh air for a few minutes."

"Why, you make it sound like an adventure," Georgiana replied, before turning to Mr Darcy in appeal. "What say you, brother?"

"The cold does not bother me," he replied, a bit startled at her sudden application. "And if you had cloaks and gloves and wraps enough, and did not tarry longer than a few minutes in the back garden—and returned immediately to warm yourselves at the fire—"

"I daresay your brother is humouring us," Elizabeth interrupted, "but I am shameless enough to take advantage. Can we go now? We have the gift of the sun to help us. This may be the brightest and warmest light we may ever see today."

In a thrice, the plan took shape, and three figures in heavy wraps emerged into the ornamental garden that bordered the kitchen patch at the rear of Darcy House. There, a fairyland awaited, with dormant rose bushes shimmering in ice on every thorny spindle, and every tree's boughs creaking with the weight of ice and snow. It was quiet in the brightness of the afternoon, with hardly more noise than the clattering feet of servants now and then passing through the kitchen door.

As the ladies meandered arm-in-arm ahead of Mr Darcy, now and again Georgiana squealed as her boots landed afoul of the icy path. Elizabeth cheered her with encouragement as she steadied her.

"I am not in the habit of dancing over icy pavers, you know. I have skated on our pond at Pemberley, however. Have you ever worn skates, Elizabeth?"

"Oh no! My mother absolutely forbade it. She had a dreadful fall as a girl, and I think her nerves would never withstand it if one of her daughters did the same. But, as you may imagine, I have always wished to enjoy the experience!"

Elizabeth let go of her friend's arm and, spying a flat paver, slid her feet experimentally across the icy surface. She allowed herself a wobble, just to tease her friend, who watched her with widened eyes. Elizabeth laughed, and the sound echoed.

The rear of the garden was bordered by beautiful stone walls and a heavy gate that hindered the view from those in the neighbouring row of houses. The young ladies ambled towards it as they chattered through clouds of breath. As Elizabeth turned to peek through a chink in the stone bordering the gate, she noticed Mr Darcy looking over the top of the wall.

"Should the streets stay impassable to riding mounted, I wonder now about calling on foot on a neighbour, a widow, who lives just that way." Mr Darcy tilted his head to the east. "The lower level of that fine house has been let to her. It may be the sole kindness her estranged son has sought to provide for his mother. I have found Mrs Jamieson lives quite meagrely, despite the fine trappings around her. I do not know if her servants have put aside anything for such an event as this."

Elizabeth at once felt ashamed that her only thoughts had been for their amusement during their wintry confinement. Those pitiful poor would surely suffer from it and, of course, they ought to do something for them!

Georgiana, attuned to her brother's mind in like kindness, suggested a basket for the good lady. Mr Darcy seconded this with his concern that Mrs Jamieson get enough firewood to last her through this spell.

When the ladies returned inside, red-cheeked and pulling at their wraps, Mr Darcy rang for his butler and made known his wish to visit his elderly neighbour.

"See that Mrs Gaines puts together a basket from the larder, Hainsbrook, and have John make up a litter with firewood—whatever is suitable from the dry storage."

"Yes, sir," said Hainsbrook. He bowed and extended his gloved hands to take the ladies' wrappings. "Shall I summon a boy and a footman, sir? It could be sent over with two easily enough."

"One footman is all I require. I shall await him here, as I am already dressed for the outing. The back gate will serve."

At the realisation that he meant to call on the woman himself, Georgiana began in a worried tone, "Brother—"

She stilled when he reached over and put a hand on hers. At that moment, a footman arrived, as though summoned by magic.

Mr Darcy regarded him impassively, standing silently as the footman bowed. He was a tall young man and sturdy of build in his felted livery, but as Mr Darcy continued to regard him, to Elizabeth's eye, the footman's proportions seemed to diminish a little in his master's presence, for Mr Darcy looked very grand in his great black coat.

"Davis, Mrs Gaines will prepare a basket for Mrs Jamieson

at the end of the street, and John is putting together a litter with kindling. As soon as they are finished, you are to report to me. Dress warmly. We shall go together to ensure that Mrs Jamieson is not in distress."

Once the footman was gone, Mr Darcy dismissed his butler with a gesture. As he turned to face the young women, Elizabeth could see that his expression was utterly unperturbed, as though this sort of kindness, this lordly mastery of household and self, were merely a part of his unconscious grace, a mere touching of the cloak of the greater power he wore.

As he stood both lofty and easy in his slick boots, Elizabeth could not help but reflect on how differently he had seemed to her in Hertfordshire. There, he had been a gentleman of quality, above her neighbours in many ways but rendered by his reserve as separate and remote. Here, in his domain at Darcy House, he was more than a gentleman. To his adoring servants, he was more than master. He was a benevolent deity in his realm.

Within a short time, he had left with the footman into yet another volley of snow, carrying a heavy basket.

Elizabeth turned to Georgiana with a sigh. "Well, I suppose now we must find some amusement with which to entertain ourselves."

"I believe I know just what to do."

Thus passed an agreeable hour—then two, then nearly three. When the clock chimed seven, Georgiana ordered a light supper tray to be brought up with some hot tea. "Surely my brother will be home soon. I will ask for another meal when he arrives. No doubt he will be hungry again from the exertion and the cold."

"You are a dear sister to take such good care of him," Elizabeth remarked.

As the two young ladies returned to their previous conversation and shuffled the magazines and fashion plates into some form of order, Elizabeth could not help but notice how often her friend's eye settled anxiously on the clock. It was a quarter past the hour, and it was very dark beyond the tall window drapes.

"Perhaps Mrs Jamieson is simply lonely and keeping them captive for companionship," Elizabeth quipped.

"Perhaps," said Georgiana, "but what if my brother fell? The ice is so treacherous!"

"Not likely, I should think. Come, my dear, all this worrying will not hurry him home. Shall we practise a song or two while we wait for him?"

Georgiana readily acceded to this suggestion. They were halfway through the second movement of one of Georgiana's favourite pieces when they heard an unceremonious bang from the kitchen door downstairs.

"He is home!" Georgiana exclaimed, leaping up. "Come, Elizabeth! Surely he is frozen! Of what have I been thinking? I should have gathered blankets and stoked the fire!"

"I shall stoke it, if you can find the blankets!"

Georgiana flew out the door. When she entered again, it was with her windswept brother on one arm and a mound of blankets in the other.

"Come in, come in! You will catch your death! Your face is still so very red!" Georgiana said.

Mr Darcy rubbed his hands and blew on them. "Is the fire still high?" he asked, and then he turned and saw Elizabeth bending to tend it. "Ah, I see you have been busy, Miss Elizabeth!" he said with appreciation.

"There is hot supper coming up, too," his sister replied breathlessly as she nearly pushed her brother's large frame into the wingback chair by the hearth. "Now stay still a moment," Georgiana commanded, piling him with blankets. "Would you like a brick for your feet?"

"Certainly! Hainsbrook took away my boots as soon as I walked in and put me in slippers. I still cannot feel my toes."

Elizabeth dutifully removed a hearthstone with the tongs and dropped it on another blanket, rolling it into a fine, warm cushion for his feet.

As he settled in with almost comical contentment, Mr Darcy muttered, "Ah, ladies, what have I done to merit such care and attention?"

"What have you *not* done?" mused his sister sweetly, pressing a tray of warm food into his lap.

"Mrs Jamieson was indeed glad for the visit," Mr Darcy reported, as he lifted the cover off an ecuelle of soup. "She was quite unprepared for this storm. Her house was decidedly cold. It gave me satisfaction to ensure she had a hot blaze going in the fireplace by the time I left."

"Then I am glad you went," said Georgiana, who had settled another tray of dainties before herself and Elizabeth.

After finishing his meal and taking some hot tea as he listened to the ladies' reassurances that their evening passed well despite their concern for his safety, Mr Darcy soon appeared drowsy.

At a lull in their conversation, he noted the time, and with a look aimed at his sister, he softly urged the ladies to their beds. Georgiana gathered her skirts as she rose and wished her brother a goodnight, her eyes drifting to Elizabeth in invitation to join her.

Elizabeth stood, but Mr Darcy forestalled their guest by rising from his chair with a sudden gesture towards Elizabeth, all while nodding his sister onward in her retreat.

"It shall only be a moment. Just a word," Mr Darcy reassured her.

Once Georgiana had gone above stairs, he addressed Elizabeth. "I must tell you the other pertinent goal of my errand. Mrs Jamieson, as I mentioned, has been provided with all her comforts for the night ahead. However, given my long acquaintance with the widow, I took an additional liberty and gave her to know that her presence as a respectable companion in my home tomorrow would be invaluable, as a certain young lady has been stranded here by the storm. I hope you do not think I overstepped, but nothing seems to delight Mrs Jamieson more than proving useful. I will send a sledge down to collect her in the morning if you approve the scheme."

Elizabeth was astonished. She coloured and bit her lip. "I should hate to have word get out about my circumstances here, when our isolation so far has been to my benefit."

"As you may imagine, given her reduced circumstances, Mrs Jamieson no longer traverses fashionable circles. You will find her quite frank in her character, yet she is unlikely to gossip. I do think she was in earnest in wishing to return my kindness with some contribution of her own."

"If Mrs Jamieson has merited your trust, then I am happy to accept her aid," Elizabeth said. "It will ease my mind if your servants and my own relatives can vouch that you quickly added a respectable chaperone to join me."

"Whatever can add to your comfort, I am vastly contented to do, Miss Elizabeth."

The sincerity in his voice should have reassured her despite the embarrassment such a topic portended. Instead, it served as a heavy reminder of all the reasons she had to esteem him and all the ways she felt herself indebted to him. Elizabeth's voice trembled as she thanked Mr Darcy and wished him goodnight, and then she quickly quit the room.

CHAPTER TWENTY-SEVEN

*D*arcy returned to his chair by the fire, unwilling to give up the warm cocoon he had created there. Once he was comfortable again, he allowed himself the pleasure of reflection. He had seen so much today to admire in Elizabeth—and all close at hand. Her playfulness, her kindness, her boldness, and even a bit of her maidenly shyness, for she had blushed and blushed again when he spoke of the necessity of procuring a chaperone for her stay in his home. Oh, how bitter was the irony of him finally having Elizabeth so near again, yet being forced to keep apart for the sake of her reputation!

As he stretched his toes towards the blaze, Darcy gave thanks that he could at least provide comfort and shelter to her. He found satisfaction in the knowledge that at this very moment, Elizabeth was likely warm and nestled deeply into the downy softness of her coverlet, the air around her heated by the coals in the brazier in her room. In such a glow of heat, the very air would become perfumed with her scent.

In his imagination, he could envision her long, dark hair spilling about her on the soft pillow, her face rosy and sweet in sleep—a sight he could envision well, having once seen it. For an idle moment, he placed himself there with her, just beside the bed, his fingers drifting into the dark waves of her hair, pausing to trace the curve of her cheek. The pleasure of this image carried him into sleep, only to be broken by the chiming of the midnight hour in the old towering clock by the doorway. Sighing, Darcy resigned himself to his chilly bed.

THE DETERMINED, AFFABLE RESPECTABILITY OF MRS Jamieson only added to the bleakness of the widow's plight, Elizabeth decided. It was hard not to like the old woman, who treated the Darcy siblings with such indulgent, grandmotherly affection that even Georgiana had abandoned formality in her dealings with her.

Mrs Jamieson swept in shortly after breakfast in her wool pelisse and widow's weeds, her gown decorated with bright pins and tucked within a vibrantly painted shawl that Elizabeth noted was more than a little ragged. In her shadow came a younger woman who Elizabeth presumed was a domestic, carrying a band box with bare hands. She had a velvet sheen to her dusky skin and an elaborately wound turban over a riot of dark curls. This young woman took up her lady's gloves, curtseyed to Miss Darcy, and whisked away without a word of dismissal. A Darcy footman followed her upstairs with a small trunk.

As they departed, their guest looked around for a comfortable perch. "I never could stand the winters in England, you know," Mrs Jamieson said, easing herself down before the fire. "What good luck that we should have the Darcys for our neighbours these many years, for they always keep Darcy House as warm as springtime! I must thank your brother again for his indulgence, Georgiana."

"Not at all," she assured her. "It is good to have you here.

This ice and snow have kept my friend and me lonesome for more female company."

"And an old biddy would suit?" Mrs Jamieson replied, her eyes twinkling above cheeks red and round as apples. "Two young girls like yourselves must surely have no wish to hear of the troubles of the aged, not when you must settle yourselves to tending the worries and wonders of youth. Ah yes, I do remember them! Now, you must tell me about all the beaux you like and the most beautiful hats you have seen this season."

"I confess I do admire a well-trimmed winter bonnet," replied Elizabeth with equal humour, "but I am afraid I left most of the young men my sisters tend to favour behind me back at my home village of Meryton."

"You do not strike me as a girl whose heart is easily caught," observed their visitor, nodding like a sage and setting her cane carefully against the arm of the settee.

"I—" Elizabeth began, not at all sure how to respond.

"Gracious, listen to me!" tutted Mrs Jamieson. "Pulling at your secrets like that. You must swat me off when I overstep. When it is only myself and Tabitha, we must amuse ourselves with speculation on matters of the heart. You will find her quite gifted in such arts too. Did you know Tabitha has something of the second sight? She reads faces and palms nearly quite so well as Madame Lenormand, but do not hand her any cards."

Georgiana turned to her in fascination. "I have never had my fortune read. My brother says it is all stuff and nonsense."

Elizabeth laughed. "Mr Darcy has firmly styled himself a man of science, I believe, much like my own father."

"Oh, I would think so," Mrs Jamieson nodded. "Yet, how sad. So much of this world cannot be comprehended through science, you know. It must be experienced to be perceived, and alas, it cannot be measured in its value."

"I think I should like to try it," Georgiana confessed, her eyes large and eager. "Having my fortune told, I mean."

"Well then, I shall ask Tabitha," Mrs Jamieson replied before cautioning, "Mind you, she is my paid companion, not a bondwoman. I shall never compel her." The old woman nodded to a footman, who went to seek out that very woman.

Mrs Jamieson did not speak further on the matter, and conversation veered to less awkward topics until Tabitha entered the sitting room. Regal in her well-starched dress and bright turban, Tabitha might have bested Miss Bingley through her manner and cadence of speech, her tone of address, and the small yet telling expressions found in her bold features. Elizabeth could not help smiling at her, despite finding her a little fearsome.

Tabitha had chatted just long enough with Mrs Jamieson to become aware of the need for her talents. "So, you wish to have your palm read, do you, Miss Darcy?"

"Yes, um—Miss—"

"Miss Jamieson will do," Tabitha replied evenly, arching her brow and pulling out a chair for Georgiana at a table Mr Darcy favoured for cards and extensive reading.

She drew near the chair and sat, and Miss Jamieson sat opposite her. With sparkling eyes that drew in the light like two wells, Miss Jamieson examined Georgiana's face, and then she held her hand out to the younger girl across the table in a beckoning gesture that made her bracelets clack together.

Georgiana's pale, elegant fingers came to rest gently in her grasp, and for a moment, the room fell silent. Elizabeth and Mrs Jamieson both edged a bit closer.

"Such a long and soft hand, Miss Darcy. There is much water in you, both depth and sensitivity in your soul and spirit. You must feel things very keenly. And see here, at the base of your ring finger, what a wonderful conjunction of skills! You are an artist, I believe—or mayhap a musician."

When Georgiana nodded, Miss Jamieson continued. "Let us look to your history, Miss Darcy. Hmm, there is no surprise here.

By the length of your line of fortune, you come from a burden of high breeding and its expectations, but I see here in this faint break in the line that it was nearly taken from you. How very curious! Oh! Ah! I see it in your face—there, a kiss that quivers on your lips! The threat came in the guise of a lover!"

Elizabeth would have laughed at the absurdity had Georgiana not gone nearly so white as the tucker in her gown.

Elizabeth speculated wildly for a moment until, with a jolt, she recalled her discussion about Mr Wickham, and how Mr Darcy had alluded to some near harm to his sister.

Drawn by dawning understanding and then by a sense of outrage and compassion for her friend, Elizabeth settled herself against the edge of the fortune-teller's table and took Georgiana's free hand. She gave it a gentle squeeze, and Georgiana's startled eyes met hers in the next instant.

"Do not let me frighten you, Miss Darcy," Miss Jamieson broke in, tempering her voice with some alarm. "I never speak of what I discover. In any event, you are safe now, I see. Let us look instead to your future."

Georgiana nodded, releasing a breath and turning a small, grateful smile to Elizabeth.

"By these marks, you appear to have had some childhood illnesses. A weakness in constitution which you overcame. It may come to visit you again, but you must not fear it. Your vitality is sufficient to sustain your life line. And in the lines of love—ah, well, I cannot say how well your marriage does you in terms of fortune, but I doubt you need any assistance there. Your marriage seems fairly long, a nice crease here, and there is but one. You may expect to be content."

"I must say I am relieved," Georgiana said, drawing back her palm. "Thank you, Miss Jamieson."

"My pleasure, Miss Darcy," replied Miss Jamieson, settling back in her seat and smiling in satisfaction. She then turned to

Elizabeth and added an invitation. "Miss Elizabeth, is it? Might I presume you would like a reading as well?"

Elizabeth smiled in amusement, as Miss Darcy eagerly gave up her seat and pressed her into it, exclaiming, "Oh yes, you must! I am so eager to know what will become of you!"

"Very well," she acceded, extending her hand.

"Come then," said Miss Jamieson, taking it up. "Let me look at your face too."

For an unsettlingly long moment, Elizabeth bore the phantom sensation of Miss Jamieson's large, dark eyes moving in scrutiny over her features before she turned that gaze downward to Elizabeth's waiting palm.

"Ah, your hand is a different shape from Miss Darcy's. Fingers like air, a palm like fire. You are an odd mixture of curiosity and passion. And by your brow, such a mind you have, Miss Elizabeth! It must always be occupied, else it feeds mischief. And your hands are alike in that they are industrious. You do not like idleness."

Elizabeth nodded in acknowledgement that what she said was true.

"Well, now, looking closer, your hand bears a mark. A scar. This will make your hand hard to read. However, the mark in itself is distinct. It crosses several mounds below your fingers—Jupiter, Saturn, Apollo—but it does not touch your Mound of Mercury. No, your quick wit and your ability to adapt are very much intact. I could read your other hand if you would like, but I tend to believe that scars like this on one's dominant hand are very important. Shall I go on?"

Elizabeth smiled. "Of course. Pray continue."

"Yours is a passionate nature. Even marked as they are by this scar, the mounds on your palms are all very high. You have many gifts, Miss Elizabeth. Gifts of the mind, the heart, and more strengths besides that. Yet by your chin, you also have an obstinate nature, which I think will serve you well. It is very striking how all these features meet my notice at once."

Miss Jamieson continued to eye Elizabeth's face for a moment. "It may be a learned trait, that obstinance, for I see now that your fate and your life line intersect very early, perhaps very recently, young as you are. And here, this faint branch in your life line shows that you might have had a second journey that was interrupted by the fate-change of the first. Your life's story puzzles me a great deal. Did something change abruptly in your youth? Let me look closer at your hand again."

Elizabeth kept silent, but she raised a brow to old Mrs Jamieson, who was chuckling in amusement by the fire as Miss Jamieson's face became more and more absorbed. Georgiana leaned closer to see what she was so carefully examining on Elizabeth's palm.

At length, she spoke again. "It does not appear to be an intrusion from your relationships—no one is there to force you onto this new path. Could it be a death? Some kind of loss? Wait! Do not tell me. Let me attempt to hit on the sign I must be missing."

Elizabeth watched her interviewer's expressions, and she thought she could perceive the moment her insights started to come together. All at once, Miss Jamieson's face lit with success.

"Of course—your scar! This palm that is shaped like fire is also touched by it! You have had an accident! You were burned!"

"Why, yes," Elizabeth confirmed, her tone surprised. "Yes, there was a fire."

"One that altered things considerably but not, I think, irrevocably. Your fate line is intact, unbroken, although it did change your life line by intersecting it. Indeed, I think your ultimate place in the world would be the same, regardless of your accident. You are where you should be, Miss Elizabeth. And by your bold marriage crease, I can say you may still expect happiness."

"That is a vast relief!" Elizabeth exclaimed with a laugh. Georgiana, obviously delighted by this news for her friend, clapped her hands in excitement.

"Good morning, ladies," called a voice from the door. Turning, Elizabeth saw the gentleman her ear had already identified. Mr Darcy bowed to the ladies within and then approached the little table on which Miss Jamieson held Elizabeth's palm upturned. "Dare I ask, Miss Elizabeth, what has brought you relief?"

"Just a little palmistry," offered Mrs Jamieson, a hint of mischief in her voice. "You will find Tabitha here most talented in the art."

"You will forgive me if I find such arts to be little more than a clever collection of observation, deduction, and mummery," Mr Darcy replied with an air of indulgent caution. "The idea that markings on our bodies offer witness to our future seems quite suspect. I do, however, think the phrenologists have something of merit in their belief that the past—and our families' pasts—may influence our present character. Such a power arises from two sources in our histories: our inherited familial characteristics and our upbringing in the homes of our origin."

Elizabeth glanced at Miss Jamieson, who was watching Mr Darcy with an air of conspiracy, as though she suddenly knew something about him that the rest of the room did not. It was somewhat unsettling. For a moment, Elizabeth thought she saw Miss Jamieson purse her lips and prepare to speak, but as her dark eyes flicked up again to Mr Darcy's visage, something seemed to make the young lady think the better of it. It could not be fear of him, surely, Elizabeth surmised. He had only ever seemed to show these neighbours kindness. No, Miss Jamieson's reserve might come from presuming that Mr Darcy, as a gentleman of high status, liked to have his thoughts left uncontested.

Elizabeth took back her hand gently, murmuring her thanks. She was unable to resist the urge to both put Miss Jamieson at ease and demonstrate Mr Darcy's willingness to bandy words.

"I do not conform to such robust boundaries of past, present, and future as I comprehend my experience," Elizabeth declared. "For the ever-fading present soon becomes our past, and the future quickly arrives in the next breath as our present experience."

Mr Darcy stared at her a moment. "That is indeed a fearful symmetry your perspective places on the framework of human experience—a chain of present moments, snatching the future in the next breath, leaving the past in its wake. I tend to think of the past and present as divided entities. You suppose mutability as a point to unite them."

"You have stated it more succinctly than I, sir, but yes, that is my perception. And as to your comment on phrenology, do we not mark ourselves by our present predilections, accidents, and burdens? And do we not carry the changes wrought upon us forward into our futures?"

Mr Darcy chuckled. "How you do play the devil's advocate, Miss Elizabeth! Next, you will tell me that 'our torments also may in length of time become our elements', I take it?"

Elizabeth answered far more soberly. "I speak as one who has experienced a bit of my own *Paradise Lost*."

"Gracious," muttered Mrs Jamieson in an aside to Miss Darcy which, due to the speaker's ageing sense of hearing, was loud enough to be heard across the room. "They could chat their way through Cambridge's Faculty Library and the entire School of Athens between them, I think."

With a smile, Georgiana admitted, "My mind is never as

quick as Miss Elizabeth's or my brother's, so I leave them to their amusements."

Elizabeth coloured slightly to be so discussed, but she found composure in the forgiving grace of Mr Darcy's smile, which he directed indulgently towards the old woman.

"Well, then, Mr Darcy," said Miss Jamieson suddenly, "I take it you do not wish to have your palm examined?'

He bowed to her. "At this moment, no, but I thank you, madam. If Miss Elizabeth's view holds, then the future will arrive quickly on the heels of the present. In any case, I should like to be surprised by any forces still at work."

In response to this, such a smile overspread Miss Jamieson's face that Elizabeth found herself looking twice. It was clear to her that whatever Mr Darcy had said it had amused the lady for reasons no one else could comprehend.

Just when Elizabeth might have taken the opportunity to ask for Miss Jamieson's perspective, a light repast arrived for the ladies. Georgiana, recalling her duties as their hostess, immediately set about to serve her guests. Mr Darcy stayed just long enough to take some tea and then excused himself again to his correspondence.

At his departure, Miss Jamieson smiled again, this time directed towards Elizabeth, and then moved to neatly snatch up Mr Darcy's empty cup and saucer.

Mrs Jamieson clapped her hands. "Oh, you clever dear! Do tell us what his leaves say."

The ladies in the room all stilled in suspense as Miss Jamieson upturned the cup on its saucer, then studied the dregs for a moment. At last, she boldly declared, "Well, Mr Darcy is certainly a singular gentleman! His heart and mind orient him like a compass, and in matters of his happiness, they will be united in the force they exert. How delightful that he cannot turn aside from that which pleases both his powers." With that, she delicately set the cup down on a tray, curtseyed to the bemused group of ladies, and quit the room.

The fantastical potential of Miss Jamieson's revelations left Georgiana's mouth agape for a moment, and Elizabeth, in no less astonishment, stared after her.

"Well, Georgiana," declared Mrs Jamieson, "it is a good day when a household can receive three such encouraging readings from Tabitha. I hope you may feel at ease now. I was afraid I would have to smooth things over after she pronounced some terrible omen."

"The thought quite terrified me as well, once it occurred to me. I was all relief for you, Elizabeth, to hear of your happy fate —and, of course, my own."

"And the reading of the leaves," Elizabeth put in. "I had never heard of such a thing, but it was quite an interesting way to reveal something in Mr Darcy's character that might guide him."

"Tabitha undertook some study of the art from a lady here in town, down by the docks on the Thames," Mrs Jamieson explained. "It was not very long after I brought her with me from Jamaica that they discovered each other. I am afraid I cannot say when or how it was. There was so much happening in my own life that distressed me at the time. For you see, I had just left my husband—yes, I left him, and he did not see fit to die until some years later. My children did not understand why, after so many years, I should choose to leave him, and at such cost. Beyond the growing uneasiness I felt in our way of living on the island, I had discovered some villainy in him that I could not forgive, except that it gave me my Tabitha, who you might guess was his child."

Miss Darcy's mouth opened in shock.

"Oh, dear! Georgiana, are you well? I should not speak of such things before a girl your age! I forgot myself. You are not yet out, nor yet a woman by society's reckoning. I fear there is no way to tell my story that will not outrage innocence."

Elizabeth nodded, then said, "I confess that I had wondered, and I had guessed enough to suppose. In any event, the truth is better than my impertinent supposition. You did us no wrong, Mrs Jamieson, I assure you."

"I agree with Elizabeth," Georgiana declared, once she had found her voice. "It is better to know than to risk assuming a fact. And what's more, I find myself glad you could leave and take Miss Jamieson with you. I am sure it took courage."

"Every ounce of hers and mine—but some things are worth a terrible risk," Mrs Jamieson said. Reaching forward, she patted Georgiana's cheek. "Bless you, child, for your kind heart."

So passed their morning in deep concentration upon the mysteries of both future and past. Their intimate conference had held them in such thrall that the ladies hardly noticed the sun gaining strength as the afternoon arrived.

When the footman entered to announce that Mr and Mrs Gardiner had returned for their niece, Elizabeth met this news with both rejoicing and regret. Much as she loved the Gardiners, she had enjoyed her time at the Darcys' home immensely.

Elizabeth and her hostess greeted the street-weary pair with delight and concern for the state of the roads, and upon their reassurances of slow progress in the traffic, Georgiana allowed herself to be persuaded to release her friend into their care once again.

"We have had ever so much fun during this impromptu visit," Miss Darcy admitted, before turning in abrupt embarrassment to the lady near the fire. "Forgive me. I am neglecting my other guest! Mrs Jamieson, may I present to you Mr and Mrs Edward Gardiner? They are Miss Elizabeth's aunt and uncle."

Mrs Jamieson received them like a duchess, amusement dancing in her eyes. Grasping her cane, she declared, "A pleasure, such a pleasure. We have had a delightful time here with your niece. I suppose you have not yet heard greetings directly from the master of this house, but Mr Darcy is the cause of my coming. When he found himself quite on his back foot with the honour of your young lady in his care, he sought me out and sledged me through the snow. I must admit that this has been the most adventure I have ever had as a chaperone to any young lady, and yet I cannot regret the circumstances. Miss Elizabeth is an extraordinary creature."

Mrs Gardiner's astonishment was evident. "That he could think of such a thing at such a time! We are most indebted to his care. How very kind and very careful Mr Darcy has been."

"It is my brother's nature," Georgiana put in, smiling.

In another moment, Mr Darcy emerged from his study to greet the Gardiners, whereupon they repeated their praise and gratitude to his face.

Elizabeth could read the discomfort in his manner, but he genteelly averred. "No thanks are needed, except to Mrs Jamieson. By sheer force of habit, I could do no less, having the care of my sister's credit these five years. Now, on a matter more pressing, please tell me of the roads. I cannot like you trundling off across the city in a hackney with no knowledge of the temper of your horses or their jostler. No, you will have the coach and my greys and my careful driver—and for that, you may thank me and have done."

CHAPTER TWENTY-EIGHT

Their slow and stately ride home in the opulence of the Darcy carriage, along with the misadventures the storm had caused, gave the family party at Gracechurch Street much to discuss in the wintry thaw that followed. Soon, more delight arrived on their doorstep in the form of Mr Bingley, who presented himself at Jane's side with an eagerness equal to the longing inspired by their ice-bound separation.

Mrs Gardiner's kind pity could do no less than contrive a way to allow the engaged couple to steal a moment or two to themselves in the crowded house, but invariably, each room had at least one occupant. On this occasion, she was able to place them with no one but the children to mind them while she whisked her sister-in-law and nieces off to discuss yet another detail pertaining to the upcoming wedding.

When the two lovers emerged from their tête-à-tête, Mr Bingley approached the elder matrons, fairly bursting with news.

"Dear ladies, you will never guess what arrived with my post this morning."

He procured a crisply folded missive edged about the linen-weave in pale blue ink, still bearing the dark stain of a seal. Mrs Bennet shuffled forward, anticipation coming alive as she recognised the signals of some important invitation.

"It comes from Darcy's uncle. The Earl of Matlock knew my father—was an investor in our family business in Scarborough, in fact—and I grew reacquainted with him more recently through my friendship with Darcy. He was very keen on my taking an estate like Netherfield, just far enough from Yorkshire and close enough to town to establish myself.

"Now that news has reached him of my impending nuptials, his lordship has astonished me exceedingly by his recognition and this invitation. I have often heard of these famous Fitzwilliam fêtes, but have never been invited to one of their Twelfth Night balls. Along with a note from the earl, the countess included an invitation for my intended's family as well."

Bingley paused to glance meaningfully at Jane. "They wish to meet you. The short note from the earl makes it clear that he knows nothing of you other than what the banns this week had said, and he is of a mind to make known his approval as word gets about. It is such a kindness to us, Jane. I did not know what to say, but here I am to do my duty to extend his very personal invitation."

Mrs Gardiner quickly stepped aside from the suddenly intense conference and sought Mr Bennet. Meanwhile, Mrs Bennet took some time to overcome her astonishment. When she did, she was as voluble in her exultation as she was quick in grasping at this opportunity.

"Oh, Jane! Such an honour! Such generosity! Such fortunate luck! And you must be chaperoned, of course. Yes, I shall take you. We shall meet the earl and his family, all of us, for I should like to take Lydia, too. She has so longed to dance! And what quality gentlemen there must be attending such a ball with such lofty connexions as the Earl of Matlock!"

As Mrs Bennet's excitement raised awareness throughout the house, the rest of her daughters entered the room to ask of the news from Jane and Mr Bingley. Lydia and Kitty gasped and clamoured to know more. Mr Bennet then came into the sitting room armed with his sister-in-law's good information and his own discernment.

He spoke suddenly but clearly. "In such a case as this, there can be no question that the earl and countess should meet Jane's parents together. I shall be sure to accompany you, Mrs Bennet. If Jane requires a sister there to look after her during the dancing, Lizzy is just the one. With one daughter engaged already, it is perfectly acceptable to have our second born out in society. That way Jane will have no distractions but her own nerves."

At this remark, Lydia howled a protest and darted up the stairs. Kitty, torn between compassion for her younger sister, disappointment for herself, and joy for Jane, managed to squeeze Jane's hand before taking herself off to follow Lydia.

Despite the tempest of Lydia's temper, which continued well into the evening, the happy preparations for the ball began the very next day with Mrs Gardiner at the helm. Mrs Bennet was vastly happy to attach some rich new lace to her favourite ball gown and to wear a fetching new cap of Mrs Gardiner's, which was trimmed in a similar lace and boasted a pearl and jade broach at the temple. Both Elizabeth and Jane's wardrobes were assessed, and while their dancing shoes were deemed acceptable, their gowns required some careful consideration and alterations. Elizabeth's year-old gown, the one she had once hoped to wear to Netherfield's ball, gained both a more fashionable sleeve length and some well-placed whitework embroidery to hide some discoloration from the smoke of the fire. Jane's own, newer gown that had been better stored away and was certainly pretty, had the wrong weight of material for a winter fête, and its overall silhouette belied her roots as a 'country miss.'

In its place, Mrs Gardiner sacrificed one of her own gowns, one she had purchased for a special engagement with her husband's most important business associates only a Season ago. The expensive satin material's muted blue tones brought out the colour of Jane's lovely eyes, and the delicate seed pearls that traced the embroidered patterns around the neckline framed her angelic face like a portrait. Jane was fortunate that she and her aunt were of a similar height, so Mrs Gardiner only had to relocate the buttons at her back to make it fit Jane well through the bosom and shoulders. The overall effect when she was through was nothing short of transformative.

"Oh Jane," Elizabeth gasped, surprised by sudden tears, "you look as though you have already left Longbourn far behind. I feel as though we are meeting *Mrs Bingley*, as genteel and elegant as you please."

"You will look just as you should as you move about in your intended's circles," seconded Mrs Gardiner. "I hope it gives you courage."

Jane turned from the looking glass and embraced her favourite aunt, her good heart too full of feeling to offer gratitude in any other manner. Elizabeth, patting her eyes with a handkerchief, had to offer it afterwards to both women.

WITH CHRISTMAS THAT VERY WEEK, AND THEN MORE momentous preparations to follow for both the ball and a wedding in quick succession, the time passed with a great deal of noise and industry. There was much merriment as well as plentiful visits between the Bingley and Gardiner homes. During these happy times, a brief morning call from the Darcys brought yet more valuable information to the Bennets as they prepared to meet Mr Darcy's most lofty relations, who would now stand as Mr Bingley's most distinguished friends in society.

"I had no notion that my aunt and uncle invited Bingley and Miss Bennet as his intended, but it is certainly fitting with their character. They have always had a fondness for my uncle's Yorkshiremen, as he invested much of his time there while rebuilding his own estate's holdings. I imagine his curiosity to meet you is only rivalled by my aunt's," Mr Darcy mused, as he accepted a cup of tea from Miss Bennet's hands.

"Are they much to be feared?" Elizabeth teased. "Their fame proceeds them, for I have heard lately of your uncle's influence in Parliament, though I know next to nothing of him except that he is a proud Whig. And in my girlhood studies, I learned he once served the Crown in Ireland during the height of the Catholic troubles. But there you see my knowledge complete."

"Should you speak to him of Ireland, prepare yourself for a long panegyric of the political disputes there. I would avoid it," replied Mr Darcy, setting down his cup with a frown. "Despite all his good intentions, I fear it was his greatest disappointment."

"Then I shall instead extol the virtues of my sister and hope for enough introductions to give me sufficient opportunities to dance. I cannot imagine a country girl will easily fill her dance card among such high society, but I am determined to at least pin up my train in readiness."

"Oh, Elizabeth," interjected Georgiana at once. "You must not fear! My brother will dance with you, will you not, Fitzwilliam?"

"Certainly," replied he. "That is—if the lady does not refuse my hand this time."

Elizabeth struggled to correct him. "I did not refuse you!

Truly, I thought you were only humouring Sir William! He had quite surprised you with his demand, if you recall."

Mr Darcy smiled a little at the memory. "Well then, let me put you at ease during your debut into high society. Reserve the supper set for me, and you will not have to fear any offending topics of discussion over dinner."

Elizabeth could scarcely conceal her delight. "You will have it, sir, and gladly."

THE IMPORT OF THE OCCASION OF THE TWELFTH Night Ball, combined with the immensity of the grand house that opened its doors to them, made Mrs Bennet circumspect and demure as she entered on her husband's arm. Even Elizabeth and Jane, following after them, could scarcely conceal their admiration as they were received into a hall unlike any they had entered before.

Time, wealth, history, and influence were all reflected in architectural form, and the graceful glass ceiling poured the heavens' own beams into the constellations of chandeliers that cast their glow onto the marble floor. Congregating among the Palladian columns of the grand salon, the crowd around them fairly glistened with rich fabrics and dripped with gemstones, and commensurate with Elizabeth's expectation, she perceived not a single face she knew.

As the Master of Ceremonies conducted them to their host and hostess, Elizabeth was at once struck by the unassuming face of the earl, whose only resemblance to Mr Darcy was his serious mien and his understated elegance. Next to him, the countess was fairly coated with jewellery above her sumptuous gown, and the earl, with his tidy, clean-shaven face over his snowy cravat and dark evening coat, seemed nearly austere in comparison.

Cheered at least by this small bit of the familiar, Elizabeth squeezed Jane's arm as their family party approached. The Master of Ceremonies gave their parents' names in introduction, and Elizabeth could only feel relief when her father's careful bow and mother's practiced curtsey lent them every appearance of elegance.

"Well met, Mr and Mrs Bennet. And who are these charming ladies you have brought with you tonight?" asked the countess.

"Lady Matlock, may I present my two eldest daughters—Jane, who is Mr Bingley's intended, and her sister Elizabeth," replied Mr Bennet.

Jane rose up to find the countess's gaze upon her. Instead of blushing or wilting under her ladyship's inscrutable look, Jane smiled earnestly. Elizabeth felt a swell of pride at her sister's sweet bearing.

"Miss Bennet, I see you will do very well for Mr Bingley. We have known him since his boyhood, and he has the sweetest temper," said the countess.

"Yes, indeed, your ladyship," replied Jane a little tremulously. "I find he is just what a gentleman ought to be."

"I stand in agreement!" remarked the earl. "His own merits have raised him to the claim. It is my hope that men of Bingley's sort will be the height of influence in their generation. Fair-minded, kind-hearted, unafraid of the taint of hard work and responsibility—that is my notion of a gentleman. You will do him credit, Miss Bennet. Where again was it that you hail from?"

"Hertfordshire, my lord, near Meryton," replied Jane with more courage.

"Of course! So, you met when Bingley came into the neighbourhood to lease his estate there. Thus, I meet not only his bride but his neighbours. You are welcome, certainly welcome."

"We thank you for the kind invitation, Lord Matlock," Mr Bennet added warmly, his gratitude evident.

More polite courtesies followed and the Bennets were led on towards the grand ballroom.

"That went well, I think," Mr Bennet remarked. "And with far less condescension than real grace. I rather like our hosts."

"Indeed!" chirped Mrs Bennet, coming out of her daze and uttering her first words of the night. "And her ladyship's gown was most becoming."

Elizabeth, ambling with Jane on her father's arm, merely smiled at her mother's remark while she cast her eyes about the enormous ballroom, edged by alcoves boasting priceless sculptures, and surmounted by a balcony promenade that already teemed with guests.

"Do you see Mr Bingley yet, Lizzy?" Jane asked. "He feared his party might be made late."

"I am sure he will arrive as soon as Miss Bingley's lady's maid allows," Elizabeth teased softly. "Do not worry. He would never abandon you on so important an occasion."

"Mr Bennet, Mrs Bennet," called a familiar voice.

Elizabeth felt her arm abruptly twisted back by her father as he turned their party all at once.

"Ah, Mr Darcy. How good of you to find us," Mr Bennet greeted him wryly.

At Darcy's side was an officer of rank, nearly gleaming in his crimson regimentals. Mr Darcy bowed and his companion did the same.

Mr Darcy turned to indicate the newcomer. "Mr Bennet, may I present my cousin, Colonel Fitzwilliam, the son of the earl."

"You honour us, sir," said Mr Bennet.

The colonel replied with the ease of evident good breeding. "The honour is mine, sir. I confess I was curious to meet your family. I know Bingley as a mutual friend of Darcy's and I have lately had correspondence from my cousin, Miss Darcy, describing her new friendship with the Miss Bennets."

Here, he turned to Jane and Elizabeth and bowed again. "I am joined with Darcy in guardianship of Miss Darcy. Any friends of hers are most welcome in my acquaintance."

"How very kind of you to recognise us so," replied Elizabeth. "I must echo the sentiment. You have raised a very sweet young lady. It is very good to know you, Colonel Fitzwilliam."

These pleasantries exchanged, Elizabeth was happy to discover that the colonel, though not so handsome as Mr Darcy, was every bit as gentlemanly as his polished manners declared. He readily entered into conversation with her family, and more than that, he proved a font of information regarding their new surroundings and the notorious individuals of London society among the teeming crowd.

"There, you see the advisor to his royal majesty, Lord Hardenton, and on his arm, be warned, is his official mistress. She is an amiable sort, but you might pardon my saying, keeping company with her overlong might cast a shadow upon an eligible young lady by association. And there—ah, to their left, you will find his lordship's son. He is a jolly, ribald fellow, much to my liking, but alas, a bit rough in his sensibilities for delicate company," the colonel remarked.

Elizabeth tore her curious gaze away from the woman distinguished by his remarks, surprised at hearing her referred to as an 'official' mistress and mixing so openly with respectable company. For all appearances, she seemed every bit the lady, no less refined than any other, only noticeably younger than her lordly protector. As the colonel continued to point out some other potentially adversarial or unpleasant company, Elizabeth pondered the circumstances that might lead so young a lady to seek to place herself before a powerful man as his mistress and not as a wife. In her ignorance of the harshness of the world from even a year ago, she might have judged such a woman.

Now, it seemed to Elizabeth less like a tale of scandal, and more of sadness.

The colonel had continued much in this vein, indicating a few more interesting members of the *ton*, until, with an instructive look from Mr Darcy, the colonel seemed to catch himself and grimaced. His good-humoured grace was such that he had thus far been able to pass off his bits of gossip as advice.

"I fear I have said too much, ladies. Forgive me. You must not take all my commentary as gospel. I am sure you will take your own measure of tonight's company."

Elizabeth smiled gently. "With such personages before us, I feel particularly lucky in meeting someone so willing to expose what may be said of their characters. They seem far less daunting now."

"You will have the advantage of being new faces in this crowd. They are, therefore, less likely to approach you without an introduction," Mr Darcy pointed out. "Alas, for myself, there are some here whom I may wish to avoid but cannot."

"Poor Darcy!" The colonel laughed. "I see Mrs Warwick is already coming this way with her new husband. No doubt he has some investment that has turned his fancy, which ought to come to your attention, and Mrs Warwick still has a daughter unwed."

"If I am their quarry, I had best head them off," Mr Darcy sighed, already weary.

"Aye, do! I still have some duties as a host to dispense to the Bennets beyond imparting my questionable wisdom. Introductions, first, as a necessity and as a pleasure." Colonel Fitzwilliam turned a broad smile to the Bennet clan, much to their amusement. "Such is my lot! I had best see to it."

Mr Darcy grumbled indiscernibly as he bowed and melted away into the press of the crowd, and Elizabeth could only be comforted by the charms of his cousin, who soon gained the promise of her hand and her sister's for some upcoming dances.

As the honourees of the evening, the former Miss Carlisle, now Lady Seaton, led the first set with her new husband as the signal of the opening of the ball. The colonel explained that the Carlisles had long been affectionate friends of his family, and that his parents always sought to sponsor the unions of their children with a ball to ensure their recognition in society. Elizabeth was content to watch from her stance beside the punch bowl as the young lady gracefully accepted the attention of the crowd, while she navigated the figures of the dance across the beautifully patterned floor.

Before the dance was through, Mr Bingley and his family made their appearance at last, and he was quick to apologise to Jane for his delay.

"Caroline was beside herself to be attending such an exclusive event. I daresay she changed gowns four times this evening," Mr Bingley laughed, even as he pressed Jane's hand. "I may not have opened the ball with you, my dear Jane, but may I have the next set? And, Miss Elizabeth, may I have the one after?"

Both ladies gave their consent, and soon Mr Bingley spirited Jane away to dance. Elizabeth would have enjoyed watching them had not Colonel Fitzwilliam raised his hand to hers with a wink, and whisked her off to the floor as well.

They took their place in the set with cheerful faces. Once Elizabeth began to feel comfortable in the pattern of the dance, she allowed herself to look around at the dazzling beauty of the chandelier, the gilt-on-white ceiling and walled alcoves, and to both follow and feel the enchanting music, played so skilfully. Her eye also sought the tall figure of Mr Darcy, who was higher up in the set and dancing with a lady she had never seen before. She turned in the set, only to find the colonel watching her with sly amusement.

"Poor Darcy! Dancing with a lady with whom he is hardly

acquainted at all. I know he abhors the practice," Colonel Fitzwilliam said with a laugh.

"How well I do know it," Elizabeth replied, her own laughter nearly making her breathless as she passed around the colonel in the figure.

"Oh, do you? I wish you would tell me of it. I should dearly wish to hear how Darcy behaves around strangers."

"The first time of my ever seeing him in Hertfordshire was at a ball, and what do you think he did? He danced only four dances, though gentlemen were scarce, and to my certain knowledge, more than one young lady was sitting in want of a partner."

"I can easily picture him standing about, looking as unapproachable as thunder. Ah, Darcy! That inimitable reserve!"

"And I quite mistook it for the worst kind of pride," Elizabeth admitted. "I can only regret how it coloured my view of him for quite some time thereafter."

Colonel Fitzwilliam offered her clemency with a knowing smile. "Darcy is not an easy man to know. Were I not his family, I wonder if I should know him half so well."

"It took a stay under the same roof with him for above a week before I had any notion of his character and still more trials and time to gain an appreciation of it."

"I can well imagine. He has learned to be guarded, but that heavy armour comes with his position in life."

"And does not an earl's son require the same careful protection?"

The colonel laughed again outright. "Not at all, if he is the *second* son. I have the freedom to put myself in harm's way, and I have done so often in service to His Majesty. Moreover, I have the pleasure of meeting whomever—and saying whatever—I like and of having any carelessness attributed to the freedom of my unburdened state. My brother, the viscount and heir, must play the game of politics more carefully."

"Ah, I see," said Elizabeth, perceiving herself beyond her experience now that the earl and his elder son's connexion to Parliament had become the topic.

The dance was drawing to a close, and Elizabeth parted from the colonel with the pleasure such courteous and engaging company had earned. She was then claimed for the following set by her soon-to-be brother, and this dance, too, held its own charm for her as she listened to Mr Bingley describe with anticipation some plans to travel with Jane after they were wed.

Elizabeth was obliged by lack of immediate introduction to sit out the next, but on returning to her parents, she was relieved to find that her mother continued to conduct herself with moderation in meeting the other ladies. Their topics of conversation encompassed fashion, the fashionable, and talk of upcoming nuptials within their sphere, all of which delighted Mrs Bennet. Her father was likewise engaged listening to some of the elder gentlemen in debate on political matters, and Elizabeth witnessed with satisfaction his acceptance of an invitation to join them in another room for cards and cigars.

The matrons keeping company with her mother soon discovered in Elizabeth an opportunity for a companionable and pretty partner for their sons, and they graciously introduced her. Their kind endeavours helped Elizabeth return to the dance floor and brought new characters to study.

As the evening progressed and she again experienced a shortfall of partners, Elizabeth contented herself with watching her sister, who experienced more success as her betrothed and his connexions introduced her and passed her into new and very willing hands in the dance. Elizabeth could well understand her sister's popularity, for even among those who represented the very first stare of fashion, her sister's beautiful face and gentle bearing drew enraptured attention.

With her mind thus engaged in enjoyable observation, Elizabeth was startled to find Mr Darcy beside her, smiling at her contentment.

"Miss Elizabeth," he said with a bow, "it is my understanding from the Master of Ceremonies that the table is being laid even now. Did you forget our supper dance?"

CHAPTER TWENTY-NINE

"*F*orget our dance? How could I?"

Elizabeth took his proffered hand with an eagerness that might have embarrassed a more refined lady. Mr Darcy replied only by tucking her hand into his arm and leading her towards the forming set.

As they joined it, Elizabeth recollected they had never danced together before, despite so many near attempts in their shared history. To her delight, Mr Darcy moved with an elegance equal to his stature. She felt all the honour of the attention they drew from the nearby pairings as they turned and turned again through the line.

Once they came into a closer figure in the dance and could speak again, Elizabeth ventured, "It was very kind of your uncle to invite my family."

Mr Darcy's look was one of both amusement and understanding. "I do not believe it was done on my uncle's account."

"Oh?"

"My uncle, like most men, positions himself first when

thinking of political or social strategy. I often find that women will seek to position others with their careful planning."

"Your aunt, then?" Elizabeth guessed, stealing a brief glance at the countess as she made another turn.

"Her ladyship's fondness for Bingley is of some duration. She entertained his family at her table with some frequency in his boyhood, and upon his parents' deaths, recommended him to my notice while I was above him at university. If it is known that the Fitzwilliams approve of his entry into the gentry, things will go well for him—and for his future family."

Elizabeth considered the milestone that Mr Bingley had reached that year. "It is very kind of them to sponsor Mr Bingley in this way."

"They also recognise your sister's gentle birth. His marriage to a gentleman's daughter does well for him."

The pinning of Mr Bingley's status upon her own family's suddenly struck Elizabeth as a perilous thing. When next she faced Mr Darcy, her eyes were wide.

"Sir, do they know?"

He took her meaning at once. "Not yet, no. I did not divulge your family's circumstances to my aunt. I suspect she may gain hints enough to surmise that your estate is not of the significance of those you see here represented."

Elizabeth nearly missed her next step. Her mind was a whirl of sudden anxiety for the interests of her family. If only these fine people knew! She could only be grateful they did not.

Mr Darcy perceived her sudden silence, and his hand pressed hers when he next took it up in their dance. He patiently awaited the return of her composure as Elizabeth reclaimed her steps.

So softly that the music nearly covered her speech, Elizabeth admitted, "I suppose I had not counted on their ignorance, although I had hoped against their knowledge. I confess I did rather wish to pass myself off with some degree of credit among their circle tonight."

"You need not worry on that account," Mr Darcy replied. "You and your sister are everything gently bred ladies should be, and they can ascertain that plainly. I have heard nothing but praise for the Miss Bennets tonight."

Elizabeth let out a breath of relief despite herself, even as their dance came to its conclusion. The effect was jarring, for no new song started up to follow their supper set, and abruptly, the ballroom became loud with talk and busy with walking feet. The crowd began to arrange itself for the table by consequence and partner, and Mr Darcy reached for her hand.

"When we were first brought in, I found myself nearly terrified at the prospect of mixing with this company tonight," Elizabeth confessed, taking his hand. "I have heard of the way your uncle spreads his fortune generously about the city, from charities, to dinners, and balls like this one. And when I beheld such grand personages here assembled, I began to fancy I might see the Prince Regent himself! I am glad you came, else my courage might have failed me."

"Even had I been absent, you would have been perfectly safe in the company of my aunt and uncle as your hosts. I know you to be a quick study of character. Did the earl and countess not receive you tonight with every air of civility without the distance of rank?"

"Certainly," replied Elizabeth. "In fact, when speaking to Jane, Lord Matlock said something rather bold about his hope that men like Mr Bingley would be the influencing leaders in society someday, despite the taint of trade in his past, or rather because of it, for it impressed a strong sense of industry into his character. I wholeheartedly approved."

Mr Darcy smiled and with pride in his voice, he said, "When my uncle inherited his estate at Matlock as a youth, the debts were astounding. You will find him a bit of a radical for his generation, for he began to embrace connexions in trade far and above what others in the peerage would consider proper in his day. In two decades, he not only surmounted the debt, but he laid a path to fortunes far more vast than many in this room can now boast. And he did it without succumbing to greed.

"In Ireland, the earl took the estate granted him there from a festering moulder of a house complete with tenants with no direction, to a pearl among castles with tenants educated in the latest farming and shepherding methods on his insistence—and all of them better paid and with lower rent than the surrounding villagers. In my youth, I also saw him bolster the men of Yorkshire behind Napoleon's blockade by bringing thriving industry to the area through his partnerships with men like Bingley's father. It seemed there was nothing my uncle could fail to achieve, at least where his influence might have any reach."

Mr Darcy paused in his reflection to join the line of escorts parading their ladies to the table. Elizabeth was happy to tuck her hand again into his arm, keeping pace with him as he led them into the grand dining hall.

As they entered, Mr Darcy continued his musings, and Elizabeth strove not to be distracted by the feel of his chest expanding as he breathed and spoke against her wrist wrapped in his arm.

"I doubt you will meet a better landlord and master on English soil. When I am managing my own estate, I often feel like a boy does wearing his father's hat and tailcoat, mimicking a greater man. I know I shall never equal him, but I certainly have been happy to emulate the earl since my father died."

Elizabeth cherished the earnestness in his voice. "You do wisely to emulate such a man, sir," she affirmed, "for even if you fail to match him, you will at least have aimed to do far more good than most."

The signal for seating was called, and Elizabeth was

delighted to have been caught up in Miss Darcy's careful planning so as to find herself neatly escorted from her dance in the supper set with Mr Darcy and straight to his side at the table. There, among the boisterous crush of guests, amidst the many laden trays and plates bearing their delicacies, and under some slight effects of some very fine wine, Elizabeth's conversation with Mr Darcy shifted to shed its weighty tone in favour of liveliness.

Elizabeth was flushed, and her ripostes to her companion's deft retorts tripped almost too freely from her lips as the two of them leaned towards each other to better hear and confine the delightful wildness of their speech. Words darted between them like sparrows in a hedgerow, too quick and hidden by the noise around them to be much overheard. Elizabeth's cheeks felt warm as she spoke and looked at him, feeling herself very close, nearly touching him, as their conversation coloured the very air between them with brushes of pleasurable insight and mutual amusement.

To her eye, Mr Darcy looked warm himself but certainly no less handsome for it. His heightened colour, the bright lustre of his gaze, and the scent of his skin were a heady mixture in close confinement—and it delighted her, held her, and nearly distracted her from their talk.

As she shifted forward in her chair when the other guests across the table grew louder, Elizabeth felt a strange sensation, as though a slow-burning flame grew inside her. When Mr Darcy reached for his wine, chuckling resonantly at the last thing she said, and sipped from his glass with his clever mouth, the heat within her licked at her spine and made her sit up straighter in her chair.

Dessert was soon brought out, and with it, a hubbub of excited talk accompanied their hostess as the first cut was made in the massive cake to celebrate the Twelfth Night in the old style. Once the slices of the grand confection were passed, it took only moments for a young gentleman seated far above them at the table to find the bean in his slice. His compatriots immediately cheered and tapped their glasses.

As Elizabeth bent to her own plate to taste the heavy cake, she gasped at finding herself in possession of the pea, speared neatly upon her own fork. Mr Darcy urged her to hold her plate aloft, and her tablemates erupted with a clattering of silver tapping against crystal to herald the discovery. The Master of Ceremonies approached Elizabeth to lead her to the unknown gentleman.

He took the young man's wrist, and to shouts, applause, and stamping feet, raised it as a fist in the air, and declared, "Lord Apsley, the King!"

Turning from the young lord, the Master of Ceremonies approached Elizabeth, and with a deep bow, murmured a request that she kindly repeat her name.

"And Miss Elizabeth Bennet, the Queen!" The guests answered with a rousing cheer.

To Elizabeth's continuing amazement, two liveried servants came forward with painted crowns, and with great aplomb, situated one on each of the new royals' heads. Elizabeth turned to Lord Apsley with a smile. The young man, who seemed near an age to Elizabeth, returned it, bowed to her, and offered her his arm.

Elizabeth took it, and upon examining her royal companion more closely, she determined that he made a very fine king with his long, elegant nose, straight mouth, and serious gaze. As he led her to the floor to begin the dancing anew, Elizabeth's courage had risen sufficiently for her to speak.

"Your lordship, or rather, Your Majesty, I must confess my ignorance. Might you tell me where you and the Apsley holdings hail from?"

He was kind enough to answer, biting his narrow lips as though hiding his amusement, for the holdings were vast and grand to her ear. Then he observed, "I take it you are not from town."

"My father's estate is in Hertfordshire, near Meryton."

"I have had fine shooting not far from that area of the country. Very fine. Pretty country, too. I am pleased to make your acquaintance, Miss Elizabeth."

They continued on in much the same pleasant way until their dance was ended, at which time the Master of Ceremonies presented them with a glass of some rich cordial to take as refreshment after their dance.

Lord Apsley at once raised his glass in the direction of Lord and Lady Matlock in a toast of salute before dutifully quaffing his fill. Elizabeth followed suit, eyes stinging at the strength of the sweet distillation. Lord Apsley smiled at her compassionately.

"I might also presume that you do not often imbibe spirits," he teased.

"Hardly at all. A glass of sherry, taken very rarely, is all the experience I can claim."

"Note carefully, then, that our hosts have generously laid the refreshment tables with a rum punch and more besides. We might all need a wee bit of caution with our next glass, aye?"

Elizabeth nodded her agreement and looked for a place to discreetly set down her half-finished glass. Finding a footman nearby to aid her, Elizabeth was able to return to the floor in time to receive a request for her hand from one of Colonel Fitzwilliam's companions.

Feeling rather lightheaded, Elizabeth muddled her way through the dance, then begged her partner's pardon. She had just escaped to the cooler air of an alcove away from the dancing when Mr Darcy once again appeared at her side.

"I hope you are well, Your Majesty," he quipped, looking more concerned than his flippant remark implied.

Elizabeth took a breath and gratefully leaned her back

against the cool column behind her. "I find that such a whirl-wind of royal duties has left me breathless."

"Might I retrieve something for you? Some cool water or shall I get your sister?"

"No, I am well. I merely need to find my footing again. Might we walk a bit? I have scarcely had the opportunity to appreciate the fine sculptures here."

Mr Darcy obliged her most willingly and offered her his arm. She slipped her hand around his sturdy forearm, trusting in his equanimity until she felt some of her own return. Their perambulations took them around the perimeter of the ball-room and towards many graceful sculptures of Greek heroes and minor deities. As they walked, the noisy carolling of revellers in the hall drew their attention, and they chuckled and shook their heads before they circled a particularly stunning statue of Perseus.

There was peace to be found in surveying such artistry. Darcy's quiet companionship was also soothing after so many surprises, and Elizabeth had just begun to relax when the revellers from the hall made their cacophonous way into the ballroom through the entrance just beside her.

"The Queen!" called one, offering a bow, while his companions continued their raucous songs.

"The mistletoe!" cried another fellow with a round, flushed face, pointing with a hand heavy with rings to the chandelier hung with greens and white clusters just above Elizabeth's head.

"I say, Darcy!" the fellow continued, calling out, "if you do not kiss the Queen, we lads will be happy to oblige!"

Elizabeth immediately flushed with alarm. Mr Darcy guided her to turn their backs on the interlopers. He released his hold enough so that he could face her.

Elizabeth stood stock-still. Such a thing was not beyond her experience, for at a Twelfth Night at Lucas Lodge some four years ago, Charlotte's younger cousin had stolen a kiss from her upon the same pretext, a lapse in propriety that was quite overlooked as a harmless game justified by the celebratory mood. But he had been only a boy and Elizabeth a girl of sixteen.

She was a woman now, and this was Mr Darcy.

He stood close enough to her that she could see her own face reflected in the darkness of his gaze. It was hard for her to read what was in his eyes, which only a moment ago had held such evident concern. As she watched, his gaze fell to her mouth, and without pausing for thought, she shifted onto the toes of her shoes.

"Ah, there you are, Mr Darcy, Miss Eliza!" came a voice like a knell.

In an instant, they each withdrew—Mr Darcy to the bombardment of amused mockery from his friends, and Elizabeth to the attentions of the new intruder.

Miss Bingley came towards Elizabeth, and with an expression of civil disdain accosted her.

"So, Miss Eliza, I hear you are to be my sovereign for the evening's ball! Do you not find such wild diversions found at this sumptuous event to be rather overwhelming?"

Elizabeth, still in a dither of distracted feelings, made no answer. Her eyes strayed again to Mr Darcy, who was deftly fending off his rowdy friends.

"I see you *are* quite overwhelmed! But of course! Such decadence is beyond your experience," Miss Bingley observed, coming alongside Elizabeth and taking the position of a confidant. "As a friend, let me recommend that you not give implicit confidence to any overtures that certain gentlemen may give to you this evening. Much as it pains me to remind you, you must recall that while your birth may make you a gentlewoman, your circumstances, I am afraid, may give such a man as Mr Darcy considerable pause.

"I should tell you, Eliza, that the wagging tongues of the *ton* are not kind to young ladies who set their cap for gentlemen too far above their reach."

Elizabeth's answer was hot with vexation. "I thank you for the warning, but not for the presumption. Mr Darcy is quite safe from me, for I left my cap at the door."

"I beg your pardon," replied Miss Bingley, turning away in dark amusement.

"Insolent girl! You are much mistaken if you expect to influence me by such a paltry attack as this. I see nothing in it but your own disappointed hopes for securing Mr Darcy!" Elizabeth murmured to herself.

As she made to walk off in a temper, Elizabeth's heated cheeks began to cool as she noted several stares directed at her, including the widened eyes of Mr Darcy. In a fever of mortified anxiety, Elizabeth wondered what he might have heard, and what he made of it. There was no discreet way to address such confusion, however, for their party had attracted some notice, and she now perceived still more unwanted looks followed by inclined heads and whispers. She turned aside again, instantly awash with the worst embarrassment of her life.

Elizabeth paused to smooth her gown and sought to regain her composure by re-joining her sister. She found Jane sipping punch and laughing most cheerfully with her beloved Mr Bingley, but such a sight did little to restore Elizabeth's spirits. The longer she lingered by Jane's side silently churning in distress in the tide of their merriment, the more she wished for her sister's sole attention and consolation. She wished most ardently for Jane's compassionate advice.

Ought she seek out Mr Darcy and apologise? Would such an action, in the eyes of any observers, only add to the preponderance of perceived immodesty on her part? Worse still, her heart added anxiously, would an apology imply to Mr Darcy that she meant to take back her words, or would it confirm them? Elizabeth could be happy with neither course, which might present a calculation to trap him or would misrepresent the full truth of her feelings. And what of the incident beneath the mistletoe? If she were to apologise for that, would he take it to mean that she regretted her wish for such a kiss?

Every route felt closed to her but one, so resolving to display every appearance of maidenly virtue for the sake of Jane's credit and her own, Elizabeth refrained from any more marked attention towards Mr Darcy for the remainder of the evening.

She accepted more dance partners, maintained her duties as the Queen by calling the last dance for the night, and gave her warmest gratitude and regards to the earl and countess when the carriage came to collect her party in the wee hours of the morning. Elizabeth consoled herself with the thought that she would soon have opportunity, by virtue of her sister's upcoming wedding, to see Mr Darcy again and perhaps by the length of her meditations in his absence, discern the best manner to seek their reconciliation.

CHAPTER THIRTY

*I*t was with great joy that Jane Bennet was married to Charles Bingley in her own parish church in Hertfordshire the week following the Epiphany. It may not have been the day that Mrs Bennet imagined it to be—for, boasting only half-finished rooms for dining and sitting at Longbourn, she was obliged to hostess the wedding breakfast at her sister Philips's house. But it was executed well, and their gathering overflowed with happy guests eager to wish the beaming bride and groom the good wishes their sweet natures deserved.

Once toasts had been made and guests began to chatter and mingle again around the second round of refreshments, Elizabeth, with some trepidation, sought out her new brother's dear friend, who had stood up with him at the altar.

She had not seen Mr Darcy since their interlude at the Twelfth Night Ball. Her shame at her own brazenness that night had thus far kept her silent and separate from him, but now, as she captured his gaze across the room, Elizabeth found herself moving towards him by the force of a longing stronger than her modesty.

Just before she could advance to his side, her steps faltered for fear he would not acknowledge her. Their last parting had been awkward, and the lapse in their intimacy had made the uncertainty between them all the more unbearable.

Mr Darcy set aside his cup and stepped forward with a bow. "Miss Bennet, I hope you are well," he said with halting graciousness.

"I am. I thank you, sir," Elizabeth replied reflexively. She took a breath. "And are you well? And your sister?"

At this enquiry, the last of Mr Darcy's reserve retreated. "Oh yes. I left Georgiana comfortably situated in London with our cousins, but at our last meeting, she pressed me to remind you to write to her when you can. I believe she already misses you."

"Of course, I shall! I do not know how I shall manage, with no Georgiana and no Jane!"

Mr Darcy stared at her a moment. "I had not thought of it, but you are sure to miss your sister very much. I do not like the thought of you friendless at Longbourn."

"I shall not be friendless," Elizabeth amended for him, "for I shall have my father. However, I shall miss my confidant, my confessor, and my comforter, but seeing Jane happy in her marriage does much to bring me comfort of a different sort."

"They could not be more fortunate in their union. I sincerely wish them happiness without end—for they have already captured it at the start."

At this most charitable reflection, Elizabeth could only smile. There was more she might have said to Mr Darcy if they had been alone, perhaps even offering her apology for her behaviour at the ball, but in the face of his unyielding and forgiving warmth, Elizabeth could find no purchase in her heart for such regrets. Such a realisation should have mortified her, but her feelings were fixed on one immovable point: she had nearly kissed him and would gladly take such an opportunity again.

All too soon, the carriage arrived to gather up the new Mrs Bingley and her doting husband, bound for their new home at Netherfield. The crowd of well-wishers advanced to the road to bid them farewell, and Elizabeth strode forward to embrace her sister.

"Goodbye, Jane dear," said Elizabeth, surprised by her own tears. "I wish you joy, and I am sure I shall see you soon."

"Should all your endeavours at Longbourn grow too tiring, promise me," Jane pleaded suddenly, "promise me you will come to Netherfield and stay, or go into Yorkshire with us when we leave next month."

Elizabeth nodded until she could find her voice. "I shall."

Elizabeth released her sister and stepped back from the carriage door. As the driver urged the horses onward, she noted that Mr Darcy's own team was stamping impatiently not far behind. She swallowed hard as she considered yet another loss to face, and one that came without the easy remedy of a mere three miles.

FOR THE FIRST FEW WEEKS SHE SPENT AT HOME, Elizabeth had the energy in body and mind to resist the promise she had made to Jane. She had a great deal of work to do at Longbourn and was glad of some help from her sole sisterly companion, Mary. Her mother and youngest sisters, having declared Longbourn still too sooty for easy breath and depressing to the spirits, had quickly decamped and soon resettled at the Philips's home, where they enjoyed happier surroundings, complete with the good company of the officers in town.

This arrangement suited Elizabeth, Mary, and their father amply, for the constant noise and complaints had been a distraction beyond forbearance in a house still unsettled by destruction. In the renewed quiet, Elizabeth gathered her diligence and bent herself to the work of restoring her home. She had never been a strong seamstress or been proud of her needlework, but she turned her attention to covering over browned and blackened furniture cushions and to replacing screens. She was no artist, but Elizabeth found herself employed in painting newly plastered walls. She even experimented with bleaching agents and laundry work, which she discovered to her humility was quite a physically taxing task, as well as one that required some rare knowledge of chemistry. This was all an education Elizabeth had never thought to direct her energies to before, but which now seemed so necessary.

Mr Bennet met now and again with the workmen who continued to repair the walls of his library and the charred back stairs that had delivered Elizabeth, Kitty, and their rescuer to safety. When her father was not ensconced with the workmen, he was often alone, often in the dark, as candles were an unnecessary expense, and to Elizabeth's distress, quite often in his cups.

In consequence, Mary became Elizabeth's primary companion, and together they engaged in various housekeeping endeavours. One afternoon, while they were crowded at the kitchen fire to do the messy work of dipping tallow to make into rushlights, Mr Bennet emerged from his solitude and ambled into their midst.

He stopped and stared at them a moment, and then said in a strained tone of compassion, "Ah, my girls, with such privations as we have taken upon ourselves, I wonder you do not seek some solace with your sister."

"If you mean with Jane," Elizabeth replied, "she has offered such, but I feel myself more useful here."

"Hmm, yes," Mr Bennet agreed. "Very useful. A great help, in fact."

"And the Lord is a present help in times of trouble," added Mary with an air of assured sufficiency.

Mr Bennet regarded his middle child over his spectacles. "Quite so."

With no more words forthcoming from their father, the girls returned to their employment. "We shall be glad of these lights tonight, I think," said Elizabeth suddenly. "I know Mary has missed reading and so have you, Papa."

Mr Bennet offered a nod of agreement. Then at last, he seemed to come to his point. "Lizzy, might I have a moment? There is something I must discuss with you."

Elizabeth wiped her hands and willingly followed him into his study. Rather than settling himself in the newly reupholstered chair Elizabeth had lately finished, he stood before her in some agitation.

"Given how attentive you have been, I do not think what I must tell you now will come as a surprise. I have worked over the figures again, and the fact of the matter is that until our payments on the restoration of the house are complete, we cannot retain all of our servants. I had hoped in sending Sarah with Jane that we might be fortuitously spared from such a decision, but tomorrow, I shall have to dismiss our scullery maid as well as Mrs Linville."

Elizabeth nodded sadly. It was not unexpected, but she forced herself to acknowledge another loss and a new burden.

"I have submitted an advertisement in hopes of finding someone who can undertake most of the kitchen and the cleaning, but I am afraid Mr and Mrs Hill will have to accept more duties than they are accustomed to managing."

"I understand, Papa."

Mr Bennet shifted uncomfortably. "Might you be willing to meet them, to discuss what division of tasks would be suitable?"

Elizabeth agreed. "And if you wish it, I can also provide a

writ of character for Esther and Mrs Linville. I cannot be grateful enough for their service."

"That I have already managed. It was the least I could do," Mr Bennet confirmed grimly.

As Elizabeth and Mary sat together in the glow of sputtering candles that evening, Elizabeth broke the news about the servants to her sister as gently as she could. She did not know what to make of Mary's silence at first, until her sister reached for a handkerchief.

Although Elizabeth was almost never alone, she found herself growing lonely as the winter drew towards spring. The dizzying society she had found in December in London, combined with all the joyful noise and company of her family there, proved a sharp contrast to the cold and dreary quiet of her days as February arrived.

She received a small reprieve from her cloistered situation when a letter came from her friend Charlotte Lucas, who was now Mrs Collins and no longer her close neighbour, Elizabeth reminded herself. She opened her letter with as much apprehension for Charlotte's uncertain happiness as eagerness for news.

> *My dear Eliza,*
>
> *I missed your wit almost as soon as I unpacked myself at the parsonage. It was hard to dress for my wedding this December without you here to critique me! It was harder still for me to disembark without a farewell or even a direction to give you!*
>
> *I know your life must be difficult at Longbourn, and so I am hesitant to place aught upon you as burdens beyond these two wishes I hold: that I hear from you often and that you would consent to visit me when my father and sister come in March. Indeed, Eliza, you will be as welcome here as either of them!*
>
> *My wish to see you is heightened by my concern. These past*

months for you have been times of trouble, and the ease of a friend's ear would, I hope, be welcome. Please write when you can of all your news and any resolutions you may have regarding a visit to Hunsford.

You will find—as I have—that our parsonage is very comfortable with such improvements to the house and its domestic arrangements as I think any guests will find pleasing. The furniture here is serviceable and comfortable, and the quiet roads are very like the ones that welcome your walks in Hertfordshire. The neighbourhood has some agreeably genteel families, hardworking tenant farmers, and reasonable merchants. Lady Catherine is also very obliging and has had us to dine. As a woman who values information, I fancy she would be curious to meet a cousin of Mr Collins and a dear friend of mine. Furthermore, Mr Collins assures me that the beauties of springtime at Rosings Park are not to be missed. I hope I have said enough to tempt you, and so I remain,

Your dear friend,
  Charlotte Collins

Brightening thoughts of the novelty of visiting Charlotte grew within Elizabeth. Her work at Longbourn, after all, must have an end, and time away from Mr Collins had dulled Elizabeth's distaste for the man and had sharpened the longing for her childhood friend, in whom she hoped she could still confide her burdens as readily as before.

Yet, therein lay her struggle. Elizabeth had valiantly sought to pretend, first to herself, and then most especially to her low-spirited father, that her troubles did not weigh on her.

And so it was when she first came to her father with Charlotte's proposed scheme, Mr Bennet balked at it, saying brusquely, "No, Lizzy. You are much needed here. I cannot fathom sending you away."

His immediate refusal gave her an unexpected pang of disappointment. Elizabeth acknowledged that perhaps what her father said was true. She alone had carried forward the tasks of restoring the household to some function, even taking on her mother's mantle by directing their reduced number of servants regarding the considerable consolidation of their roles within the house. There were still days of confusion in these assignments that required her attention, yet they grew less with every passing week. Once the servants became habituated to their new duties, surely then she could find some reprieve.

"Might we reconsider the invitation in mid-February? Mayhap things will feel more settled," Elizabeth offered, surprising herself at how she clung to her resolve.

"That much I doubt," her father muttered darkly, reaching again for his port. "Away with you now, child. I have to attend to more pressing matters."

As she stepped into the hall and closed the study door behind her, dejection descended upon Elizabeth. She could neither account for the way tears suddenly scalded her eyes, nor for how her heart now felt as if it might burst from some phantom pain.

Her feet led her outside where she breathed in the frigid air and struggled to calm herself. As she wiped her eyes, she attempted to scold herself into cheerfulness. Finding little success, Elizabeth wrapped her woollen shawl more tightly about her shoulders and began to walk, seeking peace with her feet. As she picked past the mud in the kitchen garden and came around the side of the house towards the drive, she began to acknowledge a sinking sense of despondency, a cheerless admission that she was not content in her situation. Worse, she began to feel desperately unhappy the more she ruminated on it, and that desperation only grew as she comprehended how powerless she was to change her circumstances, and of how dependent she remained on the will of her father.

A clatter of stones drew her from her miserable thoughts as a carriage rolled up towards the house. Elizabeth recognised it at once, and she quickly wiped the evidence of her distress from her cheeks.

"Jane!" she called as soon as she saw her sister alight.

Jane eagerly strode forward to embrace her. "I hope you do not mind, Lizzy. I am just come from Meryton and thought I would call as I made my return."

"You are always welcome, of course!" Elizabeth affirmed, clutching her tightly.

"You are frozen!" scolded Jane in her sweet way. "Whatever are you doing outside with not even a hat on your head? Let us go in the house."

As her sister ushered her inside, Elizabeth felt her spirits begin to revive under the balm of Jane's sisterly affection. She only released Elizabeth so she could divest her wraps and greet Mrs Hill. Then Jane led her directly into the sitting room.

"We might go to the kitchen instead, if you do not mind," Elizabeth said with some embarrassment. "We do not light the fire in this room until sundown. With so few of us here, it seems unnecessary."

Jane's face was at once alive with surprise and dawning concern. "Of course, Lizzy."

She trailed behind Elizabeth through the house until they came to sit side by side on stools near the old stone hearth, where Elizabeth grew increasingly aware of Jane's gaze.

"My sweet sister," Jane began. "You are pale and you do not look well. Will you not tell me your troubles? I can see that there are indeed more difficulties at Longbourn than I thought."

At this gentle application, Elizabeth's eyes welled again. She turned and drew in a quavering breath before she answered. "We must economise just now, so we can be sure to put more resources towards the planting in the spring. We are being prudent, Jane. Papa believes that with a good harvest, things will be better."

"I see."

"And under our father's direction, our domestics have been reduced. The Hills are still here, of course, but Esther is gone, and we also let Cook go in favour of a maid-of-all-work who has some experience as a kitchen maid. She makes simple meals, and she also washes dishes and helps with the cleaning. We have a laundress who comes once a week."

Jane nodded solemnly.

"Mary and I do what we can with what we know—mostly mending and sewing and stillroom work. Truly, Jane, it is not so difficult. I can bear it."

"Yet, you are unhappy," Jane said plainly.

Elizabeth bit her lip as unbidden tears threatened once again. She looked away into the fire as she admitted, "It is only a disappointment I had today. I shall regain my cheerful spirits, I assure you."

"Will you not tell me of your disappointment?" Jane pressed gently, placing her hand atop her sister's. Jane's fingers were warm from her fine gloves. Elizabeth's were ice cold. Jane knitted her brow and wrapped her hands gently around Elizabeth's.

That sweet, soothing touch was Elizabeth's undoing. Her tears fell and she dashed at them as she admonished herself.

"I was such a foolish girl. I asked our father for permission to go with Sir William and Maria Lucas into Kent, for Charlotte has invited me to come to her this spring. But of course, it is impossible. I should not have asked. I am needed here."

"Oh Lizzy, I came to ask you to come away with us on Tuesday into Yorkshire, to my husband's family in Scarborough. But whether in Kent or Scarborough, those who love you miss you, and that presents a need too. Yes, you have been of help to our father, I am sure, but spring is soon to come. Mama can take back the management of the household while he oversees the planting. You have done what you can, dear sister! Now let me do what *I* can to ease some of the burden."

Elizabeth shook her head as if to object, but Jane pressed on. "What if I were to take our sisters to Scarborough with us? Would they not enjoy an adventure by the sea? Their liveliness would not be unwelcome. Charles has cousins their age who would enjoy their company, and our father could have the quiet he craves while he focuses on the estate."

"Do you truly think Mr Bingley would not mind the responsibility, Jane? You know our Lydia can be a handful."

"It might be good for Lydia to be exposed to new society. Indeed, she may find herself well-suited to the merriment to be found in a seaside town, yet quieted by its peaceful environs. I shall broach the idea with my husband. I am sure he cannot object. He has been in a jumble of concern for our family, yet baffled by our father's unwillingness to allow his help. In this way, Mr Bingley could be of great assistance, and in such a form that it would be hard for our father to refuse." Thus resolved, Jane stood. "Leave this matter to me, Lizzy. You have enough cares to mind."

Elizabeth expressed her gratitude as warmly as she dared without full confidence in their plans, but she found that even the offering of hope for a reprieve was in itself a boon.

After Jane had spoken with Mary and greeted their father, her call ended. She embraced Elizabeth one last time before she boarded the carriage for Netherfield ahead of a cold rain.

WHEN JANE RETURNED TO CALL AGAIN THE NEXT DAY, she brought her husband with her. If Mr Bennet was surprised by their request to speak with him in his study, he did not show it.

After a brief conference, the couple departed his book

room, and Elizabeth stole a glance at her father from the hall. His bewildered visage gave Elizabeth all she required as evidence of his concession, for against the united affability of Mr and Mrs Charles Bingley and their kindest plans for the entertainment and care of his daughters, Mr Bennet could surely muster no well-meaning objection.

Before February waned, the three youngest Bennet girls departed in a flurry of excitement in the Bingley carriage that would take them to the seaside to enjoy the coming spring. And Elizabeth, too, would see the change to spring while on holiday —in Kent.

CHAPTER THIRTY-ONE

*I*n the short weeks before Elizabeth left for Kent, the chilly, wet days at Longbourn went on in simplicity, if not serenity. Mrs Bennet returned to resume the management of Longbourn's domestics, and she had been greatly perturbed at discovering two of their valued servants missing.

"Why was I not consulted in this, Mr Bennet?" she cried in outraged offence. "Was I not to be told? And was I not to be allowed to give my farewells when our servants were turned out from our doorstep?"

"I did what had to be done," her husband replied tiredly, removing his glasses to press the bridge of his nose. "It was not done joyfully or maliciously. But the fact is, if we cannot reduce our expenses, we shall be forced to take on considerable debt."

"So, you have reduced our comforts and our domestics to lessen the load of debt we hand to the creditors," she said coldly, "but had I been consulted regarding my own servants, I might have found other ways to economise—at least so that we might have kept on dear Cook. That girl you hired can barely turn toast without blackening it, and I am sure no one has taught her how to dress a chicken properly or to make the most of a small cut of beef. You cannot comprehend such things, having hardly set foot in a kitchen in your life."

"What is done is done!" Mr Bennet declared sharply. "If you take issue with the girl's efforts, then you may teach her better yourself."

"Very well, since you give me no other choice," his wife retorted before taking herself to the kitchen like a Fury.

TWO DAYS LATER, ELIZABETH AND MR BENNET partook of a quiet breakfast complete with toast now blessedly unburnt, served with the proper place setting. As she finished her last bite, Elizabeth could only smile at this proof of her mother's industry in teaching their young serving girl. She excused herself and removed to the parlour to begin a letter to Georgiana, when Mrs Hill announced two visitors.

The men who entered were prosperous looking, despite being rather short and plain. The accent of their speech was unusual, and Elizabeth assumed them to be American or perhaps Canadian, judging by the French surname that they shared—Gabin.

"Mr Bennet, dare we be so bold as to presume upon a shared connexion with Mr Edward Gardiner and request a few minutes of your time?"

Elizabeth merely stood by as Mr Bennet consented to their request and invited the men to follow him into his book room. She was left to her unanswered curiosity and to her correspondence.

My dear Georgiana,
  I am delighted to hear of your attempts on the harpsichord, and I hope to hear you play something for my pleasure one day. Life at Longbourn continues very quiet with only myself, my

mother, and my father here seeing to the business of restoring order to the house, and yet I confess I am eager for some diversion.

I had wished for this very thing when I received an invitation from my friend Charlotte Collins—recently married to Mr William Collins, rector of Hunsford Parish in Kent—to come and visit her in March, when her younger sister, Maria, and her father will make the journey. I confess myself excited by the prospect of seeing spring in a new place, and my father has finally given consent.

So that our correspondence may continue uninterrupted, be advised that Sir William Lucas has set our date of travel for Friday next. I promise to write from the parsonage to expound upon the beauties of nature I am sure to find in Kent and to relate all the amusements of company with so old a friend married to—dare I say it—so very silly a husband. You will think me cruel to say such a thing, but should you tell your brother that I shall soon be visiting the house of Mr Collins, observe for yourself if by his looks he does not intimate something of the same! The man is known to Mr Darcy by virtue of our common Hertfordshire acquaintance, and I assure you that Mr Collins left an indelible impression upon the whole neighbourhood while he was here.

I understand the Collinses are very grateful to their patroness, your aunt. I do not know if I shall meet Lady Catherine, but her rector has impressed upon me that she is an educated woman, obliging in her care, free with her opinions, and who keeps company only with your cousin. Do be kind and tell me of them, so I may be better prepared should any invitation or audience be forthcoming.

After half an hour of such employment, Elizabeth paused, her attention drawn away by the noisy disturbance of her father and his callers coming down the hall in a hubbub of convivial talk. She followed her curiosity to the door, and after the Messrs

Gabin took their leave and bowed very courteously as they went away, her father turned back to her, his face bright.

"Well, Lizzy, your uncle does seem to have an open mouth about our troubles," he said wryly. "But at least he has friends willing to look for opportunity to advance us."

"Who were those men?"

"Businessmen of some international means, although they now make their home in London. They have built canals for the Americans and seek to build more in England, like Mr Brindley's but with better locks. They are very near their goal to raise funds for this new series of canals. They have already begun construction. If we invest now, we could see a return this coming autumn on one completed branch of it."

"Speculation, then? How much do they require?"

"Five hundred pounds, which is all I hold currently from my investments and pitiable savings, plus the *in extremis* that is permitted to be withdrawn from your mother's settlement—and this, only if I shift some expenses from our restoration to our creditors."

"Such a sum!" Elizabeth's distress could scarcely be concealed. "But can the investment be sound?"

"I acknowledge that I had never imagined myself a speculator on principle, but many men I have known have engaged in it to great benefit," Mr Bennet said with a resigned air. "With a plan so careful as the one laid out by the Gabin brothers, and with their assurances of such a return—at double our investment—I feel myself quite satisfied. We can do without the money for the summer and harvest before we are made uncomfortable by the pinch. And then, to have it returned before the winter in such plenty, why, no one would even have cause to know of our troubles come this time next year."

"But if it is late or brings less than promised?"

Her father blew out a breath before biting out a sharp reply. "The decision and responsibility are mine. You must leave them to me." Without another word, Mr Bennet returned to his library.

Elizabeth, left alone with anxieties that seemed to mount with every moment, turned herself on the spot, and then set her feet towards the sitting room and paced the floor.

"Five hundred pounds—all we have!" she could not help repeating, even as she looked about her at the shambles still left behind from their great disaster—the cracked glass in the windows, the rug patched with tufts from rags, a table painted over to hide its blackened wood, the smoulder marks still imprinted on the ceilings and hardwoods, and her own sorry work basket, overflowing with her attempts to reclaim cushions and draperies.

There was more that did not meet the eye—the privations of their cupboard that only carried simple fare and where sugar and tea were becoming scarce, the shoes soon to be worn out in need of cobbling, the servants to be paid with bed and board besides, and in a few months, the feeding and care of the rest of the daughters of the house come home for the summer.

In such nearly desperate conditions, was the promise of a good return on a clever investment truly a terrible risk to take? After all, Uncle Gardiner was apparently on good terms with these men, or so they had claimed. Perhaps all would be well.

But if it was not, her family stood to lose too much.

On the little worktable, Elizabeth spotted the letter she had begun that very hour to Miss Darcy, opened so happily with news of her upcoming journey with the Lucases to Kent. Now, she could only marvel at her naivety in planning such a frivolous expedition simply for her pleasure. How very close her family hovered to the edge of poverty! How much her father was willing to lose to gain back what they once had!

How she wished she knew more of these men and their assurances! She could write to her uncle, perhaps, but her father's short temper just moments ago had made it clear that any meddling on her part that reached him would evoke only greater heights of displeasure. Elizabeth certainly could not tell her mother, who would either reproach her father beyond his ability to bear it or side with him out of hopeful folly. No, she could not bring her father further embarrassment or encouragement by refusing to keep her place.

And yet, her place—her small, shrinking place—was a pit of helplessness.

Blinking back tears, she took up her unfinished letter, intending to crumple it. As she glanced one last time at the cheerful words she had written that now almost shamed her, Elizabeth's eyes landed upon a line of her own writing: *'tell your brother...'*

Here was something to consider. Being a man of so much property and so shrewd and responsible in business, Mr Darcy might have already heard of the opportunity put forward by the Messrs Gabin. Surely, these canal builders had already presented their scheme to the men of means in Mr Darcy's circle, seeking their investment. If he had heard of them, if he knew good of them, how much it would soothe her nerves to hear him say so! And if they were men not to be trusted, Mr Darcy would, perhaps, have knowledge of that too.

She was wild to fly to London to seek his advice! As it was, she saw only one mortifying option. She laid out her letter to Miss Darcy and picked up her pen again.

AS HAD OFTEN HAPPENED SINCE HE HAD LAST SEEN Elizabeth Bennet in January, Darcy caught himself in the midst of cherishing some memento that brought fancies of her to the fore. Most recently, it was a piece his sister was practising at the pianoforte as he awaited his solicitor's visit. The faint strains of the song tugged at him, so much so that even the footman's announcement of the arrival of Mr Woods could not quite disengage him from the melody. He could only nod his permission, and before long, his man of business presented himself, and Darcy was forced to recall his wits and his manners.

As he made his greeting, the sound of the pianoforte blessedly ceased, and Darcy imagined his sister had begun to read through her correspondence. Darcy borrowed this cue and presented some of his own steward's letters to Mr Woods.

With his careful acumen, his solicitor turned over the figures from Pemberley's steward.

"While last year's harvest and rents might be slightly lower than previous, I can concur with Mr Atkinson that your latest income from your investments alone will more than cover amply."

Darcy nodded. A knock on the study door interrupted them. "Come," he called.

Georgiana, wide-eyed, stepped into the room. "I am terribly sorry, Fitzwilliam." Her eyes flew from Darcy to his solicitor, and her pale face made him start. "But I have just received a letter—from—from Longbourn that requires your notice."

He could not mistake her meaning, for who else would write from Longbourn but her most dutiful correspondent, Elizabeth? He suddenly feared the worst—that perhaps yet another disaster had befallen the family in their delicate state.

"Might I have a moment, Mr Woods?" Darcy said, even as he beckoned Georgiana to him.

The solicitor bowed and went out, and Georgiana came around his desk, laying on its surface her letter, with one fold reversed so that the pertinent lines faced him. What Darcy read in Elizabeth's hand arrested him completely.

Since writing the above, dear friend, something has occurred of a most unexpected and serious nature, but be assured that we are all well here in Hertfordshire. What I have to say relates to a business matter brought just now before my father by some visi-

tors. I admit their offer has beset me with some anxiety, which I hope better information can alleviate. I am ashamed to make such an imposition, but with no other sources of aid available with my new brother Bingley gone to Yorkshire with Jane and my sisters, and my uncle Philips often unreliable in matters of finance, I must petition you, if opportunity and courage allow you, to bring this letter before your brother, that I may beg his counsel.

Just now two men, Messrs Gabin, called upon my father to present a business proposal. They are apparently acquainted with my uncle, Mr Gardiner, who made known to them our situation. Thinking perhaps to draw nearer to their goal while also providing greater opportunity for us, the gentlemen invited my father to join in a speculation that will fund a project of theirs, the construction of a new canal, which promises a double return on his investment before the coming winter, once the first portion of this project is complete. My father, who thinks highly of any associates of my uncle, seems willing to take up their proposal.

Being as we are in the country and quite sheltered from such sources of insight and information as the many circles of business-minded men in London can supply, I am hopeful that if Mr Darcy has heard of these men or this scheme, he might be so good as to give what assurances he can of their trustworthiness and prospects. His word on this matter would be greatly respected by my father—and by me, greatly appreciated.

In making such a request, I know I place an unfair burden on our friendship, and I most sincerely regret the circumstances that formed my action. If you feel I have wronged you, pray forgive me and know that I would fully understand if you would rather not become involved in this matter. My father, with or without Mr Darcy's advice, will do as he deems best. I shall look forward to your next letter to cheer me, regardless of whether or not you have acted on my impertinent and officious request.

Your friend,
Elizabeth Bennet

Knowing Elizabeth's independent nature and the privacy she cherished, this letter and the impropriety of its application spoke volumes of her desperation. Although Darcy's heart demanded he reply immediately to comfort her, he recognised that even now in her distress, Elizabeth's courage had not failed her.

Far more than his useless platitudes or perhaps unwelcome declarations of devotion, he decided her far greater need in this moment was for his action and influence.

Darcy reached for his sister's hand and pressed it. "Georgiana, you did well to bring this matter to me. Please tell John to call back Mr Woods."

FIVE DAYS OF UNEASE AND DISQUIET PASSED BEFORE A large and momentous delivery of post arrived. Elizabeth was still reading a novel and dawdling over her breakfast at the table when Mr Hill presented her with two thick epistles addressed in Miss Darcy's hand with coins for their postage lodged thoughtfully in the heavy wax seals of each.

Elizabeth strove for calm as she accepted her correspondence and broke the seals on them just enough to retrieve the coins to pass back to Mr Hill to give the postman. She pretended a desire for one last sip of tea before excusing herself to the solace of the sitting room.

Assured of privacy, Elizabeth immediately brought the pages of each missive before her eyes. Those in the first letter were indeed from Miss Darcy throughout its entirety, and as Elizabeth spread open the second rather lumpy packet, she saw that the enveloping page was covered over in her friend's same dainty hand as well. With hopeful trepidation, Elizabeth removed the first sheet and caught her breath as she glimpsed a word written in a firm, bold hand she had seen several times. She let out a gasp when she realised that Mr Darcy had written only *Elizabeth*.

She knew not what to think. She could only stare at her own Christian name and wonder what he meant by using it. Absent was not only her formal title or surname but any endearment, and yet it was still, to her mind, an intimate address.

Shaking hands bade her lay his letter down on her lap as she pressed her palms to her cheeks in an attitude of confusion for a moment before she carefully unfolded the page. As she did so, yet another letter fell out into her lap, tightly folded and sealed. Elizabeth swallowed when she saw that Mr Darcy had addressed this new missive, very correctly, to her father.

Her curiosity enflamed, she turned back to Mr Darcy's first note and began to read.

Elizabeth,

I am grateful for your conscientiousness in sharing your concerns with me by such means as are at your disposal. The apology you tendered at your 'imposition' was unnecessary as the term is unmerited and unjust. You sought my advice with the purest motives on a matter which could gravely affect your entire family's future. Your application, rather than presenting an imposition, bestowed upon me the gift of your confidence and evoked my reciprocal concern. I now find myself with pen in hand, imposing upon you. I must, therefore, rely upon your generous nature to pardon the freedom with which I demand your attention in light of that which I must relate.

Enclosed, you will find a letter addressed to your father which contains no intimation of your confidence, yet at the same time, offers him the careful disclosure of my recent discovery of some speculative schemes in popular circulation in and around

London—schemes which include the one presented by the Messrs Gabin—that represent return margins and their timetables of allotment quite falsely, with the design to entice those seeking to invest.

Your father's perspicacity is such that he may come to regard the precipitous nature of such a missive with suspicion, however much I endeavoured within it to also impress upon his notice other, better investment opportunities, as well as matters pertinent to the reconstruction at Longbourn in an effort to preserve his autonomy in these concerns as head of your family. Being that disguise of every sort is my abhorrence and therefore against my usual practice, I cannot be certain of the convincing powers of this epistolary 'piece of cleverness' as you once called a previous interference of mine.

In this case, I determined that I ought to take the risk. My friendship to your father and my own character demand nothing less than this well-intentioned and reasonable attempt to alert him to the dangers of his present course. I trust in your discretion to divine the best means of delivering this cautionary message into his hands.

I must thank you again for your courage in relating the whole of these circumstances to me, for I know the disclosure must have generated some feelings of mortification. Indeed, your suspicions of this speculation have been proven wholly warranted, the fact of which I hope will gratify you and remove any lingering burden of distress for having resorted to my gladly rendered assistance. Rest assured that even had your judgment erred and my investigations proved this proposed scheme fruitful, it would have been my delight to send news that might have cheered you.

Being of use to you would and does please me. I, therefore, urge you not to be remiss in applying to me for any assistance in the future. For those occasions where my service would not avail, I must add, God bless you, Elizabeth.

Fitzwilliam Darcy

What a tempest of feeling did his missive bring! In every well-formed letter, Mr Darcy had thoughtfully traced the weight of the gravity of the matter, his care for her family's well-being, and even his concern for her anxious feelings. Where one line would raise Elizabeth's sense of alarm as to her own impropriety in so directly appealing to him or to the very real danger in which her father had placed her family's fortunes, the next line would soothe and flatter her. And with this example of kindness, came a strangely mortifying joy. For what a privilege it was to have his assistance, and to have it given so unreservedly! That Mr Darcy should own himself pleased to be of use to her in any hour of need was astonishing! Still awash in her appreciation of Mr Darcy, she picked up the smaller epistle intended for her father and secreted it into her work apron's pocket.

Hearing her father moving about in the hall, Elizabeth hastily slid Mr Darcy's missive to her under the pile of correspondence. She smoothed open the rest of it hurriedly, to better conceal and appear occupied should her father walk in. His footsteps, however, passed innocuously by the door as they took the well-worn path to the cellar for more port.

In what felt like her first in days, Elizabeth took a calming breath, released it in a sigh of relief, and collected her letters. Palming the smallest one, she dashed for her father's book room where she placed Mr Darcy's note with prominence upon the desk.

That done, she sidled quietly up the stairs to her chamber, skirt pockets rustling with the other sheaves of her correspondence. Glancing about the room, Elizabeth decided upon her prayer book as the place to hide away Mr Darcy's other letter— a perfect spot for further meditations. With a sigh that spoke of the now rare delight of contentment, she settled herself by the window in a lumpy chaise and began to read her far less weighty missive from Miss Darcy.

It was a happy, long letter, which began with a recitation of some of the enjoyments and trivialities of her friend's recent days. In the second part of Georgiana's letter, she included more direct replies to Elizabeth's last missive, along with her promises to seek immediate assistance from Mr Darcy and her heartfelt prayers for a quick and timely resolution to Elizabeth's concerning matter. Just as feelings of shame began to creep and then to bear down to overpower her, the last lines of Georgiana's letter did much to raise her spirits.

> *And how glad I am to read that you are soon for Kent this spring! What lovely timing your friend Mrs Collins has, for my brother and my dear cousin Colonel Fitzwilliam are planning even now to make their yearly Easter pilgrimage to Rosings Park to visit Lady Catherine. I shall apply to my brother immediately for permission to accompany him this year. I daresay he will be surprised by my request, for I find our aunt so very fearsome that I usually beg leave to stay home. With you in attendance, however, I shall not be afraid. I shall have someone to talk to who will not sit in such awful dread of her ladyship as I! I shall write more once I have secured all permission.*
>
> *Ever fondly, your friend,*
> *Georgiana Darcy*

With a lighter heart, Elizabeth laid aside her letters, deciding that she would keep her trunk open in readiness for her journey to Kent after all. But first, she had to return to her work in preparing Longbourn for her absence.

Elizabeth's resolve stirred her enough to hasten her return below stairs, where she donned her work apron and made her way to the back of the house to prepare pots of seedlings for the kitchen garden. She spent a pair of quiet hours in this dirty work before her father sent for her. She had made time to wash her hands before she hastened to his study.

"Well, Lizzy," said her father, his words slightly slurred, "it seems you may have been right to caution me about the Messrs Gabin. There will be no investments made in any canals."

Elizabeth's heart swelled in relief. She took her father's hand. "I am sorry for such a disappointment, but I am very glad you looked further into the matter."

Mr Bennet raised a brow, considering both his daughter and her words, but then he pressed on, waving his hand as if swatting the matter aside. "I should also tell you that your aunt Gardiner has written to me for permission for you to join them in their travels to the Lakes this summer. If all goes well this spring for the planting, I may consent, but I shall certainly miss you."

With a sigh, Elizabeth mused aloud. "I wonder now if my life will be thus until our home is restored— invited by one well-meaning friend into one home or another, like a rolling rock never able to settle."

"Take cheer, my Lizzy, that at least you have such friends at your disposal."

Melancholy made him silent after this observation, and so Elizabeth squeezed his hand in farewell before taking herself off to her room to wash and rest. Unwilling to face the decision of dressing herself in clean clothing, Elizabeth went to the bed and lay down, feeling unaccountably wretched. She yearned for the calm and peace she had known as a child. She yearned for another soul's understanding, for the warmth of care she once knew with Jane. She missed the good sense of the Gardiners and the advice and direction they gave her. And, thinking of today's letters, she yearned for the thoughtfulness of the Darcys, in whose company, she realised, she had enjoyed a home-like peace, even when she was in the less familiar surrounds of Darcy House.

Within her breast jostled the burdens of bereavement, heavy like stones. Her old life was gone in sweet youthful memory. She ached for the serenity and fortitude that now eluded her, and when she allowed herself to dwell on her fancies, miserable longing pressed its aching weight within her heart for a future life she could never have with a man she admired and adored above all others.

Knowing this, could she bear to see Mr Darcy again? In mere weeks, Elizabeth would have her answer. She wrestled with her courage, even as her weary eyes fell closed.

CHAPTER THIRTY-TWO

*T*here was no way to feel at peace without knowing something of his success. To Darcy's mind, his letter to advise Mr Bennet might have been written in vain, for the man might have chosen to ignore such officiousness and go his own way. Worse, he might have been a dilatory reader of correspondence, as seemed his wont, and so he might have made his commitment to the Gabin brothers' scheme before even opening it.

So, when Darcy discovered his sister had obtained yet another letter from Elizabeth, his curiosity and anxiety demanded at least a polite enquiry into the matter.

"I hope Miss Bennet is well," he said, pausing by the escritoire as his sister sat writing.

Georgiana turned to him. "It certainly seems so. While her letter does not speak of her—of her troubles at home, it does confirm that she is off to Kent to visit Mrs Collins, likely today." At her brother's look of astonishment, she continued. "Did I not tell you? It must have slipped my mind, for I had learned of her plans when I read her last letter. But then her pressing need was so great, I did not tell you all I knew."

"To Kent?" Darcy could only repeat dully. In just a few short weeks, his own visit to his aunt would bring him to Rosings. There might be opportunity anew to secure her regard —and this time, he would not miss the chance.

"Yes! And I know it is not my usual request, but might I go with you to visit Lady Catherine this year? Elizabeth's visit will extend past Easter, and I should so like the chance to visit with her."

Darcy smiled. "How you must be missing your friend, for you have never volunteered such a request! However, I am sure it will please our aunt and our cousin Anne."

"Then I may go?"

"Most certainly. I shall ensure the arrangements are made and perhaps seek an earlier date to begin our visit," he said eagerly.

Silently, Darcy worked over in his mind the difficulties of dividing his time between his aunt's demands upon him for attendance and estate matters, his duties to his sister, and opportunities to speak alone to Elizabeth. Some of his conundrum must have appeared on his face, for his sister's pleasure transformed into concern and then dawning understanding.

"If I am likely to be in the way," Georgiana began, "then perhaps I ought to stay home. I had not thought of it, but of course, you might want some time with Elizabeth. I must not be constantly *de trop* in matters that concern more than myself."

"No, no, you will be very welcome. In fact, if you are bold enough, I might task you with sitting with our aunt, should a chance to speak with Miss Bennet arise."

Georgiana gasped and clasped his hands. "Oh, Fitzwilliam! Do you mean—will you make her an offer?"

Darcy looked down to meet Georgiana's hopeful gaze,

unsure how much to unburden himself to his sister. The truth of it was that the intolerable uncertainty of regard in which he stood with Elizabeth had to end. "It is an offer long overdue, if my heart has had anything to say about it. Will you wish me well?"

Georgiana beamed. "How can I not, when I have been wishing for this very thing?"

As the carriage conveying Elizabeth, Sir William Lucas, and his daughter Maria bounced along the ruts in the road on their way into Kent, Elizabeth attempted to put her mind and heart at ease.

It had been difficult for her to leave Longbourn behind, to leave her father to his burdens without her aid, with only the caustic complaints of his wife to urge him to greater success in estate matters.

At least in bidding farewell to Mary and her other sisters as they prepared for the enjoyment of the sea, there had been lightness of heart.

"Jane and our brother Bingley are come!" Lydia had sung, and they had all been met with the warmth of Mr Bingley's smile and the sweetness of Jane's kindness and care, for she came bearing thoughtful gifts of new gloves and a bonnet for each of her sisters. As they exclaimed over these delights, Elizabeth tried on her new bonnet and turned to show Jane her appreciation.

"I see you remembered my preference for a deeper brim."

"All the better for your complexion as you take your walks! And I do hope you will take the opportunity as often as you can," Jane replied. She went on admiring each of her sisters in their new hats until Mr Bingley brought news that the trunks had been loaded on the carriage.

Mrs Bennet excitedly ushered them all into the entry hall

where she made her last admonishments to her children and wished them a fair journey whilst Jane kindly helped her younger sisters secure their ribbons and button pelisses. If the young ladies' reticules had suddenly jingled with new coin, Jane did not admit to it, but Elizabeth had witnessed all. Jane had been far more conspicuous when she turned away to press Elizabeth's portion directly into her hand and express her hopes for a happy visit to Kent.

Elizabeth smiled to herself as their conveyance slowed and swayed. The carriage that bore her turned from the high road, and she soon beheld the palings and handsome trees of Rosings Park. The lane then drew up to a gravel walk and gate, which led into a sloping garden that raised up towards a fine cottage. And there, opening the parsonage door and stepping into the walk, appeared Mr Collins and Charlotte. Maria Lucas gave a little squeal of delight as the carriage trundled to a stop, and she surged up from her seat beside Sir William to go and greet her sister.

Their greetings expressed all their delight in their reunion. Mr Collins, happy at last to have visitors to his domicile, at once urged them into the house with ostentatious formality. It pleased Elizabeth to see Charlotte more amused than vexed by this bit of ludicrous fervour, and she allowed herself to be shown around, pressed to eat and drink, and tidily settled into her modest but comfortable chamber.

Once Maria and Sir William had likewise been shown to their rooms, Charlotte returned to Elizabeth, who had begun unpacking her trunk.

"It does my heart good to see you looking well," Charlotte declared. "You seem a trifle thin perhaps, but you are not so pale as you were when last I saw you. Is all well now at Longbourn?"

Elizabeth's answering smile was a conscious one. "When I left it, the house had been put to better order, but the occupants of the house, I fear, are not well-suited to harmony. My mother is home alone with my father now, you see. Did I not tell you that Jane and Mr Bingley took my sisters off to Yorkshire?"

"You mentioned such a holiday in your last letter," Charlotte replied, adding with a wry sort of smile, "and that was very kind of Mr Bingley. I think your sister married very well."

At such a remark, Elizabeth's grin widened as her spirits gained a little of their former, happy spark. "Of that there can be no doubt. Whatever might bring Jane happiness is done on the instant, as whatever Mr Bingley does, he does in haste."

Charlotte laughed good-naturedly and came around the bedside to help Elizabeth slide her trunk against the wall. She sighed in a sort of relieved satisfaction when she said, "It is so good to laugh openly again, my dear Eliza. You cannot know what your visit means to me."

Elizabeth bit her lip, recognising some dejection in her friend's words. "Charlotte, do tell me you are happy. I must admit I was surprised by your engagement, although I have wished only joy for you."

Her friend hesitated before she made her answer. "Mr Collins is not so very difficult a husband. He asks very little and is not a complicated man. But I sometimes find that my position here—most especially my role as the parson's wife—brings an abundance of complexity and caution to my personal doings. I cannot feel easy when I am often under scrutiny."

"Are your parishioners here so ready to cast judgment?"

"Most are far too humble for that, although they do keep a careful distance just the same. Perhaps in time, I may bridge the gap, but for now, Eliza, I am so glad to have a friend here with me."

Charlotte's sense of isolation fixed a new kinship between them, and Elizabeth clasped her hand in understanding. When she went off to bed that night, Elizabeth felt at peace for the first time in many weeks.

Such tranquillity would be disturbed the very next day, when Miss de Bourgh and her companion, Mrs Jenkinson, surprised them—or as Mr Collins declared it, *honoured* them—by stopping by in their phaeton in the drive by the lane.

For the first time, Elizabeth observed Charlotte acting publicly as Mrs Collins. Her friend was so wary of giving offence that, rather than request that the ladies come inside, she stood outside the phaeton in the chilly wind while the ladies from Rosings enjoyed warm lap-rugs. Their visit was otherwise cordial, and Mr Collins expressed his delight that they would deign to stop and talk for so long.

To this bit of condescension, Lady Catherine de Bourgh herself added still more by inviting them to tea and an evening's company at Rosings when she met them all at Sunday service the following day.

Large in frame and imposing in manner, Lady Catherine presented herself much as Elizabeth had pictured. To her consternation, Lady Catherine's dominance of the conversation did not allow for Elizabeth to politely address that great lady's seemingly frail daughter. This bit of vexation gave way to rising anxiety as it became clear to Elizabeth that Lady Catherine prized the information she had heretofore gathered of all of Mr Collins's relatives and their unfortunate affairs. It was this which Lady Catherine sought to discuss.

"I take it, Miss Bennet, that your father's estate is not over-large or prosperous, and this fire has placed great strain upon your family," Lady Catherine mused aloud after interviewing Elizabeth for a quarter of an hour.

As Elizabeth pondered how best to respond without either shaming herself or her impertinent hostess, Lady Catherine continued. "Well, while you are here, I hope it lessens your father's burden. You may stay on as long as you desire, and should you tarry past a month, I could ensure your conveyance home in my own barouche."

In some astonishment, Elizabeth expressed her thanks, while also remarking that her father would need her soon at home.

"Has he no bailiff or steward to run his estate? Must he send for his eldest daughter still at home?"

Elizabeth replied, "In this matter, your ladyship, you may take my word upon it that I serve as my father's faithful assistant both in the house and on the estate. In such times as these, you may imagine, convention may be overthrown in favour of necessity."

"Upon my word, you give your opinions very decidedly," Lady Catherine observed.

Elizabeth was glad when their conversation was interrupted by the arranging of the card tables when Mr Collins and Sir William Lucas returned. The chief speakers of the room—the gentlemen and Lady Catherine—then dealt as much in anecdotes and observations as in cards, and Elizabeth was content to keep out of their way. The call for the carriage came not long after, and at this release, Elizabeth nearly gasped with relief.

In the weeks to come, Elizabeth experienced long stretches of happy freedom exploring Rosings's groves—punctuated only by some outings for morning calls with Charlotte, as well as twice-weekly evenings for tea or supper at Rosings, which passed better with Elizabeth attending to the pianoforte more than to her hostess.

But on her fourth evening at Rosings, Lady Catherine's mention of the catastrophe at Longbourn once more unmoored Elizabeth from her peace.

"Mr Collins, did you say that Longbourn expected full repairs within the year, or do some outstanding debts remain on the estate that would preclude it? I was speaking just this morning of your prospects to my steward, and I could not recall where your portion stood."

Mr Collins turned pale. "I—that is, my cousin Bennet has assured me that things are well in hand. I—'"

"Come now, Mr Collins, have you not inspected your inheritance? Did you not return there in December when you took your wife?"

"Alas—no, your ladyship, it was only—"

"It is mostly complete, ma'am," Elizabeth interjected with some heat. "The house is in order, or so it was when I left it. My father may answer further questions for Mr Collins."

"And well he might," said Lady Catherine with a severe look at her rector. "If only Mr Collins would take the trouble of writing or visiting to ascertain it."

Elizabeth bit back a retort intended to defend the veracity of her own word. Instead, she stared up at Lady Catherine until that older woman noticed the offence and challenge she had written upon her expression. Elizabeth's silence stood in their midst like an obstruction in a road. When Lady Catherine next approached Elizabeth with a question, it was with more caution than before, querying her again regarding her expectations for her stay as the weather changed to spring.

Visits to Rosings were henceforth more brief affairs. Elizabeth took pains to observe rather than speak, and so kept the harmony among those present. Without meaning to, she had adopted the mode of the delicate Miss de Bourgh when in company with the great lady of the house.

These habits of silence sometimes followed Elizabeth back to the parsonage and thence into her meditative walks in the grove. On one fine, bright morning, Elizabeth was alarmed to find Mr Collins walking in the lane and seemingly eager to follow her towards the grounds of Rosings.

"Did I not tell you, Cousin Elizabeth, that Lady Catherine is expecting her most esteemed visitors at any moment? Mr Darcy, Miss Darcy, and the second son of the Earl of Matlock are soon to arrive! I have every intention of moving towards the lane leading to the manor, so as to acknowledge them as they pass."

Elizabeth found herself divided between embarrassment and affinity upon hearing his wish. Her own excited longing caused affinity to carry the day.

"Well, then," she replied with a smile, "shall we not walk this way?"

In half an hour, Mr Collins had his wish, and he made his bow as a great coach-and-four swept down the lane in their direction. Elizabeth, with less dignity, rose upon her toes and waved.

As it passed by, there was a shout from within the carriage, and to the alarm of Mr Collins, the conveyance slowed and came to a stop.

CHAPTER THIRTY-THREE

To Elizabeth's delight, Mr Darcy emerged from the coach, looking decidedly amused as his gaze swept over her where she stood dumbfounded in the road.

"Mr Collins, Miss Bennet!" he called. "Well met. Might we prevail upon you and have the honour of calling at the parsonage before we head on to the manor house?"

Gasping his acceptance, Mr Collins offered to conduct them on towards his home.

"The horses are still hot, so I think they would object at being so slowly led. You had best come aboard, Mr Collins, and you too, Miss Bennet, while we break them from their lather. Would you join us?"

Elizabeth bit back a grin at Mr Darcy's easy handling of the rector. As she raised her eyes to his face, she caught the hint of his familiar smile, and she knew they shared the same entertainment. As she approached, he offered her his hand to board the carriage, and Elizabeth took it unreservedly. Miss Darcy, Mrs Annesley, and Colonel Fitzwilliam greeted her within, each expressing delight at the happy surprise.

It had been a quarter of a year since she had seen the Darcys. Such a small span of time, and yet how in those months Elizabeth had changed! Her eyes had been opened to the struggles of human existence, she had learnt to endure disappointment and deprivation, and she knew herself to look a little careworn from the efforts of this strict tutelage. It pleased her to see that Mr Darcy looked as magnificent as he ever did, while Miss Darcy seemed the picture of contentment.

This journey with her friends was brief, however, and Mrs Collins came out to greet them. Her eyes grew wide at the sight of the party now assembling by her gate. Her self-possession quickly returned, however, and she welcomed the road-weary travellers inside while calling for tea and refreshments.

Mr Darcy was quick to make introductions, and Colonel Fitzwilliam just as eagerly set his hosts at ease. "I hope you will forgive us for calling so unexpectedly, Mrs Collins. You are very gracious to welcome such an invasion."

Charlotte offered immediate clemency with her smile as she greeted each in turn.

"Mrs Collins, what good fortune it is for us that you have included Miss Bennet in your party," said Miss Darcy when she was through. "It is such a joy for me to see her again, as I am sure it is for you as well, having so long been her friend."

The colonel declared, "And I am vastly contented to know that Miss Bennet will be in the neighbourhood to enhance the enjoyment of our visit. I have my own fond recollections of our meeting in London, and of course, my cousins know her so well. Georgiana has brought sheaves and sheaves of music, and I do hope you will play and sing, as she has talked of little else that brings her more pleasure than a duet with Miss Bennet."

"I shall be happy to oblige you, if I am welcome to practise with Miss Darcy at Rosings or play duets there in an evening party," Elizabeth agreed, with a soft look at Georgiana, before turning her gaze from sister to brother with some new mischief brightening her smile. "We have already visited with your aunt and cousin there some evenings, and I have displayed my meagre skills at the instrument. I am sure with Miss Darcy's fine playing to overshadow me in our duets, her ladyship's assessment of my capabilities can only improve!"

Elizabeth's faithful young friend decried this poor self-reflection, but Elizabeth let out a breath and gave her an honest confession. "Of late, I admit, I have been most neglectful, having lost our little pianoforte to the fire at Longbourn."

"Ah, but I know you have employed your time much better. You have sacrificed your pursuits in favour of serving your family's needs, which is most admirable," Mr Darcy remarked.

"My own comfort is bound up with my family's, and I believe it often mingles with my nobler sense of duty. You must not think me a slave to devotion."

"And yet, I have often seen you devoted to the detriment of your comfort—or safety," he maintained. He paused a moment as he searched her face. "I hope you have been well, Miss Bennet."

"I—thank you, yes, I have," she replied, flushing at this mark of attention. "It was a long winter with much to be done, but it was well done, sir. And I thank you for your part," she added meaningfully.

The soft rumble of his voice betrayed his satisfaction at her revelation. "I am glad to hear it."

As their visitors' company was soon expected up the lane, Elizabeth was disappointed that there was not much time for further talk beyond pleasantries, reflections on the condition of the roads, their plans at their destination, and entreaties from Mr and Mrs Collins to call whenever convenient. Elizabeth saw her friends to the door with regret, for she knew she had only the good grace of Lady Catherine on which to ground her hopes of meeting with them soon.

ELIZABETH WAS FORCED TO BE PATIENT, FOR TWO days passed before Lady Catherine was sufficiently satisfied by the companionship of her visiting family to issue invitations to others or to release them to make visits. Upon observing her relations mingling merrily with the Collinses' guests at church on Sunday, she finally approached Mr and Mrs Collins and very civilly invited them to bring their party to Rosings for the evening.

At sunset, they took the lane towards the manor. The party from the parsonage was quite aflutter with talk. Maria, anticipating a meeting with Miss Darcy again, spoke her hopes that they might strike up a friendship, if only to share the woes of being a similar age. Mr Collins reflected on the importance of his role as clergyman in preparing for Easter and the implied compliment of her ladyship's invitation. After giving answer to her husband's comments, Mrs Collins then took Elizabeth's arm.

"You are very quiet, dear Eliza."

"Am I? I do not intend to be. I aim to please this evening, if our company is of a mood for it."

"I have no doubt of your reception by her ladyship's guests. I still cannot believe they called upon us straight from the road. I must thank you, Eliza, for that civility. Mr Darcy would never have come so soon to call upon me, and I would have been obliged to wait a week to meet the famous Colonel Fitzwilliam and Mr Darcy's young sister."

That visit had surprised Elizabeth as well, and it had taught her to hope that perhaps in defiance of everything, Mr Darcy did indeed hold her dear. But then there had been no calls and no happy encounters on her walks for two days, and such oversight had done much to temper her fancies.

"You might place too much stock in supposition, Charlotte. His consideration of my condition, I believe, led him to be curious and concerned. My apparent good health gave him all the satisfaction he sought, and so he has made no other attempt to visit. Now I feel I can conclude what I have asserted to you from the first. Mr Darcy has no more than a friendly interest in me."

Charlotte raised a brow. "You might have underestimated the influence of Lady Catherine. She has every means at her disposal to occupy him, even to unseat his plans by compelling his interest in matters of estate and family business."

"Perhaps."

When they were shown into the drawing room, her ladyship received them with civility, but it was plain she was almost entirely engrossed by her niece and nephews, speaking to them, especially to Mr Darcy, much more than to any other person in the room.

Elizabeth's eye caught Mrs Annesley's, who directed her gaze with a gesture towards a cluster of chairs in the corner by the instrument, where Miss Darcy had sought refuge. Finding the heiress of Rosings present there as well, Elizabeth approached and sat down between her friend and Miss de Bourgh, who seemed a bit startled at her choice.

Elizabeth sought to put her at ease. "I hope I do not startle you by sitting so close. I promise to be well-behaved, and you should have no fear of me. Miss Darcy, I think, can vouch for my ability to conduct myself with decorum despite my wilder inclinations."

Georgiana laughed at being put forward. "Indeed, Cousin Anne, you should have no fear of Elizabeth. She will talk and talk but never bite!"

Miss de Bourgh surprised them both by emitting a chuff of a chuckle. "So I see."

Encouraged by this small spark of liveliness, Elizabeth settled herself more comfortably, and with the assistance of Miss Darcy, began the hard work of drawing out their reticent young hostess.

Elizabeth had just discovered the kinds of music Miss de Bourgh most liked to hear when Mr Darcy approached, his face a portrait of curiosity.

"Do you mean to frighten us, Mr Darcy, by coming all this way to hear our conversation?" Elizabeth teased him, once she saw that his appearance had, indeed, intimidated Miss de Bourgh back into silence. "I think you know by now, sir, that there is a stubbornness about me that can never bear to be frightened at the will of others. My courage always rises at every attempt to intimidate me."

"I shall not say you are mistaken," Mr Darcy replied with a smile, "because you could not really believe me to entertain any design of alarming you." Here, his gaze fell to his frail cousin, who seemed to struggle to find her composure and did not know where to look.

Elizabeth laughed heartily and then admitted, "Oh, you have caught me out, Mr Darcy. I am not afraid of you."

Elizabeth continued on in this teasing vein, at times appearing to alarm Miss de Bourgh with her vivacity, but she also seemed captivated by the amity it implied between her cousins and their friend from Hertfordshire.

Their merriment was interrupted by the sound of a cane rapping the floor. Elizabeth looked up to find herself the focus of Lady Catherine, who watched them from the great winged chair by the fire. Such scrutiny forced Elizabeth to consider how her lively display had appeared to that lady—and most especially how her ladyship's prized nephew's attentions towards herself might be perceived by a woman who held high hopes for her family's connexions.

In recent visits, Elizabeth had detected a tepid amiability directed towards her from Lady Catherine, who no doubt viewed her as an unfortunate young woman worthy of some charitable consideration. But now, Elizabeth felt the swell of her ladyship's compassionate condescension shrinking away and her ire flaring brightly as though it had struck flintlock.

Lady Catherine turned away her gimlet eye, and then she abruptly dismissed Mrs Jenkinson with the observation that the hour was late, and Anne had grown tired. As her daughter gave her companions a regretful glance and retreated slowly from the sitting room, Lady Catherine turned again to Elizabeth.

"I believe my niece has said something about wishing for your cooperation in a duet. If you and Georgiana would oblige us, I should find that a satisfactory way to end this evening."

Elizabeth's enthusiasm had dimmed the instant she perceived her ladyship's sudden turn of attitude, but she complied with her request. She gently led Miss Darcy, who had gone a little pale, to the great instrument. After some whispered conference, they determined it best that they play a song they had worked up some months ago in London, rather than attempting the new sheets at Rosings.

Opening the instrument, they shared a glance, then a breath, and began to play. They had not gone far past the first movement when Elizabeth heard Mr Collins rise and begin to talk.

"Now this is an exemplary manner of producing music! Such cooperative talents, I am sure, are to be pleasing when the skill of one such as Miss Darcy is involved..." On he went, persisting in his extemporaneous sermon until Lady Catherine shushed him with an abrupt gesture. It was not long afterwards that she called for a carriage to escort them all to the parsonage.

Mrs Collins was fully surprised to find Lady Catherine quite alone at her door for a morning call at the parsonage the next day. Inviting her patroness inside and giving her the best parlour chair with great civility, she begged her ladyship to take some refreshment, but Lady Catherine very resolutely, and not very politely, declined anything to eat.

Elizabeth, who had come into the room out of polite courtesy to their guest, curtseyed to their visitor. She was then astounded to be addressed.

"Miss Bennet, there is something pressing on my mind regarding last evening's events. I would discuss it with you here and now, if you will favour me with your company."

"Gladly, ma'am," replied Elizabeth.

"Mrs Collins, you may stopper up that teapot. I have no need of it," declared Lady Catherine abruptly. "However, I must avail myself of this room for my interview, if you would accommodate me."

Charlotte expressed her certain acquiescence and quit the room.

To Elizabeth's growing alarm, Lady Catherine rose and shut the door behind her parson's wife. Without preamble or ceremony, the great lady turned back to her and began, "You can be at no loss, Miss Bennet, as to why I have called upon you for a private interview."

"Indeed not, madam," answered Elizabeth in honest surprise. "I can neither account for this honour, nor imagine that you might have much to say to me that should necessitate our privacy."

"I do not seal this room out of any respect for your modesty of character," answered Lady Catherine in a tone beyond even her usual insolence, "but I had hoped your own conscience might tell you why I must speak to you now. You ought to know that my powers of perception are considerable, and that I am not to be trifled with. But however insincere in your pretended innocence you may choose to be, you will not find me so. My character has ever been celebrated for its sincerity and frankness, and in a cause such as this, I shall not depart from it. I shall say it plainly. I have witnessed the way you have imposed yourself on my nephew and his family, with all your arts and allurements, and have succeeded in your insinuation insofar as drawing Mr Darcy's attention and engaging the affection of his sister. Having witnessed your behaviour, I instantly resolved to make my sentiments known to you.

"Let me be rightly understood. Your schemes shall not succeed with my nephew. This match, to which you have the presumption to aspire, can never take place. Oh, you might draw him in for a moment, and he may forget all that he owes to himself and to all his family, but at that moment's end, he will rue his error and immediately repair his course, for Mr Darcy is engaged to my daughter! It was arranged by his mother and myself since they were in their cradles. Your upstart pretensions can amount to nothing when familial duty, honour, and prudence must claim him. I speak now to urge you to spare him from making such a degrading error by removing yourself at once from this familiar position within his circle, for you are as decidedly beneath that sphere as your wishes are misplaced within it."

Elizabeth took an unsteady breath. "Your ladyship, if I have had any such aspirations, I shall be the last person to confess it. Your speculation is offensive. I must beg at once to return to my room."

"A moment more! I insist on being satisfied and shall be satisfied only by your penitence. I must make my point now in such a manner as might make even you—heartless as you seem —feel it."

"Your ladyship knows nothing of my heart. Again, I beg to be excused." Elizabeth moved for the door.

Lady Catherine cut into her path, grabbing her arm. "You refuse to oblige me? You are determined to ruin him in the opinion of all his friends and make him the contempt of the world!"

"These are heavy misfortunes, but they would be of the

world's making, not of mine." Elizabeth struggled to free her wrist. "I do not agree that our union would bring any such misery as you describe."

"It shall never take place," replied Lady Catherine haughtily, "because his honour, decorum, prudence—nay, even interest, forbid it. Yes, interest! Do not expect to be noticed by Darcy's family or friends if you wilfully act against the inclinations of all. You will be censured, slighted, and despised by everyone connected with him. Your alliance will be a disgrace. Your name will never be mentioned by any of us. You will bring him nothing but isolation—to Georgiana, nothing but ridicule and shame, affecting her prospects for a good marriage."

Something jarred Elizabeth from within—her memories of the harsh words from Miss Bingley's lips at the Twelfth Night Ball and the whispers that had followed after she parted from Mr Darcy there.

But Lady Catherine was not done. "Nothing will create more abhorrence in the peers of our circle than your pretensions to gentility and your ambitions to ascend through so unequal an alliance. Such wishes are as disgusting as they are ill-considered! It is common knowledge that your family's estate is nothing more than a ramshackle shell. That your family has subsisted for months wholly on the charity of others. That your 'connexions' as you call them, are to tradesmen, to whom you will soon—if you do not already—owe increasing debts."

Elizabeth made no reply. She had already seen much of this to be true and had carried it all within herself as a painful source of shame.

"What are you now but a parasite?" Lady Catherine abruptly released Elizabeth's arm. "Gentle birth means nothing without a birthright to accompany it. Darcy will be pitied as a fool for taking you on. A position of educated service is the only respectable post to which a woman of your reduced circumstances can be recommended!"

"Your ladyship has said quite enough," said Elizabeth in a shaking voice. Stung to the soul and stabbed to the heart by the dowager's words, she immediately turned her back to shield herself from further mortification. She had until now been determined not to cry, and Elizabeth struggled against the waves of humiliation and grief rising like floodwater in her throat.

"I see now that you are not so unaffected as you pretend. I am relieved that you have some natural feeling in you, and that your display now confirms what I suspect—that my nephew, being wise, has not and will never make you an offer of marriage. My fears, it seems, have been for naught."

Elizabeth shook her head. "No, he has not." Her heart was breaking, for she now felt she understood the mystery of his behaviour in these past months.

Lady Catherine took up her cane with some satisfaction. "Then let me conclude by saying only this—and I say it to you out of my condescension and charity—remove yourself at once from a connexion that can only disappoint your misplaced hopes. You must promise to me now that you will endeavour ever onward to become no more than an indifferent acquaintance to my nephew and niece, for their sake as well as yours."

Elizabeth straightened her spine. "We are friends, your ladyship. I can give you no such promise."

"Friends, indeed!" she scoffed. "Such flimsy connexions are easily sundered, yet you still refuse to oblige me. You are an obstinate, headstrong girl, and I am ashamed of you!"

With that, Lady Catherine swept from the room and slammed the door. It would be nearly half an hour before Elizabeth could collect herself sufficiently to open it again.

When at last she emerged, Elizabeth's bleeding heart had been hollowed out by resolve. There was nothing else she could do but concede to her fate and leave Mr Darcy to his.

CHAPTER THIRTY-FOUR

*D*arcy and his sister were on the point of going out when the colonel found them pulling on their gloves in the foyer.

"Are you to call upon the ladies at the parsonage?" Colonel Fitzwilliam asked.

"Why, yes," said Georgiana, glancing between her cousin and her brother with an anxious expression.

Darcy gave her the barest shake of his head, which the colonel seemed to decipher at once.

"Ah, well, I shall not interfere in such a call," he said, "but it might make what I have to share all the more imperative, for our aunt returned just an hour ago from the parsonage. When I enquired on the need for such an early call, she spoke of her visit with great satisfaction. She had dispensed some advice there and felt those within to be very indebted to her, for Lady Catherine told me that she now congratulated herself on having lately saved a young lady from a most imprudent attachment. I suspect it was Miss Bennet she had so directed, as our aunt then voiced some very strong objections to the lady. If you visit her, I hope you will attempt to soothe any injured feelings."

Darcy started, and Georgiana gripped his arm. Disbelief quickly gave way to anger at the meddling of his aunt, and then, in almost the next hasty breath, Darcy's mind turned over in panic at the thought of Elizabeth's mortification and the real danger that any tender feelings he had so long worked to build in her might be destroyed by so unwelcome an invasion. He steadied his sister and then loosed her hold on him.

"I must leave immediately. Georgiana—"

"I understand. Go now, Brother!"

Half fuelled by anxiety for Elizabeth and half by rage at his interfering aunt, Darcy made quick work of the trek down the lane, and he was nearly winded when he reached the parsonage door.

Mrs Collins herself answered it, her expression grim. "Ah, Mr Darcy. How good of you to call."

"I understand my aunt to have lately visited. Is—is Miss Bennet—"

"Sir, she is not here," Mrs Collins cut in with urgent compassion. "She has left the parsonage. She took the gig with our manservant. She was truly distressed."

"But where? Where did she go?"

"Her only object was to find a conveyance at Bromley that would bear her to London."

"I—I thank you. I beg your pardon, Mrs Collins. I must go."

Darcy reeled away, aggrieved to the heart and nearly overwhelmed with the double burden of panic and pursuit. His desire to hurry made him curse his decision to leave his curricle behind in town. As he charged back down the lane and took the gravel track back towards the carriage house and stables, Darcy spotted the stately barouche his aunt had lately used still standing nearly ready to hand, but decided immediately to forgo it. Requiring utmost speed, he snatched up his tack and went to the stalls to seek his mount.

It was only seven miles to the coaching inn at Bromley, and if he rode his horse at a gallop, he might reach Elizabeth before she made for London.

ELIZABETH ARRIVED AT THE BELL WITH ONLY minutes to spare before the Bromley post left at eleven. As John wrangled her trunk, Elizabeth bought her fare. In her distress, her haste to escape was so great that she was glad to claim the last place remaining on the crowded coach, which was on the outside, near the guard at the rear of the conveyance.

She climbed aboard with hardly a backwards glance, attempting to keep steady to her purpose. She had wallowed in her grief just long enough that morning to realise that she could not stay in Kent, for she would have her broken heart crushed anew at every look of admiration from Mr Darcy that came to nothing and at every dashed hope for a sign of tenderness from him. It was impossible to stay and to be exposed again and again to such torment, made more painful by the kindness of his sister and the continued disapproval of his aunt.

Elizabeth could not go to Longbourn where she risked having the great rents she had torn in her heart pried open most indelicately by her mother and then teased at by her father. No, she was decided. To the good sense, the compassion, and familiarity of those who resided in Gracechurch Street she must go.

Elizabeth tied her bonnet against the wind and willed herself not to cry. It was necessary simply to relinquish Mr Darcy altogether. She finally believed she rightly understood why he had been so silent on his feelings despite the signs of his attraction, for what a predicament he faced! The conscientious Mr Darcy she knew would never shirk his duties to his situation in life, to the grand legacy of Pemberley, and he would not expose Elizabeth to the contempt of his peers. His own honour —nay, even his own kindness to her—surely forbade any union between them.

She felt the carriage shifting a little beneath her, so Elizabeth clung to her seat in anticipation of their departure that came with a sudden lurch mere moments later.

As she settled herself, she found she was being studied by the guard perched upon the high seat nearby.

"Where are you off to today, Miss?" he asked her, in a gruff voice made rougher by the need to raise it above the noisy carriage.

"I have relations who live near The Eagle on Gracechurch Street. That is our destination, is it not?"

"Aye, that it is," he confirmed and said no more. Elizabeth merely nodded at his grizzled, sun-beaten face with a tight smile.

As their carriage gained speed, further talk became impossible, and Elizabeth was forced to distract herself from the jostling discomfort of her journey by watching for other travellers and transports along the road.

They had not been ten minutes along when she heard a shout from behind them, and Elizabeth turned her head to look for the source.

What she saw stole her breath, for behind the carriage came Mr Darcy on one of his greys, thundering down the highway towards them. Her hope surged at the sight, even as disbelief warred within her.

The guard posted near her back suddenly roused himself to turn around, narrowing his eyes at what appeared to be a thrill-seeking young sportsman trying to make a run for the ribbons of the coach. In a quick gesture, he ensured that his pistol could be seen at the ready.

Mr Darcy gave just enough rein to match the pace of the

coach, and he followed, calling out to the guard and to Elizabeth.

"Halt! Halt! Sir, halt the coach! Miss Bennet! Miss Bennet, pray have him stop!"

At the distress now plainly visible on his dear face, Elizabeth's resolve slipped and fell deep within her and shattered. She burst into wretched tears, and she added her voice to his, crying out for the coachman to stop, even rapping upon the conveyance on which she clung to gain his attention.

The guard shouted, "What are you doing? Who is that man? This coach does not stop! I say, this coach does not stop! The route is straight to London!"

She turned her face to him and cried over her tears and the wind. "Sir, there has been some mistake. I must get off! Please! Please!"

The clamour of her distress apparently had reached the ears of the other passengers. One older fellow stuck his head out of the window and exclaimed, "Stop that pounding! What ails you, Missy?"

Elizabeth swiped at her eyes and cried, "I must go back! He has come for me!"

The old man's face creased as his eyes shifted from Elizabeth to the rider on the horse, and he withdrew into the cabin, where a buzz of voices began to rise. They built into something of an uproar, led by one elderly matron.

"We should make the driver stop! Stop, I say!" she bellowed.

"Are you mad? These coaches never stop!"

A flurry of gossip arose from within, speculations on why the gentleman was chasing the coach, and what the pretty young lady atop the conveyance had to do with it.

Elizabeth did not care—she only hoped they might prevail upon the better nature of the driver to halt.

The old man's face appeared again, this time in the window

below the driver's seat, and he barked towards their coachman. "Stop, man! Stop! There has been a crisis!"

Elizabeth continued her own pleas to the guard at the rear of the conveyance, adding to the din. To her dismay, when next she looked to find Mr Darcy, he and his horse were gone. It was the guard's gaze that helped redirect her, for the horse and rider had now moved apace on the left side of the carriage.

Elizabeth watched in a terrible suspense as Mr Darcy's grey, its sides heaving, tore ahead of the coach, giving just enough head to their jostler's own team that the driver was forced to draw in some rein.

"What the devil!" he shouted in shock. "The man is mad!"

But it was plain that Mr Darcy's skill as a rider and his own experience driving a team had enabled him to maintain the gap just enough to become a moving obstruction in their path— one that continued to drop down from a gallop, to a canter, to a trot, in a decrease of speed by degrees. Even as the post-driver strained to outmanoeuvre him, Mr Darcy would edge his grey into the path of the team until the driver was forced to retain his place.

Having herded the team into position, Mr Darcy reined up his mount to forestall them further, causing the coachman's team to buckle. At an alarmed shout from the driver and a blast from the guard's horn just above Elizabeth's ear, their coach was forced to stop.

Elizabeth gripped the ladder and flung herself down immediately, and the guard, seeing her desertion, obligingly threw down her trunk into the dirt. She shouted her thanks to him, and the outraged driver, seeing her on the ground, urged his horses straight on. Elizabeth stood beside the road still quivering from shock as Mr Darcy came to her at a trot and dismounted.

"Forgive me, please, forgive me," he said without preamble.

"I could think of no other way to halt your progress. Are you hurt?"

She forced herself to stop trembling. "I am not, sir."

"I could not have you leave Kent in such distress, with no sense of aid or comfort. I fear that my aunt—my horrible, meddlesome aunt— has done you such a wrong, and I did not prevent it."

Elizabeth shook her head, her breath catching again most painfully at the remembrance. She released it in a mirthless laugh. "You could not have prevented it. Lady Catherine's determination was such that I doubt anyone could have opposed her."

Mr Darcy's troubled expression hardened into cold confirmation. "And so she did, I take it, say or do something that led to your distress."

"Yes, and I quickly realised I could no longer remain in Kent." Her embarrassment at the fact that she had chosen to run away from him kept her from unburdening herself fully. She also had no wish to pain him further with the tale of his aunt's cruelty when she herself was still reeling from it.

Yet, he persisted. "What did she say to you?"

She turned aside from him a moment, wrapping her arms around herself to ease some of the ache—an ache in heart as much as in body—that was steadily growing from the wish that he would comfort, rather than question her.

Her hopes, nearly dead, had been resurrected at the sight of him coming after her on the road. Why had he come, if not to claim her? Why must he now press her to reveal her feelings, her despair, and share none of his? Why did he come at all? She was cross with him, Elizabeth realised, and her anger tempted her into giving her answer.

"My interview with your aunt this morning did me at least one kind service. It forced me to acknowledge the bitter truth before me: that I am nothing—no one—and ought not persist in my foolish wishes to once again hold the place I once had in the world, which languished just within the bounds of a gentleman's sphere. Moreover, she reminded me of the facts of your familial obligation: that you belong to circles far beyond any of mine—you and your sister both—and that I must cease any further attempts to hold you in friendship, much as it pains me, for your friendship has been the honour of my life. But with such a realisation, I knew my best course was to withdraw immediately from your company."

Mr Darcy, snatching up his horse's lead in distressed agitation, began to walk beside her. "And why should my aunt say such a thing to you in the first place? To what end or purpose would she do so but to wound you? I have known Lady Catherine to be an obstinate fool but never intentionally malicious. This, however, is proof of the cruelty in her nature, and it is not to be borne! What right has she to interfere in your affairs or mine?"

Mr Darcy shook his head, and Elizabeth struggled against her own discomposure as she paced along beside him. When he turned his face to Elizabeth again, he must have seen how unsettled she felt, for his outrage softened into concern.

He offered her his arm as he began to lead the horse farther down from the road into a low stretch of pasture dotted with clusters of campion and cow parsley. Elizabeth went willingly, glad to be off the edge of the busy main road. In the relative privacy of this patch of countryside, she stopped and met his aggrieved gaze again, and she had to swallow back the sensation of drowning as she recalled that he was still awaiting an answer.

"Lady Catherine may claim a right to interfere because she has a reason to believe she will soon have a connexion nearer to you than as your aunt," said Elizabeth in a tone of forced calmness, as she swiped sudden wetness from her eyes at this reminder of where he rightly belonged. "Her offense was performed on Miss de Bourgh's behalf. As a mother, that is her right. It is I who have no right to persist in any more girlish fancies that might undermine her daughter's plans. I ought to own my position in life and adhere only to the opportunities attendant upon such a situation."

Mr Darcy seemed at once astonished and bewildered by her revelation, and he beseeched her, "I have no notion of any plans, or of these fancies you hint at, and since I have no way of discovering them, I beg you to speak plainly. You need not fear me."

Mr Darcy took up her hand, and Elizabeth saw some of the affection she had detected from him before in his expression of earnest compassion. Before she could check herself, she answered in a trembling voice, "I have been a foolish creature these many months, Mr Darcy, but when I left Kent today, I had come to an understanding about what I must do, which was to leave you to your destined bride. But now that you are here, I find myself unwilling, so helplessly unwilling, to bear the pain again of enacting such separation." She looked up tearfully at him.

Mr Darcy drew in a breath.

Elizabeth continued with unburdened boldness. "I have said enough to make my feelings plain to a man of your intelligence, so I have no reason to withhold further confession, now that I have begun. You must allow me to tell you how ardently I admire and love you."

Seeing him now shocked and silent and reading in these signs some painful sort of surprise, Elizabeth poured out the fullness of her own despair. "In declaring myself thus, I know I unfairly burden you with my feelings. Indeed, even if you do return them, I know full well that any alliance between us would be viewed as reprehensible to your family, to the world, and even to your own better judgment. What is more, since you have an arrangement with your cousin, there is nothing else you might say to me. So why have I spoken when I promised myself

I should not, when I know very well I am the last woman in the world you should ever marry?"

Tears pricked the corners of her eyes, and her courage, exhausted by her shameful speech, now failed her. Elizabeth turned and paced away from him towards the road, wringing her hands as the sinews of her heart twisted within her breast. "You should have let me leave for London!" she cried.

Quickly, Mr Darcy strode forward and took hold of her. "Elizabeth, no! Do not go away again! Pray, stay and be sensible."

"But I *am* being sensible," she protested. "I am all sensibility, it seems, and this is what it has done to me!" She was openly crying now and tugged away from his gentle hold, eager to flee in her mortification.

Mr Darcy turned Elizabeth's trembling figure to face him and pulled her firmly against his chest to both restrain and comfort her. In the shock of this unexpected embrace, she felt him begin inexplicably to chuckle.

"Have I made myself ridiculous to you?" asked Elizabeth, her flushed, wet face pressed into the wool of his coat.

His voice was a mirthful rumble at her ear. "I do not laugh at you, my dearest, but at us."

Us. The word held even greater hope and promise than his endearment. Elizabeth peered up at him, and he released her for but a moment to retrieve his handkerchief. Returning her to the circle of his arm, he used the bit of lawn to carefully dab at her face, turning her countenance before him with two fingers pressed under her chin as he worked.

"Dearest, loveliest Elizabeth," he murmured down at her, pulling from her an unexpected smile. "Whatever am I to do with you?"

"That is the question, is it not, my dear Mr Darcy?" she said archly, sniffing a little but growing steadily much more composed.

His fingers moved softly against her face, finding their place along the curve of her cheek and drifting into her hair. He smiled down at her and answered, "I have considered all you have said in your argument and find many articles of it so utterly ridiculous as to move me to both compassion and amusement at this latest expression of your propensity towards wilful misunderstanding. You have constructed your offer upon numerous false premises. The first being that I am engaged to my cousin. I am not! Anne and I have spoken of our mutual lack of desire for marriage to each other. It is only Lady Catherine who belabours the point and attempts to force our alliance at every turn. I am my own master and the head of my own house. She has no influence over such a domain, not even, as she presumes to claim, the wishes of my mother as inducement."

"Even if it is as you say, it does not change the fact that an alliance with me would be looked down upon most strenuously by society. To be ensnared by such a pauper! They will think you an appallingly besotted fool at best and a reprehensibly cuttable connexion at worst. I would not cause the honour and reputation of your family to be so abandoned, when Georgiana is soon to come out and needs all to work for her advantage. I could not do that to my dear friend."

Mr Darcy shook his head. "Who would cut us who mattered, Elizabeth?"

"Everyone whose standing is of consequence! Why, your aunts and uncle—"

"I tell you this in utter truth, Elizabeth—Lady Catherine's opinion has never mattered less to me than it does today. And the earl and countess have known of my friendship with you, of course. They saw enough of us dancing and speaking together at the ball. They hardly dislike you."

"Yet they *will* if they think a fortune-hunter has attached herself to you."

"Would a temporary misunderstanding—for such thinking could only be temporary—be worse than forgoing a chance at a lifetime of happiness?"

Elizabeth could barely breathe. She was suffused with warmth by his words, at his persistence on the topic of their marriage, despite her own caution. "Your honour, sir, is such that I fear you might think it incumbent upon you to offer for me because of the immodest, unladylike impropriety I have displayed today, but there is nothing you must say or do. The fault is mine, for the cause is my own inability to control my feelings for you!"

"You cannot know how much it delights me to hear that you cannot restrain your feelings for me," Mr Darcy replied, his eyes dancing as they gazed at her. She began to tremble as the tip of his thumb upon her chin began to stroke lightly down along her neck. "I have long felt unable to rein in my own."

Suddenly frowning, he released her abruptly and tore off his hat to rake his fingers through his hair. "I understand your confusion now, Elizabeth—why you might think that the disapprobation of society by my marriage to you would seem a bane to me.

"I have been silent for too long, merely because I was made anxious by my belief that you did not have feelings for me, and that by marrying you, I would curse myself to misery with a wife who only married me out of gratitude and who could not return my love."

He came back to her and took her hands. "But your feelings change this. With your feelings for me secure, I can bear anything. I *will* bear anything, and society would be rendered foolish to fail to perceive that ours is indeed not a mere match of one-sided convenience but of mutual regard."

To her utter surprise, when Mr Darcy finished this speech, he knelt before her on the ground. "Will you marry me, Elizabeth, despite my failings? Will you forgive me, dearest, for not speaking until now? I love you so utterly and completely and have lingered these many months in hopes of someday receiving your love in return."

He looked up at her then, holding her gaze so earnestly and endearingly, that her heart, 'til now in a bind of anxiety, released with the fall of several tears. "Yes—yes, I will marry you," she managed at last.

In the relief and joy of her declaration, Elizabeth joined him at his level by sinking to her knees before him and pressing her cheek against his neck, wrapping her arms around him, and clinging to him earnestly.

After a moment to savour this nearness, he took hold of her waist and turned her in his arms, pulling her onto his lap, pressing her closer still and touching his lips to her hair as she lay her cheek against his heart. He let out a breath that, to Elizabeth's senses, seemed to come from a deeper fount of feeling than relief.

"Marry me soon, Elizabeth," he whispered at length. "That is all I ask."

She lifted her eyes to him in amused understanding and heartily agreed, laughing at herself a little as her hands found their way inside his coat to wind her arms around his waist.

As if freed by her boldness, Mr Darcy's hand raised her chin so that he could finally kiss her.

The initial touch of their lips was gentle, tempered by their lingering disbelief at the suddenness of their new understanding. But as the heat of the sensation swept over them, the intimacy of their connexion secured them in their regard, and passion stole at once into their midst.

His mouth moved over hers with assurance as his hands spanned her waist and stole caresses, while Elizabeth's fingers slid from the silk of his waistcoat upwards, beyond his lapels, and into the dark curls at his nape. As they each tasted and touched each other and found more to be desired, it was only a heavy rattling from a cart passing on the nearby road that returned them to their senses.

"Good lord, we are in the dirt!" Mr Darcy exclaimed, as he tried to catch his breath. "What a scene we are making!"

He engaged the strength of his arms about her as he stood, bringing her to her feet with him. He released her waist before clutching both of her hands in his again.

As he stood before her, Elizabeth took a moment to take in the bright colour in his cheeks and the dark, heady expression still lingering in his eyes. The spell holding them both seemed to weaken as she drew in another ragged breath.

"I suppose we ought to either return to Rosings or go on to London. There will be speculation, I am afraid, either way, once we are seen travelling together."

"Yes, you are right."

He did not move; neither did she. They merely continued to gaze at each other, fixed in the suspense of wonder. Elizabeth's smile grew, until at length, she squeezed his hands. "Might Bromley be closer? I had thought we had several miles to London."

"You are right, my love, perfectly right. We should return to The Bell. I shall lead you on Incitatus, and once we reach the coaching inn, I hope we may find transport that is more comfortable for you while I ride him back to Hunsford. Forgive me. I am—I am so distracted. Do you see what kissing you does to me?" He laughed at himself in astonishment as he turned to ready his mount to receive her.

Elizabeth, who was never at ease with horses, and even less certain of her skill at riding on a man's tack, confessed, "I hardly think we are more than two or three miles from The Bell. Much obliged as I am to Incitatus, I would much rather walk with you."

Mr Darcy's ready smile showed all his pleasure. "Then I

shall take this opportunity to secure your trunk as his burden. It is still in the middle of the highway."

"I had quite forgotten it—and so you see what your kisses do to *me*," she said, and her laughter followed him up into the road.

CHAPTER THIRTY-FIVE

By the time Mr Darcy delivered her to the parsonage in a hired post-chaise much later that evening, Elizabeth had already realised their understanding could have no hope of secrecy. Even though her beau had ridden separately on his mount, his retrieval of her and his subsequent proprietary escort home made plain his intentions. The way he took her hand at their parting made his claim evident, even as the long look he gave her before he rode away spoke eloquently of what it meant to him to have secured such an understanding.

Charlotte had kindly received her again without a word beyond a welcome and an exclamation of relief at her safe return. Rather than alerting the house, she quietly manoeuvred Elizabeth up the stairs to grant her some privacy to wash and dress for sleep.

It was not an hour after Elizabeth had wrapped herself snugly in bed when Charlotte, having been an intimate confidant of Elizabeth's since childhood, felt it her duty and right to knock lightly on her chamber door and let herself in. The warmth of her candle's glow illuminated the pillow by Elizabeth's head.

"Eliza, you are not asleep. I can see you hiding a smile under the covers, closed eyes or not."

Elizabeth blinked her eyes open and guiltily met her friend's assessing gaze. "You have caught me out."

Charlotte came straight to the point. "Well, I am glad to have you back and looking so much better in spirits than when you ran off this morning. Might I assume correctly that Mr Darcy's success in retrieving you from the road heralds yet another significant achievement? Will you not give me some satisfaction, or must I be left in suspense?"

"I admit I was still distressed when he overtook me just as I was leaving Bromley, but after we spoke of Lady Catherine and our own misunderstandings, I felt better. He acquitted himself as a friend very well."

"And?"

"And. . . he is no longer a friend."

"Is he not?" said Charlotte, giving Elizabeth a sly grin.

"No. He is now my intended until he can call upon my father, and we can be officially engaged."

"Oh, my dear, dear friend!" cried Charlotte exultantly. Elizabeth, in shared delight, sprung up to allow the two of them to embrace. "I am happy for you both, and I confess, also pleased to have been correct in my conjectures. It certainly took you two long enough to come to an understanding!"

Elizabeth settled back on her pillow with a smile. "It did indeed. We both confessed ourselves utter fools. Does that satisfy you?"

"Very much! And did you also, in addition to such foolishness, confess undying love?"

"Most decisively," said Elizabeth, with a blush of remembrance at her ardent words—and his—and what resulted after.

"I see. You will both be happy then. How soon will you be married?"

"Soon," she avowed.

"Eliza, should I worry that there may be a reason for a quick wedding?" asked Charlotte in some alarm.

"Mr Darcy was everything honourable, I assure you. We kissed, I confess it, but that is all—but that was enough to confirm that we would do better not to wait overlong."

Charlotte patted Elizabeth's hand in some relief. "I knew it must be so. Good girl."

Elizabeth fought the urge to protest a little, for surely, her friend should have more faith in her modesty, but then she recalled the passionate embrace she and Mr Darcy had shared beside a public road and decided to leave the subject alone. Instead, her concerns turned to the day to come.

"Will you promise me to keep our understanding from Lady Catherine until I am gone away from Kent? I am sure she will not find any happiness in such news."

"Yes, of course. I would not make you uncomfortable should her reaction be less than joyous."

"And I would not have it do damage to her trust in her parson and his wife." She looked at Charlotte earnestly. "I hope she will not sink to accusing you of helping me to *entrap* him, or any other such nonsense."

"If she should, I would point out to her that you have been my friend for many years and had every right to visit me. Moreover, I could provide evidence that Mr Darcy had been paying his addresses to you for months without your acting to solicit them in any way. If this alliance is made now, it was made because Mr Darcy chose it."

"I thank you, Charlotte. You are a good friend to me."

"And you to me, Eliza. You have given me much comfort and pleasure with your visit, and it brings me joy to see you so well-matched. Your Mr Darcy will vex you and make you deliriously happy in turns—just as it should be in a relationship of equal minds and affections...or so I am told."

"With such uncommon wisdom, how am I to argue?" She embraced her friend warmly, both in celebration and consolation, for she recognised in Charlotte's words a trace of sadness. "Dear, dear Charlotte!" was all she could say.

When at last she bade her friend goodnight, Elizabeth found that her joy, wonder, and longing made it hard for her to find rest. She lay awake for some hours until she found a cure for her restlessness in envisioning herself nestled in a quiet, sumptuous bedroom at Darcy House, restful and warm, drawn close in the arms of her beloved.

ELIZABETH GOT UP WITH THE SUN AND WENT OUT, meditating on her happiness and giving thanks for every small thing blooming in the fields and hedgerows as she walked, swinging her bonnet absently in her hand. After several minutes of such delightful contemplation, she found herself arrested by the appearance of, and then running towards, the object of her delight, whom she espied striding purposefully towards her from the path that led to Rosings.

He laughed as he caught her in his arms and, kissing her soundly, set her down. "Good morning," Mr Darcy said, with all the emphasis of a benediction.

"It is indeed wonderful, is it not?" Elizabeth mused, tucking herself under his arm and against his heart as they took again to the path to the trees. She could not find it within herself to be shy at all with him.

Mr Darcy's deep voice buzzed at her ear where it was pressed against him. "Is it? I believe I first called it 'good'. *Wonderful* is rather more expansive, would you not say?"

Elizabeth pouted playfully. "If it does not merit the term in your eyes, then I suppose I could go inside again, and let you enjoy the merely 'good' morning by yourself."

"Or, you could convince me of its wonder," he rejoined impishly, stopping and sliding his arms around her waist as he leaned down to kiss her once again. Having kissed her soundly only moments before, it seemed his intention was to savour her now, and he did so, slowly and deeply. They did not part until both were flushed and out of breath.

"I stand corrected. This morning is *sublime*," Mr Darcy said at last as he pressed her against his side once more and began to walk on with the sound of Elizabeth's laugh ringing in their wake.

After they had gone some distance in the silence of spirits too uplifted for words, the sight of the manor through the trees spurred their thoughts towards the rest of the world reaching into their own joyful sphere.

"I could not hide my happiness from Charlotte when she came to my room to attend me last night," Elizabeth confessed as she unwound herself from his embrace, only to take his arm up primly. "She certainly had every reason to be highly suspicious."

"I think she knew what I was about as soon as I came to her door in search of you yesterday," he said, shaking his head, "but now that you have confirmed it, I hope the news goes no further for now. I wish you would come away from Kent with Colonel Fitzwilliam, my sister, and me as soon as you may. I fear only distance will protect you from my aunt's anger once she learns of our understanding. Indeed, I wish we could protect the Collinses from it, for I know it will reach them as well."

"I expressed just such a concern to Charlotte." Elizabeth nodded. "When might we leave?"

"If you will write an express this morning to Mr and Mrs Gardiner informing them that I am taking you to them in London a few days early, I can have arrangements made with

Colonel Fitzwilliam and Georgiana to collect you from the parsonage at first light tomorrow. I will also bring Mrs Annesley, of course."

"As much as I have enjoyed Kent, I find I am not sad to leave it, especially since I will travel with your party. But my leaving with you might arouse suspicion in others. Have you told Colonel Fitzwilliam and Georgiana of our understanding?"

"Of course. It was Colonel Fitzwilliam, you know, who told me about my aunt's interference. Georgiana and I had been readying ourselves to call on you when he found us. When I returned last night, I could not hide my good fortune from them, and I confess I did not wish to."

"I hope Georgiana was made happy by the news. You must relay to her my delight that we shall soon be sisters."

His only response was to smile and bend down again to kiss her briefly.

"Mm. Shall we, either of us, be creatures of good sense ever again, do you think?" Elizabeth mused, once he had released her impertinent mouth.

"I find I have little motivation to care, if this is my reward for foolishness," said he, grinning as she expressed her own pleasure on tiptoe with a kiss to his cheek and the brightest of looks from her eyes.

As they crossed the road and headed back towards the parsonage, Mr Darcy grew more sober. "Once we reach London, I will set out again for Longbourn. I would like to ask your father if we could marry in two weeks," he said abruptly. "Will that—will that be sufficient?"

Elizabeth stopped mid-stride, causing him to pause likewise. "Sufficient for me, of course," she agreed. "Poor Mama will be disappointed not to have something grander planned—unless, of course, you plan to make up for it by acquiring a special license, as I assume two weeks' time would be insufficient for the banns to be read. I suppose we shall marry in London, then, as Longbourn's dining room will still be unsuitable for our acquaintance to come to breakfast?"

"If that pleases you, it would certainly be convenient for us to remain in London. Perhaps we might marry from Mayfair—at St. George's?" he offered.

"Certainly."

"And as to the marriage settlement," he stole a shy glance at Elizabeth, "it is done. Your father need only sign it. I took the liberty of drawing up a draft of the papers with my solicitor."

She took a moment to recover from her astonishment. "You did? Precisely when did you do this?"

Mr Darcy opened the garden gate and gestured for her to enter before him. "After the Twelfth Night Ball, when I nearly kissed you. Do you remember?"

Elizabeth looked at him, remembering perfectly. "I had no idea that your intentions were so serious," she confessed.

"They were set in stone when I realised how utterly lost I was. I could not be near you without temptation, so I considered I might do well to prepare to act in an honourable fashion, should I prove unable to remain a gentleman in your teasing presence."

"You were not far off the mark," Elizabeth said with a mischievous grin. "I nearly kissed you myself then, you know."

The effect this confession had on him could not be missed. He brought their progress up short before the parsonage door.

"Confound it, madam!" hissed her lover in restrained tones, tearing off his hat and glancing about them. "Mercy, I cry mercy! Could you refrain from talking of kisses so near to your cousin's doorstep? I am tempted to make such a scene that we may have to engage his services at once!"

Elizabeth gasped. "Oh, please, I beg you, no! I would not have our marriage sullied by the remembrance of him as our officiant!"

"Then allow me some measure of composure, Elizabeth,"

he whispered, tacitly reminding her to lower her voice as his hand reached for the door, "or else I shall do something that may shock your relations to witness."

Mr Darcy's announcement that Elizabeth would be taking his carriage directly to London did shock and confuse Mr Collins and Maria. Mrs Collins merely smiled with sage indulgence and called for the maid to start packing the lady's things so that she could follow with only a little delay the express sent off to the Gardiners of Gracechurch Street.

HER AUNT AND UNCLE RECEIVED ELIZABETH AND HER news with as much joy as she had hoped, and their offers of kind assistance did much to soften the pang of loss she felt when Mr Darcy hastened away to Hertfordshire to secure her father's blessing.

When Mr Darcy returned, he brought both her mother and father to her. And while her mother stood lamenting that the Bingleys and the rest of the Bennet girls seemed fixed in Yorkshire beyond the requested day for the wedding, Elizabeth felt distinctly cheered that her father's affection for her had animated him to stir so precipitously from his realm of comfort to go again into London.

"Well, Lizzy," he said, once he had drawn her aside, "your Mr Darcy came to me with a request, and I felt myself obliged to fulfil it. I have given my consent, but as I had no word from you on the matter, I felt the need to withhold my blessing until I saw you. You should not feel compelled by gratitude or obliged by any assistance he has given to you or our family. You must understand that."

"I should have sent Mr Darcy with a letter for you, Papa. I am sure it was a shock to see him suddenly at your door, but you may be assured that my affections and wishes are the same as his."

Her father nodded. "Then I must make myself content with parting from you so that you may find your happiness."

Although Elizabeth anticipated that her happiness would only be complete in marrying Mr Darcy, she felt a surge of yet more joy upon reading a letter from Jane confiding, among her unnecessary apologies, the reason for the Bingleys' prolonged need for comfort in Scarborough. It was a concession to a change in Jane's condition, and the hope of what that might mean.

In the absence of the Bennet sisters, Georgiana offered her assistance to Elizabeth, Mrs Bennet, and Mrs Gardiner as the wedding date approached. Although the time that followed was full of activity, it seemed to stretch interminably. Yet the days that separated Elizabeth from union with Mr Darcy did at last wane, and the morning of that blessed event arrived when she could finally take her place beside her beloved at the altar.

Elizabeth awoke some days later in lavish comfort at Darcy House, draped in silken sheets. Drowsy from the generous warmth of her husband's long body at her back, she blinked slowly into awareness. She stretched her toes under the covers and shuffled a little at the bedclothes to discover the source of a concentration of heat at her side—a large and familiar hand, resting in quiet possession on the curve of her hip.

These sights and sensations, although new, did not alarm her. Elizabeth breathed deeply for a moment, drawing in a satisfying awareness even as she was reminded of all that had passed to bring her to this morning and its intimacy.

Unhurriedly, she closed her eyes against the pale light seeping through the curtains and dozed against her husband upon the bed, until a desire to look upon Darcy's face in sleep inspired her to shift upon the mattress and turn herself into his embrace.

Rousing only enough to slide his hand around her waist and gently gather her closer, her husband edged slowly towards wakefulness. Elizabeth could just trace a smile at the corner of his mouth as he drifted, his features otherwise utterly undisturbed as he released a sigh that stirred the curls at her temples, and he resettled into stillness.

Until this moment, she had never appreciated fully how handsome he was, but with a span of mere breaths between them, Elizabeth could now observe every feature with exquisite leisure. The fall of his hair upon his broad forehead. His dark eyes, so expressive when wakeful, were now framed with black lashes that curled delightfully at the ends. She admired the cut of his patrician nose above a mouth even more beautiful to her now that she had discovered its skill.

It had been an exhilarating night, following on the heels of a day of enchanting ceremony and exploration of her new life within his realm. Elizabeth had never experienced before such a succession of revelations. Her life was entirely new. Indeed, she hardly knew herself.

Nevertheless, there was joy in the realisation they had many more days unspent to face together as the chosen partners of their future life.

CHAPTER THIRTY-SIX

Mr and Mrs Darcy made their way into Derbyshire at the end of May, where they reunited most happily with Georgiana after their monthlong honeymoon. As Pemberley's new mistress, Elizabeth could scarcely recall any time in her life when she had felt more excitement to explore some new environs or more anxiety to learn well a role settled upon her.

She rejoiced in the ample assistance she received from her husband and their servants as she settled into her new responsibilities. Georgiana's warm recommendation of Mrs Reynolds's affectionate character proved itself in her care of the family and into which circle of kindness, she welcomed Elizabeth. The house was beautiful, elegant, and well-ordered, so her work with the venerable housekeeper became a source of joyful satisfaction.

However, the management of the Darcy social calendar and correspondence, a society elevated above hers by birth and connexion, seemed especially daunting. Nevertheless, as the new mistress of the house, she was anxious to attend to the responsibilities that now awaited her.

"Heavens!" she declared, beholding the overflowing basket of letters on the lady's escritoire in her private sitting room.

Darcy, who had wandered in to take his coffee with her that morning, nearly laughed outright at the look on her face, but restrained himself for compassion's sake. "I could sort through them, if you would like. I can parse the names and characters for you," he offered, strolling over to the desk and sitting down.

Elizabeth shook her head. "You have kindly performed this exercise with me once already in London when we sent out our new calling cards to your acquaintances. I should like to test my recollection and ensure I have learnt what you have taught me. Should I struggle, I will seek your aid. You may depend upon it."

"Very well," said her husband, making to rise from the chair. But Elizabeth, with a wicked expression, pressed him back into the seat and settled herself on his lap.

"Minx," he muttered, but he was smiling broadly as testimony to his willing compliance. Elizabeth turned to kiss him, and then reached across the desk and pulled his cup and saucer nearer his reach.

Darcy chuckled and settled in contentedly, sipping from his cup and observing her at work. Now and again, she peered over her shoulder at him and asked for clarification regarding a connexion or his opinion on accepting some invitation, but beyond that, her husband seemed to keep himself entertained with his delightful observation of her.

"Fitzwilliam," said Elizabeth, drawing his attention to a tidy little missive. "Now, here is a name and a direction I recognise! It is a note from Mrs and Miss Jamieson." She opened it and read.

Dear Mr and Mrs Darcy,

How very well such an address sounds! You may imagine my surprise, and Tabitha's delight, at reading the notice of your marriage in the newspaper. You know it is in my nature to pry, so I hope you will indulge this old woman by telling her the tale whenever your many duties may allow it. A very little will suffice —just enough to tell when and where such a conquest of affections took place.

Tabitha asserts that your engagement was a quickly done thing and was reached as swiftly as your marriage followed it, while I hold that you were secretly engaged throughout the entire winter!

There was too much evident delight in your looks and bandying of words, and too much grace as you traded blows, for there to have not already been a strong understanding between you. My sight is not as precise in guessing the succession of events as my Tabitha's, but she owns that in essentials of the heart, I am often the more right.

When next you are in town, I do hope you will pay us a call and give me a chance to crow victory over my more talented companion.

Yours ever,
Hannah Jamieson

Elizabeth, in laying aside the missive, could only laugh at the affectionate audacity of the old woman. Darcy, evidently not so used to having women speculate into the matters of his heart, frowned at first as he took up the letter. Elizabeth watched his eyes narrow and then soften.

"Might I respond by telling them we shall be happy to pay a call in the late autumn and say nothing of the circumstances of our engagement? Or would such suspense, in their solitude, be cruel?" Elizabeth asked lightly.

"You may reply and tell them they are both right, but they

will have to hear the tale in person," said Darcy at last. He set aside the letter next to her hand and captured it, gently turning up her palm. His eyes traced the scar blazed upon it before bringing the tender flesh to his lips. "In essentials, Mrs Jamieson had the right of it. Not long after the fire, I knew I was as good as bound to you. There would be no other for me."

"Nor for me," Elizabeth admitted, turning to catch his cherishing glance. She could well remember how acute her longing for him had felt, even as she had prepared to leave Netherfield in November. "But I had no notion you wanted me then," she added with a sigh.

"Elizabeth, I directly intervened in another man's offer for you. Clever as you are, I could not divine how you overlooked such an important piece of evidence of my decided affection."

"Ah, but I counted it then as more a kindness than a claim. Mr Collins's attentions presented a horror equal to the fire to my sensibilities and since you had proven yourself my champion against the blaze, I likewise imagined it was in your nature to assist a friend by averting so disastrous a marriage."

Her husband bit his lip rather consciously at these words, but Elizabeth, rather than press him for his thoughts, hummed to herself as she smoothed out Mrs Jamieson's note on the desk. As she did so, her gaze landed on another missive nearly sliding out of the basket. It was addressed to her in a hand she knew immediately.

"This note came quite quickly from my sister Mary. She must have anticipated my coming to Pemberley and sent it on ahead," she said, hastily breaking the seal. "I do hope nothing is amiss."

Darcy shifted a little forward and rested his chin upon her shoulder, concern written on his brow as they both read together.

Dear Lizzy,

You might imagine me in some state of vexation as I write this. Forgive me. I do not wish to complain but to seek advice. Mama has been insistent on the hiring of some sort of chambermaid, for she finds our maid-of-all-work cannot manage the burden now that three daughters are at home for the summer. I do confess, I had never noticed how decidedly untidy Lydia and Kitty are and that they have nary a care for their clothing. They are forever asking me to add to my work basket. They will not lend their aid to any pressing or to any other tasks I have taken on to ensure the ladies of Longbourn appear as presentable as ever.

Papa maintains that we shall never keep ourselves out of debt if we add an additional retainer to the household and has applied to poor Hill, who already must now tidy most public areas of the house, for more assistance. That dear lady has not the eyesight nor the back to attempt such work. It seems most unfair to ask it of her, but I am unsure how to express the injustice without the risk that our father will view it as yet another complaint.

Should you have suggestions for me, I would be content to read them all. I am sure you must now be very busy managing your own household, so I do not expect to hear from you soon. Be assured that you are quite missed.

I remain your loving sister,
Mary

"Mary is so very conscientious," Darcy observed. "I wonder if your father would view it as an overstep if I were to place one of our maids in his household. I am sure the right one would embrace the chance to gain experience as a kind of lady's maid for the mistress and daughters of Longbourn. Mrs Reynolds may know just the one."

Elizabeth might have called him officious at another time,

but now that she knew Darcy's heart so well, she was glad for this generous aspect of his nature that would seek to remedy the cares of those within his reach and to defend their interests and make all matters well. It was much like her own way of loving, and the delight of this familiarity and understanding could only endear him more to her.

She smiled up at him. "If you write to my father first and offer it as a temporary means to help train the maid you send for other service in your own household someday, perhaps his pride may allow it."

He kissed her forehead. "Clever as always, Elizabeth."

"And you are very kind to ease Mary's troubles. I must say she has grown through this difficulty into a remarkable young woman. We should have her next to Pemberley, I think. She has so longed to learn more of the German composers from Georgiana, and they had no chance to practise together while we were in town over the busy winter."

"I am always content to secure any pleasure of yours. Moreover, I think the notion of bringing another companion for my sister has considerable merit. I rather like the idea," Darcy confessed.

Elizabeth had tucked herself cosily against his chest, but now lifted her face in concern. "Surely, you do not think Georgiana is lonely. Between Mrs Annesley and myself, we have been doing our best to keep her entertained."

"That is exactly why I should send for Mary," Darcy replied as he toyed with a curl by her ear. "For when you are off with Georgiana, I find myself lonesome for my wife."

"Ah," remarked Elizabeth at once catching his meaning. "Well then, I find it only right to extend the hospitality of Pemberley to all my sisters, as soon as may be."

She had intended to write such a momentous letter with her best penmanship to set a fine precedent for herself as Mrs

Darcy. Her husband, however, would have none of her energies so diverted.

The invitation was hopelessly smudged, but Elizabeth found the remembrance of writing it nevertheless pleased her, for not many months later, she would find herself again in that chair, writing to Jane of all her joy in expectation of an heir to Pemberley.

Finis

Quills & Quartos
PUBLISHING

Subscribers to the Quills & Quartos mailing list receive advance notice of new releases and sales, and exclusive bonus content and short stories. To join, visit us at www. QuillsandQuartos.com

ACKNOWLEDGMENTS

This work took roughly eight years to complete, from 2012-2020. It spent its early life as a half-finished post on the Derbyshire Writers Guild forum, and I received great encouragement from its reception there among lovers of Jane Austen's works. I am glad to present this completed novel to the wider Jane Austen-loving world after a long birthing process that met some difficulties in the labor—namely career shifts, an out-of-state move, two babies, and an unforgettable worldwide pandemic.

I am very grateful to the encouragement of my own "Mr Darcy," most especially for his help in keeping our two small boys busy so that *Fearful Symmetry* could be as well-written as circumstances might allow. Thank you, Zachary; I did well when I married a man who understood my passions. I must also thank his wonderful family—his parents and my sisters-in-law, especially—for their help gaining time to write while they gave my children beautiful memories of their special playtimes.

There are also many peer readers of the manuscript I wish to thank—including my former roommate and fellow writer Stephanie Gail Eagleson, historical romance-reader and dear friend Hannah Young, former English professor Dr Margot Tomsen, and yes, even my husband and my mother, Janie Fulton—whose early responses helped me make this story into a more memorable tale. I am grateful to each of you, who span connections built over my entire lifetime. That kind of invested encouragement nourishes like no other—for who else would read a 130,000-word rough draft but someone who cherishes our connection?

I am also indebted to the English Department of Hanover College, and in particular to those professors like Dr Tomsen ("Dr T"), Dr John Smith, and Professor Melissa Eden who encouraged me to write my way through tragedy in 2009, when my own sense of childhood security seemingly went up in flames after my own excellent father died during my senior year.

This story, which touches on so many themes of recovery, growth, and rebuilding, was healing for me to write but quite challenging to shape. In this process, my gratitude to the wonderful team of editors at Quills & Quartos Publishing is endless. Amy D'Orazio, Jan Ashton, and Debbie Styne all patiently worked with me to creatively and deftly shape and polish this work into something that shines and brings joy. The emotionally striking cover art by Susan Adriani only added to this particular tale's glow.

I thank you *all* from my heart for your part in the making of this story.

ABOUT THE AUTHOR

Gailie Ruth Caress has been a lifelong adaptive dabbler hailing from Indiana in the United States. As an English major who won prizes for her literary essays at her alma mater, Hanover College, she also explored opera, ballroom dance, and journalism. Her career path took her into educational marketing and communications, and then later into non-profit social work, and ministry with her husband, a pastor. She has two small boys and now lives in rural Illinois. Writing has always been her joy; crafting *Fearful Symmetry*, her first novel—in a genre of her own pleasure-reading—has fulfilled a lifelong dream.

Learn more about Gailie Ruth at her blog, GailieRuthWrites.com

f facebook.com/GailieRuth

a amazon.com/stores/Gailie-Ruth-Caress/author/B08Y5ZFW8F

ALSO BY GAILIE RUTH CARESS

AN INDUCEMENT INTO MATRIMONY

AN INDUCEMENT INTO MATRIMONY is an anthology of short stories which are variations of Pride & Prejudice. All are set in the regency era and follow a different path to happily ever after for Mr Darcy and Elizabeth Bennet.

Sixteen Days At Pemberley by Susan Adriani

When Elizabeth Bennet's journey to Derbyshire with the Gardiners results in an extended stay at Mr Darcy's estate, new depths of understanding grow between them—but it takes longer than either had hoped.

The Pleasure of Understanding Her by Mary Smythe

The sudden and shocking ability to read minds gives Darcy some much needed insight into Elizabeth Bennet's heart, and into his own faults and behaviour.

The Heart's Consent by Paige Badgett

Both Elizabeth Bennet and Mr Darcy must overcome regrets and recrimination if he is to win her back from another seemingly ardent suitor.

No Charm Equal by Jan Ashton

The enchanting qualities of Elizabeth Bennet drive Darcy from Netherfield earlier than expected, but encounters in London with friends and relations quickly remind him why she pierced his reserve and captured his heart.

United by Happenstance by Gailie Ruth Caress

Lady Catherine brings Elizabeth Bennet unexpectedly to Mr Darcy's doorstep but when her ladyship recognises she has brought the enemy to the gate, she turns vitriolic. Darcy and Elizabeth unite against his aunt's wrath but will the union lead to more than either anticipated?

The First Moment of Their Acquaintance by Amy D'Orazio

Darcy's cousins believe that they can fabricate a second chance for him to make a first impression on his beloved Elizabeth. He returns to Meryton hoping the disguise he wears will make the man he is more plain.

Speaking the Truth by Nan Harrison

Elizabeth leaves the Netherfield ball desperately ashamed of her family's behaviour and wishing to escape the censorious eye of Mr Darcy and Miss Bingley. When Darcy follows her however, truths are spoken freely...and a new chance at love emerges.

A Duet in Dispute by Michelle Ray

A shared love of music results in a more amiable relationship between Darcy and Elizabeth but complications arise. Will his love for her be enough to overcome the challenges that face them?

What Might Have Been by Kay Bea

It's been five years since the Bennet family was sunk beneath Lydia's disgrace. Elizabeth has learnt not to regret Mr Darcy—that is, until a chance meeting makes her think that what might have been still could be.

www.ingramcontent.com/pod-product-compliance
Lightning Source LLC
Chambersburg PA
CBHW011430240626
47153CB00011B/2921